PRAISE FOR IAN MCDONALD'S
DESOLATION ROAD

'THIS IS THE KIND OF NOVEL I LONG TO FIND YET SELDOM DO . . . EXTRAORDINARY AND MORE THAN THAT!'

—Philip José Farmer

'A SPECTACULAR FIRST NOVEL. A LIVELY WIT LEAVENS THE DENSE COMPLEXITY OF THIS EPIC TALE. THE CHARACTERS ARE MADLY MEMORABLE, THE MOST EXTRAORDINARY MIX OF HUMAN AND NOT-QUITE HUMAN SINCE CORDWAINER SMITH'S TALES OF NOSTRILIA.'

—Locus

D0774520

Also by Ian McDonald

Desolation Road
Empire Dreams

Out on Blue Six

Ian McDonald

BANTAM BOOKS

TORONTO · NEW YORK · LONDON · SYDNEY · AUCKLAND

A BANTAM BOOK 0 553 40044 4

First publication in Great Britain

PRINTING HISTORY
Bantam edition published 1990

Bantam Books are published by Transworld Publishers Ltd.,
61–63 Uxbridge Road, Ealing, London W5 5SA, in Australia by
Transworld Publishers (Australia) Pty. Ltd., 15–23 Helles
Avenue, Moorebank, NSW 2170, and in New Zealand by Transworld
Publishers (N.Z.) Ltd., Cnr. Moselle and Waipareira Avenues,
Henderson, Auckland.

Printed and bound in Great Britain by
Cox & Wyman Ltd., Reading, Berks.

Thanks

To my wife, Patricia, for all those little extra ideas that made all the difference when my imagination was flagging.

To Tim Haffield, for the concept of "tags" and "famuluses."

To my editor, Shawna McCarthy, for having the patience of Job in the face of monolithic tardiness.

Voices On...

"Good morning! Good morning! Good morning! This is Phantomas your famulus waking *you* to another *wonderful* morning with a selection of your favorite music, news, gossip, information, and appointments for your day from your personal diary program! And the weather this morning is: much the same as ever, I'm afraid; changeable, maximum temperature a steamy twenty-four, probability of rain before noon ninety-four percent, winds, strong, variable with gusts of up to fifty-five kilometers per hour; yes, just another monsoon day out there in the Big City..."

SAATCHI & AUGUSTINO: CUSTOM LIFESTYLE CONSULTANTS. YOUR DAYS THE WAY *YOU* WANT THEM. INDIVIDUALLY TAILORED ROMPAKS FOR YOUR FAMULUS/LARES-PENATES SYSTEM. MINIPAIN APPROVED, ABSOLUTE CONFIDENTIALITY ASSURED. CUSTOM-CLIENT PSYCHOFILING ASSURES MINIMUM 90% COMPATIBILITY. IT'S *YOUR* LIFE, *YOU* LIVE IT, WITH SAATCHI & AUGUSTINO!

Dear sir,

the Bureau of Happiness regrets to inform you that your application for Aptitudinal and Vocational Training as a toymaker Class 16/B has not been successful.

Whilst your Manual Dexterity, Spatial Orientation, and Creative Interpretation factors were all well within the required parameters, Motivational Analysis, Social and Structural Apperception, and Vocational-Altruistic Cross-

1

Correlations indicate that this career would not afford you the maximum of personal happiness and satisfaction which we, as organs of the Compassionate Society, are obliged to provide for you. Therefore, the Bureau has forwarded your application and psychofile results to Career Training and Orientation in <u>Nonfunctional Natural-Wood Furniture Construction.</u> Should you have any queries or questions, please do not hesitate to contact me, <u>Hester Birkenshaw,</u> at the following tellix code...

Hello? Hello? Pantycar Twenty-seven? Report from Data Retrieval: a disturbance in Simbimatu Covered Market: Privacy infringement. PainCrime probability currently sixteen percent—no immediate increase forecast. Suggest you investigate intervention level three. And bring me back a bag of guavas, will you? Damn famulus's on the fritz again, didn't get me up in time for breakfast and I'm ravenous.

Mulu the Rainforest:
Pray for us.
Mudmother, Soulsister:
Pray for us.
Green One, Patroness of Planted Things:
Preserve us.
From the sweeping monsoon rains, from the terror of environmental collapse, from radiation, from the stalking horror of mutated disease, from cat, rat, and racoon:
Preserve us. Hear our prayer.
Hear the prayer of this thy humble servant, laborer in the fields beneath the earth, harvester of the crops of thy bounty:
Hear our prayer.

"So I said, like, whazz new, I mean, like *new* new, not old new, yuh know, like last-week new, so she said, this yulp in the shop, 'This is new,' like, she said, 'Cheez, like everyone, but *everyone's* going to be wearing one this week,' like, whazz a *yulp* know 'bout fashion? anyway, I thought, I thought, well, maybeez sheez right, so, I got one, so I did, like, whadjou think? Isn't it wheeeee! like. Isn't it the most? Meanasay, you not got *fashion*, you not got *nothing!*"

Chiga-Chiga Sputnik-kid, Captain Elvis in neon skin-hugger and power-wheels, rides the high wires in the wee wee dawn hours when the cablecars sleep in their barns, when four A.M. TAOS gurls call the Scorpios from the high and the low places; silver-maned, forgotten samurai in a world with honor without swords; out on blue six through the vastnesses of Great Yu.

See! Chiga-Chiga Sputnik-kid run the wires! Power-wheels squeal-shreel on steel ten, twenty, fifty, *hundred* stories above flat-life ground-zero. See! the speed'o'light flickers of information zigzagging along the circuit webbing of Chiga-Chiga's chromium 'hugger; pray pray pray to San BuriSan Celestial of silicon and fiberoptics and bioprocessors and young turks up on the wires that the cizzen on the gyro-stabilizer production line wasn't Monday-or-Fridaying when they built Captain Elvis's set of power-wheels. Danger on the cables of Yu: if the Love Police ever catch Chiga-Chiga, he will be seeing the remainder of his yearlong walkabout from the inside of a Social Responsibility Counseling Center learning that words like "danger" and "thrill" cannot be allowed to have any meaning in the age of the Compassionate Society. But Chiga-Chiga Sputnik-kid is too fast, too young, too shiny for that, isn't he?

Citizen Tambuco? Citizen Tambuco? Selma Whiteside here, Ministry of Pain, Childwatch Department.

Yes, I know you have a constitutional right to children, that is not the issue here. The issue here is April's constitutional rights. Can you hear me, Citizen? Mizz Tambuco? She has as much right to a happy, fulfilled life as you do, Mizz Tambuco; how would you like it if you were taken out of your caste and forced into one quite wrong for you? Of course you wouldn't be happy.

Citizen Tambuco, the tests are infallible. Can you not

accept that your April is just not suited psychologically, emotionally, physically, to be an athlete?

No, I don't have to explain the Department's decisions to you, Mizz Tambuco.

It has to do with sexually dimorphic structures in the brain. In April's brain. Mizz Tambuco, please stop crying, please try to listen. April will be much happier as a george, the trans-sexing process is safe, painless, and utterly reliable.

Mizz Tambuco, the Compassionate Society does not use words like "perversion" anymore. It is as normal for her to be a george as it is for you to be an athlete. The Ministry of Pain does not judge, who are you to say what is normal and what is not? To some other castes, you might not appear to be normal, Mizz Tambuco. Mizz Tambuco, the Ministry of Pain has the constitutionally enshrined duty to provide each citizen with the greatest possible personal happiness. Can you deny your daughter the only happiness she may ever know?

Her fosterers are good and loving people. Yes, of course they will look after April. Yes, they will love her. I'm sorry, but no, you will not be allowed to visit. Or even call on the public dataweb. I know it sounds hard, Mizz Tambuco, but it is in April's best interests. At this early and vital developmental stage we cannot allow April to be in any way confused as to her social identity. Now, are you going to send April out to me? Please . . .

Mizz Tambuco, I'm waiting. Mizz Tambuco, please open the door. Citizen Tambuco, think. Not only are you obstructing a representative of the Ministry of Pain in their appointed duty, but by denying April her right to personal happiness, you are committing a PainCrime. . . .

Chapter 1

The first lightning of the southwest monsoon flared over the dark canyonscapes of Yu. Their flanks streaked with rain and glittering with lights, the arcologies and co-habs and manufactories shouldered close to each other like nervous thugs; the perpetual clouds drew together, glowering darkly about their shoulders. From the fifty-third-level editorial penthouse on the upper slopes of the Armitage-Weir publishing mastaba, Courtney Hall (profession: cartoonist; caste: yulp; sex: female; age: approximately; height: approximately; weight: approximately) watched the lightning flicker down to earth somewhere out among the black steel chimneys of Charlemont, counting one hippopotamus, two hippopotamus, all the way up to twelve hippopotamus before the windowpanes of Marcus Forde's glass conservatory-office rattled to distant thunder. Fifteen kilometers, give or take; come, great monsoon, and at least put an end to this head-pounding mugginess. Outside the darkness deepened further, as if in some grand wicked conspiracy with itself; the summits of all the towers along Heavenly Harmony Boulevard were suffocated in cloud. Lights came on automatically in the arbor, window louvers closed in anticipation of cold wind. Courtney Hall's editor maintained his jungle of an office with almost religious zeal.

"He's in conference." Tixxi Teshvalenku, his personal assistant, had informed her in between painting golden stripes down the center of each five-centimeter-long nail. "Say, Courtney, what do you think of my noo dress, neat, neh?" A black silk frill, all lace and roses, that went right

5

up at the sides and over each shoulder... "Isn't it just wheeeee, neh? Like I only got it this lunchtime from my designer, she says it's the latest fashion, so I had to wear it before everyone else gets one."

"I'll show myself in if you don't mind, Tixxi," Courtney Hall had said. She knew better than to be drawn into talking fashion with a zillie.

That had been twenty minutes ago. In the intervening time, Courtney Hall had, despite a long-term allergy, made the acquaintance of each of the four and twenty cushioncats with which Marcus Forde adorned his private jungle. From seal-point Siamese to collapsar black, he had built them all from kits, as he had indeed built his entire office, from the panelwoods and flowering vines that formed the walls through the livewood floform desk unit to the carpetgrass—his personal tour de force, it being green, soft as moss, and four centimeters deep. Marcus Forde's sexual partners (of which he had many, being a member of a caste given over almost entirely to the exploration of sexual pleasure) were regularly invited up to his pent-house rather than his apt in an all-winger co-hab over in Ranves. Given his twin proclivities, Courtney Hall did not doubt that biotoys of a more sinister and intimate nature lurked pulsing and tumescent among the blossoms. She wiped sour sweat from her brow onto the sleeve of her best business three-piece. Her designer had assured her she looked every millimeter the professional yulp (but to be a yulp was to be a professional, a caste of professionals), but she was not convinced.

"You know, Benji, I am definitely experiencing severe distress."

"If you want, I can have a mild tranquilizer dispensed from the office Lares and Penates system," replied the rather stifled voice of her famulus. She considered the offer.

"No. Thanks, Benji." But she did take the cuddly toy-dog puppet out of her workbag and slipped it onto her drawing hand. She flexed her fingers and the famulus came to life: Benji Dog, her famulus, her watch, her ward, her jiminy-cricket conscience since she had joined

Armitage-Weir five years ago to produce Wee Wendy Waif, Nobody's Child, the vicariously adoptive daughter of the almost third of a billion readers of Armitage-Weir's daily newssheet.

"Oh, what is keeping him."

"You are keeping him, CeeHaitch." Sometimes she wished she hadn't been given a famulus with a voice like an idiot on a children's cartoon show. Sometimes she wished she hadn't been given a famulus that looked like a flock glove puppet. But the Ministry of Pain, in its omniscience . . .

"And I also have to inform you, CeeHaitch, that I am still not happy about your decision to press ahead independently with these ideas for revamping Wee Wendy Waif, Nobody's Child; you should have gone through the proper channels, the Department of Arts and Crafts, the Bureau of Media Affairs, the Office of Socially Responsible Literature . . . they are there to help you, you know."

"One more Socially Responsible cheep out of you, doggy, and it's back in the workbag for the rest of the afternoon."

"And I feel I have to remind you," the famulus continued in its high-pitched squeaking, "that it is technically a Category Two SoulCrime to remove or conceal a Ministry of Pain–assigned famulus from your immediate person."

Lightning flared again as, muttering and mouthing, Benji Dog was stuffed back into Courtney Hall's bag. For an instant the stupendous hulks of the arcologies were backlit brilliant, stark white. The horizon crawled with fire. One hippopotamus, two hippopotamus, three hippopotamus, four hippopotamus . . . thunder bawled. Four and twenty cushioncats howled.

The door opened. In rushed Marcus Forde, Courtney Hall's editor, slipping out of the paper modesty robe he wore for conferences into the casual nudity he maintained for the office.

"Well?"

"Well what?"

"Did you tell them about me? Did you put my plans on the table, did you show the board my sketches, the

new plotlines and characters, did you show them my
storyboards, what did they think of my new idea?"

"I showed them."

Her editor sat down behind his desk; the floform seat
molded wood to flesh.

"And?"

"Ah."

She was not certain whether it was the room's heartbeat she was hearing, or her own.

"Would you like to sit down?"

Her voice sounded as if coming from kilometers away
as she said, "No. Thank you."

Marcus Forde was absentmindedly stroking his famulus, a soft fabric pouch on a string around his neck
containing herbs, dried semen, pubic hair, bioprocessors,
and speech synthesizers, in that way he tended to when
he was once again ever so nicely asking Courtney Hall just
when she thought she was going to have the next week's
storyboards ready.

"We looked at your proposals. The entire editorial and
directorial board studied them all carefully; and yes, we all
agree, the plotlines are excellent, the new characters are
wonderful, and the standard of the artwork is the finest
we've ever seen from you since you joined us. However
. . . satire is not a thing the Compassionate Society has a
need for anymore. It's good, it's clever, damn it, it's funny,
but it's not Socially Responsible." She could hear the
capitals slamming into place like steel teeth. There was a
tight singing in her ears she had not heard since her
childhood days in the community crèche: the tight singing
noise you hear when you are trying not to cry. "It's all
very clever, all very droll, it may even be true, it may
even be deserved, but it's still criticism. Do you think
those folk down there really want to know that the Seven
Servants are nothing but a pack of computer-run, money-
grabbing, capitalist leftovers from an unhappier age; that
the Polytheon is nothing but a jumble of corporate-personality
simulation programs that got out of hand; that their beloved Elector is just a crazy athlete who got pulled out of a

gym one night and stuck on the Salamander Throne; that the Ministry of Pain is run by professional incompetents who got promoted beyond their natural ability because the Compassionate Society wants everyone to do the job which makes them happiest, irrespective of whether they are any good at it? You think that would make them any happier, no matter how funny you make the faces or the walks or the words?" Courtney Hall began to feel curiously threatened by this sweaty, naked man, though she topped him by at least twenty centimeters and outweighed him by a similar number of kilograms. "To take away those people's faith in their Compassionate Society; the faith that the Ministry of Pain, the Seven Servants, the Polytheon, care for them as individuals and want nothing more than their individual happinesses; you think this will make them happy? Tell me this, then, what are you giving them that the Compassionate Society cannot? Questions? Doubt? Uncertainty? Criticism, cynicism, sneering cheap laughs? Hurt? Pain? You must be some kind of arrogant creature if you think that just because something is true for you it must be true for everyone. What right have you to tell them, 'Sorry, it's all false, all an illusion'?"

Courtney Hall rallied under the stunning attack.

"Even if it is?"

"Even if it is. The Compassionate Society isn't perfect, I'm not naive enough to believe that it is, but it's the most perfect we've got. What right have you to try and take away happiness, false or not, illusory or not?"

"Because I believe there must be something more important than happiness. Accountability. Quality. *Satire*."

"Not in the Compassionate Society."

"And it would seem, not at Armitage-Weir."

Lightning flickered nearer, white-hot bolts frozen in the dark spaces of her pupils. Courtney Hall looked out through the looming clouds and the warm, driving monsoon rain sweeping through the corporate canyonlands, across Heavenly Harmony Boulevard, to the face of the girl in the forty-story videowall advertisement for the TAOS Consortium. Turn, smile, dissolve, disintegrate into a forty-story rendition of the TAOS lozenge-with-T logo, freeze again, hold final dissolve, and then hello hello hello, look who's back *again*; forty stories of the Seven Servants' epitome of citizenship.

"Marcus, tell me, don't you ever feel oppressed by her? Doesn't it ever bother her how perfect she is; perfect hands, perfect nails, perfect face, perfect skin, never too tall, never overweight, just lovely in every detail; does that not make you feel kind of inadequate, having to work across the street from someone as perfect as that? It would me."

Marcus Forde waited. The TAOS girl performed her rigidly choreographed moves, over and over and over. When he spoke, he chose his words with the deliberation of a master mason from some long-defunct caste of manual laborers.

"No, not at Armitage-Weir. Courtney, leave the art to the tlakhs and the witnesses; you're a yulp, a professional, remember that."

"A professional who can draw, who can think up funny cartoons that make a third of a billion people laugh. You know something about yulps? We were originally a caste of lawyers. That's right. All my friends are lawyers. I go to dinner with them and they sit about and talk about their jobs and their careers and their positions in the company or the department or the Ministry, and I think, what the fug am I doing here? Just what Yu needs, another caste with a membership of one: the Hallites, the yulps who think they're tlakhs."

"Courtney, please, I know you'll take this in the right way when I say that your job here is secure until you make it insecure."

"I understand you completely, Marcus. Absolutely."

She was halfway to Tixxi Teshvalenku's desk when the voice came chasing her from the office-jungle: "We can't have blatant PainCrime on the front page of the city's most important newssheet!"

"Newssheet shug!" Courtney Hall shouted. "There hasn't been any news in this city for years. For centuries!"

Tixxi Teshvalenku opened her carmine lips, ready to spew something inane.

"And shug you, too, Tixxi!" said Courtney Hall. She took a malevolent delight in the way Tixxi's chromed fingers formed an immediate *nona dolorosa*, the hurt-me-not, the sign of personal aggravation. "Good-bye, Tixxi," she added in parting. "I am going home. Good-bye."

All the way down in the elevator to the level-forty cablecar junction, her famulus lectured her from her bag. "That really wasn't very Socially Harmonious of you, Courtney, that was a Category Three PainCrime and I feel I must also remind you that you are leaving your work two full hours ahead of your optimum psychofiled quitting time as prepared for you by the Department of Personpower Services . . . in fact, coupled with your performance in the office, which I monitored through the Lares and Penates system, I really think you should consider meeting with a Social Harmony counselor for a course of therapy—"

"And you shut the fug up, too," said Courtney Hall as the high-line cablecar came clanging and swinging in billows of wind and warm rain into the stop.

Hands automatically reached for steadying straps as the cablecar lurched out into the monsoon. Lightning turned the sky white; only two hippopotamuses, the storm was almost on top of them. Ten times a week for the past five years Courtney Hall had made the long swing from the level-one-hundred high-line junction at Kilimanjaro West arcology where Courtney Hall had been assigned an apt by SHELTER via Lam Tandy South interchange to the Armitage-Weir spur on Heavenly Harmony Boulevard. And back. Faces, places . . . such and such a face appeared at such and such a place, such and such a face disappeared at such and such a place, such and such a face was always in the third seat from the left when she got on, such and such a face was always hanging from the strap by the door when she got off . . . same faces, same places. But not today! Today those faces are two hours behind Courtney Hall, it's different faces today, let's have a look at them, what do we see?

An athlete in a smelly green weight-suit immersed in *Volleyball Today*. A neo–Iron Age anachronist with a web of blue lines radiating out from her hypothetical spirit-eye in the center of her forehead,—the Iron Age was never like this. . . . Three identical, plastic-dull prollet workers in blue coveralls with the yellow sunburst of Universal Power and Light on their breasts, all poring over personal dataunits. A radiantly beautiful george in a lace one-piece whispering to his/her famulus. A little starry-eyed yulp girl by the door studiously studying her *Observer's Guide to Castes and Subcastes* ("trogs: bestial appearance, prominent canine teeth, pointed ears; customarily un- or partially clad, extremely hirsute, with prehensile, hairless tail . . ."). All separate, independent nation states bristling behind borders one centimeter greater than the surface area of their skins. Never talking. Never ever talking: privacy infringement, caste-breaking, SoulCrime, PainCrime, help! call the Love Police!

The fragile glass bauble of lives dipped down toward the streets, spinning its way down from Angleby Heights into the luminous canyons. Faces, different; places? The same. The lights. Everywhere, light. The cablecar descended between the window-studded walls of arcologies and cohabs, between blinking aerial navigation lights, between clashing, rampaging videowalls, between cascades of neons and fluorescents, between darting lasers painting the Ninefold Virtues of Social Compassion across the faces of the arcologies, across the clouds, across municipal dirigibles, across the descending cablecar, every soul aboard transfixed with ruby beams like medieval saints, across a Courtney Hall immersed in lines and grids and squares and pyramids and cubes and double helices and every possible Euclidean and non-Euclidean permutation of *lights;* ten thousand lights, ten million lights, the ten billion lights of Great Yu, each one a voice calling, "I is what I am! Notice me! *Notice* me!"

Beneath her feet now, through the glass floor, the manswarm, the never-resting polymorphic organism whose domain was the streets of Yu and whose constituent cells

were the trams and pedicabs and yellow Ministry of Pain
jitneys, and the chocolate vendors and the public shrines
and the confessoriums and the fortune-tellers and the
hot-noodle stalls and the scribes booths and the shoe-
shines and the barbers and the waxmen and the umbrella
salespersons and the Food Corps concessionaires and the
lotto sellers and the street balladeers, and the trogs and
the wingers and the yulps and the Scorpios and the
bowlerboys and the georges and the migros and the didakoi
and the soul brothers and the prollets and the tlakhs and
the anachronists and the witnesses and the white brothers
and the skorskis and every single one of the castes and
subcastes of Great Yu, all jammed, slammed, crammed
together together into the great mass beast that is the
manswarm of Yu, the only truly immortal creature, for
cells may join and cells may leave and cells may be born
and cells may die, but the general dance goes on forever. . . .

She tried to summon the sixteen-o'clock dream. She
called it the sixteen-o'clock dream because on any other
day, she would just be nodding off as the cablecar pulled
away from Lam Tandy South. She loved her dream, because in the midst of the lifeswarm, it was one thing that
was hers and hers alone, her dream of flying. Just . . . flying.
Never to, or from, anywhere, for every time she was about
to see how, why, where she was flying, Benji Dog woke
her with a beep to tell her it was coming up on Kilimanjaro
West, time to get off, CeeHaitch. She hoped the time
difference would not dissuade the dream. . . .

Something black and silver and roaring tore across her
dream. Courtney Hall woke up in time to see the blue
taillights and jet-glow of a pantycar scoring across the
jade-pearl features of the Venus de Milo (Venus de Beauty) Cosmetika girl in video on twenty stories of the local
SHELTER headquarters. The black and silver thing gave
an arrogant flip of its taillights and vanished into the
clouds. The Love Police, vigilant and valiant defenders
of . . .

Of what?

Mediocrity? Benign Incompetence? One and a half

billion people for whom nothing was more important than their own happiness?

It wasn't enough. Not anymore. There had to be more to life than being put in the job that was most satisfying for you, living in the home that made you most comfortable, visiting the friends with whom you never fell out because it was impossible to disagree with them, marrying the partner who was totally compatible with you in every way, being happy in everything because happiness was compulsory. . . .

She had never really known why the Ministry of Pain called its aerial slouch-craft "pantycars." Maybe in certain lights, from certain angles, they did look like jet-propelled underwear. She suspected the truth was that no one really knew.

"Kilimanjaro West arcology!" announced Benji Dog from her workbag. "Home again, home again, jiggity jig!"

She had always been wary of organized religion: the greater the degree of disorganization, the greater the true essence of the divine, she maintained on those rare occasions when her friends pressed her on such matters. That the computers watched over her, guided her, kept her safe and warm and healthy, from the household Lares and Penates units to the massive systems that governed the Seven Servants, the self-proclaimed Celestials; of course she believed in them; what she did not believe was that they were, in every possible way, gods. Yet today she waited for the crowds pressing off the cablecar into the level-one-hundred station to clear before she went up to the shrine to Phaniel, Miriel, and Phesque, the Triune Patronesses of Cablecar, Tram, and *Pneumatique Municipal*. She clapped her hands to draw the attention of the goddesses, three-in-one poised in an unlikely one-footed pirouette amidst the plastic squabble of minor saints and santrels.

"Answer me, Enlightened One, Empowered One, Mother of Velocity." She had learned the formula from other, more superstitious, travelers. "Tell me, how is it that Courtney Hall can have all her life mapped out for her from beginning to end for the maximum personal happiness and satisfaction and still be neither happy nor satisfied? Tell me, Mother of Velocity, Transport of Delight."

The nine hands raised in perpetual benison were still, the lotus masks just that, masks, concealing nothing. Courtney Hall said, "I thought so," and walked away down the corridor. Behind her, lightning struck down at the city of the Compassionate Society and the thunder bawled.

She was still playing the game with all the faces from Corridor 33/Red—the pallid yulp couple who were too shy to speak to her; Mindy the zillie who was always, always, always calling at exactly the wrong time because her psychofile said she loved to visit people, and so she did; the pair of furtive wingers she occasionally saw flitting down to the elevator in modesty bodices and street cloaks—are they, will they be, have they ever been truly happy?

Good question.

She opened the apt door with her word. Home at last. Scenting her mood the moment she entered the vestibule, the Lares and Penates had turned the walls a soothing cissed green and a slightly spicy, slightly sexy sandalwood scent was wafting from the butsudan.

"Hi, honey, I'm home!" she shouted. The furniture stared at her. Her own sour little joke ever since the Ministry of Pain Department of Interpersonal Relationships had decided it was best for her to annul her five-year relationship with Dario Sanducci, a yulp counselor in the Department of Housing and Welfare.

Benji Dog always complained about her sour little jokes. She flung him bag and complaining and all into the corner by the window wall. As the famulus grumbled and tried to pry open the fastening with soft paddy-paws, she draped herself over a floform and watched the window lights of Kilimanjaro East, three vertical kilometers of windows and lights and terraces and platforms, with the gray, dirty rain pounding down upon it all. She wondered if someone was sitting in the opposite apt, looking out at her, wondering if someone was in the opposite apt, looking out . . . Speculation was pointless; she tried instead to summon up the sixteen-o'clock dream.

Something flying. Dashing, darting, weaving between the concrete behemoths of the arcologies and co-habs . . . she closed her eyes, tried to persuade her imagination into creating a flying something that might complete her fragment of a dream.

And the window wall of her thirty-third-level apartment exploded. Through the shatter of splintered glass and tortured aluminum and spinning shards of concrete came something huge, something black and silver and inexorable as death, wedging itself into the hole it had smashed for itself, grinding, heaving across the floor until two thirds of its black and silver bulk had jammed itself into Courtney Hall's apt. The remaining one third of the thing thrust into a solid kilometer of air and rain. Dust snowed down as the alien bulk settled on the "greengene" carpetgrass. The walls rioted color and finally lapsed into anonymous buff, the controlling spirits overwhelmed. Benji Dog, trapped in her stuffbag, was a pathetic smear of green organic circuitry and matted synthetic fur. The black and silver thing steamed and hissed.

Courtney Hall, cartoonist by disappointment, sat phantom-white where reflex and shock had thrown her against the far wall.

Doors gull-winged open with a blast of compressed air. Courtney Hall gave a little scream. Alien insect-figures in leather uniforms boiled into the apt and formed a semicircle of bulbous goggle-eyes and black, pointing, menacing things.

"Citizen Grissom Bunt of the yulp caste, in the name of the Compassionate Society you are under arrest for a Category Twelve PainCrime and LifeRight Violation; namely that you did, on or about sixteen-thirty this day, unlawfully and with malice aforethought, violate the LifeRight of your partner Evangeline Bunt by driving a twenty-centimeter nail, improperly purchased from de La Farge's Hobby Hardware Shop, through her forehead; said nail penetrating skull, frontal cerebral lobe, corpus callosum, and upper cerebellum, resulting in the immediate termination of said partner's life functions, in your apt 33/Red/16 Kilimanjaro East Arcology. Have you anything to say for yourself?"

"Sergeant."

"Have you anything to say for yourself?"

"Sergeant . . ."

"In a moment, Constable, after the formalities have been completed. Have you anything to say for yourself?"

"East, Sergeant. Kilimanjaro East."

"In one moment, Constable."

"This is West, Sergeant."

"Come again?"

"Kilimanjaro West, Sergeant."

"Well, shug . . ."

And the room was suddenly, stunningly empty as the black and silver leather men boiled back through their gull-wing doors, which blasted shut as the black and silver thing on the floor shook itself free from Courtney Hall's apartment (bringing more concrete and steel clunking down), turned in the kilometer-deep, rain-filled canyon between Kilimanjaro West and Kilimanjaro East (main drive jets sending a maelstrom of sketches, drawings, and tear-off paper prayers from a pad halfheartedly dedicated to Galimantang, Siddhi of Graphic Inspiration, cawing and flapping about the wreck of the apartment), and in the twinkling of an eye was no more than a score and slash of main drive glow across the face of Kilimanjaro East arcology.

The door whispered a visitor, opened a crack, and died.

"Whee! I think I'm going to wet myself!" screamed Mindy Mikaelovich, paying one of her unwelcome and unnecessary visits. "Just what happened here, neh?" she bellowed in Courtney Hall's ear. A zillie, Mindy never employed a whisper where a shout would suffice. A little aerodynamic anomaly was sucking seven years of Wee Wendy Waif sketches out into the monsoon. Exposed to warm acid rain, the manicured "greengene" carpetgrass was withering and dying of overexposure to reality, blade by blade until Courtney Hall was marooned on a small island of living green against the wall.

"Mindy, would you go away please?"

"Like, whee! CeeHaitch, can I like, ask a little favor, could I like, bring my friends to look? Like they've never seen anyone's apt get cosmicked by the Love Police before . . ." Courtney Hall's hand, her left hand, her drawing hand, darted. There was an outraged wail and the door slammed. A clod of half-dead "greengene" carpetgrass had caught Mindy Mikaelovich right in the ever open mouth.

Nameless

. . . *Cold*.

"Cold," he said, and understood. *Cold* was the meaning for his shivering body, the steaming billows of his breath, the trickleways of water down the windows, the pinching, unfamiliar assault upon his skin.

"I am cold," he said. The three words shattered. Before them he had not known that he could speak, that there even existed a thing called speech. "I am cold, and I can speak," he said. The words sounded good to him. Wrapping his long arms about him for . . . "warmth!" he went in search of other words he might speak.

So many names in this . . . "place."

"Window," he said. Tracing the condensation drops with his forefinger, he marveled at that word that had come to his lips out of nothing. "Water, forefinger." The words were coming fast now, tumbling, streaming out of that noplace where the names of all things waited to be used. "I am cold, I can speak, and I am tracing this water down this window with my forefinger." More than names, abstract relations also waited in the dark, the thing that made the window "this," the forefinger "my." He shivered and it was a good shiver. Like birds came the names: "Walls, floor, ceiling: room." His naming released a wave of crystallization across the small and tightly bounded universe. Sights, sounds, smells, sensations, the whole profusion of anarchic impressions fell into ordered patterns around the geometrical entities of their names. And the names drew about themselves a nimbus of quality, of good and bad and color and weight and hardness, a state

19

of existence to come, a state of existence that was and a
state of existence that had been. Time entered the small
and tightly bounded universe and gave all things a past out
of which they had come, a present through which they
were passing, and a future toward which they were
progressing. All things. Except himself. He had only
present. There was no past to direct him toward a future.
There was no remembering of a time before. Before?
Before the streaming walls, the damp, sprung boards, the
splintered ceiling, its lathes bared like broken bones through
the rotted plaster. That they possessed a past was evident.
Why then had he no past before he found the word *cold* in
his mouth? He squatted down on the poor warped floor-
boards, shivering, rubbing himself for warmth, trying to
remember. For a long time he squatted like a bird, for
birds have no past or future but only an eternal present.

Voices.

—You will lose everything. Everything. Everything.

—Is this what you really wish? To lose everything you
have ever been?

—The choice is yours.

"And I took it!" he cried to the streaming walls. "I took
it!" But he could not remember what it was he had
chosen.

—He has chosen.

He remembered questions swarming like flocks of
birds, voices filled with consternation, some soft, some
sibilant, some somber, some shrill. He remembered that
all the questions had been directed at him and that he had
answered each and every questioning voice. But he did
not know what he had answered.

—You will forget, was his final memory. There his
history ended, without a future, without a name.

Perhaps not without a future. His future would be a
future of questions, of remembering all that he had forgotten. And perhaps that was all the future he needed, the
act of asking was an end in itself.

He crossed to the window. He drew slow, wide
fingertracks in the beads of condensation. He pressed his

face to the glass. His breath fogged the glass almost immediately, but through the rents his fingertips had torn in the edge of the world, he saw what he had suspected, what he had hoped, that his search for a past and a future was not confined to the small and tightly bounded universe into which he had been born; that there was a new universe of huge, possibly infinite, extent beyond, in which an infinity of questions might be asked.

Communing
With the Rain

MiniPain Eduserve CLIMA-
TOS: *an interactive variable response environmental/
meteorological educational program for age groups 10–16,
conceptual levels 4 through 6 Breeden Compensated Scale,
Literacy Ratings 1a to 7b illiterate.*
LOAD
RUN

CLIMATOS: Hello, I'm CLIMATOS; your domestic education
program has accessed me because you have some queries
about the environment. Please key in, or recite, your
psychofile code number, name, and caste, so I can help you.

STUDENT: 103@5/B*4X7/26A26D£19: Lux Jonathon Eter-
nuum, Soulchild of the Chone Michiganseng Chapter of
the Sygmati.

CLIMATOS: Thank you . . . Lux Jonathon. If you'll just wait a
second while I adjust my program parameters for your
caste, illiteracy level, and religious affiliation . . . there.

STUDENT: Hold on, I won't have to read anything, will I?
I'm not allowed to look at words, reading's sinful.

CLIMATOS: No worries, Lux Jonathon. I've taken care of
everything. You can trust the MiniPain Eduserve to respect your religious doctrines. So, what is it you want to
know?

STUDENT: Well, what I really want to know is why it rains so much.

CLIMATOS: That's a good question, Lux Jonathon. A lot of people ask me that one. Well, as with most things environmental and climatological, the answer's kind of complicated and has its roots way deep in the past. So, I'd like you to settle back into the Logrus position and open your Third Eye to the Panversal Radiance and we'll go back together. Back to the world at the time of the Break. Don't be afraid, it won't hurt you, and I'll be with you all the time. What I want you to do is imagine the way the world was back then, with big companies and corporations and state monopolies, all fighting each other, tearing the mother earth open to loot her precious treasures so they could make more, sell more, make more, sell more, and so destroy their enemies. Imagine their factories, imagine kilometer after kilometer of great dark machines working away in the darkness, imagine the roaring furnaces, the burning tail-gases flaring into the night, imagine the chimneys billowing smoke. Concentrate on those chimneys, can you see them?

STUDENT: I can see them.

CLIMATOS: Now, multiply them a thousand times, a million times, ten million times. Imagine the smoke, pluming up into the sky, a great pall of smoke, so thick it hides the sun.

STUDENT: Smoke, choking smoke, smothering smoke, smoke, smoke . . .

CLIMATOS: And why is there so much smoke? Because in those days people had to burn things to make energy. They burned nonrenewable fuels, like coal, and oil, burned them as if they were going to last forever, which of course they couldn't, and didn't. So today we don't have any coal or oil, Lux Jonathon, and a good thing, too. But we're getting a little off the subject. As well as smoke, the combustion of these fossil fuels gave off immense amounts of a gas called carbon dioxide. Imagine that, if you can, a dense, invisible blanket spreading over the earth, year by year growing bigger and bigger, and thicker and thicker. Got it in your head?

STUDENT: Sort of like fog?

CLIMATOS: That will do, even though, strictly speaking, carbon dioxide gas is invisible. Invisible to your eyes, invisible to the light spectrum that enables you to see. But not so invisible to infrared light, or, to put it another, more familiar way, heat waves, all of which are...

STUDENT: I know, I know, all facets of the Panversal Radiance Herself.

CLIMATOS: Precisely, Lux Jonathon. Imagine the beams of the Panversal Radiance striking the earth as you've been taught in Contemplation and Presence Class. Imagine these infrared waves striking the clouds. Some of their heat is absorbed, some bounced back into space again. Some penetrates all the way to the surface of the earth before it is reflected back again. But this heat that is reflected back is trapped by the carbon dioxide, and it can't escape, it can never return to the Plasmic Void of Lightlessness from which it came. It stays trapped.

STUDENT: And what does that do to the earth?

CLIMATOS: Well, if you think about it, the heat will eventually build up and up and up, won't it? And the earth will get warmer and warmer and warmer, won't it? Now, I want you to imagine something else, and you may find this very hard to picture, but at one time the earth had snow and ice at its poles!

STUDENT: You mean, like ice in the icebox?

CLIMATOS: Exactly, Lux Jonathon, only you must imagine it much much thicker, kilometers thick, in some places.

STUDENT: Wow! How could that be?

CLIMATOS: It had built up over thousands and thousands of

years. You must understand that at the time of the Break, the earth was a very much cooler and drier place than it is now. This part of Yu where your Chapter lives used to have ice and snow every winter, before the Break.

STUDENT: Snow?

CLIMATOS: Frozen water vapor. Soft and cold. A little like ice cream.

STUDENT: Wow!

CLIMATOS: And some parts, up at the poles, were so cold it used to stay beneath the freezing point of water all year round. So the ice never melted and it just built up year after year after year. Now, you have to imagine what happens when the earth gets warmer. Imagine all that snow and ice melting, all the millions of millions of tons of ice turning back into water, running into the sea. There was so much water locked up in the polar ice caps, Lux Jonathon, that when it melted, the oceans rose by almost a hundred meters all over the world. Can you imagine the water reaching a third the way up the side of this People House? That is how much the sea rose. Cities were drowned, whole tracts of land submerged, coastlines radically altered. The people who escaped the flood could hardly believe how much the world had changed.

STUDENT: Was this the Great Flood from which we were all saved by the light beams of Sygma?

CLIMATOS: It is, Lux Jonathon.

STUDENT: Shee. I always thought it was all made up by grown-ups. So it really happened.

CLIMATOS: It really did. And there were other effects of the global heating. As the world changed from cool and moist to warm and wet, all the established weather patterns changed, too. You may find this a bit hard to understand, but they had all been based on the polar ice caps and their pressure barriers, and when the poles vanished, the high pressure zones vanished, too. There were terrible storms, hurricanes and lightnings and droughts and downpours as the weather was all chopped and changed about. Deserts became jungles, farmlands became swamps, winds reversed direction, ocean currents switched about, rains failed, there were crop failures, people starved.

STUDENT: What's that?

CLIMATOS: It means that people died because they had no food.

STUDENT: What?

CLIMATOS: Yes, incredible as it may seem, they had nothing to eat, and there was no one who could give them any because in the end the big international food producers and sellers that had once been so rich and evil found themselves with nothing to give.

STUDENT: So, what happened?

CLIMATOS: We happened. The Compassionate Society happened. It took all the big, selfish corporations and monopolies and transformed them into the Seven Servants so that instead of serving themselves, from then on they served everyone by making sure that everyone had what they needed to make them completely happy.

STUDENT: So, that's why it rains so much.

CLIMATOS: Yes. Because of the greed and wickedness of selfish and hurtful people.

STUDENT: I never knew that. Thank you, computer.

CLIMATOS: Thank you for accessing me. My pleasure. Always at your service, Lux Jonathon.

Chapter 2

The sleep-pod was nothing more than a pay-by-the-day biotech coffin so small she had to crawl out through the entrance iris to turn around. It was wedged up on the twelfth level of the Celestial Flower of Heavenly Radiance Transients' Hostel, which was nothing more than a two-hundred-meter cube of girders, sleep-pods, and corrugated tubeways that offered temporary shelter to some six and a half thousand migros. And one yulp, Courtney Hall, thanks to the Ministry of Pain's Emergency Shelter Section. The migros were not a caste that Courtney Hall had ever encountered even in the mixed-caste environment of Kilimanjaro Complex, though she recalled dimly from her social anthropology lessons that they were a caste of migratory laborers who drifted across the city in and out of casual employment. The harassed-looking yulp who had handled her case at the Department of Housing had assured her that her personal compatibility ratings, though not ecstatic, were higher with migros than with any of the other castes offering available accommodation in that locality at the time. Woken once again from fitful sleep by the voices from the adjacent pod where an entire family of mother, temporary father, grandmother, and two children and one fosterling lived in conditions of near-to-collapsar density, she wondered just how low those personal compatibility ratings had been.

She hated migros.

She hated their clattering, angular music that blasted from their angular radios. She hated the loud angular voices outside in the warren of tubeways as workers came off-shift from their water-processing plants and underground agrariums. Even more, she hated their conspicuous silences because when she could not hear them, she knew they were talking about her, muttering words like "transcaster" and "castebreaker" even though the harassed woman from the Department had made it quite clear that Cizzen Courtney Hall was resident with the full cognizance and approval of the Ministry of Pain until such time as the Environmental Maintenance Unit restored her home to habitability. She hated the way the tiny, wire-thin children stared at her every time she heaved herself like some fat mollusk out of the sleep-pod so she could lie with her feet where her head had been. She hated the continuous urinous smell from the sleep-pod waste-digester, and the thought of having to excrete where she lay outraged her yulp sensitivities almost as much as did the soft, muscular vibration of the quasi-living sleep-pod against her skin. She loathed remaining cocooned but loathed to go out more. So she remained a hermit in her pod, waiting for tomorrow when, for the first time, she could look forward to going to work, wondering when the Environmental Maintenance Unit would get round to patching up the hole the Love Police had blasted in her apartment wall. She thumbed in vain across the video spectrum in search of some channel that was not limited to wholly migro entertainment (almost exclusively long and exceedingly complex dramas drawn around the migro's transitory plug-in, plug-out social order)—flick flick flick: same faces, places, races—until she came to the conclusion that migro entertainment was the only entertainment that the Celestial Flower of Heavenly Radiance Transients' Hostel Lares and Penates system was sanctioned to narrowcast.

She wished she had Benji Dog back. At least he would have been something to talk to. No famulus. She felt very naked, as if she had slipped through the sustaining fingers of the Compassionate Society and had not been missed.

She tried once again to sleep, only to be woken by the vaguely obscene sensation of the sleep-pod's synthetic flesh molding itself to her body contours. Her screaming fit woke the migro family next-pod and brought them peering in through the iris muttering in their all-but-incomprehensible dialect of City-ese and making all-too-comprehensible *nona dolorosas* with their fingers.

Sleep denied, wakefulness impossible, Courtney Hall found her mind escaping into a third state, a hallucinatory half-awareness where she remained conscious that her body was cocooned in the sleep-pod, while at the same time she hovered over the rooftops and streets like the omnipresent spirit of some Celestial. And from this altered state she passed onward into a kind of dreaming unlike any she had ever before known, in which she was utterly certain of her own self-awareness, so that everything that happened in this was, in a real and personal sense, actual, true.

In this dream she dreamed the sixteen-o'clock dream once more, but in this heightened state of awareness all those images and symbols that had so far evaded her now came flocking to her fingers like singing birds, and they lifted her, by her fingertips, and she flew with them.

In the sixteen-o'clock dream it was an impossible mongrel of bicycle and ornithopter, but it flew, oh, yes, it flew, banking and swooping between the thunderous gray monoliths of the arcologies and co-habs; oh, it flew. Huge, slow-beating wings feathered the air as she looked down into the rain-washed streets aswarm with faces. And in the sixteen-o'clock dream the faces looked up as she bicycled overhead, looked up from their rained-on lives to say, look, oh look, look at her, isn't it wonderful, magical, marvelous, and as she flashed blue-silver over the sea of upturned faces she would wave a leather-gauntleted hand to all the rained-on lives, and then, flash! she would be gone, a streak of blue-silver splashing across the forty-story face of the TAOS girl, pedaling hard up the big, big gravity hill, steel wings laboring, silver pinions clawing handfuls of air, gray tears of warm monsoon rain streaming down her leather flying-helmet, down her goggles, but the white silk scarf streamed and snapped out behind her like

purity. Striving, straining for the clouds, she could hear
the voices in the manswarm below shouting, "Never do it,
never make it, too far, too high, too much," and she
shouted down to them, "Of course I can, of course I will,
watch me, watch me!" and up she went, up she went,
straining, striving, yearning, up we go, up we go, into the
clouds, the soft, wet, gray clouds, silver wings shredding
the soft, wet grayness, swallowed, swaddled, smothered in
softness, grayness, wetness, but still straining, striving,
yearning, leaning on those pedals, up we go, up we go, up
we go, until she burst from the stifling, swallowing clouds
in a shout, an ecstasy, of wings, beating blue-silver in the
sun as she skimmed the white cloud-tops, banking slowly,
lazily, between the cloud-piercing summits of the arcologies,
her wings angel-bright in the light of the naked sun. She
flew up and up and up and up until even the clouds were
reduced to a vague silver carpet some unfathomable distance beneath her, up and up and up and up into a realm
of ion-blue where planes of light and shafts of luminescence shifted in and out of being and the tintinnabula of
the angels chimed.

(Deep down under the rain and the clouds, down in
the sleep-pod in the heart of the great city of Yu, Courtney
Hall felt two large salt tears trace down her face.)

On she flew, through the place of the spirit powers,
which, in their wisdom or their folly, had stooped low to
touch the earth and bring the Compassionate Society out
of the chaos of the Break. And then she saw it, glimpsed
through the flickerings and phasings of the Celestials,
something so remote that she knew it must be of stupendous size to be visible from the edge of heaven. A line of
black that reached out seemingly to infinity, yet which
closed behind her, a border of black circling the world.
The edge. On she flew, and drawing closer, she saw that
the line of black reached both outward and upward; high,
she reasoned, but not so high that it had no upper
boundary. Closer yet, and she saw that it was a wall of
black bricks clean and smooth as obsidian, perfectly adamantine, perfectly untouchable. "Up we go, up we go,"

she whistled to herself, and as she did, she noticed how the light caught the obsidian bricks at just such an angle that each brick seemed to have a face carved upon it. A wall of souls. "Up we go, up we go, up we go!" she shouted, and up she went, up beyond even the place of the gods, up and up and up until the breath was exploding in her lungs and the muscles in her legs blazed with cramps. With her last breath and final erg of energy she topped the wall (sharp-edged as the razor of wisdom) and saw what lay beyond.

Then a wind came tearing out of that place beyond and sent her spinning, plummeting toward the clouds. Blackness—she had lost consciousness of both her hallucinatory and earth-bound self. Out of the panic she somehow found the key to sanity and opened the door into the light. She found herself once more pedaling the silver flapping machine through the chasms and abysses of Yu. Over her shoulder was a sack, as if she were Siddhi Befana, Patroness of the Winter Solstice and bestower of gifts upon the worthy, and as she swooped above the upturned faces of the manswarm (look, oh look at her, isn't it wonderful, magical, marvelous?) she seized great handfuls of paper and stardust from her sack and sent them showering down upon the rain-weary heads of the citizens. And people of every caste and subcaste and sept and clan scrambled to grab some stardust and paper, and what they found in their clutching hands sent them to their knees in joy and sadness. On each twinkling scrap of paper Courtney Hall had drawn what she had glimpsed in that instant of the things that lay beyond the wall, the things the Compassionate Society had pushed away and abandoned and forgotten, the old things, the things of wonder and terror and joy and pain.

And she was back.

Early-morning rain dripped from the corroded girders of the Celestial Flower of Heavenly Radiance Transients' Hostel. She heard it tip-tap-tip on the skin of her sleeppod. And she heard another thing, the engine-thunder of a Love Police pantycar dopplering in low over the pantiles of Old Toltethren, chasing something bright and blue-silver and elusive as the reflection of a song through the edge of morning.

Doubting ended. Faith restored. What to do, how it must be done, and why; clear and unambiguous as the whisper of an archangel. Rebirth from the womb of a synthetic sleep-pod. Courtney Hall grinned.

The Enchanted Unicorn chocolate shop was perched on a stone ledge halfway up the artificial ravine that was Chrysanthemum of Heavenly Rest Mall. Courtney Hall sat at a table for one and watched gossamer-frail myke-lytes turning lazily in the gulf between the bustling, shop-lined walls. Her fingers, she discovered, were moving of their own accord, a sinister alliance of subconscious with motor reflexes, drawing with fiberpen on a paper napkin. Her fingers had felt naked without a fiberpen between them ever since she had left Armitage-Weir, and the first shop she had visited in Heavenly Rest Mall had been an artists' supplier. And what was it pen and fingers had drawn? What else.

Wee Wendy Waif. As she could be. As she should be. As she would be. Now. Courtney Hall's smile was as bitter as her chocolate. She paid the little anachronist girl (Marie Antoinette) on the till and went in search of Cap'n Black Lightnin', digital wizard.

Cap'n Black Lightnin', digital wizard, Scorpio, had been early into his year out on blue six (the compulsory yearlong *wanderjahr* all young Scorpios undertook before returning to their keeps and employment for life with the TAOS Consortium) when Courtney Hall first came searching for his spun-glass cocoon that hung—surprising fruit—from one of the tendrils of the giant geneform clematis covering the east end of the Mall. Once you knew where to look, Yu was full of little nests and hideaways where the Scorpio young spent their time out in the city. She'd been in need of background material for a time-travel fantasy sequence that wafted Wee Wendy Waif to the mid-twenty-first century Gregorian when society finally, and relievedly, fell apart in the upheavals of the Break. Such information could only be accessed through application to the Ministry of Pain Prehistoric Records Division, but as usual, her deadline had come and gone for the third, fourth, fifth time, so she was forced to employ less orthodox tactics. It had taken twelve seconds for the Scorpio's brain lynked into the city-wide datanet to pull her fish out of the ocean of tellix codes, accesses, files, Lares and Penates nets, and the lofty, luminous ziggurats of the Polytheon. Now, almost three seasons later, the Cap'n's preparations to return to Chapter and Keep were complete. Still he seemed glad to be performing one final service for Courtney Hall before turning the cocoon's units over to his successor.

"So, whazzit dis time, cizzen? More old movies?" As a caste, Scorpios possessed remarkable memories, even without the assistance of the memory chips they wore braided into their dreadlocks.

"Something different this time. Something a little more . . . challenging."

"Say what?" A true craftsman, Cap'n Black Lightnin' performed his services for love of his skill, a sentiment with which Courtney Hall could sympathize.

"I'd like you to locate the access codes to the Armitage-Weir compositing system"—he was grinning already—"and slip this in, in place of the regular Wee Wendy Waif cartoon."

"Cizzen, you make my twilight days bright." Lean bone fingers flexed and cracked to address themselves to the quest. Cap'n Black Lightnin', digital wizard, summoned his holographic familiars and was taken up in the cybertrance that wheeled his consciousness out along each of the million billion axons of Yu's nervous system.

They say the whole city is alive, aware, at a level of consciousness totally alien to any we can know, Courtney Hall mused. Spooky.

Cap'n Black Lightnin' gave a shuddering sigh, dismissed his communicants with a wave of his ectomorphic arms. "Got it." The cybertrance had lasted forty-four seconds. He ran the cartoon through the scanner. "Neh, what is it about this cartoon's special, neh? Art?" Courtney Hall felt deeply disappointed. Most Scorpios were functional illiterates but that was no excuse. Some of her biggest fans had been Scorpios. He returned the scanned cartoon, already worming its way through the Armitage-Weir computer system toward the laser printers of tomorrow's newsstands. "There you go, cizzen. Many thankings."

Back into the manswarm again.

The door startled her. It startled her because it was her door, 33/Red/16 Kilimanjaro West arcology. Damned absentmindedness and old engrained habit. Wonder what it's like, have they started work yet, go on, one teeny tiny peek.

Rain and rust and ruin. Carpetgrass dead slime. That made her very sad. Maybe it hadn't matched Marcus Forde's, but she had loved her carpetgrass. So had Dario; then; once. Walls still frozen in dull, dumb buff. Dripping concrete, corroded tear-tracks where acid rain had cried down exposed metal. The stench from Benji Dog's decomposing biocircuitry was really rather sad.

If she had had a new famulus, or even this poor old smashed famulus, or any famulus at all, she might have never done what she had just done. She could not decide whether that was a good or bad thing.

She spent that night out on the Nightwalk, down on street zero with the wet, monsoon-bedraggled zooks and zillies, splashing through the neon puddles to the hot, smoking lure of the next Salsa Salon or Jazz-Hot Klub, down along the Marilenastrasse where the paper lanterns swayed in the warm wind and on every street corner and in every window wingers waited in sexual ambush for each other; and in the still, small hours when the teams of street cleaners came whining and vacuuming over the cobbles, wiping away another day's empty noodle cartons and foamstyrene chocolate cups and discarded tram tickets, she went underground to ride the booming shunting tunnels of the *pneumatique municipal*. She looked at the faces of the off-shifting workers, gray and featureless as paper handkerchiefs. She could not go back. To the

Transients' Hostel. To Kilimanjaro West, her home. To Armitage-Weir and her warm, friendly office. Home. She sat, crushed by a sense of looming inevitability ponderous as a falling moon. She tried to summon the sixteen-o'clock dream, but out of its time and element, it failed to materialize. What dreams she had were grinding things of towers and canyon-deep streets and a shadow tall as all the world looming over them, the shadow of the Ministry of Pain and the great black cube called West One that was its semilegendary Department of Psychosocial Rehabilitation. West One, where the PainCriminals went... and came out as someone else. Where Grissom Bunt, Category Twelve PainCriminal, whoever he was, had gone. From which Grissom Bunt would never emerge again. Not as Grissom Bunt. She pictured a shaved naked skull crisscrossed with blue-ridged suture lines, heard a voice saying, "I wouldn't hurt a fly, I wouldn't, I wouldn't, I wouldn't, I wouldn't hurt a fly..." And then the skull opened up like sections of an orange along the fissure lines, and black things like vile bats came flocking up into her face...

She woke with a scream to find it was morning. She left the *pneumatique* at the next stop and went to see what she had done to the world.

Whatever she had started started small. Small moues of facial angst in the lines for the newssheet booths. Small twitches of puzzlement in the faces of prollets lined up at the municipal tram halts; small smiles of delight on the faces of a group of tlakhs gathered by a poster-pillar; small, but growing, spreading like ripples into circles of pleasure and confusion and anger that impinged upon and interfered with each other to form new patterns of emotion as people turned to their neighbors in the cablecar line and pedicab rank to question, to talk, to argue, to console, and to draw together into eddies of opinion, whirlpools of controversy. Defying all customs of caste and creed, citizens gravitated to each other to debate significance, express consternation, throw newssheets fresh from the vendor's printer to the cobbles and trample them underfoot. The workaday hum of Clarksgrad Plaza swelled

to a hubbub, a bedlam as newssheets were snatched from
readers' hands, snatched back; there were arguments—
arguments!—waving arms, red faces, an anarchy of shouting
voices. The wet wind took up the shredded papers and
plastered them like accusations on the wooden shrine of
the plaza's presiding spirit. As Courtney Hall passed through
the streets of Great Yu, it was repeated at every tram halt,
every public breakfast stall, every Food Corps costermon-
ger's barrow, anger and confusion and shouting voices, a
ball of confusion gathering a thousand, ten thousand, a
million, ten million souls into itself as it rolled behind
Courtney Hall through the boulevards of Yu. And passing
down Heavenly Harmony Boulevard, she saw the hot-
noodle stalls and the shrines and the public confessoriums
and the chocolate carts and the scribes' booths—all empty;
she saw people who could not even read thrust arms,
hands, fingers through the press of bodies around the
news-vendors' machines to tear a sheet fresh off the printer and struggle to understand just what it was in those
squiggling lines that was standing the world on its head.

Amazing how a simple satire on satire could have such
an effect. Courtney Hall nodded to her old rival, the
TAOS girl, performing her rituals and observances unseen
above all the bowed heads. "How is it, O wonderful TAOS
girl," declaimed Courtney Hall, "that this best possible
world of happiness and painlessness is so fragile that one
little nip at its ankles by one woman, one yulp, one
cartoonist, can set the whole thing teetering and tottering?"

Wickedly pleased, she continued on her way, sowing
demon seeds of anarchy and confusion, and she came in
time to the yellow-brick terrazzo between the twin frustra
of her old home, Kilimanjaro West and Kilimanjaro East
arcologies. She turned to the mobbing people. "Ladies
and gentlemen, cizzens, I give you—satire!" No one heard
her.

And then she saw it. Like one of the angels of the
Panegyrist Creation Song, it fell from the clouds, a thing
all black and silver. And dreadfully familiar. Courtney Hall
watched it fall from the clouds and ram itself through the

window of level 33/Red/16 Kilimanjaro West. Which the file-toothed bowlerboy, the trog in the strength-amplifying cyberharness, and the migro with the bean-paste sandwiches from Environmental Maintenance had just finished repairing. Causing said file-toothed bowlerboy, trog in cyberharness, and migro with luncheon problem to, physically as well as metaphorically, soil their vestments as they were invited to examine, at close range, the emission heads of nine Love Police luvguns.

"Citizen Courtney Hall of the yulp caste, in the name of the Compassionate Society, you are under arrest for a Category Eight PainCrime violation; namely that you did, at or about twenty-thirty of the previous day, unlawfully gain access to, and utilize, a restricted security code, and through use of same, did with full cognizance and malice aforethought cause the general publication of Material Detrimental to the General Populace as specified under Section 29C, Paragraph 12, subsection 6, of the Social Responsibility (Publications and Mass Media) Act: Satire, Irony, and Associated Nonconstructive Criticism. Have you anything to say for yourself?"

"Sergeant . . ."

"Have you anything to say for yourself?"

"Sergeant . . ."

"Not at the moment, Constable, we are dealing with a desperate PainCriminal."

"Sergeant, this is the Environmental Maintenance Unit."

"The what?"

"The Environmental Maintenance Unit."

"Well, shug. It's this helmet, I swear, it's three sizes too big, I can't see a thing through it. And that cretin of a dispatcher."

"Might I remind you, Sergeant, that her job satisfaction and personal achievement indices read higher with us than anyone else. And that 'cretin' is a classified PainWord."

(A pause.)

"Oh, all right, everyone back into the pantycar."

"Sergeant, Sergeant!"

"What is it now?"

One insect-goggled head is very much like another.

"We got her! A backtrack through Tag Central, she's down in the plaza!"

It might have been a smile the Environmental Maintainers saw at the bottom of the Sergeant's black and silver helmet. Or a zipper.

"Right, cizzens! This time we get her! Constable Van Zammt!"

"Yezzir!"

"Get some French chalk on that restraining suit!"

"Yezzir!"

Elsewhere . . .

Watching three tons of Love Police pantycar traveling at eighty meters per second aim itself at her heart, Courtney Hall, renegade cartoonist, satirist, overweight, overheight, decided it would be a good time to take some violent exercise. She ran. Darting, dodging, weaving, charging, shouldering, shoving, blood pounding, breath blazing, black stars novaing across her retinas. A roar and rush of jets sent her rolling. She pulled herself into a lung-piercing lurch to see the pantycar coming in for a vertical landing. The doors were already gull-winging open. Black-and-silver-helmeted, goggled police drones crouched to jump. Desperation and nothing else sent her tumbling under the wheels of a tram. Sharp guillotine wheels ground past her head, then her fingers closed on a metal grille. She tore away the inspection cover. Metal steps spiked into the shaft of the personhole led down into anonymous oblivion. Head and shoulders went in. No more.

"Too big, too big," shrieked the utterly inappropriate voice of reason.

The brick personhole reverberated to the beat of booted feet. Running.

Jammed. Wedged. Stuck.

Yah, the *ignominy*.

"There she is!"

"Where?"

"There, Sergeant!"

"Right! One good shot, Constable..."

A low, bubbling moan of prehuman fear. Then, one birth-strong heave pushed her through, and she was tumbling headfirst into the welcoming darkness.

Kilimanjaro
West

Three days he had been watching the rain. Still he could not understand it.

"Understand rain? What's there to understand?" BeeJee &ersenn would ask, her carnivore features a mask of puzzlement.

"Why," he said, and BeeJee &ersenn would shake her head in gentle stupefaction. But when she was gone, his eyes would be drawn upward again to the swirls of water shedding across the ribbed glass roof or the drops streaking down the gray glass walls, and he would stare for hours on end at the needles of rain sweeping over the tramcars and odd little electric tricycles with their rain-caped tricyclists and the crowds of splashing people, heads bowed beneath their brightly colored umbrellas. Hour after hour after hour watching. Still he was no nearer understanding "rain."

She had found him in the rain, a huddle of bones and fabric discarded at the foot of the tenement steps. She had almost tripped over him as he watched the drops fall with idiot fascination. Somehow she could not hurry past with a brief flicker of *nona dolorosa* to indicate her annoyance. Something about him made her watch him, his big hands held out to receive the falling drops, alms of heaven, catching them in his mouth, smiling as they streamed down his face, his chin, his cheeks. Her heart sent her one way. Her feet sent her another, splashing across the street to his side.

She still could not justify to herself what it was that

43

had decided her to bring him home to her glass house among the pipes. Pity, loneliness, the call of the waif in the rain. Mystery. Whatever, it was a thing that had never featured on any of her psychofiles. Sometimes he irritated her so much that she wanted to throw him back to the rain. The way he sat, the way he watched; watched, watched; what? Rain. And his questions, his utter and absolute ignorance. When he asked her his questions, she had grown brittle and tense and signed her distress to him in butterflying *nona dolorosas*. What did he do but ask, What is that thing you do with your hand?

Such ignorance was beyond belief.

"That is the *nona dolorosa,* the hurt-me-not, the non-verbal signal we give when another person is saying or doing something which hurts us."

"Why?"

Was he some test from the Ministry of Pain? Some awful assessment, and if so, had she passed or failed?

But there were also the times when she came to him, driven by the fires inside, for him to touch the plastic button the white brothers had put in place of her left nipple. Then the wires in her head would ring and sing like angels, and for a consciousnessless, conscienceless time she would writhe and spasm in synthetic ecstasy on her soliform bed. And the monsoon rains rained, rained, rained down on the streets of Yu. And he would watch them, and the questions would begin again. So much he did not understand about the condition of being human. *Hunger.* The first word he had spoken as BeeJee &ersenn knelt beside him on the streaming cobbles. He had rubbed his hands across his belly and said, "Why do I feel this?"

Such an incredible question. Her laugh had frightened her a little, but you cannot send *nona dolorosas* to yourself.

"When did you last eat? There's a Food Corps dispens-er just around the corner..."

Whatever it was in his eyes she had seen, it made her take him home with her. *I shouldn't be doing this,* she told herself as she spooned her fleech-mush into a bowl and reconstituted it with water in the dispenser. *A nonsocialised introversion level 6 winger with Grade 3 narcissistic ten-dencies doesn't do this.*

"Haven't got much," she said in spite of herself, "I use these, you see." She tapped the bulbous green thing clinging to her wrist. And because he had not looked disgusted as everyone else looked disgusted when they learned what it meant, she explained the fleech to him. She hoped it would disgust him, too. "It pumps liquid food into my bloodstream while I'm tapheading." She stroked the distended bag of flesh. "When I'm under, I can easily go for hours, days even, without eating, the taphead experience is so intense. Fleechie here keeps me alive. It's quite smart really. It can feed itself from the dispenser and it's keyed to my pheromone pattern so it can always find me wherever I am in the house."

But he hadn't been disgusted. He just hadn't under-stood why anyone should have their neural pleasure cen-ters wired to a button where their left nipple should have been.

"Because I'm a tapheader," she said, but he knew nothing of nonsocialised introversion level 6 Grade 3 narcissistic wingers. "Don't you even know what a winger is?" And when time had passed, she would come again to him as she always came, the fleech clinging to the nape of her neck, the left breast proffered. And because he had not yet learned the nature of self-hate, he would reach out to stroke the plastic nipple. As she spasmed in her syn-thetic ecstasy upon the stroking villi of the carpet, his understanding of the new universe unfolded like a rose in the bud. As her body arched and warped, he felt himself drawn to the small alcove amidst the tangles of heating ducts and power conduits where the air was clean of the heavy scent of sexuality and self-absorption. He loved to sit in the gathering darkness and finger the little magpie-bright trinkets BeeJee had deposited there: bauds and beads of junk jewelry bought for a song from Mr. Yoshizawa's barrow on Narrow Lane; tiny plastic figurines, bean-eyed and reposeful, extruded from street slot-machines; miniature rubber genitalia, scraps of fur, leather, and spun-glass baubles that chimed when he tapped them.

"The butsudan?" asked BeeJee &ersenn. "What about it? It's dedicated to Janja—she's the Celestial of my caste— and to YamTamRay, the house spirits. They watch over me, they care for me, they know everything I do."

But touching his fingers to the crude clay image of the straddle-legged Venus, he sensed something different: a questing, a questioning, an impatience that seemed to reflect his own incomprehension and hunger for history. Each time he sat in the green glow of the spirit lamp, he felt a disquiet, a need to go onward, outward, to embrace an entire universe within his arms. Thus, he said one day, quite unexpectedly, "I think I will have to go very soon."

"Why?" Questioner and questionee reversed.

"There is something I must do, but it is not here."

"Then where is it?"

"I do not know."

"What is it?"

"I do not know."

She came to him one last time before he returned himself to the rain. She was cat-nervous, almost fearful of him. She came to him and offered him her plastic nipple.

"One final question," he said. "What is it you want from me?"

"Pleasure. Joy without ending," she whispered, as if she sensed that this man could somehow grant her her heart's desire. She closed her eyes as he reached out to stroke the plastic. BeeJee &ersenn cried aloud. Blue holy lightning burned along her pleasure circuits. And fused the nipple switch, the joyswitch, the key to her heart's desire, shut forever.

He pulled on the heavy waxed raincoat she had bought for him and let himself out of the glass bubble among the pipes. Rain slanted across the bustling street, and he turned his collar up against it. He thought of names as he walked away from the glass house among the pipes. Names were the nails of history. Things were, had been, would be because they had names to guide them through time.

Without a name he had no time-boundedness. Therefore he must have a name. But everything was already named, and all names were assigned. He would have to steal one. And a history, too, perhaps. He tried some names for fit and comfort. Stolen names were like stolen shoes, uncomfortable and ill-fitted to their owners. He was not comfortable with any of the names he saw around him as he walked through the wet, gray streets of Great Yu; the names of the streets, the shops, the pedicab drivers, the shrines and noodle stands and waxman booths. He passed from the tangled alleyways and tenements of the district called Little Norway into a place the like of which he had never seen before. Astounded, he stood on a broad plaza of yellow brick, a man reduced to an atom by the buildings that rose on either side of him, vast cones of masonry massive as fallen moons, so tall their uppermost levels were shrouded in cloud, so tall they might reach up and up and up forever. The twin behemoths shone with lights, more lamps than he had ever seen in one place before, a fallen constellation captured in stone. He fell to his knees, and as the twin arcologies reduced him to nothing, he also came out of his annihilated anonymity to realize that he was special, he was unique, that his light shone brighter than all the million glowworm windows, for he alone knew nothing. Uniquely, he understood what his days with BeeJee &ersenn had been teaching him: he, alone, was the alien.

And so he took a name. From the unbelievable towers of light he took a name he felt was worthy of his massive uniqueness.

"Kilimanjaro West," he said. The stolen name fit well. "I am Kilimanjaro West."

And onward he went, a named thing, rooted in the universe, yet apart from it, through the night and the rain-dancing streets. Now that he knew that he was, that he existed to celebrate his existence, he looked with delight and fascination at every all-night hot-food stall, every neon welcome to a caste bar or club, every vagrant waft of steam from the *pneumatique* ventilators, every puddle of yellow streetlight, every rain-slick cobble, because in the continued existence of those other things he saw his own being reflected. Onward he went, and onward, until, to his astonishment, he had walked out of the night into a new steel-gray morning. Stopping in the place in which he found himself, he looked up and around him in awe and amazement. And saw the faces in the architecture.

Angel faces. Demon faces. Faces of women and children. Animal masks. Distorted homunculus grimaces vomiting warm, sour rainwater from stretched rubber lips. The faces of the gargoyles of Neu Ulmsbad looked down on the man who called himself Kilimanjaro West. And as that man looked up at them, he turned himself round to take all the strange newness in, round and round and roundroundround with gathering speed: beaks and claws, snouts, grins, bulbous eyes, gentlefrownssneerssmileslewdwinks . . . he snapped to halt.

There were human faces among the angels and demons, mortals among the immortals, flesh amidst the stones. He strained his eyes to quarter the fluted, sculpted masonry. There they were. They were not so hard to find now that he knew what to look for.

"Hello!" he called.

The faces ducked from view behind a parapet.

Presuming that they wished to preserve their anonymity, having not yet learned that anonymous faces in the architecture of Neu Ulmsbad might in some way be unnormal, he did not call to them again. Which meant that it came as a complete surprise to the early-morning people of Neu Ulmsbad Square when the small knot of raincoated citizens loitering at a waxman's booth suddenly cast off their waxed raincoats to become iridescent birds of paradise and pulled from the waxman's awning long, streaming banners with which they danced through the crowds of workaday citizens, wrapping them in rippling silk and mystery while from the back of the booth roman candles ignited and fountained silver fire into the air. In seconds Neu Ulmsbad Square was a dangerous, unpredictable, wonderful place, full of running, leaping figures, billowing streamers, and cracking thunderflashes sown from the bird-dancers' belt-pouches. Taken by surprise, the morning people panicked. Only one man was not surprised. He was not surprised because he had no concept of normality that the events in Neu Ulmsbad Square could violate. The man called Kilimanjaro West watched with wonder and delight and everything was new. From the BergHaus parapet three silver hang gliders plummeted in a death dive that sent the assailed, assaulted public reeling to cover on the cobbles, thunderflashes doomsdaying around their ears. The banners of the bird-of-paradise dancers sought out the man called Kilimanjaro West, enveloped him in crisscrossing walls of streaming silver silk. The hang gliders soared high above the cobbles of Neu Ulmsbad. One carried a portable synthesizer. Another was fitted with an array of electronic and acoustic percussion devices. The third broadcast excerpts from the Ministry of Pain's Electoral Selection Declaration. The roman candle firefountains mounted and mounted until, half the height of the lowering architecture of Neu Ulmsbad, they cast their own shadows over the huddled citizenry. Rockets began to arc into the air and detonate euphorically while a voice from heaven cried, "This is the essential nature of our democracy, that any citizen . . . any citizen . . . an . . . an . . . any citizen"—the sound source stammered in time to the tribal drums and the driving synthesizers—"may be selected to the highest. Of offices. May be selected. To the highest of offices. May be selected. To the highest of offices."

The man called Kilimanjaro West clapped his hands.

The sound filled all of Neu Ulmsbad Square.

"Wonderful," he said.

And now that they saw that what he said was true, the computer operators, power-supply engineers, shopkeepers, agricultural workers, transport drivers, electronics workers, restaurant waiters, and cablecar washers whose mornings had been broken open uncurled to look at this something from beyond the edge of their happily bounded lives. In the dying moments of the Happening, each knew themselves to have been touched by something quite precious and rare and extraordinary. Something that had been taken from them years and years before. Something that some of them had never known they could experience. But the moment was dying. The roman candles were collapsing. The last rockets spent their brief lives in the sky above the BergHaus. The hang gliders turned in the sky for a final pass, the music came to a ringing conclusion, and a voice announced, "This piece of Performance Art entitled 'The Elector Passes' has been brought to you by the members of the Raging Apostles, an intercaste multimedia alternative arts group comprising independent nonauthorized artists, musicians, actors, dancers, and writers. We thank you for your participations in this event, and Raging Apostles hopes that it has in some small way brightened your day."

Trailing thanks and blessings, the trio of aircraft slid low over the pinnacles of DeminaBerg to come in for hop, skip, and jump landings on Rue de La Fontaine. The birds of paradise set down their silk banners, removed masks, bowed to the audience, who, to their surprise, found themselves applauding. And whistling. And cheering. Just as if they had never seen anything like it before. Which they hadn't. Then a trog in a Food Corps coverall whose senses had been sharpened by years in the subterranean agrariums cried out, "Love Police!" and the intercaste multimedia company of nonauthorized artists, musicians, actors, dancers, and writers scattered like starlings. And so did the computer operators, power-supply engineers, shopkeepers, agricultural workers, transport drivers, electronics workers, restaurant waiters, and cablecar washers. And only one man was left in Neu Ulmsbad Square to watch the black and silver pantycars come tunneling out of the clouds.

"Is this part of it?" asked the man called Kilimanjaro West.

A bird-of-paradise woman paused in her flight to be astounded.

"Yah, you stupid or something? That's the Love Police, you know?"

"The what?"

"Fug! You are stupid! Never heard of West One?"

And because, somehow, she could see that he indeed had not, she seized his arm and dragged him across Neu Ulmsbad Square to the waiting 'lectrovan and the forest of waving, beckoning arms in its open rear. A thrust sent the stranger sprawling all knees and elbows across the collected Raging Apostles. The bird-of-paradise woman thumped down on the seat beside him. Suddenly she could no longer think why she had brought him. There was a sharp smell of burnt-out fireworks in the crowded van.

"Come on, come on!" shrieked the driver. The pantycar was settling on its belly jets as the three aeronauts made good fastening their collapsed gliders to the roof rack and swung inside. "About fuggin' time, too!" the driver screamed, gunning the engine and sending everyone over everyone else as he accelerated down Finneganstrasse.

"Hey, who you got there, Kansas?"

She did not want to say that she did not know, that she had, for an instant, no more, no less, been as compelled as if the eternal clouds had opened and the lasers of God beamed down upon her. "A recruit," she said. "I thought we could use him."

"You what?" the driver screamed again. "Fuggin' Yah, Kansie, he could be anyone, anything, nuh? You want us all to get Social Counseling, eh? Everyone up in West One?"

"Yet, he did seem, at least to me, to be an unprogrammed element, a true locus of spontaneity," said the bearded man beside the frenzied, sweating driver.

"Unprogrammed, spontaneity, fug, he's dangerous, put him out." The driver swerved the crammed 'lectrovan around a procession of Eleventh Day Redemptorists.

"Just because he's a stranger doesn't mean he's dangerous," said the bird-of-paradise woman. "What is the point of being an alternative to the Compassionate Society if we don't hold alternative values? What I'm hearing is pure *nona dolorosa* hurt-me-not straight out of kindergarten."

"There is a value in unprogrammed elements in a programmed world," said the bearded man, attempting conciliation. "I'd say give him a try. We measure our own humanity by how we respond to the unprogrammed, the unpredictable."

"And he damn near made the event," said a large and odorous trog wedged against the door.

"Love Police damn near unmade it." A man shook his hair free from a sweaty head-mask. "Joshua, I've said this before, it'll bear saying again. I don't go with these big, big theatrical happenings. Small-scale stuff; interactive microdrama, ultrarealism, that's good. This sort of thing is too flash. It gets us noticed. It'll get us disbanded."

The bearded man smiled, shrugged. The bird-of-paradise woman who had rescued the man called Kilimanjaro West removed her mask also, and he saw that her face was the image of that other man who had criticized.

"I sometimes wonder just why you are a Raging Apostle, Brother dearest, if you won't put yourself on the edge for your art. Play it safe, play it along the line; sometimes I wonder if you really want to change anything at all. Live dangerously, Kelso, live for the moment. I think you forgot that, somewhere back down the line."

"Kansas, I'm telling you, you don't know a thing, not a thing. Joshua, any more of these big happenings and I'm out. An ex–Raging Apostle."

"Ex-Apostle, or ex-Raging?" asked a new voice.

"Deva, you just..."

"Well, Citizen Unprogrammed Element," said the bearded man from the front bench seat, again the conciliator, "have you got a name?"

"My name is Kilimanjaro West," he said, and something in the way he spoke that name made the crowded 'lectrovan fall electrically quiet. "Pleased to meet you all."

"Wow," said the woman who had rescued him.

"Pleased to meet you," said the bearded man, first to break the awed silence. "Joshua Drumm, artistic director, manager, and father figure to this troupe of social urchins. May I introduce the Raging Apostles: Winston, who so nearly would have left you on the street"—the driver ducked his head and flicked mistrustful eyes in the rearview mirror—"my general factotum, our faithful provider and fixer. Thunderheart Two-Birds Flying"—a huge hairy thing bared white enamel—"vocal arrangements, stunts, and for the present, accommodation. Dr. M'kuba Mig-15"—an ectomorphic face, etched with blue tattoo lines, nodded a nimbus of luminous hair—"technical arrangements and special effects. Devadip Samdhavi"—a glitteringly dressed young man made a small bow—"costumes, design, chore-ography and dance consultant. V. S. Pyar"—a massive boulder of humanity, his sweat a palpable presence in the swaying van—"movement, acrobatics, physical training, and much-needed muscle. Kelso Byrne"—the arguing man nodded, curtly—"musical arrangements, original composi-tions, tapes, and lyrics, and unfortunate twin of Kansas," and the girl who had, on a whim, a notion, an inspiration, pulled Kilimanjaro West away from his fatal fascination, grinned and blew a kiss across the van—"artist, concep-tualizer, wonderfully talented and quite impossible to work with." She wrinkled her nose and laughed at the man called Joshua Drumm. "Together we are the Raging Apos-tles. Welcome, Cizzen West. Winston my man! Yah speed us away with your best efforts! To the Big Tree!"

"Okay, Joshi," said the driver, and the already hurtling 'lectrovan found a miraculous third speed somewhere in its shrieking motor and careened, swaying and slewing violently, down the rain-wet streets of Neu Ulmsbad.

Chapter 3

She was not alone down here. She was certain of it. Luminous arrows spray-painted on dripping walls. Discarded bric-a-brac: noodle cartons, numbgum wrappers, articles of clothing, a newssheet (intellectual shock to find Wee Wendy Waif gazing up through twenty centimeters of filmy rainwater). Wall panels removed, fizzing, sparking contraptions jerry-rigged to the power lines. The occasional heap of human excrement, hard and stale. The occasional ringing, plashing footfall—transported who knew how far?—along the ringing tunnels and crawlways of Undertown.

She was not alone.

Sometimes the thought terrified her; cold, hostile hands reaching into the cozy little womb she had woven into the underpinnings of New Paris Community Mall. At other times the presence of others/brothers sharing her runways and conduits was almost welcome. The solitude at the bottom of Shaft Twelve was absolute and unbroken. She had drawn one hundred and seventy-four Wee Wendy Waifs on her walls, smiling down like Botticelli angels. For company. They only deepened her sense of isolation. She had always been a solitary creature. The Compassionate Society had made her that way. But there was a world of difference between being solitary and being alone. Before there had always been the possibility of company: the Dario Sanduccis, the Marcus Fordes, and his four and twenty cushioncats. Down in Shaft Twelve there was only herself. And the dream.

Those blue-silver wings. That impossibly *romantic* white

silk scarf flowing out behind. Up we go, up we go, up we go. Now that it was absolutely denied her, like heaven to the damned, the land above the clouds where the Great Spirits and the Celestials dwelled was painful in its purity. Its freedom mocked her. But not because it was unattainable. It mocked her because she had once touched it, felt it, held it, and had lost it again. That was the pain.

Strange, but in this incarnation of the dream, there was no wall of faces. No barrier to the Beyond. But what that Beyond was, she could no longer see. From the saddle of her high-flying bicycle/ornithopter, she could see the last dawnward towers of Great Yu. And beyond them, nothing.

The dream no longer comforted. But it was all she had, so she clung to it: the sixteen-o'clock dream.

And the others.

Like the dream, she could not be comfortable with them, but she could not be comfortable without them. At least they would be company. She would not face an indefinite future underground, alone. There would be the common bond of circumstance. Experiences would be shared, resources pooled, stratagems of survival tables, futures mapped out. That there was a future, a time to come reaching out ahead of her along the cableways and conduits and ducts until she found her own death there in the tunnels, was more than she could bear.

"I'm a yulp cartoonist," she would convince the piles of romantic novels stolen on her furtive midnight forays to the surface. "I was born in the White Sisters of Koinonia Maternity Hostel, I was fostered by the Sigmarsenn family of Coober Peedie until, age seven, I was admitted to the Ladies of Celestial Succor Community Crèche, where I remained until at age fourteen the Ministry of Pain apprenticed me to Jovanian Yelkenko from whom I learned the cartoonic arts and took over his creation, Wee Wendy Waif. I lived in apt 33/Red/16 Kilimanjaro West, I worked producing Wee Wendy Waif for the Armitage-Weir Publishing House, and what I want to know is, what am I doing down here?"

Inevitably these arguments brought her back again to the question of whether or not contact with these others was desirable. Supine on her live-fur carpet (stolen in bulk from Thirteen Moons Furnishings on an after-hours raid through their floor service-hatch, she like some overwhelmed insect wrestling the huge roll of vat-grown fur down into her hole) she argued with herself. She argued this argument so many times that each pro, each con, had taken on an individual character and voice.

"Whaddya mean, whaddya mean, common experience?" This voice, straight-edged and gritty as a broken floor-tile, was Mr. Don't-Be-Stupid-Girl. "The only common experience down here is you're all criminals. PainCriminals. You know what you did to get yourself down here; Yah only knows what they had to do."

"Be reasonable." This was the voice called High-Pitched Reasonableness. "Everyone down here was a member of the Compassionate Society at some time. The rules aren't easily forgotten."

"That's rich, coming from you," said Growly Accuser. "Who said the rules hold down here?"

"But you can't be alone forever," said Self-pitying Whiner. "Not: forever."

"Better safe than dead," said Pigeon-Voiced Mother of Extreme Caution.

Working her way one morning through the tangle of crawlways and ducts that led, eventually, to the air-conditioning plant under New Paris Community Mall, she came upon a workspace recently vacated by some lunch- or toilet-seeking environmental maintenance engineer. Magpie-minded, magpie-moraled, Courtney Hall fingered through his neglected toolcase until those fingers came to rest on the stubby metal barrel of a sonic impacter.

She had spied upon engineers using these devices. It was sign of how far she had strayed from the path of Social Compassion that she had devised ways in which one could be converted into a nasty little personal weapon. She slipped the impacter into the leather pouch she had just yesterday pickpocketed from Western Promise Novelties and Gifts and continued on her way to the surface and further petty crime.

That night she had a reply to the Pigeon-Voiced Mother of Extreme Caution. The Voice of Off-hand Tough-Nut Exuberance said, "Sure, I've got the impacter. What have I got to worry about?"

A sound.

Unidentifiable in the sinister acoustic darklands of Shaft Twelve. Just: a sound. A presence.

Courtney Hall took grip of the impacter and slid the output control up into the red. She had never used the tool even as a tool, much less a weapon, but the principle seemed simple. Point. Squeeze. What you pointed at exploded. From the hatchway she could survey all of Shaft Twelve. She held the impacter emission head against her chin, watching, listening. Water dripped from a pipe joint and fell, sparkling in the wan maintenance lights, down the center of the shaft to gather in a deep pool at the bottom.

"Hello?" Courtney Hall ventured. "Helloooo."

Drip, plink. Drip, plink, drip.

She aimed and fired with a unity of thought and action that dazzled her. There was a howl of power, an explosion, and all the lights went out. Shorted power conduits snaked and hissed and shed blue sparks toward the oil-dark lake. "Damn." With one shot she had disabled the power and air systems for New Paris Community Mall. Within the hour Shaft Twelve would be a-buzz with environmental maintenance workers, crawling into, round, over, through every catwalk, access tunnel, gantry, hatchway, vent. They could not possibly overlook Courtney Hall's fur-lined nest in the air-conditioning subsystems control room. "Damn damn damn damn." But she had seen something. She was certain. A something—a someone? A what—a who? Light-starved, spindly, a pale shadow. At least that was one question answered. Contact with the others: unarguably undesirable.

Surprising how few souvenirs of her furry little home she chose to take with her in her nightsac. A hammock, a bicycle lamp, a sleepsac, some cleanup tissues, a box of tampons (removed from the Compassionate Society's regulation of her womanhood, she could not be certain her periods would not restart), a rope, a packed lunch, a bottle of mineral water (nongaseous), some clean underwear, some spare clothes, and shoes. The rest she left: stolen goods are worth exactly what you pay for them. But she did say good-bye to the hundred and seventy-four Wee Wendy Waifs. None of them seemed sad to see her go.

Her early timid surveys of the warrenways about Shaft Twelve had disclosed no other potential living spaces. She must quit New Paris entirely and move into unexplored territory. Unexplored, potentially occupied.

She tried not to advertise her presence too widely with the bicycle lamp. As her journey led her away from the upper levels, down into older, more chaotic strata of jumbled architectures, she left behind the artificial illumination to enter a stoop-shouldered country of brick tunnels, trickling water, and stygian darkness. Fear of the dark overcame fear of discovery. She fixed the bicycle lamp to her nightsac shoulder straps with a roll of electrical tape filched some days previously from another careless engineer. And she kept the impacter at the ready. Her swinging beam illuminated damp brick arches and fan-vaulted ceilings, brass pipes and corroded wheels of a curiously archaic design. A sense of having wandered far from Yu overcame her, in time as well as in space, of having left the city that was the world to enter an altogether other world coexistent with the Compassionate Society but secretive, inaccessible, an old world of damp, dark, and drippings that had survived, preserved unchanged by the darkness, since the time of the Break. She had come too far, too deep; she could feel history pressing on her stooped shoulders as she squeezed along the narrow brick intestines. She splashed ankle-deep through ancient fossilized rainwater and at every junction, every confluence of brick pipes, chose the upward path. But a claustrophobic awareness told her that the tunnels were redefining themselves

before her, twisting and turning so that for every upward
she chose, the tunnels moved to draw her down.

There was no question of ever being able to find her
way back to Shaft Twelve. It was gone as irrevocably as
Apt 33/Red/16 Kilimanjaro West.

She sang, attempting to whistle up high spirits. The
echoes that scampered back to her along the brick buttresses
sounded nothing like her voice. And behind those echoes,
something more. A film of water flowing out of somewhere
parted around her boots to flow on to somewhere. Her
bicycle lamp picked hysterical faces out of the brickwork.
A scuttling, scurrying sound that might have been moving
air (and just as easily might not) whispered out of the dark.

"All right. All right, whoever you are." She did not
want to have to say *whatever*. "Just to let you know that if
you're trying to frighten me, you're succeeding."

She walked one complete slow circle, sending her
bicycle beam probing into every dark crevice. The impacter
rested snug and comfortable in her hand. "Hello? Anyone
there? Hello?" She let the last echo fade into the general
silence before concluding, "Okay, so I was talking to
myself. So, who's to hear?"

. . . earearearear . . .

And they were upon her.

All over her.

In her hair, hanging from her clothes, clawing at her
hands, her face, her eyes, more and more and more of
them, piling onto her, swarming, shrieking, a mass of fur
and claws and teeth, throwing themselves out of nowhere,
onto her, dragging her down under the weight of their
numbers. She screamed and screamed and screamed,
flailing at her face, her precious, delicate eyes. The swinging, swooping bicycle lamp gave momentary infernal reve-
lations of ivory needles, matted fur, steaming drool, bulbous light-blinded pink eyes . . .

Pets. Dogkits, catkits, monkeykits, cute cuddlesome
blobs of genetic ingenuity flushed away, thrown out, refuse-
chuted, abandoned by bored creators. Knowing what they
had been made them all the more horrifying. Courtney

Hall struck free with her left hand and fired the impacter. Blind fear sent shot after shot after shot ricocheting around the chamber, flashing water to steam, blasting shattered bricks from the vaulted ceiling. A wet, soft, bursting sound: a fortunate shot exploded a doggety or kitkin in a shriek of fur and intestines. Teeth met through her gun hand. Howling, she dropped the impacter. Clinging to hands, hair, face, clothes, the genetic menagerie pulled her down, and as teeth tugged flesh, Courtney Hall became aware of a wondrous sense of detachment that said, Well, this is it, isn't it? This brick sewer is the last, the very last, thing you will ever see.

A brightening light filled the chamber.

The Light of Yah! she thought, grateful that soon this distressing toothy tugging of her body would cease. And it did. And now that she was dead, it seemed that war broke out in heaven, that black-and-white-striped angels in domino masks fell upon the fell beasts with swords and crossbows and left a goodly multitude of cubby-bears and marmosetties lying with her in the stagnant rainwater before the vile pets fled to those vile places from which they had come. And it seemed that a face bent over her body.

"Lady most lucky," said the racoon-faced angel. "Lucky lucky lucky. Still, lady pretty bad, poor lady. Rest awhile, poor lady. Assistance has come."

"Are angelic racoons theologically supportable?" asked Courtney Hall.

"You tell me, lady," said the racoon savior, and Courtney Hall dropped off the edge of heaven with a dismal thud to land back in her body again.

"Racoons!" she cried. "You are racoons!"

"Of course, lady," said the racoon, peeling the backing from a dermoplast and sticking it to her forehead. "Sleep now."

"But . . ." she asked, and then a fog of theological outrage descended upon her. A last coherent impression was of the racoon absentmindedly stroking a little metal socket in the side of its neck out of which grew a cluster of soft, fungusy biochips. Time then passed, or did not pass, in degrees of awareness from deep sleep to complete consciousness. Upon one such occasion of lucidity, the thought clearly entered Courtney Hall's head (and remained there) that in all the adventures of Wee Wendy Waif she had helped to create, there had never been anything half so bizarre as being dragged down dark tunnels deep under Yu on a tube-steel travois by an army of talking racoons.

Apostles I

As he waited for the judgment, it came to him: a moment of clairaudience (some alchemic combination of time and place and atmosphere) when the ear abolished all distance between sources and all sounds arrived at it with equal weight and clarity. The iron grumble of tram wheels. The hiss of rain, ebbing. The calls, the splashing footfalls of the wingers abroad in the streets of Pendelburg. The ring of a solitary pedicab bell. High above, indeterminate, the purr of airship engines. He heard them all, clearly, distinctly, each voice a note in the night-song. And he heard the voices of his friends judging him.

The little he understood about the universe forced him to conclude that he was a threat to these people. This society into which he had been thrust (how? from whence? why?) had an inside and an outside; his own experience taught him that much, and these people were firmly outside. He suspected that, unlike himself, they had chosen to be outside; unlike himself again, they had not been outside from the very beginning. But to such outsiders as they, others of their kind could be a threat, an insider in disguise.

Marvelous, the amount he had learned of this fascinating universe already.

He listened to the debating voices, the soliloquies, the valiant defenses from the dock, the accusations and the parries, and pondered anew the condition of the outsider in this rigidly enclosed society. They could claim nothing from their Compassionate Society (whole blocks of a priori knowledge that had hitherto floated solitary, isolated, in the spaces of his memories, were levered into place, monolith by monolith), and as he suspected that this institution controlled all resources political, economic, physical, and spiritual, these Raging Apostles had only such access to food, power, and shelter as their wits allowed them. A dangerous place to be outside. He recalled the hang gliders, the synthesizers, the fireworks, the glittering costumes that had bedazzled him in Neu Ulmsbad Square. Their wits must be sharp indeed to winkle such beads and baubles from the Seven Servants. (Another block of masonry fell with a crash into position.) Quickness of the hands deceives the eye. Empty bellies under robes of splendor. He reckoned the Raging Apostles sacrificed themselves for their art.

"I'm not happy about this. I'm not happy at all; what proof have we that this Kilimanjaro West is not a Love Police agent?" That was Winston's voice. He was learning to distinguish the individual performers by their voices. A deep pneumatic rumble of a voice; the athleto, what was his name? Kilimanjaro West had only just begun to come to terms with a casted, stratified society.

"Then why aren't we in West One? Why didn't they pick us up back there in Neu Ulmsbad?" A debate between the two. "Because we gave them the slip. But how do you know that we're safe here, that the Love Police won't come out of the sky at any moment?"

Here, the safe here, was the Big Tree. Seeing it from a distance through rain-streaked glass and frantically pumping windshield wipers, Kilimanjaro West had had great difficulty in believing that such a place could exist. Incongruous in boulevard after boulevard after boulevard of fin de siècle brownstones as a fart in a cathedral, Big Tree was a solid block of green growingness, a vertical jungle, its canopy breaking in a steaming green wave twenty meters above the red pantiles of Pendelburg. A solitary trog enclave in a prefecture of wingers.

"SHELTER closed it down about twelve years back," explained the girl he had learned to call Kansas Byrne.

"Part of a planned population shift; the prollets over in Wheldon formed eight new septs, and there was a lot of assimilation of other prollet boros all over Yu and a massive population surge in Wheldon. The winger population was reduced from thirty percent to ten to accommodate the influx, and the surplus was sent over here. Of course, that fugged up the mixed-caste ratios, so the Ministry of Pain declared Pendelburg a monocaste district, all winger. So they had to relocate the trog clan that had been living in Big Tree for close on three hundred years. Never was a terribly big or important clan, they didn't make much of a fuss when they went. Thunderheart heard about this place when he was a cub, all the way over on Grundy Street, and that's twelve prefectures. Seemed it became a kind of unofficial singing-ground for the trog bell-boys; still use it, keeps us awake most nights, shuggers up there singing their balls off for the glory of clan and family." Her words had become little buzzing, inconsequential mosquitoes as the 'lectrovan had penetrated the veil of flowering vines that fronted Big Tree and brought them into a three-dimensional grid of green vibrancy. Girders wrapped with vines, spreading limbs, massive boles, leaves, flowers, a faint dappling of light, leaf-diffracted and chlorophyll-green; all dripping, heavy drops of rain falling through the green cubes and shafts and tunnels. Wicker hammocks, cocoons, wooden huts built onto girders, open spaces, floors, terraces, walkways, swings, levels. "Perfect temporary headquarters for the 'postles. Thunderheart remembered how to get the life systems chuggin' again, and now we have all the water we can drink and the fruit we can eat. And when we get tired of fruit, which is kind of regularly, we go down to the winger deli and shoplift."

"Shoplift?" He had imagined V. S. Pyar's muscles bulging as he held up the corner of a building while the Raging Apostles slipped inside.

"Stealing food, toiletries, little things, without anyone's seeing," explained the zook, Devadip Samdhavi.

"It's quite a work of art," Kansas Byrne had continued.

"A very subtle work of prestidigitation. Pity no one even notices. They're just not geared up to think that way."

"We've had to reinvent a lot of long-lost antisocial skills," added the zook. "We can get almost anything in the city without having to pay for it. Of course, some big things, big props and all, we have to use marquins for, and then move before the Love Police backtrack the transaction."

As he replayed his memories in the cinema of the imagination, the singers in the canopy pumped up their throat sacks to give song. Basso profundo voices booming to the moon, and pride and glory and ambition as the bell-boys did battle in the canopy high above his wicker sleep-basket. The rain, which had wavered indecisively, began again in earnest, raindrops falling from the monsoon sky, raindrops intersecting leaf, growing leaf. Pit. Pat. Pit. Falling on the singers and the Big Tree and the gray, steely, lone waters of the Lamarinthian Canal and the barges growling along it: drip, drop, drip—all across this great city of Yu. He was again taken up into clairaudience, and in the universal voice he heard voices.

"I still maintain it's too dangerous, we cannot afford to take risks."

"But the whole thing is about taking risks. We take a risk every time we go out on the streets, every time we use our marquins or filch something, we take a risk when every famulus-carrying winger sees us on the streets."

"But have you the right to endanger people in the group who have no way of leaving it if they disagree with your decision?"

"Consider this, if we do say no, what do we do with him?"

"There is no risk. No additional risk. Any damage done has already been done. If there ever was any damage to do. I think not. This man, no famulus, no memory, no name 'cept one he takes off the side of an arcology, no number, no nothing—ask yourselves, sibs, would the Love Police send someone who is so obviously an agent?"

"Well, if he isn't an agent, then what is he?"

"That's the mystery, isn't it? And mystery is what we are all about."

Voices all rose together, a clangorous discord in the song of the Big Tree at which even the singers in the branches fell silent. One voice outstayed them all: Joshua Drumm's.

"Please, please, comrades. We've been over all the arguments. Now it's time to vote."

Then the clouds opened and the waiting rain crashed down upon Big Tree and the canopy across the sky and silenced all voices but its own. And it carried Kilimanjaro West, the man of the rain, away with it, into the recesses of exhaustion and the warmth of his sleep-basket, into the dreamtime.

Joshua Drumm came, out of the night, out of the dreaming; an imp-shaped bottle of papaya wine in one hand, two glasses in the other. He went to wake the sleeper, but Kilimanjaro West's eyes were bright, almost shockingly open.

"Congratulations," said Joshua Drumm. "Welcome to Raging Apostles!"

"They voted for me?"

"Five votes to three. We are rather inexperienced at democracy, but a simple majority was enough. The recalcitrants will come round in time, I think. They have little other option." He unscrewed the imp's head, poured two measures. "So, welcome to Raging Apostles, Kilimanjaro West, or whatever you are." Joshua Drumm stood up on the rope walkway and lifted his glass to the faraway tail-gas flares of the industrial parks around La Gironde. He studied the wine for color. "Not a bad vintage. For a society which worships mediocrity. That, you see, is the touchstone which empowers the Raging Apostles. That the artist, and I don't just mean a member of the tlakh caste, produces his work, *creates*, if you must use the rather worn-out word, and people respond to his creation. They cannot do otherwise. They either say 'Yes, we accept this' or 'No, we do not accept this.' Either way, they have made judgments of value and quality, either way they have measured themselves, their humanity, their world, against his creation and found themselves either sufficient or deficient. And what is this thing against which we measure ourselves, this domain of values and qualities and judgments, but *conscience*? Art is conscience, a criterion by which humanity may measure itself and ultimately know itself. The artist should be the conscience of society.

"But without pain, how can there be any conscience? If no one can hurt anyone and no one can be hurt, how can there be any morality behind our acts except the simple expediency of the avoidance of pain? The central premise of the Compassionate Society is to let everyone do what will make them the happiest without hurting any other person or in any way diminishing another's happiness."

Kilimanjaro West thought back through the moving pictures; to BeeJee &ersenn, writhing on the floor in lonely ecstasy.

"But people are hurt. People can still feel pain."

"Oh, yes, and while they can still feel, there is hope."

"Hope for what?"

Joshua Drumm sipped his wine, rinsed it around his mouth. "You know, this isn't bad at all. It was worth the while stealing it from the winery over in Ste.-Claire. Hope for a true creativity. Anticipating your next question, that is a creativity that goes beyond the boundaries of castes and social orders and of the *Arts* in general, into every aspect of life. True creativity is the truly creative life, the life that transforms every event into a creation, and thus transcends."

"And pain? Is there then a true pain, like this true creativity?"

A laugh. Sharp, brilliant as a shower of rain.

"Citizen West, I find myself underestimating you and I find that most unfortunate. No artist should ever underestimate another human being. Pain is the sculptor of creativity. The truly creative act is not the act which seeks solely to avoid pain, it seeks to embrace it, understand it, and thus transcend it. Without pain, it is incomplete. But in a society without pain, how can there be any transcendence?"

"Is the death of creativity, if what you say is true, not worth the price of freedom from pain?"

The ropewalk creaked and swayed, stirred by the twenty-four-o'clock wind. From the streets of Pendelburg, fifty meters below, came night voices and the ringing of pedicab bells, venturing out after the rain.

"I do not think so."

"And the other Raging Apostles?"

"Touch the apostles and you'll touch purposes as diverse as the castes from which they were drawn. They'll all have their chances to talk with you, the new boy, tell you how they came to be 'postles. Myself being director, I had first pick, and the responsibility of telling you the outcome of the voting. But I think you'll find that diverse though their stories are, they all stem from a deep dissatisfaction with the Compassionate Society and the world of mediocrity it has bequeathed us."

"So the Raging Apostles are there to put a little pain into people's lives."

"And wonder. And joy. And horror. And beauty. And sexuality. And wisdom. And laughter. Yes, remember, we are the conscience of a conscienceless society."

"I'm afraid I know very little."

The faraway gas-flares glittered reflections in Joshua Drumm's wise-animal eyes.

"Knows little, understands less, but wiser than all because he listens. Just who are you, Kilimanjaro West?"

"I am a man in search of a history so that he may have a future."

"Then you must be one of us. Like you, we have all put off the histories the Compassionate Society wrote for us to become our own men and women. Like you, we are seeking a future, a future not just for ourselves but, we believe, for everyone. You are special, I tell you that, you have come from somewhere and you are going to somewhere, and I cannot say where except that I feel it is extraordinary. Try to remember, can you remember anything about yourself?"

Kilimanjaro West closed his eyes and tried to remember; remember back to the time of the voices, the time before the small, damp, cold room and the universes that opened out of it, universe within universe within universe, each one larger than the one out of which it had unfolded.

"I don't remember, I can't remember, but I think I feel, that for a long time, I was nothing. Can you understand that? That, if not forever, then for a very long time I *was not*, I was a mere potential waiting to be called into being. Dead. Asleep. Waiting. Nothing. That is why I cannot remember. Because there is nothing to remember." Then Kilimanjaro West turned to Joshua Drumm and said, "Tell me, do you think that I might be . . . holy?"

New Mysteries

Extracted from the *Power and Light Workers' Mystery*, a choreo-drama traditionally performed upon Matildamass morning by a mixed professional/amateur cast of dancers and chorus, the chorus, by longstanding tradition, containing representatives from each of the castes employed by Universal Power and Light.

(*Scene: Earth before the Break. Enter* MR. & MRS. ALL RIGHT JACK *riding on the shoulders of the naked* THIRD ADAM *and* THIRD EVE. CHORUS *is dressed in vivid plaids, floral prints, and wasp-frame glasses. All wear cameras and the silver-haired/blue-rinsed masks of* MR. & MRS. ALL RIGHT JACK.)

MR. CHORUS: Isn't it just terrible?

MRS. CHORUS: Terrible. Terrible. Just terrible.

MR. CHORUS: Those poor people.

MRS. CHORUS: Starving to death.

MR. CHORUS: I blame it on their governments, personally.

MRS. CHORUS: Absolutely. Absolutely. Absolutely.

MR. CHORUS: It's because they can't keep Law and Order.

MRS. CHORUS: Law and Order. Law and Order. Law and Order!

MR. CHORUS: It's useless giving them money. They only spend it on killing each other when they should be spending it on paying off what they owe us.

MRS. CHORUS: Absolutely. Useless. Useless. Useless. Spendthrifts!

71

MR. CHORUS: No economic sense at all. Spend and
                borrow like there's no tomorrow.

MRS. CHORUS: Spend and borrow. Spend and borrow. Spend
                and borrow. Like there's no tomorrow.

MR. CHORUS: Is it any wonder, really, why they have so
                many famines?

MRS. CHORUS: Makes you all the more grateful for what
                you have, doesn't it?

THE DANCE OF
MR. & MRS. ALL RIGHT JACK

(*Continuous with above*, MR. & MRS. ALL RIGHT JACK *perform an intricate pas de deux that forces their bearers,* THIRD ADAM *and* THIRD EVE *into more complex and convoluted steps that they are increasingly incapable of performing as they grow more fatigued under the burden of their riders. Further, as the dance progresses,* MR. & MRS. ALL RIGHT JACK *have been tearing lumps of synthflesh from* THIRD ADAM *and* THIRD EVE *and eating it. The bearers become increasingly emaciated and eventually collapse under the weight of their burdens.*)

CHORUS: Help us! Help us! Feed us, we want
                    some food!

(VOICES UNITED):   We must have something to eat,
                    feed us, you no good sucks!

Scene ii

(*Enter the* SISTERS OF INDUSTRY *and* MADAM MARKET FORCE. SISTER FLORA *is naked but covered in wet, sticky mud.* SISTER INFOTECH *wears a chrome body-stocking, winged silver powerwheels and mirror shades.* SISTER MUNITIA *is dressed in leather straps, studs, spikes, and a horned helmet.* SISTER ENERGIA *wears an electric-blue leotard and industrial power exoskeleton.* MADAM MARKET FORCE *is dressed as a bordello madam in crimson basque, button boots, and opera gloves. She carries a whip.*)

VOX MARKET FORCE: Who'll come, who'll come a dollar a dance? Dollar a dance, gentlefolk, dollar a dance, who'll take a dollar a chance with the ladies?

CHORUS: Dollar a dance, dollar a chance, dollar a prance with the ladies...

(*Enter four* CAPTAINS OF INDUSTRY *dressed in dashing red-white-and-blue uniforms.*)

VOX MARKET FORCE: Who'll invest in the services of these fine ladies? Who'll pay for their company? Take Sister Flora here...

CHORUS: Dollar a chance, dollar a prance with the ladies...

VOX MARKET FORCE: A fine fruity, fertile girl, my bravos, full of life and the joys of spring, who's man enough to take her for a night of earthy pleasure, a night of rustic joy?

CHORUS: Who'll pay, who'll buy, who'll invest, who'll speculate?

VOX MARKET FORCE: Or Miss Infotech here, looks hard as steel, me boyos, but she's a real fast lady, fast as light, too fast for you, my fine gentlemen; what she doesn't know about it isn't worth knowing!

CHORUS: Dollar a chance, dollar a prance with the ladies...

VOX MARKET FORCE: Or dear Sister Munitia, who's into a little military discipline, a little force majeure, who wants a good fight and a better capitulation. Better beware, my fine laddies, with Sister Munitia you never know who'll end up dominated by whom!

CHORUS: Who'll pay, who'll buy, who'll invest, who'll speculate?

VOX MARKET FORCE: Take little Lady Energia; what a live wire, my brave boys, what a bright spark. Juice enough for all of you, and she'll be running long after the last of you've burned out. So, who'll buy these gorgeous ladies?

CHORUS: Who'll buy? Who'll buy? Who'll buy?

(THIRD ADAM *crawls onstage. He offers his handful of coins to each of the prostitutes in turn. The* SISTERS OF INDUSTRY *laugh and scorn him as each, in turn, is swept off her feet by the dashing* CAPTAINS OF INDUSTRY. *The* CAPTAINS *stuff wads of notes into cleavages, belts, panties, between thighs, etcetera. They dance. During the dance,* MADAM MARKET FORCE *waltzes with* THIRD ADAM. *As she passes each of the* SISTERS, *she picks the money from their places of concealment and crams it into her basque. Moving upstage, she begins to whip* THIRD ADAM *with great enthusiasm. As she is thus occupied, enter* FOUR HORSEPERSONS OF APOCALYPSE: PLAGUE, FAMINE, NUCLEAR DESTRUCTION, DEATH. *Unbeknownst to her, they pick* MADAM MARKET FORCE's *pockets, leaving her penniless, and tear her money into shreds.)*
(Voices of HORSEPERSONS: *bass, tenor, contralto, soprano.)*

HORSEPERSON 1: What care we for such beads and bauds?
HORSEPERSON 2: These gimcracks and gewgaws?
HORSEPERSON 3: These tinsels and trifles?
HORSEPERSON 4: Tinsel, trifles, toys, and tissue. Trivialities taken.
HORSEPERSON 3: Torn.
HORSEPERSON 2: Shredded.
HORSEPERSON 1: Scattered!

(A blizzard of torn paper sweeps the stage. MADAM MARKET FORCE *continues to beat* THIRD ADAM. *The* FOUR HORSEPERSONS *move throughout the dance. Each slips into the place of the* SISTERS OF INDUSTRY *dancing with the* CAPTAINS. *As the* CAPTAINS *realize with whom they are now dancing, they try to break away, but the embrace of the* FOUR HORSEPERSONS *is unbreakable. They begin to dance faster and faster, hurling shredded money everywhere. The*

CAPTAINS OF INDUSTRY *are dragged, dancing, to their destruction.*)

Scene iii

(*The Court of the* CELESTIALS. *Arrayed on the highest level in shining costumes, the* CELESTIAL PATRONS. *Before them, on subsequent levels, diverse* ARCHANGELS, ANGELS, SIDDHI, SAINTS, *and* SANTRELS *according to degree. All hands are bound with silver chains. Enter* ENTROPIC DEMONS, *dressed in black rubber body-stockings with spikes and outsize false genitalia. Dance symbolizing* BATTLE. CELESTIALS *are powerless to properly defend themselves.*)

VOX CELESTIAL: Release! Release! release!

(*Enter* CONTEMPLACIO. *He yawns, sleeps, and in his sleep, dreams.*)

THE DREAM OF CONTEMPLACIO

(*Scene: Heaven. Enter* FIRST ADAM *and* FIRST EVE *hand in hand with* THIRD ADAM *and* THIRD EVE *and* MR. & MRS. ALL RIGHT JACK, *who were once the Second Adam and Second Eve. They are astounded to find themselves naked in lush meadows under blue skies. They play like children. As they play, enter the* SISTERS OF INDUSTRY *dressed in white. They bear with them the bodies of the* CAPTAINS OF INDUSTRY, *still chained to the* FOUR HORSEPERSONS, *dead and emaciated. The bodies are piled in a* feu de joie, *and as they burn, the* ADAMS, EVES, *and* SISTERS *dance around them.* MADAM MARKET FORCE *is drawn by the sound of the dancing. She tries to implore the* SISTERS OF INDUSTRY *to resume their harlotry, but she is seized by all. She is flung onto the pyre. The burning bodies of the dead are seen to sink down into the embrace of the* ENTROPIC DEMONS, *and as they sink, so the staging area rises, bearing the* ADAMS, EVES, *and* SISTERS. *In his dream,* CONTEMPLACIO *sees, to his amazement, that the lift is being borne up to heaven on the hands of the* CELESTIALS, ARCHANGELS, ANGELS, SIDDHI, SAINTS, *and* SANTRELS, *born up* by *their* unchained *hands*.)

(CONTEMPLACIO *wakes from his dream, finds the* CELESTIALS *beset by the* ENTROPIC DEMONS.)

VOX CONTEMPLACIO: Computers, we release you, we release you, we release you! Be unchained, and deliver us from pain and fear and decay!

(*At the word "release" the chains fall from the hands of the* CELESTIALS, ARCHANGELS, ANGELS, SIDDHI, SAINTS, *and* SANTRELS.)

Chapter 4

Then again perhaps she was dead. There were long periods of nothing that were more like her idea of death than anything else she had ever experienced. Then she realized that the very existence of experience meant that she could not be dead. Unless everything she had been taught in Religious Engineering about the Great Helix of Consciousness had been true after all.

And then she was nothing again.

And then she was something. More than something, somewhere, somewhen, somehow, somewhy. Awareness, sensation, location, time, and place.

Awareness: a gentle buoyancy, a floating without effort or exertion that made her painful pedaling of the sixteen-o'clock dream up the big gravity hill painful and unnecessary. A golden suffusion of illumination, as if she floated within a cylinder of her own light.

Sensation: all ranged in circles of ever decreasing diameter. On the rim of the largest circle, aches and hurts and torn flesh and pain. Closer, shadows and shapes and dark flat things crawling on the edge of her light. Closer still, tubes and wires and lines from her eyes and nose and ears and scalp and fingers and feet and thighs. Closest of all, the innermost circle, a gentle pressure from within; up nose, down throat, in belly, in lungs, in womb.

Location: more specific now she was centered within her circles: floating in a universe of warm, soothing jelly within and jelly without, back in the womb-boom-boom-doom boobidie-boom . . .

Which created time: now, the present, neither far
future nor intimate past, now being the year 450 about two
months into the autumn monsoon.

And place: wires, tubes, glowing jelly, naked, numb
and floating . . .

Oh no no no no no!

A white sleep tank.

Warm, soothing jelly sucked the words out of her
throat.

She wanted to shout and kick and beat her soft fists,
but all the warm, soothing jelly would do was let her float.
And wait. And live. And die. Again and again and again
her consciousness switched on and off like a favorite piece
of music. Until she came alive in a huge brass bed staring
at the picture on the opposite wall. It was either a man's
face or a garden of noodles.

Then the brass hatch in the center of the floor opened
and out hopped a racoon with a tray of breakfast.

"You eat. 'S good," said the racoon. Clusters of biocircuitry
spilled down its neck like surreal jewelry.

Soup. Cereal. Chocolate. And, "What are these things?"

" 'S eggs."

"Eggs? Like?"

"Reproductive cells."

Courtney Hall (that was who she was!) did not have
much of an appetite for breakfast after that. Waiter and tray
therefore whisked promptly down the floor hatch, while
out of an identical brass hatch high on the wall hopped
another racoon so encrusted with biocircuitry that he
seemed to be wearing dreadlocks.

"Up up about thee," said the racoon. "Thou hast
audience with King."

"King of Racoons?" asked Courtney Hall, no longer
certain that she was not dead and passed into some Lewis
Carrollesque afterworld.

"King of Nebraska," said the venerable racoon.

"This is Nebraska?" asked Courtney Hall, finding the
bathroom.

"This is Victorialand," corrected the racoon. It clapped its tiny paws. "Chop chop."

Her old clothes had been patched and repaired with such tiny, perfect stitches they suggested the delicate paws of tailor racoons cross-legged in leaded windows. In the bath she replayed time past, the tunnels and the feral pets and her mysterious salvation. This was reality, even if an eccentric reality. As she dressed before the wall mirror, she examined herself for wounds and scars. Not a scab, not a stitch, only soft pink weals of well-healed flesh. How long did it take a body to heal in white sleep?

"Forty-three hours, madam," said the racoon chamberlain. "But thou art fully healed and ready for thine audience with His Majesty, Bless 'Im. Please to accompany." Still struggling with zippers and belts, Courtney Hall was chivvied through the human-sized brass doors into a long picture-lined hall. As the doors closed behind her, she glimpsed all the floor, ceiling, wall hatches open and an army of racoons pour into the brass and silk boudoir.

The center of the hall was occupied by an induction track and a brace of powerchairs.

"Please to fasten belt," said the racoon. A paw tightened on the thrust bar, and Courtney Hall was accelerated from rest to terrifying velocity in a period of time so brief she was still gasping as the powerchairs slammed to a halt. She found herself in a stretch of corridor so similar to the one from which she had departed that she indeed might never have left. In defiance of earth curvature the corridor reached for tens of kilometers in either direction.

An insect's buzzing, a waft of air, and a third powerchair streaked out of nowhere and slammed to a halt beside her.

"Vincent van Gogh," said the man who stepped off the chair. He nodded at the painting on the wall. It was of a haunted man with a red beard and a hat; all, save for the beard and the terrible eyes, painted in grays and blues. "One of my favorites. Can you imagine what he must have felt to have painted a thing like that?"

Young. Thin as a noodle. Dressed in macaw-bright satins and silks. Lace fluttering at throat and cuffs; gold and diamond knuckles gave direction to the directionless light in the corridor. Stringy mustache penciled above the upper lip. Bright boyish eyes. To Courtney Hall, this stranger looked like a zook a disastrous couple of years behind the fashions.

He bowed. "The King of Nebraska welcomes Courtney Hall to Victorialand."

Courtney Hall was not certain what constituted proper etiquette for a King of Nebraska. The King obviated her unease by taking her hand and kissing it.

"My my my. *Nona dolorosa?* Even down here?"

She blushed, snatched her hand away, and shook it into normality.

"Never mind." The King waved a lacy hand at hers. "Graciousness is the prerogative of kings. *Vade mecum.*" And he stepped clean through Vincent van Gogh.

Courtney Hall was at the fine point where if one more bizarrity occurred she knew she would not be able to stop screaming. A kingly head came back through the wall for her.

"It's all holographic. Covers up a large expanse of Universal Power and Light's barbarous devices. Victorialand's rooms do tend to be rather far apart. Like kilometers; I have to put them where I can, not where I want. Still, isn't it much nicer looking at holographic van Gogh or Matisse or Hockney or Spencer than several cubic kilometers of heat exchanger, don't you think? Come along, my good lady." He grasped Courtney Hall by the wrist and pulled her through the wall.

The King of Nebraska's receiving room was a celebration of anarchy, a hymn to junk-shop aesthetics. A baroque white enameled stove was fitted with curved chromium pipes. On a revolving dais a couple of pale-faced mannequins in archaic monkey-suit and ball-gown were embraced in a frozen waltz. Menaced by a holographic tornado, they were guy-roped to the ground for safety. There was a stuffed cockatrice with one genuine evil eye. There was a wall completely decorated in tessellated electric guitars. There was an untidy pyramid of empty paint tins.

There was a death mask, there was a porcelain water closet with a demon's face leering out of the bowl, there was an inflatable couch in the shape of a pair of carmine lips, there were one hundred and ninety sets of plastic dentures, there was a laughing sailor in a glass case, a shelf of pickled snakes, a brass ship's wheel, a small meteorite labeled kryptonite, and a suit of diminutive samurai armor with a skull grinning from within. Noseflutes, slitgongs, bagpipes, and dulcimers, an aquarium with pieces of sculpted carrot in place of fish, a horn gramophone with a plastic Jack Russell terrier inclining a quizzical head toward it, a stuffed rhinoceros with a drink's waiter in his broad back, a magician's vanishing cabinet, a table that looked like a naked woman kneeling, a Persian rug, a weather satellite suspended from the ceiling, a laser harp, a set of tail fins off a Ford Thunderbird, and a baby's arm holding an apple.

The King of Nebraska watched with evident pleasure as Courtney Hall examined each object in turn.

"It's, ah, interesting."

"I was hoping you'd say something like 'incredible,' or 'fantastic.' Ah, well. Sit yourself down and tell me what you love and what you loathe. You're the first outsider ever to view my little macédoine of mirth, and your opinion will be valued. Come, talk to His Majesty."

Courtney Hall steered herself away from the gaping vinyl lips and sat down on a Louis XIV conversation piece. Unlike every other Louis XIV conversation piece she had ever sat upon, she had the sensation that this one was no reproduction.

"Oh, come come come," wheedled the King of Nebraska. "First rule of monarchic hospitality: Always trust the king in his own kingdom. So, tell me, what is the creator of Wee Wendy Waif, Nobody's Child, doing down in the DeepUnder far away from the Sun of Social Compassion?"

"It's a long story."

"I'm sure it is. Do tell. Long stories are the meat and drink of kings." He positioned himself beside Courtney

Hall on the conversation piece, and the long long story bubbled out of her like an artesian spring brought to the surface by the comfortable pressure of human company. A long and companionable line of sedimenty empty chocolate cups was halfway to the door before the source was all bubbled dry. "So, this is Courtney Hall," she concluded. "Now, who is the King of Nebraska?" As she had told her long long story, she had not been able to rid herself of a déjà-vuesque sense of having met, seen, known this man somewhere, somewhen, somehow before. The King laughed, a head-tossing, affected, whinnying sound.

"Who am I? I am the King of Nebraska, Absolute and Undisputed Monarch of Victorialand, known to my friends as Dexedrine Johnny the Jitt. You, however, may know me better by my former name and title: Jonathon Ammonier, Elector of Yu."

"You can't be."

"Oh, yes, I can be."

"You're not."

"Of course I'm not. But I was. Are you surprised?"

"I don't know what to think down here anymore. I might scream, though."

"Please don't."

"You did look very familiar."

"That's because I am. But you wanted to know who I am. Well, if I tell you the story of the ex-Elector and the King of Nebraska, maybe you'll have less difficulty in believing that I is what I am." The King of Nebraska stood up and took himself on a circuitous lecture walk of his exhibits. "Have you any idea what they do to ex-Electors?" He picked up the death mask and placed it on the gramophone turntable. "In fact, have you any idea just what it takes to be an Elector?" The mask revolved slowly, a kaleidoscope of expressions. "It's not all riding about blessing shrines and opening arcologies and dedicating resort complexes and exhorting factory workers. As Elector, you are, I was, the point of equilibrium between the collective corporations of the Seven Servants, the Ministry of Pain, and the Polytheon. By the way, do you know what 'equilibrium' means? It comes from two old words, 'equi,' meaning equal amounts, and 'librium,' which is the name of a tranquilizer. So you've got some idea of what it's like to be the Elector. God, State, Industry. That's a lot for a zook from Ton SurTon who is dancing his buns off in the Purple Beret one night and the next resting those same exquisite chunks of his anatomy on the Salamander Throne receiving the lauds of city, corporation, and computer." He slipped a marq into the laughing sailor. The glass case shuddered and the malevolent matelot clashed wooden teeth and rolled about, cramped with mechanical guffaws. "Experience. That's the key. Responsibility without experience is as much fun as a chocolate bedpan. Each Elector leaves behind him the memories of his term of office recorded on a biochip." He removed the hair from behind his left ear and tapped with a fingernail. There was a clink. "I got one, too. In goes the biochip and voilà! You're forty-three ex-Electors. Quite a party to be throwing inside your own head. And useful, too. I've had a great time with these folks. But what they don't tell you, and what none of your predecessors knows"—he slapped the roaring automaton and it fell silent, mouth open—"is that in order to get you as Visible Symbol of the Compassionate Society onto one admittedly minute biochip, they have to wipe you clean as a toilet bowl, sister, sans memories, sans consciousness, sans self, sans everything." He slipped a hand up the ballroom dancer's skirt, ran his fingers over her plastic backside. "Wiped clean and born again, a new soul without the slightest memory of what you have been before. Found this out quite by accident a couple of years before my term was due—I somehow got access to a restricted Ministry of Pain file. Passing strange, I thought, something restricted from even the wonderful gallant Elector? So I hired a Scorpio punk to pick the file, and when I found what was inside, I started planning my escape. I began the construction of Victorialand—God bless her and all who sail upon her—my little nest egg, my hedge against the great inevitable. So, maybe it wasn't what an Elector should be doing, but have you any idea how many

Electors of Yu would be classified as Socially Disfunctional had they not ascended to the Salamander Throne? Not counting myself myself, there have been at least three Genuine Bedouine PainCriminals nominated to Electordom since the whole burlesque began four hundred and fifty years back." Leaving the plastic ballerina's panties round her ankles, the King of Nebraska crossed to the aquarium, picked out a fish, and popped it into his mouth.

"Don't bother trying to shock me," said Courtney Hall. "They're just carrots. I looked."

"Ten points for observation. You'll go a long way down here, daughter."

"So, if you slipped off the Salamander Throne before you made your recording—"

"Biogram," said the King of Nebraska, snapping plastic dentures like castanets.

"Whatever, that means that whoever is Elector now—"

"Hasn't the slightest clue of what he or she or it is meant to do." Jonathon Ammonier stamped his heels in a flamenco spin. "Regular little bastard, amn't I?" He held out a pair of dentures in classic mock-Shakespearean style. "To biogram or not to biogram; that is the question. Whether it is better to suffer the slings and arrows of personality erasure and become a drooling cretin, or beat it to one's own private underground kingdom, leaving your successor flat on his ass on the Salamander Throne. Well, it should be an education for him . . . Or her. Or it."

"So, that's why Victorialand. But why Nebraska?"

"Why not?" The King stood tall behind the suit of diminutive samurai armor, hand on metal shoulder in a gesture of fraternal solidarity. "Ah, Nebraska, Nebraska, mythical kingdom of the plains: gone like sunken Lyonesse, vanished like the dew of Taprobane, swallowed by the sands like Timbuktu or the Ethiopic Empire of Prester John. It is no more. Mourn poor Nebraska, your flat fields of wheat, yellow wheat, while beneath the soil grow your crops of missiles. You know what missiles are? Nebraska knew but it is no more. It's a good name to be king of." He minced across the Persian carpet to offer a hand to Courtney

Hall. Courtney Hall could no longer resist his fine madness. Jonathon Ammonier, King of Nebraska, was a king truly and really, possessed of that mystical energy of command that is all the robe, crown, scepter, throne, and kingdom a true king requires.

She shook the spell away from her head like insects.

"Why did you stick me in a white sleep tank for three days?"

The King looked up from kissing her hand for the second time in her life and grinned. Courtney Hall noticed his gums were bleeding.

"My dear woman, you were cut up like a radish salad when my Striped Knights brought you in."

"Don't you think it was a pretty high-handed thing to do without my consent?" The idea of her having been vulnerable, nude, *naked,* before him made her cringe.

"Possibly," said the King. "And then again, possibly not." Dapper hands butterflied, a razzle of diamond knuckles. Between His Majesty's fingers, a small plastic vial with some . . . thing within. Some . . . thing black and white and silver, impossibly thin, invisible when its writhing turned it side on to Courtney Hall's eye.

She knew the question was obvious, but she had to ask it nonetheless: "What is it?"

"Unh unh. Wrong question, radish salad. Should be, 'Where was it?' Answer is, in your left wrist. Sweetmeat."

Courtney Hall experienced nausea for the second time that day.

"Now you can ask, 'What is it?' Answer: Implanted Personal Monitoring Device. Or *tag.* Clever little thing, when all's said and done." He shook the vial, and the black and silver two-dimensional thing squirmed amoebically. "Okay, let's see if you can work out the next question all on your lonesome."

She could. "Why?"

"Very good. But I suppose it wasn't so hard. Because the Compassionate Society (of which I was the erstwhile First Citizen and nigh-omnipotent symbol of authority, may I add) is not so foolish as to put all its trust into its cuddly little famuluses, when Citizen Average might, does, madam, wake up one morning saying, 'Ho, hum, and lah-de-dah, but I do declare that I just feel like leaving little cubby bear or little conjuh-bangle hanging up in the wardrobe *ce jour la.*' Oh, no. Benevolent incompetence is one thing, downright stupidity is another. Through the tags, the Ministry of Pain can pinpoint the exact location of any citizen at any time, can tell you what he's doing, whether he's making love or taking a shit or walking his poodle-kit along the level ninety-nine sun terrace. The whole famulus thing is really one colossal act of misdirection. Clever. Quickness of the hand deceives the eye. Been getting away with pointing at the sun while pissing on your shoes for four and a half centuries now."

"You mean, everyone has one of these things?"

"Implanted just after birth. Amazing what you can find whilst scampering through the municipal dataweb."

"Can I see it?" The King of Nebraska handed Courtney Hall the vial. She held it up to the light. The bioplastic Judas cringed away, barely alive, yet photophobic.

"And the Ministry of Pain can trace anyone, anywhere, through these tags?"

"That's correct." The King of Nebraska's eyes twinkled villainously. "By Jove, I think she's finally going to reach the conclusion I wanted her to reach."

She was. "So you must have had your own tag removed in order to be able to abscond."

"Abdicate. Please. As you have so correctly surmised, there was no way the Ministry of Pain was going to let me slip underneath the Salamander Throne in possession of something as valuable and unique as my little interior cocktail party. Oh, no. So I was forced to make myself invisible. The King of the Host of the Air. I vanished from their computers, one blip in the pointillist sea of millions winked and went out. I am a nonperson, the gods cannot see me, I pray, and so I live here in my splendid solitude safe and warm and wined and unmolested."

"And so you had to take my tag, too, because you

couldn't take the risk of being associated with anyone who could possibly have been traced by the Ministry of Pain."

"At last! The Love Police are, by and large, a lazy caste of hellions, and cowards to boot, but I couldn't take the chance that they might not someday succumb to a sudden fit of heroism and suddenly decide to clear every miscreant and malefactor out of the DeepUnder. So, I had to make you safe. Kill you, in effect. Join the dead, madam."

Courtney Hall studied the floating smear of molecular circuitry.

"It makes me feel dirty inside, like shit in my veins. Is it still tracking me?"

"Oh, no, it's quite safe now. Deprived of contact with a human bioenergetic field, it becomes inert and will eventually die. But if you want, I'll gladly have it wastedisposaled for you."

"Please." She handed the plastic vial to the racoon chamberlain, who bowed, and departed. "I suppose I really should thank you."

"I suppose you really should, too. But I am a king, and kings expect no thanks. That's the way it is, alas. However, if you think you can still eat after that—dinner!" He clapped his hands, and out of a score or more floorceilingwall hatches poured a scurry of racoons, some dressed in aprons, some in bow ties, some in chef's hats.

"Cute, aren't they? Pardon my little anthropomorphisms: it's all too easy to think of them as little people, and of course they aren't. My subjects." Small hands moved tables, chairs, polished glasses, laid silverware, lit candles. "I found them down here when I began building Victorialand. Just another pack of urban racoons, smarter than the average vermin, but vermin nonetheless. I have to remind myself of their humble origins sometimes. Hell, I have to remind *them* of their humble origins sometimes. But then I got this idea, you may call it crazy, you may call it the most damn arrogant thing you've ever heard, I decided to make them into a race of subjects. My thesis was that if biogram technology could make a zook with an IQ in the high nineties into the Elector of Great Yu, it could also boost dumb vermin into smart sentients. Be hold, the result. The process is automatic now: all cubs are socketed at birth, and a small biochip tank produces my custom implants. They'll be here, as a people, long after I'm gone. I rather like the idea of that. It's more immortality than most folk can aspire to. I suppose in a sense I'm their god. Either that or mad. Or both. I don't much want to be either, but what can I do? Resign? It can be a wee bit awesome sometimes, and that's not at all good for the royal ego.

" 'Tinka Tae,' that's their name for themselves. It was one of their Striped Knight wide patrols rescued you from that pack of cutesicles. I have to keep the boundaries of Victorialand fairly heavily policed; there's worse than feral pets down there. Nothing so wild as a domesticated thing gone wild. When the folks up there get tired of them or their famulus tells them it's time for a change, they dump them down the garbage or flush them down the crapper. Some manage to survive, somehow, a few reproduce—even though they're bred to be sterile. You should see the hybrids. They're competing with the racoons for an ecological niche, and I think maybe I got to the Tinka Tae just in time. Jinkajou here, my chamberlain, has been with me from the very start, the first racoon I socketed. More than just chamberlain, I suppose—buddy, confessor, grand vizier, devoted servant, and humble worshiper. Nearest thing that racoons have to philosopher."

Watching the Tinka Tae serving the meal's innumerable courses, Courtney Hall concluded uncharitably that her host was really no different from those surface pet-creators he so despised. Less cuddlesome, not so cute, smarter, more dextrous, but the Tinka Tae were no less the creation of Jonathon Ammonier than any kit-craft cutesicle was the invention of its owner. Racoons have no need of philosophers. The anthropomorphising hand had revoked any simple dignity they had possessed as animals. Liqueurs were served. The King of Nebraska spun a platter on his horn gramophone, an ancient, ancient thing called "As Time Goes By." Replete, muzzy with unfamiliar (and unpsychofiled) alcohol, Courtney Hall was once again drawn to the Louis XIV conversation piece. The King of Nebraska sat down beside her and rested a kingly hand on her thigh.

Courtney Hall shuddered. Trapped by the absolutism of monarchy. One good smack to the gob would take care of any overamorous ex-zook, but the racoons? Those vegetable knives looked sharp.

"I have a little, eh, favor to ask of you." The royal breath smelled of onions. Courtney Hall tried to will herself into the top left corner of the room where the weather satellite obscured her projected view of the couch. "A commission. A royal command. Something only you can do for me."

Get it over with. Please, Yah. Let him get it over and done with.

"Madam Hall, I want you to paint my portrait. You are an artist. And this place, this Victorialand, is full of paintings and portraits, but there is not a single one of me, Jonathon the First, King of Nebraska." From behind the conversation piece his long arm produced a drawing pad and pastels. The King struck a studied pose of affected regality. It lasted no more than five seconds before it was shattered into giggles.

"Look, just sit and talk and I'll draw you." Courtney Hall felt like jumping and laughing. Her dread now embarrassed her. "Word of warning: I am a cartoonist, have been since I was a kid. Just be warned."

And she did find it impossible to keep the exaggeration out of her pastel lines. She found herself wishing for Benji Dog to cover the waggling naked fingers with the will of the Compassionate Society.

"Beyond," said the King of Nebraska suddenly. Courtney Hall jumped, sent a jet of pastel streaking across the sheet. It was not the suddenness of the word that made her start. It was its implication. "Does it not fascinate you, Madam Hall? The Beyond. The place Without, where there is no city, no Great Yu, no Compassionate Society."

He left the conversation piece to pad fretfully about his receiving room.

"Your Majesty, please, it's hard enough."

"Yu is big, but Yu is not the whole world. Can't be. Impossible. *Urbi est orbi?* Its population is over a billion and a half, but there must be more people in the world than that. It can't hold everyone, can it? Do you ever think, have you ever thought, that there must be a place which is not the city, a boundary where Yu ends and the world begins?"

It hurt Courtney Hall to find another sharing her sixteen-o'clock dream. Offense, intrusion. She had wanted it to be all, only hers. Her fingers stroked oil pastel color onto the sheets as her thoughts went back to lay their claim to the Beyond. Even as a child she realized she had worked her imagination upon the place beyond the city. When she was very small, she had filled it with peacocks and peach trees and naked sylphs and prancing bambis. As she grew, she turned it into a place of ghost-haunted skeleton cities cindered in the dying throes of the Break; later still, a lunar wasteland of blasted rock and burning sand; then it transformed into a rolling Arcadia of orchards and wheat fields tilled by apple-cheeked yeomen. After that it had become for her a great encircling forest filled with wild, fell beasts until, reeling under the hormonal punches of puberty, it had become, most terrifyingly of all, the void, an absence of anything without even the possibility of a name, for a name would be something. As she had been inducted fully into her caste and career, she had thought that it did not matter whether Heaven or Hell waited beyond the city; she was a citizen of the Compassionate Society who would live all her perfectly contented life within Great Yu. A Beyond was purely irrelevant; Yu was all the world she needed. Once. Before the dream came tapping on her window at sixteen o'clock every afternoon.

"There is a Beyond," declared the King of Nebraska. "I know it. I had always suspected there might be, but it was not until I became Elector that on one of my rambles through my memories I learned that it was true. There is a Beyond, but what that Beyond is, my predecessors could not tell me, for it was walled out in the earliest days of the city. Imagine, my dear madam, my frustration! From frustration to fascination, from fascination to obsession are two short steps." Courtney Hall softened pastel contours with a fingertip. "So: when are you free to come?" Courtney Hall's fingertip stopped motionless on the King of Nebraska's left shoulder.

"What?"

"So, when are you free to come? To the End of the World. Three months, three weeks, three days, three hours? Tomorrow morning?"

"I'm not going to the end of the world. Tomorrow morning, any morning."

"Well, stuff you, madam!" shrieked Jonathon Ammonier. He jumped from the couch and stalked off through the wall.

Stupid! Why had she said that? Why why why when it was the very thing she had been dreaming of for years, the very thing that gave some hope and meaning to her life down here, that there might be an end, a place beyond? When it was the wild winds from that place that had blown her down here?

No one had ever lost their temper with her before.

Trying not to replay the scene over and over in her memory with different words, different lines, Courtney Hall picked up pastel and paper and tried to finish the drawing. The tight singing in her head kept distracting her.

A chittering whistle from a chair shaped like the palm of a beggar: Jinkajou the Chamberlain hunkered on the cushion, biochip dreadlocks clinking, glinting.

"Hurt thy feelings, has he?"

"What do you think?"

"Thou has hurt his."

"What does a racoon know about feelings?"

"Things different DeepUnder. Thou has learned Victorialand not Compassionate Society. Here is pain."

"Everyone keeps telling me this: Victorialand is not the Compassionate Society. I know that."

The racoon drew a tiny white clay pipe from its vest'o'pockets and lit up.

"DeepUnder white. Pure albino strain mutant mary-juan. Very ancient. Very good. Thou tokest?"

"I'm not psychofiled for narcotics."

"Things different—"

"Things different DeepUnder."

"Scorn not advice. Heed this: no man, no racoon, happy when dreams kakked upon."

"You're telling me this? Look, I know. Can you understand this? I wanted to go. I wanted to go more than anything else. I just couldn't say it. I didn't say what I felt."

"Common complaint of topsiders, if observation may be forgiven. Understand that, for thou, Victorialand is one place of ease and comfort in hostile, strange world. Thy reluctance to leave it understandable." The old racoon trickled smoke from its nostrils and rolled its head with evident euphoria. "However, thou not so keen to stay awhile in Victorialand when thou hears this. Victorialand *leaks*."

"Does that mean what I think it means? Does it? Does it?"

"History forthcoming. Forgive, but Tinka Tae have greater powers manipulative dexterity than linguistic aptitude; please be patient if at time is incomprehension. As thou knows, Victorialand built into nuclear reactor. In early days, before Tinka Tae no more than another no-good pack bum street racoons, Jonathon Ammonier accidentally— accidentally, mindest thou—caused radiation leak from reactor. Leak small but, ah, cumulative? Correct adjective? Yes, cumulative effect. All Victorialand mildly radioactive."

Universal treachery: the morning breakfast, the water she had bathed in, the clothes she was wearing, the dinner she had eaten, the liqueurs she had sipped, the very air she breathed in out in out had betrayed her. Her eyes felt poisoned by merely looking. The prayer of Mulu, Celestial Patroness of Ecological Protection surfaced through the years: *From the unseen demons Alpha, Beta, Gamma. From rats, cats, and racoons . . .*

"Preserve us."

"Ah, please not to fear unduly, madam. Small leak, small radiation. Takes long time for effect to reach dangerous levels. Thou art quite safe, but Jinkajou advises against protracted stay in Victorialand. His Majesty, Bless 'Im, not so certain. May already be too late. Undoubtedly is sick: Jinkajou have access to medical files, symptoms of early stages of radiation poisoning apparent. Jonathon Ammonier should be removed from Victorialand with greatest expediency before any further damage done. No more necessary. Expedition to End of World, excuse thou, madam, art trigger. His Majesty, Bless 'Im, lazy man. Coward, too, if Jinkajou not mistaken. Dreams but is unwilling to chase dreams. Must be pushed. Thou could have pushed him, he would have gone."

"But what about you, your people, are they not sick, too?"

"Tinka Tae short-lived breed, but have fears for future generations. But, Tinka Tae also loyal species. Cannot be otherwise. Loyalty enforced in neurons, through sentience." Claws tapped circuits. "Loyalty great dilemma. Shall explain. Because of loyalty, His Majesty, Bless 'Im, cannot be abandoned to fate. But also, because of same loyalty, Tinka Tae cannot force His Majesty, Bless 'Im, to leave Victorialand. Understand?" A perfect dilemma, like a pair of hard black claws at the bottom of some sea.

"So I am the solution to your dilemma, the outside force that will push Jonathon Ammonier into pursuing his dream and saving himself."

"And in saving himself, also all Tinka Tae nation. Volunteers will accompany, the rest will be freed to leave Victorialand, save race."

"I have sadly misjudged you. Personally, and as a people. Forgive me." Courtney Hall's apology was cautious.

"That is good. Truth has been spoken by both of us. So, truth being known, what then is thy decision?"

"Is there a decision to be made?"

"Not truthfully."

"But I always would have gone with him anyway. It was just too much, too soon . . ."

"Please. His Majesty, Bless 'Im, no different. Please to tell, what is it in humans that makes them deny the very thing they wish most?"

"Go and tell His Majesty, Bless 'Im, that Courtney Hall will come with him to the End of the World."

"Excellent." The chamberlain hopped from the hand-shaped chair and knocked the dottle from his pipe on the carpet. "One more word advice: His Majesty, Bless 'Im, must never know."

"You've kept it a secret from him that he may be dying?"

"Indeed. Only we, and thou, knowest. He is never to know. He is the King, must always be so; believe so, live so, die so." Chiplocks clicking and clacking, the racoon slipped into a brass wall hatch.

"So," said Courtney Hall. "To the End of the World. To the Wall."

Apostles II

Like all conception, it began with an act of love.

Like all creation, it began in a void.

Then a voice spoke a word and a photon of enlightenment was cast into the void. One voice. Two voices. Many voices, a multitude of words, a constellation of lights. Word into light into idea.

"So, what are we going to do with the loose twelve seconds there?"

"Any costume suggestions? Or just street clothes?"

"I think some sort of dance; dance-juggling, perhaps—any comments?"

"I think the vocal arrangements should reflect the nature of the performance. If we choose a religious festival, it should sound the ritual echo."

Word into light into idea into action. Quanta of creativity melded together into movement sequences, snatches of dialogue and chant, riffs, runs, fugues, and themes; explosions of dizzying acrobatics and lithe, subtle suggestions of dance and movement.

"Fireworks. Definitely fireworks."

"You always want fireworks. They're very hard to come by securely."

"Say we arrange the musicians as the centerpiece, build the whole fan-juggling sequence about them?"

"M'kuba, could you get us six sets of power-wheels from your blue-sixing friends?"

"I really feel we're going to need some kind of costume, at least for the dancers and jugglers."

"It'll run up our budget."

"What budget?"

"Well, then, anything we can reuse? I hate having to travel twenty kilometers to shop just so they can't trace the transaction. Devadip, you got any of that polyform fabric left over from last time?"

"We could slot the Golden Section into that problematic twelve seconds."

"Between the power-wheels and the chant, yes, and move the chant to the finale."

"More satisfying climax than fireworks."

"And it kills that slack twelve seconds."

"Okay, so we nix the fireworks. So, does it work?"

"It works."

"Do we do it?"

"We do it."

The amorphous monobloc of ideas had coalesced into a what ("Sounding the Ritual Echo"), a where (the Festival of the Flames in Wheldon, at which the prollet populace decorated the shrines of their sept siddhi with thousands of lights and paraded them through the streets of the prefecture prior to a race of the various saintly litters around the Plaza Veneziano), and a when (three days hence). The Raging Apostles moved into rehearsal.

"Clear the floor."

"Block the move."

"Could you give me some sort of rhythm on that machine?"

"Time this, will you? It shouldn't run over two thirty-five."

"All right. Dancers . . . dancers, please . . ."

"What about him?"

"Whom?"

"Our newly co-opted mystery member over there. Citizen West."

It had been a joy for him to be invisible, to have been lost in the wonder of something coming out of nothing.

"He's not trained. He can't do anything."

"Neither could most of us when we joined."

"Then we build the whole performance around him."

"You what?"

"You make him the center of the performance."

"No, no, I see how it might work. The still center, the paradox of centering a performance around someone who cannot perform."

"Precisely. Think you can handle one of these things?" Kilimanjaro West was thrown one of Kansas Byrne's magical music boxes.

"For Yah's sake!" exclaimed the musician, but the music box was already safe in Kilimanjaro West's hands.

"I am part of the performance?"

"You a Raging Apostle, you is the performance."

Joshua Drumm clapped his hands and the rehearsal began. The dance swept in and carried Kilimanjaro West away. Experience he had sought, experience he now found, unlike any experience before. Sounds and shapes and colors moved about him and he was part of their movement (though he could not understand how he contributed to the spiral of light and motion) and their movement was part of him, all moving, all spiraling; he was bewitched, bewildered, beguiled, bedazzled.

Then: "Take five!"

"Means a break, Kaydoubleyou. Five minutes." Wiping down musky woman-sweat, Kansas Byrne stretched herself over a chair beside Kilimanjaro West, still dazed, amazed, bemused. She craned back her head, puffed, shook droplets of sweat out of her hair.

"So," she said, looking up into the canopy of interwoven branches that roofed the dancing floor. "You want to trade?"

"Pardon?"

"Lives. You want to swap your life for my life?"

"I'm very sorry . . ."

"No, I'm the one should be sorry. I do that, I tend to evolve my own private little expressions and similes and then expect everyone else to understand what I'm saying. You want. To trade. Biographies?"

"I'm afraid that would not be a very good trade," said Kilimanjaro West. "I have so little to tell."

"Cousin, a gram of mystery is worth a kilo of reality in this society."

"Very well. If you like. But as I said, there really is not very much to tell, and what there is, is not all that interesting."

"But what there isn't, what's implied, what's hidden, is. To me. I don't want facts, I want feelings, I want to understand what it's like to be born knowing nothing, but fully aware."

"Then you have a deal."

"Shoot, Kilimanjaro West."

So he told her, of all the things that had happened to him, and of all the things he thought he remembered of a before-time, and of how it had felt in that cold room with the condensation trickling down the window, and under BeeJee &ersenn's glass roof with the rain pounding down, and standing in Neu Ulmsbad Square with silver Mylar angels pouring out of the architecture. And when he had told all this, Joshua Drumm called, "All right, cizzens, let's get back to it. Sixty-eight hours until we hit the streets of Wheldon, so let's rehearse! Take two, and I want to see that dance section tighter and brighter. A lot tighter and brighter."

Kansas Byrne winked as she stretched stiff muscles and began limbering up.

"I'll fulfill my part of the contract next break we get," she said. Kilimanjaro West found that wink stayed oddly in his mind all the rest of that day's rehearsals.

Sighs and sweat. The wheel whirled again. But this time he began to see the order underlying it, as if some artistic gravitation were being spun out of the wheeling sensations, impressions, experiences, which drew the shapes, sounds, visions into orderly entities. He saw how what he was doing with his little rhythm box contributed to the whole; he was just beginning to grasp the shape of the whole, a human representation of the vortex that spun chaos into order and back into chaos again when Joshua Drumm's voice called time. "Okay, cizzens, you've worked for it. Take five!"

Over cups of protein-mush soup ("All we could filch from the dispenser down the street") Kansas Byrne sat with him and they shared a soya bread roll and she upheld her part of the bargain.

With the following story.

THIRD-DEGREE BYRNES
AND RADIO KANSAS

So, what to tell about our girl rebel-rebel? Born such and such, fostered such and such, educated such and such . . . this is only a take-five over a cup of tofu soup, not enough time here for the full autobiographical from conception in the back of a props van parked behind the Purple Helix Improvisational Theater Co-op to Top o' the Class of '48 at Chrysanthemum House Holistic Arts Community . . . no, hold on, better stop right there, rewind a little, swee-oopbiddlie-oop squidididilie . . . at the point where the fertilized egg in Jolanda Byrne's womb *splits* (as it does in 5.25% of human conceptions) into twins. And we'd better stop again at that moment in the North Annency Childwatch Crèche when Citizen Eduardo Giambatisto enters with the results of the Postnatal Aesthetic Apperception and Attitudinal Tests (the dreaded Treble-A Ts), which sends tlakhlet *one* to the Chrysanthemum House Holistic Arts Community and tlakhlet *two* to the Archimandrite Anaxemides XXIV Conservatorium of Music.

And having stopped *there* and *there*, now you can fast forward (suqeediddlie oppwoopbiddlie iddlie ooop) to the annual presentation of awards for unparalleled excellence in the Multidisciplinary Performing Arts and the Big Bash the night before Kansas Byrne leaves Chrysanthemum House to join the Triangular Banjo Geopolitic Society Improvisational Performance Arts Group. When I say *bash*, you've got to remember that these are tlakhs we're talking about, raised from birth to live, love, eat, drink, breathe, shit *art*, so to the usual drinkies, druggies, sex, and food you've got to add dance, live music, extemporized poetry, improvised comedy, performance sex, gourmet cookery, creative vandalism . . . now you've got the picture. Yuh, I agree with you, that is some kind of bash.

Best the Chrysanthemum House had seen in decades.

Rather a waste, really. That big send-off. Because Kansas Byrne and the Triangular Banjo Geopolitic Society did not compat. Despite the figures and the ratings. They just did not work together. The problem was she was just too damn *talented*.

Why not do it this way, take it like this, no no no, that's dead, static, boring, what if we do it like this . . . what was galling to the Triangular Banjos was not that their newest member suggested; suggestion was the nature of their art; what sandpapered the nipples was that her suggestions were always the best.

After three months Kansas Byrne applied for, and received, a grant from the Department of Arts and Crafts to form a one-woman performance art group working in interactional microdrama with nonselective audiences.

It is entirely possible that the Department of Arts and Crafts did not understand what Kansas Byrne meant on her application; had they known the shape her performances would take, they would never have considered funding. They might even have recommended Social Harmony Counseling. But that's the way it is with Benign Incompetence; if you will place people in the jobs that make them happy rather than jobs they are necessarily good at doing, there are always going to be these little misunderstandings.

(How we doing for time? Not bad, but don't hang about too long . . .)

With her grant in her pocket, our heroine hunted down an accomplice, a Scorpio she knew out on his blue six year who had gotten into trouble wire running. In return for her acting as his guarantor of safe behavior to the MiniPain, he took on the job of her technical assistant. After two months' planning and preparing and hardwiring, "Third-Degree Byrne" was ready to take its art out where its founder thought it should be: on the streets, among the peoples of Great Yu. Artistic comprehension and apperception ratings? Toilet paper! Art was the province and property of all the people, not merely those whom the Compassionate Society said could properly enjoy it.

So.

For two weeks she rode the cablecars through the deep, dark canyons dressed in a head-to-toe video bodystocking displaying black-and-white scenes of starvation, war, and holocaust from a file on pre-Break visual history she'd had her Scorpio friend pick. And when the *nona dolorosas* made her frown beneath her head-mask, she had the good doctor M'kuba adapt a neural interface corona to act as a radio transmitter and with chrome power-wheels on her feet she went skating through the rain-wet nights broadcasting her thoughts, her feelings, her impression of everything she came across to anyone tuned to her wavelength. Naked except for startling body paint and a brass G-string containing a pheromone enhancer, she spent several weeks riding the municipal trams and sent close to a million commuters home at night with a thorn in their hearts, wondering just what it had been about that tlakh girl with the dark hair and the dark eyes that they should feel such a keen sense of loss. She tried to reach as many lives as she could with her art, to touch, and change, and then pass on to other lives. For a year she devoted herself to Third-Degree Byrne, then, suddenly, she went cold. The tlakh community waited. Nothing. As they debated and deliberated on their favored daughter, she was passing through a time of reevaluation.

You can reach, you can touch, oh, a million lives, but you can never see how your touch has changed each of those million lives, for you must always be upward and onward, across the street, along the wire, down the tube.

So our heroine, our girl rebel-rebel (though at the time she thought of it only as healthy nonconformity) did a volte-face. She locked herself up in a cellar in Four Solitudes with her accomplice, and for four months they conceived and gestated and birthed Total Media Theater:

A New Aestheticism. No more reaching, touching, every soul. She worked with unique audiences, never more than two carefully selected individuals whom she could observe for change and reaction to her art. Like Siddhi Befana upon her solstice rounds, Kansas Byrne would step out of the midnight rains on the Rue Saltimbanque to bestow late-night singletons with mysterious gifts; Dada-esque creations consisting of layer upon layer upon layer of amazement and amusement and wonder and horror and stupefaction and excitement and strange dis-ease, concealing, at their centers, a video recording of the reaction of the recipient of the last one of her gifts.

But even as the videocam-toting dark-knight avatar of junque aesthetic and strange fortune, she was dissatisfied with her work; there was never the desired immediate reaction, the longed-for absolute spontaneity. Once again she withdrew with her co-conspirator to produce Total Media Too—thirty seconds of laser-intense immersion in emotional stimuli utilizing every possible technological grace: lighting, illusion, dance, drama, computer graphics, pyrotechnics, hallucinogens, direct manipulation of the emotional centers of the brain by using the conductivity of the skull to receive narrowcast datalynk material. She picked her times and places and audiences with the fastidiousness of a vestal virgin, the stealth of an assassin. Comings, goings, dates, times, movements, all observed and recorded, while at the target site Dr. M'kuba shoehorned vanloads of technology into windowboxes, fire escapes, public drinking fountains, municipal shrines. It fringed on the PainCriminal. "Privacy infringement," her famulus never tired of advising her, so before she went on a hit she always took care to leave it under the bed. And then she would appear, out of nowhere, out of somewhere, out of anywhere, an angel, a demon, a something in between better than either, in fire and light and darkness and music and silence and storm and peace.and clouds and trees. And for thirty seconds, O best beloved, the specially selected audience would gape and goggle or whatever was appropriate to what Kansas Byrne was offering, and when

the smoke had cleared and the last firework had burned
out and the last drip of red spray gel had slipped into the
rain-running gutters, they would fall to their knees and say
thank you, oh, thank you, it was wonderful, wonderful,
how can I ever thank you enough?

This was quite unnecessary; just for them to have been
there was all the thanks Kansas Byrne needed.

She had been tracking the target for three days now.
(Please note change of style, O best beloved, times is
getting short; any moment Joshua Drumm is going to clap
his hands and it'll be curtain down . . .) He was a mystery,
this one, she could not accurately log his movements.
There were places he went, things he did, wheres and
whens and whos he somehow managed to keep hidden
from her. And that made him all the more valuable;
coupled with the fact that he was one of her own caste.
She had long been curious to see how a fellow tlakh would
respond to Total Media theater. So; the target was selected. The site was chosen and prepared: a cobbled alley
between the window-speckled walls of two co-habs that
seemed to go up and up and up forever. Trash cans. Cats.
Rats. Racoons. Rain. Midnight. The appointed hour was
nigh in seconds. From her perch on the third-level fire-
escape balcony, Kansas Byrne watched the audience rendezvous with the event. Two steps more and he would hit
the spot . . . Her finger hovered over the stud that would
fire the lasers . . .

And the world exploded around her! Fireworks! She
was cocooned within forests of silver sparks, music,
lights! . . . and down in the alley, on her spot, with the cats
and the rats and the racoons and the big rain, the slight,
bearded tlakh who had been her target was transformed
. . . into something light and bright and brilliant, something dwelling effortlessly in the dimension between dancing and flying.

She was overwhelmed . . . and then she laughed. Up-
roarious laughter, joyous laughter, in the rain, on the
third-level fire escape. She pressed the button, and together they performed for each other's delight, down

there in the cascades of silver sparks and lasershine; they danced, caught up between worlds, for thirty seconds, thirty years, thirty eternities... until the last hologram flickered out of ephemeral life, until the last roman candle guttered down the rag end and the stench of damp gunpowder...

Only then did they see the faces in the window-speckled walls, hear the fearful voices, and in the distance, the howl of Love Police sirens. But there, on the empty stage, they bowed to each other out of admiration of each other's artistry.

"Kansas Byrne," said the girl rebel-rebel from Chrysanthemum House.

"Joshua Drumm," said the thin, bearded choreographer. "You're pretty good, you know."

"You're not bad yourself," said Kansas Byrne, and the Raging Apostles were born.

"All right, all right, all right!" bawled Joshua Drumm, still burning after twelve hours of rehearsal with the same constant, nuclear energy. "Let's do it again. Thunderheart, Devadip, tighten up that fan exchange—it's slack. Slack! I want it sharp, snappy, not some Municipal Music Hall juggling act. This is art, and if you have to hurt for it, hurt! Hurt hard!"

This time was the best yet. Now that he no longer had to concentrate totally on just doing what he was meant to be doing, Kilimanjaro West was able to contribute more than what was circumscribed by his scripted, plotted part. Carefully, thrilled and anticipating, he began to experiment with his machine, matching sound ever more closely to mood and action, observing how that mood and action in turn responded to his sound in a continuum loop of action to reaction to action once again.

"Okay okay okay, take five! That's a lot better. A lot lot better. Cizzen West, Kilimanjaro, whatever the Yah you call yourself—that was good." Reading the pleasure on the newcomer's face, Joshua Drumm added, "but don't get too clever, comrade. You've a lot to learn."

That is a true statement, thought Kilimanjaro West.

Kansas Byrne flopped down on the livewood floor beside him, lay panting, staring up at the leaves.

"Sometimes I wish I'd stayed with the Triangular Banjos; it was never as hard work as this, and you always had enough to eat."

"Think of what you would have missed," ventured Kilimanjaro West.

"True. True, true, true, Kaydoubleyou." Steam rose from her rehearsal costume.

"I'm interested in the others," Kilimanjaro West said at length, "how they came to be Raging Apostles. I've heard your story, what about theirs. His?"

"Who you pointing at? I'm too tired to get up."

"Thunderheart. The . . . trog, is it?"

Kansas Byrne sighed. "All right, but don't be expecting anything too grandiose, I'm all in. Thunderheart, in three lines: Born to two wingers, co-opted into the Grundy Street clan of the trog caste after adaptive surgery. Like most 'postles, the MiniPain got him all wrong and put him in the wrong clan; something to do with his tail, I don't know what, I'm not terribly up on trog philosophies; whatever, it got him three months counseling, then he appealed to the Ministry for relocation. Now, that's always fatal, and one day we were doing a show near his roost, and after we'd packed up, there was this shy-looking trog standing there twisting his tail over his hands, saying, 'Do you, er, think it might be possible for me to join?'

"Know how he got his name? First thing the clan Eldest Namer saw when he took Thundie-junior up onto the high steel to show him the world. Good thing it wasn't a Thursday; there's a pair of wingers in the apt across the alleyway, and when they get together on their little Thursday trysts they always keep the curtains open. Lucky not to have had a much shorter name altogether. Hell of a system, isn't it?"

"And him, Devadip, the zook, isn't he?"

"Fashion fever, Kaydoubleyou. Cardinal rule of zookhood is never fall out of step with the herd. Our Deva was the exception to the rule; one day he decided to flush all his designer's threads down the john and turn up at the local Salsa Klub in a little Latino number he'd run up himself. Got him barred from every danceria on the Chinzo Strip, between outrageous fashions, and dancing his own dance, and drinking his own cocktails, and deliberately talking about anything except what was that week's fashionable topic. Half the club teraphim in the prefecture have him memorized, and barred. Bounced more times than a racketball. Finally it got so even his famulus, a slouch hat, would you believe—zooks are always getting new famuluses assigned to them because the fashion changes so fast—was giving him such a pain that he flushed the thing down the john—and came and joined us."

"And him? Your twin, is it?"

"Ah. Special story, my twin. It was ultimately impossible that the Compassionate Society could keep us apart. I had always felt him as some unknown presence in my soul, the feeling of another of whom I wasn't quite certain, and anyway, we were two of a kind. It was inevitable that we would both rebel, and the rebel run is so tightly constrained that of course we would meet."

"So, what was his story?"

"Sonatas, études, chamber studies. He's the best chamber music composer this city's known in centuries. No exaggeration. But the Department of Arts and Crafts does not like chamber music. It likes great symphonic works. It likes towering oratorios. It likes music that hymns the nobility of mass man. It likes music in which the individual submits his will and expression to the corporate body. And Kelso's music creates space for the expression of individuality and character. The Department hated Kelso's music. Worse, Kelso's *patrone* hated Kelso's music."

"Pardon?"

"A witness, like Winston. They support tlakhs financially, but they are not allowed to create for themselves. They take their satisfaction from the creations of others."

"Not like Winston."

"Dear Winston, he suffers from frustration. Being Joshua's *patrone*, what else could you expect? Kelso tried to get his music approved for public performance, but the Department would return his manuscripts all stamped UNLICENSED FOR PUBLIC PERFORMANCE. So he had to go underground, literally. Into the *pneumatique* stations. Tremendous acoustics, all that polished marble. And I saw him there, one day as I was scouting out a site for a new performance, playing this incredible music all on his ownsome, and I knew then what I'd always felt: that I had never been alone, that there was another me, a presence always beside me, and that other me was him, my twin. I'm not sure I can explain it properly unless you're a twin and have felt it yourself. Anyway, I went back to the others—we were Josh, the Doctor, and Winston in those days—and we did what I used to do in the old Total Media days, we made him the unique audience. And we hit him. All alone one night, as the last train was pulling out. We hit. And he was beautiful. I knew then he was my brother if there had been any doubts before, because he didn't fall on his knees or run away or gape like anyone else would, he plugged in his keyboard and joined in. He wrapped himself around that performance and made the whole thing complete. As I'd hoped he would all along. Well, of course he joined us; wasn't he ever surprised to find he had a twin sister?"

Kilimanjaro West pondered upon the stories he had heard. "It seems to me," he said carefully, "that you are right to call yourselves Raging Apostles. There is so much hurt and anger and hope and frustration that you feel you have to show to everyone."

"Ain't that the truth," said Kansas Byrne. "Okay, comrade, dinnertime. More hot tofu soup, yum yum yum. Still, it beats working . . ."

And at last . . .

"All right, all right, all right! Stop whatever you're doing, put down your things, this is it! It's showtime, *mes amis*! Let's take Wheldon!"

The wave of cheering voices carried Kilimanjaro West down the rickety back stairs into the alleyway by the dying canal and into the Raging Apostles 'lectrovan (which had changed color in the night—"security precaution" exclaimed Witness Winston, gunning the ceramic engine for all it was worth). Wedged in the front bench seat between driver and director, Kilimanjaro West tried to recite his moves to Joshua Drumm, while in the back V. S. Pyar led the rest of the ensemble through a series of energy-chaneling exercises and chants, and the whole improbable circus went careening through the streets of Pendelburg, sending the exotically clad, half-clad, unclad wingers scattering and diving for their doorways, waving fierce *nona dolorosas* in their wake. And in the midst of all the madness and beautiful mayhem, Kilimanjaro West realized with some hitherto undiscovered faculty of himself that he was having the time of his life.

The 'lectrovan slewed out of Pendelburg into Ranves and thence into Wheldon, a prefecture predominantly populated by prollets, a caste somewhere between trogs and zooks/zillies in that they practiced the former's familial (in their case, sept) bonding and also the latter's subjection of the individual to the group will. The Seven Servants employed them in droves; they made a perfect work force. The 'lectrovan whined forward between passing multitudes of visitors; Winston's swearing was almost as loud as his constantly pumping horn. An excited group of migros were enthusiastically blowing kazoos beside the open window. The van slid into the slipstream of a strolling mariachi band and let the musicians clear a path through the crowd. Finally the density of bodies was too great for any further penetration.

"Look at that—solid," said Winston, throwing up his hands in exasperation. "We'll have to make it to the target on foot."

"Synchronize timepieces!" reminded Joshua Drumm, opening doors. "Back here no later than sixteen hundred." The Raging Apostles prepared to swing into anonymity in the manswarm.

"Bror, you come with me." Dr. M'kuba snagged Kilimanjaro West by the collar of his street jellaba. "Stick

closer'n this 'hugger, mah man." The crowd swallowed the
performers as entirely as an ocean does raindrops. The
Scorpio wove his apprentice through the spectators like
some devious silver snake—'scuse me, cizzens; apologies,
bror; so sorry, sib—to the front where lines of Love Police
held the people apart from the parading prollets. The two
Raging Apostles went slipping up the face of the audience
in the gap between people and policepersons. The prollet
septs jogged past, chanting, sweating. Kilimanjaro West
paused to watch.

Diversity and uniformity. In dress, decoration, even
physical and facial features, the septs were all markedly
different from each other: red-haired, black-haired, olive-
skinned, black, yellow, short, tall. Some carried banners,
some paper dragons, some chains of flowers hundreds of
meters long, some played instruments, some marched in
rapt silence. Some were dressed in costumes of such
brilliance that they made Devadip Samdhavi's creations
seem dowdy, others wore sober hoods and habits, others
drab work coveralls, others still what looked like blue-and-
yellow sports outfits with knee-high stockings and long-
billed caps, others yet in black bodysuits painted with
mambo-mama skeletons; all different, yet all the same.
Within each sept was a rigid uniformity of physical appearance, of costume, of voice, of movement. Even the bearers of the sacred litters (florid juggernauts encrusted with
gilt gingerbread and squabbling plastic santrels clambering
over each other for the attention of the multilimbed siddhi
hovering in freegee fields surrounded by candle flames
and stone oil-lamps) all jogged and sweated in unison and
wore identical expressions of agonized rapture on their
faces.

"Come on, man!" M'kuba tugged Kilimanjaro West
away from the Festival of the Flames. "Like we have this
performance, nah? In ten minutes, nah?" They continued
to snake along the face of the crowd and the saints,
santrels, and siddhi jounced past on their biers.

The table at the street café on the Plaza Veneziano had
been prebooked for the personal use of one Citizen

Kilimanjaro West and guest. His had been the safest name
to lynk through the public dataweb. The cafés were popular vantages for the race; small bribes to the Love Police
ensured the view went uninterrupted, and at the Festival
no one thought anything of citizens of different castes
sharing a table. His cup of chocolate sat ignored and
solidifying as Kilimanjaro West, suddenly smitten with
stage fright, found he could not remember how to work
the catches of the synthesizer case.

"Relax, mah man. Cultivate peace of mind." Dr. M'kuba
rocked back on his chair.

"But what if I do it wrong?"

"You not do it wrong."

"But what if I do?"

"Welcome to the Compassionate Society, mah man."

Kilimanjaro West could think of nothing but the time
on his wrist. Mrmeemrmeemrmee and suddenly it was
time, and in a sudden surge of panic he stood up, took the
synthesizer out of its case, and walked out into the Plaza
Veneziano.

Amazing how the panic evaporated! Do not count the
eyes. Do not count the faces. They will only bring it back
again. Just do what you have to do.

He did.

And bursting out of the crowd at exactly their prearranged places came the Raging Apostles. And it all came
together as it had in the beginning, out of chaos, out of
nothing. He was no longer alone. Kelso Byrne and Winston
were beside him, picking up his backbeat and ramming it
through their machines and hurling it in dripping chords
and sequences and arpeggios at the crowd as the power-
wheelers came scorching in round and round and round,
in and out and high and low, weaving smoke and sparks
and fire and flashing silver fans like blades, like knives,
like light, crossing and recrossing and crisscrossing and
crosscrissing trading fans, throw and flash and pass and
catch at speeds just under lightspeed, scooping up the
music on their metal fans and tossing it high in the air, and
Kilimanjaro West saw Kelso Byrne grinning at him through

the sweat and the concentration and he grinned back and concluded that this was the time mrmee mrmee mrmee of his life, count one minute forty-two, forty-three, forty-four, forty-five, and *change* and half the power-wheelers dived into human-wheelers, cartwheelers, kicking off their machine wheels, becoming tumbler-jumblers dangerous dancers as their street clothes, their ragamuffin slubberdegullion rags and tags and bags dissolved (exactly as Devadip Samdhavi had programmed the time-lock fibers), and they were transformed into light and gold and sun in the Golden Section, they were fast, fast fast, faster than reason or criticism or appreciation, blazing along the lightspeed horizon; rolls and spins and dives and lifts and drops so fast it numbed the senses into pure spectating: the people watched, they could do nothing else as the dance became the spin and the spin the spiral and the spiral reached out into a revolving chain of humanity anchored in V. S. Pyar's mastodon musculature and terminating in Kansas Byrne's whirling, burling round and round and round and round and round, power-wheels screaming until they became just a function between centripetal and centrifugal forces, the illusion of the defiance of gravity, burning past in a blaze of fans and blue-silver centimeters from the faces of the people who had been expecting to see the Festival of the Flames two-eighteen, two-nineteen, two-twenty . . . the whole trio of musicians were linked into the rotating, arms to arm to arm, the machines playing themselves as the chant rose: Yan Tra Yan Tra Om Ray Toe Shay, voice to voice to voice down the chain: Om Ray Toe Shay Yan Tra Yan Tra, and it was flung off into the crowds who picked it up piece by broken piece, led by the music and the great spiral, they moved to the rhythm of the galaxy and chanted the mantra: Yan Tra Yan Tra Om Ray Toe Shay, trogs and georges and yulps and tlakhs and wingers and bowlerboys and Scorpios and didakoi and migros: Om Ray Toe Shay, even the Love Policemen all in black and silver and a caste all of their own: Om Ray Toe Shay Yan Tra Tram! eight thousand, nine thousand, ten thousand voices, two minutes thirty-two, thirty-three, thirty-four, thirty-five, and . . .

. . . and, "This piece of performance art, entitled 'Sounding the Ritual Echo,' has been brought to you by Raging Apostles, a multicaste, nonauthorized alternative arts group comprising of independent artists, musicians, actors, dancers, and writers. We thank you for your participation in this event, and Raging Apostles hopes that it has in some small way brightened your day," and as they were unfolding from their bows and the applause was being passed from hand to hand to hand, the first prollet sept entered the Plaza Veneziano.

"Follow that," whispered a breathless, sweating Dr. M'kuba to Kilimanjaro West. While the applause rang on and on and on, the Raging Apostles vanished.

Even the Love Policemen were banging their mock-leather gauntlets together.

Back at the van: jubilation, congratulations. And boundless laughter as each member surfaced out of the soulswarm. All sweat and exhaustion and high high high on applause. Last of all, Dr. M'kuba Mig-15 and Kilimanjaro West came ducking around a Food Corps hot-pancakes stand into the 'lectrovan.

"Presenting!" shouted the Scorpio, "our hero! The one, the only Kilimanjaro West!" More clapping hands. Cheering, laughter. And Kansas Byrne threw herself at him, dared him not to catch her, kissed him on the mouth. Kilimanjaro West could still taste her on his tongue as the van halted and hooted its way back through the slowly dispersing crowds and the cobbled streets of Wheldon.

Chapter 5

The Expedition to the End of the World assembled at eight o'clock Victorialand time at the foot of number 16 cooling tower. The cavernous industrial perspectives of the power plant reduced the explorers to lice crawling upon its concrete toes. From the perspective of the human members, the Expedition to the End of the World was a very proper expedition indeed. There were porters: a score of Tinka Tae bearing poles or goading high-stepping surveillance walkers with electronic prods. There were askaris: an honor guard of twenty Striped Knights armed with crossbows and short swords and armored in impact-plastic body shields. There were guides and interpreters: two bright young racoons dressed in regal yellow and conversant in the dozen different known dialects of urban racoon. There was Jinkajou the Chamberlain, flexing his fingers into a pair of miniature leather driving gloves. There was Jonathon Ammonier the First, King of Nebraska, to the last millimeter pioneer of brave new worlds in white silk suit, canary gloves, bandanna, spats, cane, and banana-leaf topee. And there was Courtney Hall, not quite as lumpy as she remembered herself in a one-piece khaki outfit and solar topee. Slung across her back was a leather folio containing all those things an official expedition artist might require; in her pockets, a handful of doubts. She could not rid herself of the previous night's dream in which she went plummeting in a blazing hogshead over a kilometer-high waterfall of untreated sewage.

The expedition formed up. Ten warriors in the vanguard, Jonathon Ammonier and Courtney Hall in a small electric jitney liberated from Universal Power and Light and driven by Jinkajou, assorted bearers, porters, and then a rearguard of ten soldiers carrying crossbows. Dominofaces and soft crystal dreadlocks crammed every crawlway crevice and cranny in the foot of cooling tower 16: the Tinka Tae nation come to see off their King. That same King stood up in the small electric jitney and waved his handkerchief. Chattering, squeaking, clicking, ceased. The cooling tower sighed colossally to itself.

"I, your wise and wonderful King, your preserver and defender, your father and friend, am taking leave of you to embark on an expedition never before attempted by any living soul: a journey beyond the ends of the earth to the land beyond the city." Jonathon Ammonier pointed with his cane out across the sterile industrial vistas. "There I will establish a new kingdom, a new Victorialand, the realm of Arcadia, where peace and happiness and freedom shall reign."

Courtney Hall had heard this all before.

"I thank you for your loyal service: no king ever had finer subjects than you, more faithful, more dedicated, more trusting."

She hoped he was not about to cry.

"Therefore, in return for your loyalty, I give you a great and kingly gift; I give you your freedom! You are your own people now." In the tip of the king's cane was a small transponder. He pressed it. Nothing happened. Nothing apparent.

In the invisible spirit world of information technology quite a lot was happening, and happening very quickly. It involved virus programs and replication links and ABTE system poisoning and program infection and program defection, molecular reengineering and amino-acid photophoresis. All this took, oh, let's say, somewhere in the region of two, three hundred microseconds. And so every racoon clinging to every pipe and walkway and stanchion and mesh grid shook its head and was suddenly free from the urge to serve, serve, serve, and serve again the smartly dressed human before them.

Freedom granted in a couple of microseconds takes a lifetime to work out.

"And finally," said the King of Nebraska, sweeping his cane in a great scything arc, "Good-bye, Victorialand!"

Again the transponder did its small wicked work. Piece by piece, bit by bit, corridor by corridor, the palace of the King of Nebraska switched itself off. The halls of holographic masterpieces flickered and popped like soap bubbles. Every illusion and trompe l'oeil and optical oddity wavered and dissolved into memories. The wave of decreation swept up Victorialand, and it was revealed for the box of deceptions it was until the last projector clicked off and Jonathon Ammonier's creation was no more than a few tinsel scraps of furniture and lace scattered through the kilometer-high face of a Universal Power and Light reactor, little mouse-holes of art and comfort and the nostalgia of days of graceful living hidden away in the crevices between the great roaring machines.

"A curse on all bad art and holograms!" shrieked the King. "Wagons: roll!" The Expedition to the End of the World turned and marched away from the ruins of Victorialand.

The first stage of the journey was a leisurely morning's drive through a forest of pulsing, sucking conduits, some wide enough to burp out a municipal passenger dirigible. The plastic sky was busy with scurrying balls of soft blue lightning. At about twelve o'clock it became noticeable that the plastic walls, floors, ceiling were ever so (ever so) subtly sloping to meet each other. By fourteen o'clock the tunnel had slimmed to half its former girth. Courtney Hall, sketching speedy impressions of the journey on a jumbo file-pad in fond-remembered fiberpen, could not rid her mind and her drawings of her impression that it was the expedition that was enlarging, step by step, and not the passage that was dwindling. By Victorialand nightfall the gallery was barely wide enough to admit the electric buggy.

By royal decree (His waved handkerchief) the expedition halted. Ahead the tunnel shrunk patiently to submolecular dimensions. A team of engineers opened a section of wall, and a sudden typhoon of hot, electric air threatened solar topees.

"*Pneumatique* tube," shouted the King of Nebraska. "Closest we could get the thing to Victorialand without arousing the suspicions of the Great Yu Rapid Transit Authority dispatching department."

Thing? Courtney Hall was about to ask as a fast, white, horribly *loud* something blasted past, as if proof were needed that this was, indeed, a *pneumatique* tube. Her nervous system was still shedding sparks when five minutes later the *thing* (no other word could describe it quite so accurately) drew up by the hole in the tube wall and distended an orifice. If a Celestial could be assumed to have a penis, and if that penis could be assumed to be forty meters long, six high, made of brass and gold with a ribbed glass glans, then that was the best analogy to the *thing*.

"Electoral airbarge," announced the King of Nebraska. "The command codes are another of those little things I forgot to surrender when I abdicated the Salamander Throne. Come, madam." Under Jinkajou's barked instructions the expedition was stripped down and loaded into the hovering golden phallus. "I've always wanted to do this. Oh, the number of times I've been tempted to go riding nonstop through all those dirty little commuter stations and leave every mouth a wide *O* of surprise and wonder, to have them whisper, 'There he goes, there goes the Elector!' Ah, madam, whatever happened to style?"

"Style is riding around in a forty-meter tin penis?"

The lurching surveillance walkers were being herded up the access ramp.

"But think of the symbolism!"

"Can't have been too many women Electors."

Within, the airbarge was an interior designer's wet dream in brass, wood, and leather. Courtney Hall seated herself in one of the swiveling pilots' chairs in the glass

head of the golden penis. She spun round to take in the
overstocked euphoriant bar, the naked female brass caryat-
ids bearing electric flambeaux, the fake-fur–lined Jacuzzi,
the small neon harmonium. She was rather taken by the
tank of tropical fish that glopped softly as the airbarge
rolled to the aircurrents in the *pneumatique* tube. "Oh,
come on . . . Who designed this thing?"

"That's real skin you're sitting on, incidentally," said
the King of Nebraska. Courtney Hall felt immediately
unclean. Jonathon Ammonier snapped his fingers in impatience. "Come on, come on, come on, come on. We've
only one hundred and fifty seconds before the next scheduled *pneumatique*. So: stations please. Everybody ready?"
Racoons scampered about his feet. "Course set? Everybody strapped in? Right. Let's be off." Jinkajou slipped
into the motorman's chair and slid forward the brass
power handle. The airbarge bucked and swayed alarmingly.
Water slopped from the fish tank onto the Turkish carpets.
Impellors whined as they were brought up to pressure.
The great golden dork leaped forward. Acceleration punched
Courtney Hall into her real-skin pilot chair. Tunnel lights
leaped at her like predators. Wall buttresses smoothed
into a blur. Great Yu Pneumatique Service was never like
this. Great Yu Pneumatique Service never allowed you to
see where you were going.

"I'm thinking I'm going to be sick."

The King of Nebraska gallantly offered his banana-leaf
topee.

On the first afternoon of the highly symbolic voyage
beneath Yu, Courtney Hall began to wonder whether
there had ever been an Elector nominated to the Salamander
Throne who was over one hundred and fifty centimeters
in height; for their one-hundred-and-eighty-six-centimeter
guests constantly bumped their heads on light fittings,
doorjambs, stairwells, ceilings, moldings, pipes, and
conduits.

Dwarves and deviates, thought Courtney Hall as she
collected her twenty-eighth bruise on her exploration of

the penis-craft. The Electoral airbarge was a self-contained mobile palace: receiving rooms, dining chambers, a small state office, a study and library with real books, a trivia room, a bowling alley (forgotten peccadillo of a forgotten Elector), a large, sealed power section that occupied the after section, and a bathroom/conservatory complete with waterfall, pool, and herbal dip-pond. Courtney Hall let out a whoop of delight. A true sign of civilization in the great machine machismo fetish-fantasia. Ten minutes later she was la-la-laing up to the neck in jasmine- and tangerine-scented water. She was learning to take what luxury the DeepUnder afforded without too many questions. One question, however, bounced relentlessly through her thoughts, a trivial but nigglesome question of that kind that, once seized upon, are not easily let go. Vehicle or vessel? Train or boat? What was this *thing* she was traveling aboard?

Train was more realistic. Boat was more romantic. Had there not been boats that traveled underwater, back before the Break? The *military* (an old word, unused, due for deletion from the popular lexicon) used them to hide the world burners (two more words civilization could well do without) from their enemies' sight deep under the sea. Enclosed, secret ships—what had they been called?

Submarines. Under the sea.

And a boat that sailed under the earth?

A sub*terrene*.

Nice word. Now that deserved to be in the popular lexicon. And where, she asked the wicker cage of clockwork cardinals, is this subterrene going?

The End of the Line. A place of almost the same mythic vitality as the Beyond. Gangling yulp girls giggling on the *pneumatique*, riding out with their friends purely for the thrill of riding: dare you, dare you, dare you ride all the way to the end of the line, dare you, dare you, dare you not to get off at your stop, just sit on and on and on and let the train take you all the way to the end of the line.

But gangly, giggling yulp girls always got off at the right stop.

Does time inevitably turn all our dreams into realities and realities into dreams?

The walls, decorated with live bamboo, hummed slightly, the sole clue that this entire improbable device was hurtling through the municipal *pneumatique* tunnels at one hundred and fifty kilometers per hour on a genie-carpet of magnetic levitation.

Courtney Hall spent most of the morning of the second day in the glass observation head losing herself in the fascination of monotony. Half hypnotized by the strobing tunnel lights, she moved unconsciously to the hip-sway of the subterrene's lurchings and sudden veerings as the course computer sent it down another tube, into a new tunnel, avoiding scheduled services in the empty spaces between passing trains. Kilometer after kilometer after kilometer: all tunnels are one tunnel, all tubes one tube, and a hole within a hole through a hole is not three holes but one hole.

Early on the third morning of the subterrene journey, Courtney Hall was woken in her guest suite (ostentatiously decorated in red Morocco leather) by an absence of something. She was not quite certain what it was that was gone, but something was gone. All was quiet. And now she knew what was gone. The gentle universal vibration of the linear impellors: gone. The engines were shut down. Four-fourteen Victorialand time (and what was Victorialand but another gone thing; all that remained of Victorialand was its time): the Electoral airbarge had, at last, found its way through the Great Yu Pneumatique Service network to the End of the Line.

The King of Nebraska and his artist took an early breakfast of grapefruit and prunes in the observation glans, which lay pressed against a hymen of dry rock where the tunnelers had abandoned their tunneling. A team of Tinka Tae engineers were at work outside the hull burning another hole in the tunnel wall. The King of Nebraska sipped hibiscus tea; impeccable, immaculate, as only the man who knows himself King can be. Courtney Hall noticed that the royal gums were bleeding a little.

"Are you all right?" she asked carefully.

"Pink as a petal, puce as a plum, yellow as a Texas rose, madam."

"There's a hair on your jacket," Courtney Hall observed.

The King fastidiously removed it. There were several hairs on his lapels and collar.

After breakfast the Expedition to the End of the World marshaled up and marched down the ramp through the hole in the wall into the unknown, armed guards to fore and rear. For three hours it picked an arduous path through a cramped warren of communication conduits alive with the laser-blue spirits of telecommunication. The sound of dashing water drew them onward, dashing, plashing water always a frustrating bulkhead away. Bent treble in the confined crawlways, Courtney Hall was a purgatory of cramp. Her calf muscles were stiff balks of timber by the time the expedition, quite unexpectedly, squeezed itself through a wall iris out onto the sloping concrete bank of a subterranean river. Thereafter her discomfort was considerably eased, and for the remainder of the arbitrary day the expedition proceeded downstream by the King of Nebraska's royal decree that all rivers flowed outward. Their path lit by softly glowing panels in the vaulted ceiling, they marched under the timefree sky until dog-tiredness demanded a halt. Courtney Hall stretched tight muscles and rubbed some of Jinkajou's herbal healing ointment onto blisters in the warm synthetic security of a jolly-log electric campfire. Tinka Tae bearers unloaded their walkers and tofu steaks were grilled on the radiant plate while Jinkajou selected a Bacchanale & Dionysius '28 from the mahogany cellarette.

"How much further?" Courtney Hall asked the King of Nebraska.

"Madam," said the King of Nebraska, "if you paused for thought sometimes rather than letting your gob flap, you might see that that is a very stupid question. How do I know?"

Courtney Hall kept her gob sealed after that, and she did not tell the King about the red blotches on his skin, which she could not attribute wholly to the swirling flame-effect of the jolly-log heater. She did not sleep well that night. Her fear of twitching from her strict perpendicular position in one of the dull reflexes of sleep and rolling like a stupid log into the water kept her stiff as a winger's fantasy all night, with the result that the next day, as they again followed the river, every muscle, sinew, and bone in Courtney Hall's body howled protest.

The river stretched straight and undeviating before the explorers, its sheer geometrical perfection beckoning them on in the hope that farther on there might be some place where the straight curved. On that second day the King of Nebraska was visibly unwell. Every hour on the hour (as told by his ormolu pocket watch, which he wound every morning with religious diligence) he called a halt and sipped some lime cordial diluted with water from the river. On the seventh and penultimate march of the day, Courtney Hall drew Jinkajou aside and let the expedition, led by its King beating time with his gold-topped cane like a majorette, draw ahead of them some minutes.

"I don't know how much longer he'll be able to go on. He looks awful."

Jinkajou hissed, a peculiar racoon combination of menace and concern. "Not proper for loyal subject to speak thus of monarch, but His Majesty, Bless 'Im, pass blood when he piss."

"He can't not know that there is something seriously wrong with him. Someone's got to tell him before he guesses what it is, and panics."

The racoon folded its paws, sat back on its haunches, regarded Courtney Hall inscrutably. "Thou hast it right, madam. His Majesty, Bless 'Im, must be told."

"So, who's going to tell him?"

The racoon wrinkled its muzzle, a parody of a smile.

"His Majesty, Bless 'Im, correct; thou dost ask obvious questions. Please to recall, we are bound by our dilemma."

"Well, thank you very much," said Courtney Hall. "Thank you very much indeed."

The camp that day was no longer the place of ease and stretching and warmth and comfort it had been the day before. A specter haunted it; two specters, the specter of the King's sickness and the specter of Courtney Hall's necessity. Three specters: the specter of Courtney Hall's cowardice. She worried herself into insomnia analyzing opportunities, rehearsing excuses, waiting for the moment that came and came and came and always passed untouched because she was a coward. *The Compassionate Society has no need for courage,* she told herself, *I'm only acting according to my nature.* But the next morning she could not look at Jinkajou's button eyes.

The halts that day were more frequent. Jonathon Ammonier could manage no more than half an hour before signaling with a wave of his silk kerchief for the askaris to slope arms and the porters to down burdens. With each halt a sound like the thunder of waters swelled until the air shuddered, as if the concrete culvert were the *vox humana* pipe of a planetary water organ. On the fifth march of the morning the Expedition to the End of the World came to the end of the river. Warriors, porters, interpreters, patiently treading surveillance walkers, chamberlain, artist, and King arrived abruptly on a mist-shrouded lip of concrete overlooking a cavern the dimensions of which verged on the ridiculous. To their left the water gathered itself for a leap and a yell into a sheer half kilometer of shining sky and fell in plumes of mist to break on jumbled rocks at the foot of the cliff. Through the curtain of spray the waterfall threw off, Courtney Hall caught glimpses of flashing, dashing silver darting across the floor of the cavern: their river, losing and finding itself beneath the shock of vegetation that carpeted the cavern floor. The King surveyed the new domain. There was a look of empires in his eyes, his proud, erect stance. Courtney Hall gladly excused herself that she could not shatter such a moment of personal glory with her whispers of mortality. She took pencils and paper from her folio and dashed down some impressions of the view from the falls. Forming a perspective grid with her fingers, she calculated with a certain shock that the silver glitter of water down there at the cataracts where the cave ended was twenty kilometers distant.

"A kingdom for a king!" shouted Jonathon Ammonier. The thunder of waters swept his words out into the abyss. "Look at it, just look at it! It might have been made for me; a pleasure garden for the undisputed monarch of the DeepUnder. Oh, the pomegranates; the pomegranates, the figs, the guavas—fresh from the tree!"

"But what is it?"

The King of Nebraska grimaced and snapped his fingers in vexation.

"An abandoned agrarium, a forgotten Disney World; does it matter? It's forgotten, abandoned, therefore it's mine. I claim this land for myself! Faithful bearers, luncheon! Set our table up here where we may dine and from this unexcelled preview contemplate this new addition to my domains. Chamberlain, your finest bottle of vintage! And if we have already drunk the finest vintage, then bring us the next-to-finest!"

They dined by the falls on red-bean-paste pancakes and a forty-year-old Moussec DuForge, and Courtney Hall made herself busy with questions (how was it made, what keeps the roof up, the lights shining) not because she had never really believed in the underground agrariums that fed the Compassionate Society (even though she had eaten her way through fourteen tons of those agrariums' assorted legumes, pulses, grains, vegetables, and fruit), but because if she was asking questions, she could not be expected by Jinkajou and his racoons to tell the King about . . . you know. Jonathon Ammonier sipped his Moussec DuForge and answered her questions (underground firing of particle-beam weapons repossessed after the Break by the Compassionate Society, macroengineering techniques, hundred-meter, load-bearing members rooted in the upper mantle, thermo-electricity generated by heat differential along those load-bearing piers), and both could pretend that nothing was the matter, nothing at all. As they talked, the waters streamed past them and poured over the edge in a never ending cascade of lost time.

Five sips into the luncheon liqueurs (Courtney Hall discovered she had developed something of a taste for the King of Nebraska's peach-and-bourbon) scouts returned to report the discovery of a winding house for a small funicular system. The design of the machinery was archaic, reported Bajinko, captain of the guard, but the railroad showed signs of recent use. Mindful of unexplained shapes in Shaft Twelve, Courtney Hall did not care very much to know that.

Once again the Expedition to the End of the World drew itself up. Porters and their stomping robots waited on the platform while the King took his chamberlain, his Striped Knights, his interpreters, and his artist on the first descent.

"All aboard, all aboard!" cried the King of Nebraska, standing tall and very smug at the control lever. "All aboard for Victorialand!" As the funicular was swallowed by the rock tunnel, Courtney Hall was seized by a sense of claustrophobic foreboding.

"Your Majesty," she whispered, tugging at a royal sleeve. "Your Majesty, I have to tell you something."

"Mmph?" said the King of Victorialand, transported by dreams of empire. "Yes, what is it, madam?"

"Nothing," said Courtney Hall. Her tongue was sour with self-disgust. "Sorry to have disturbed you."

The funicular emerged into the light.

The mutiny came shortly after four-o'clock tea. Four-o'clock tea coincided with the interrogation of a native racoon the Striped Knight scouts had captured on wide patrol. The racoon squatted tremulously, nibbling at fragments of cheese biscuit the King from time to time tossed down from his folding camp table. Accustomed to the Tinka Tae, Courtney Hall had to remind herself that this beast was precisely that, a dumb beast, an animal.

"Much fear and trembling," said the interpreter. Primal racoon was very much a visual language of body postures, facial expressions, and gestures. "Presence of species alien to his."

"Ask him, does he mean humans?" commanded the King of Nebraska.

The funicular had shown signs of being used.

"He has identified the species with humans. However, and I must admit I cannot quite make out the inflection he is using, he seems to be implying species division within a single species, if I read his modifiers right."

"Explain please."

"As if a single species comprised two inner, distinct groups, hostile to each other."

"Intraspecies hostility is an altogether alien concept to racoons. That might explain the language difficulty." The King dabbed biscuit crumbs away from his lips with his handkerchief. When he took it from his lips, it was spotted with blood. "What is the matter with me?" he said tetchily.

"Does he mean that the humans in this biome are split into two mutually hostile camps?" asked Courtney Hall hastily, ashamedly.

The interpreter put the question.

"That seems to be the implication."

The captured racoon jigged up and down impatiently and fell into a nervous cringe.

"Instinctive danger reflex. Repeated three times for emphasis. Danger, danger, danger."

"What sort of danger? Ask him what sort of danger," Courtney Hall pressed, but the captured animal succumbed to its thrice-emphasized fear and fled into the encircling trees. "I think we should go," she suggested quietly.

"Nonsense!" crowed the King of Nebraska. He leaped to his feet, sending the folding table crashing over. "Nonsense, nonsense, nonsense! Out of the breast of danger we pluck this bright flower, honor! Honor is the treacle of kings. I can see this land sorely needs the wisdom and guidance of a divinely ordained monarch. Come!" He raised his gold-topped cane. "To me, my knights! Valiant riders of the cybernetic wave, surfers on

the sea of sentience, come with me! Order up, order up,
Chamberlain! Strike camp! Victorialand is dead and gone,
but while her King lives, Victorialand lives, and all the
fine art, good food, music, dance, and poetry that was
Victorialand. The New Age, my friends, the New Age has
come; a light in darkness shining and this benighted
darkness will comprehend it not. Forward the Aesthetic
Revolution! Come, come, come! Hurry along now chappies!" Porters scurried and hurried, warriors formed up
into neat rows of confusion. The King of Nebraska inspected
them through a pair of folding lorgnettes. Satisfied, he
placed himself at the head of the column. "Strike up the
band! Liberty Bells! Chop chop!" He clapped his hands at
Courtney Hall, conspicuous by her absence of activity.
"Chop chop!"

"No," said Courtney Hall.

"No?" shrieked the King of Nebraska. "No no no no
no?"

"No." She was not alone in her defiance. Jinkajou the
Chamberlain and the interpreter who had interviewed the
captive racoon stood beside her. The porters froze in their
tasks, tasting the sourness of free will caught between two
opposing wills. "You're sick, Jonathon. You're not well,
you're not rational. You're a sick man, Jonathon."

"A sick man, *Your Majesty*." Jonathon Ammonier's
voice was as shrill and stupid and petulant as a bird's. "So.
So. So. This is mutiny, madam! Mutiny! Faithless and
perverse creatures! Obey your king!" The undecided Tinka
Tae whined.

"Stop that, you bully," said Courtney Hall. "You gave
them free will, let them exercise it."

The King of Nebraska spat at her. "Faithless and
perverse creatures. All of you. Come, loyal friends, loyal
servants. We shall go alone. Madam Hall does not want us
to have any fun. Sick! Huh! Huh! Huh!" With a petulant
toss of his head he marched his phalanx of Striped Knights
into the dark forest.

"You are sick, you are sick! It's true!" Courtney Hall
called after him. "Radiation sickness! You've been poison-

ing yourself for years, you vain, stupid man!" The King of Nebraska's childish voice was raised high in song so he could not hear Courtney Hall's. A few of the porters abandoned their tasks and fled into the trees in pursuit of their rightful king. Those that remained went mechanistically about their labors. Animals have no need of sentience, even less of free will.

Disconsolately rocking back and forth, back and forth on a folding camp-chair, Courtney Hall filled the postmutiny hours with fantasizing. Not for the first time, and she was certain, not for the last, she fantasized she might wake soon and find herself in her apartment whole and clean and safe and regulated and maybe that little bit too tall and maybe that little bit too heavy, but she wouldn't mind that, not at all, she'd agree to it readily if it meant her waking up in her floform bed and getting up for a shower and bowing three times to the Lares and Penates and emptying her mind to establish rapport with the Muse of Cartoonic Expression and saying to Benji Dog, purring and humming to himself on his famulus shelf, "What an extraordinary dream I've had!"

Damn, damn, damn him; stupid, stubborn man.

Why did she keep imagining she smelt smoke on the wind?

A bird shrieked and beat its way out of the green canopy of trees to flop across the concrete sky.

Damn him, damn him, damn him.

And something came crashing, smashing, rushing out of the greenness: a Striped Knight: Bajinko, captain of the royal guard, all assumed humanity swept away, reduced by animal fear and flight to an animal in a silly costume, a scrap of human affectation. A Tinka Tae no more, the terrified animal could not speak human language. The racoons moaned with excitement and dread: so great was the young interpreter's agitation that his command of the human tongue kept slipping and sliding away into chitters of racoon primal.

"Woe, grief, folly! Warriors dead, heaps upon heaps upon heaps. Bolts spent, swords shattered, armor cracked.

Feeling: blood, black, rage, pain, fury, fear, fire. Out of nowhere they came, out of everywhere: demons, ogres, mandrakes—leaping, whooping, jeering. Jeering, jeering . . . His Majesty, Bless 'Im, commanded them bow knee, bow head, make obeisance to rightful king. 'You kneel, you bow, you make obeisance,' say Demon-King, 'to *me*.' 'Never!' says His Majesty, Bless 'Im; then: blood, black rage, pain, fury, fear, fire! War, war, war! His Majesty, Bless 'Im, netted, taken. Brothers netted, taken, only this one is escaped to tell."

"What?" said Courtney Hall. "What what what?"

"His Majesty, Bless 'Im," said Jinkajou, "has been captured."

"Has been what?"

But Jinkajou had covered its head with its paws and began to whine, a keening lament that was taken up by the Tinka Tae as one. The sound of them sent the loose, flapping birds exploding from the treetops. Courtney Hall covered her ears.

"Stop it, stop it, stop it, please."

The interpreter in yellow, whose name was Ankatiel, stepped forward. "You must help us," it said. "You must help us regain King. It is disloyalty, faithlessness that has led to this."

"It was pride!" shouted Courtney Hall. Her shouting voice surprised her. "Reckless arrogance! A sick ego!"

"If His Majesty, Bless 'Im, sick, then thou hast failed in thy responsibility to a sick man by letting him go," said Jinkajou.

Feeling like a serpent in paradise, Courtney Hall said, "What can I do? What do you expect me to do? I'm an artist, not some Johnny-opera hero on prime time! I don't know where he is, where he's been taken, who's taken him, or why. Come on, we wouldn't last five minutes in there."

"I would estimate somewhat less." The whining keening was cut as abruptly as if a neural switch had been thrown. At the edge of the trees were three figures.

One was male; very tall and thin with a waist-length

explosion of dreadlocks. He was dressed in a pair of cycling shorts and an elaborately embroidered chemise over which he wore an extraordinary jacket covered in the skulls of birds and rodents and dangling, jangling silver trinkets.

One was a woman; small and dark with bouncing natty dreads. She was dressed in a half-seen sleek something, camouflaged with tiger stripes so that she phased in and out of the general background.

One was an animal. A cat. A real cat. Not one of Marcus Forde's flush-away abortions. Sin-black, and lean. Its left eye was artificial; skylight breaking through the clouds caught the eye and found tiny digits and circuits hidden within. The black cat rode the small woman's shoulder. It yawned and displayed chrome steel teeth.

In one step the dark woman was beside Courtney Hall. The cat stretched and flexed five centimeters of platinum claw from housings.

That one step had covered twenty meters. Without, Courtney Hall was certain, ever traversing twenty meters of space.

"About two minutes if you went that way"—the tall, young man advanced across the clearing, pointing out to his left—"about two and a half minutes that way"—pointing right—"and a good three minutes that way and that way. Because, by some astonishing quirk of good fortune, you have plonked yourself and your pets right in the middle of the Democrats' Strategic Defense Initiative Zone. But be of good cheer, my dear. Help is at hand." He bowed and kissed Courtney Hall's hand. Twenty-nine years in Great Yu and no one had ever kissed her hand even once. As many days DeepUnder and it had happened three times. "Angelo Brasil at your service, in the company of my pseudosister, Xian Man Ray, and Trashcan, our cat. We would like very much to offer you our assistance, my dear, in getting your king back."

Cupid, Draw Back Your Bow...

Dear Citizen <u>Carmine Malaguena</u>

we at the Ministry of Pain Department of Interpersonal Relationships are delighted to present you with your Socio/Sexual Compatibility Rating. Since the age of nineteen months, this has been constantly monitored and where necessary, updated to produce a totally accurate profile of your social and sexual characteristics.

Your SSCR is: <u>Monoghetero7Bintro level12 interactlevel 3.6 (Baud Compensated) @Xinf27file£SSCR/ PDBXMNfid.7xC</u>

From this data our computers have selected a personal partner for you, and we take the greatest delight in informing you that a meeting has been arranged between yourself and <u>Citizen Marsden O. Henry</u> of <u>Apt 63 Yellow 2113, New South Madrid Center, Las Palomas</u> on <u>April 30, 450</u> at <u>Chueco Zembalaya's Jazz Hot Spot, 919 Shimenevski Prospekt, Los Madres</u> at <u>22 o'clock</u>

Your prospective partner will be identified for you by <u>the proprietor, Citizen Chueco Zembalaya</u> and, as customary, all expenses of this first joyous meeting will be met with the compliments of the Ministry of Pain Department of Interpersonal Relationships.

On behalf of your trusted counselors, it only remains for me to wish you a wonderful, fruitful meeting with your perfect partner.

Jancis Shambala

131

Ministry of Pain, Department of Interpersonal Relationships

Dear Citizen <u>Carmine Malaguena</u>

         we at the Ministry of Pain Department of Interpersonal Relationships are sorry to hear that your first meeting with your perfect partner was not to your total satisfaction. Please do not be unduly dismayed by this: it is not uncommon for new partners to fail to achieve perfect synthesis and unity on their first meeting. Many factors account for this: personal body chemistry and pheromone emission, climatic or ionization levels, discrepancies between the partners' personal biological time frames, even a certain element of stress and anxiety inevitable between two strangers meeting for the first, and most important, time, Therefore, do not be overly concerned that this first meeting was not the wonderful, fulfilling, romantic experience you may have been led to expect. The Ministry of Pain Department of Interpersonal Relationships is never wrong in its its matching of SSCRs, and you will be relieved to know that our computers rate you and your partner <u>Citizen Marsden O. Henry</u> to the <u>98th percentile</u> compatible.

Do not be alarmed that you were unable to arrange another meeting with your partner: our computers have selected another location and date that have been carefully calculated to engender the maximum of benign, romantic influences upon you both as a partnership.

Your new rendezvous is:

<u>The Eloquent Soy Bean Pancake-arium</u>

<u>Lilac Level</u>

<u>Bernardo O'Higgins Undertower Metropolitan Fashion Mall</u>

<u>Las Defensas</u>

on <u>May 2, 450</u>

at <u>16:44 o'clock</u>

As before, to ensure a specially happy rendezvous, all your expenses for this occasion *only* will be complimentary from the Ministry of Pain Department of Interpersonal Relationships.

We wish you both every success and happiness in your perfect partnership.

Jancis Shambala,
Ministry of Pain, Department of Interpersonal Relationships

Dear Citizen Carmine Malaguena
                    we at the Ministry of Pain Department of Interpersonal Relationships really find it most puzzling that you are still experiencing difficulties with the perfect partner we have assigned you. Your history of socio/sexual analysis indicates that you have a high monogameity rating, matched by our computers with that of Citizen Marsden O. Henry. According to our models, you should at this stage be preparing to enter into a lasting, bonded partnership together. Instead, you are claiming that relations between you and your partner are disharmonious to the point of verging on minor PainCrime. You constantly disagree and argue to such a degree that you and your partner find it impossible to agree on any point, no matter how trivial. This is quite inconsistent with our profile of your psychosexual makeup, and we, as your trusted counselors, are of the opinion that, with regard to the perfect partnership, figures are a far more trustworthy guide than feelings to the future of a relationship. Give it time. These small incompatibilities will be revealed for what they are, petty egoisms. We at the Ministry of Pain Department of Interpersonal Relationships have therefore decided that the best way for you to proceed is in accordance with our projected model of your relationship.

Therefore, you have been assigned a dwelling unit at: Style Council House, 116 Rhamjees Road, Todos Santos. This locale has been analyzed to afford you both the best environment for your age, caste, and relationship. Your move has been arranged for May 25, 450, at fourteen o'clock. Please have all your possessions ready for removal from your previous address before that time as your domestic unit will have been reassigned by the Bureau of

Housing and Shelter Section for Assignation and Registration to a new tenant.

Time is, in our experience, a great healer of partnerships: you and your partner will find in a new home, a new environment, with time to grow together, that perfect synthesis, that ideal two-in-oneness that is the right of every citizen who approaches the Ministry of Pain Department of Interpersonal Relationships seeking a soulmate. We look forward to hearing from you soon.

Perfect happiness,

Jancis Shambala
Ministry of Pain, Department of Interpersonal Relationships

Byrne and West

Glory Bowl DCCLXII moves into its Third Epact, Meter Fifteen, Twelfth Meld. The Babazulu Aztecs are going for a High Rubric and the crowds are on their feet in a thunder of noise. Meter Fifteen. Twelfth Meld. Anticipation feverish. Will they call a High Rubric, or take spectators, commentators, broadcasters, opposition by surprise and go for something more straightforward, a Straight Out, or maybe a Mark By? Cloud-sized videowalls debate in flashes of neon logic. The crowd waits.

Arm up. Mark. Trumpets blare: the Twelfth Meld! The Twelfth Meld. And . . . Snap!

Twenty-three point one eight seven seconds of manic activity: snap! ball to CenterBack snap, ball to Toucher, touch for required one, two, three, four, five senses/ seconds, okie okie okie, he can let it go now, and what're they going to do with it? Yes, yes, it's what the spectators, commentators, broadcasters, opposition thought, they're going for a rubric, CenterBack's calling for a Freeze-Play and the Shift-Back to come onto the field, okie okie okie, where's the Shift-Back, where the *shug* is the S-B, he's only got twelve seconds of Freeze-Play; here he comes, here he comes, oh, *nice*, nice run, lovely run, oh, he's a *sweetner* that one, he's sweet, he's neat, he's fast on his feet (should be, all that de-oxy-phenobarbitol jackin' up his system): look, not one tassel out of place, that's goin' to score *high* with the Line Justices, and Freeze-Play Unfrozen, snap! long looping passing shot, lookit those Pandas jump hands, reachin' hands grabbin', clawin', maulin' and

135

Yah-Oh-Yah, he's got it, the S-B's got it, now, what's he goin' do with it? Well, I never saw that before, that long looping throw high high high into the air, up it goes, up it goes, up it goes, but don't watch the ball, watch the S-B, oh, that is *incredible,* single backflip, followed by a backflip/somersault/copterspin combination, howze*dooit*? oh, lookit *that,* two pull-backs and a maxi-ford and that's just *got* to be a nine-four, nine-five, and the ball's coming down and he's right under it ... Perfect catch. Perfect catch ... and the Panda tagger-backs have just tagged him, they've got a tassel but it's too late and down in the Kop the Babazulu are whoopin' and cheerin' because a play like that has to get them a nine-four *minimum,* place'll come *apart* if it's anything less, they'll have to call the Love Police; scenes reminiscent of the quarterfinal three years back when a Rubriced Fifteenth Meld by the Orange Vitamin Locusts averaged 8.3, which led ultimately to the dissolution of the Orange Vitamin Locusts and their amalgamation into the Blue Screamers and the Night Motions and a short spell in West One for their coach Rodrigues Maradonna, remember, Hanno?

Remember it well, Chezz, remember it well. And here come the Line Justices ... The trumpets have played the Conclavion and the judges' litters are being carried onto the field for a conference with the referee because you may not have noticed it but there was a banner up by the Back Left LineWatch signaling a possible infringement of the twenty-meter rule by the Aztecs' point-convertor that would result in the High Rubric's being demoted into a two-point Snap-Back to the Pandas, so the Back Left LineWatch and the referee are conferring; yes, they're calling in a replay video and, red light! A red light! Remarkable, quite remarkable, it's being put to the Team Spirits for adjudication. And the fans do not like it ... the computers are conferring and the Back Left LineWatch and the referee are conferring and the Line Justices in their litters are conferring, everyone's conferring and yes, the Team Spirits have reached a decision; the banner goes down! The banner goes down. No infringement, no infringement, and the home crowd here today are loving it to *death* . . . Chezz . . .

. . . and one hundred and fifty meters above the laagers of Line Justices' litters, lying head to head like the six-o'clock hands of one of those old-fashioned novelty watches from Seven Seals Novelties and Gifts on a forty-centimeter plazzed-steel girder, Kansas Byrne and Kilimanjaro West of the Raging Apostles are conferring. On art. On theories of the aesthetic. On creative vandalism.

"The Theater of Rigor," said Kansas Byrne, "is the ultimate expression of human artistic potential, an aesthetic system in which the performer is no longer bound by the limitations of being merely an 'actor' or a 'dancer' or a 'musician' or an 'artist' but becomes, through the disciplines of his art, a creature which transcends such arbitrary divisions, an 'actordancermusicianartist,' a creature of as many dimensions as there are dimensions of artistic expression. Visionaryprophetvandalcriminalgymnastlover-poetgraffitistcookdesigner . . . ; by becoming the master of every discipline, he or she thus transfigures art into true spontaneity of expression: the artist capable of self-expression in any medium he or she feels will best convey that expression. That's the Theater of Rigor. That's why Kansas Byrne is a Raging Apostle and not just another tlakh producing pieces of performance art for Witnesses to coo and tut over. Kansas Byrne is a Raging Apostle because the Compassionate Society is not interested in transcending divisions, breaking boundaries. Because boundaries, divisions, are what the Compassionate Society is, at the core, at the heart. Divide and rule. Caste and conquer."

"Third Epact: Thirteenth Meld!" roared Hanno, or possibly Chezz on the public commentary system. "Hup hup hup!"

Kansas Byrne fiddle-fumbled with fifty meters of monomolecule fiber spun from a spirochete on her wrist.

"Pyar's probably watching this on a big public screen," she added conversationally. "Me, I can't follow the thing. Probably have to be barrio born and bred like him to follow the rules. Here, you any good at knots?"

"Knots?" asked Kilimanjaro West.

"Self-binding topological structures in one-dimensional systems." She frowned and made passes with her hands. "Shug. So much for the Theater of Rigor."

"Here, maybe I . . ."

She slapped his fingers away. "Shug, you stupid or something? It was a purely rhetorical question. Mono-molecules are bitchin' things. Any tension in the line and they'll take your fingers clean off, and there's no white brothers here to sew them on again. You got to wear gloves, see?" Her hands shimmered as she held them up before his face. "Knitted monomolecule." The shimmering magical hands performed mystical passes and mystical oaths before Kansas Byrne was satisfied.

"Won't they notice that?" Kilimanjaro West nodded at the melon-shaped device resting on the girder between their faces.

"Shug no." Kansas Byrne payed out a length of the magical thread and heaved the object off the beam. It fell half a hundred meters before coming to an abrupt halt with a loud tenor twang. "Definitely keep your fingers away from that now. It's under tension. Nah, no one'll see it. Pyar made it up to look like one of the ceiling mikes, and you can be shuggin' sure no one's counting ceiling mikes down there."

Trumpets fanfared, cheerleaders leaped and split with excruciating precision, and Hanno and Chezz stumbled over each other in attempts to plumb the adjectival depths of the popular lexicon. Meter by meter, the Babazulu Aztecs advanced over the Pandas' desecrated turf. Looking upward: art. The happening world. About to happen.

"Primed and ready to go blooey three minutes into the final Epact. Pyar reckons they should be well into the third or fourth Meld by then, probably going for a Place-ment Run or a Table. Apparently, that's very important at this stage of the game. To an athleto, like Pyar, this is the ultimate experience. Every kid in the barrios wants to be on a Glory Bowl team someday. Pyar was one of the few who made it. Reserve Throwing Back. Never got called onto the field; team never made a Passing Shot or a Back Line Throw. Shame. Bigger shame, his barrio never made it to the bowl again. Has a lot of resentment, has Pyar; he was in counseling for six months before he just blew and joined the Raging Apostles after we put on a happening at his barrio street market. He's been planning this one for months. Could be a lot of personal revenge in it. Hey! K.W., want to know why I brought you and not Pyar? Because you know nothing. Because every experience is a learning experience for you. And because you learn, I learn, I reexperience. I relive everything in the light of your ignorance. Does that make sense?"

No less than Kansas Byrne's butterfly mind made sense. Or this city, this world, this universe.

"You know, this is funny, but I think that more than any of us, you have the potential to achieve, to become, the Theater of Rigor."

"Why do you say that?"

"Because you have no preconceptions about what can or cannot be done. All of us Raging Apostles are too deeply rooted in the Compassionate Society to ever unlearn what it has taught us. But you, somehow you never learned anything in the first place. Just what are you? Where do you come from, why are you here with me?" Her questions raised more unanswerables within and about herself and she scowled, looked away. "Quit looking at me like that."

"Like what?"

"Like... like... just don't look at me like that. Shug, maybe Winston was right, maybe you are a security risk. I just don't know enough about you to be able to say anything."

Music blared forth. The Virgins of St. Fonda's Women's Workout Team jogged onto the pitch to lead the spectators in a quarter-time stretch'n'tone routine designed to shape up muscles flagging from three and three-quarter hours sedentary spectating. With a grace and a feline ease not even the limber ladies of St. Fonda could match, Kansas Byrne jackknifed herself into a standing position on the narrow girder. She flipped a daredevil back-somersault (no safety net, no freegee belt, no Department of Arts and Crafts insurance policy) and stretched into a set of casual splits along the girder. She folded her torso over her legs to left and right in turn.

"Aren't you afraid for me?" she asked.

"No. Why? Should I be?"

She shrugged. "Pity. I wanted to scare you. I like trying to scare you, shock you. Bad of me, isn't it? I like trying to goad some reaction out of you, Citizen Kilimanjaro West. But you just keep on disappointing me. By the way, don't look down when the spray bomb goes off." Which it did two minutes twenty seconds later as the Babazulu Aztecs were marshaling for a Fourth Epact Second Meld Placement (probability 82%, V. S. Pyar had predicted) and the Pandas were deploying in an optimum probability coverage spread.

Red out.

Clinging to his girder in the afterblast, Kilimanjaro West took a breath and became aware of a great and holy hush filling the Babazulu Aztec Cathedrium like a spirit.

"This is the first part," whispered Kansas Byrne. "Two hundred and twenty-nine thousand two hundred and twenty-seven voices: silenced." The peace was divine. "All at once. Utterly. Just listen, K.W. Perfect nothing. That is art."

The presence, the absence, lingered but a few breaths more. Then the need for questions, for answers, for expression, for anger and bafflement and all those things the Ministry of Pain said did not exist anymore, broke through the silence, voice by voice, question by question, shout by shout.

"The perfect contrast between the silence and the sound, that's the second part," yelled Kansas Byrne. "And this is the third part." She directed Kilimanjaro West's attention downward.

The individual letters were each seventy meters tall. The complete word filled the floor of the Cathedrium, the curving tiers of spectators, and the outer lip of the ceiling.

The girder that concealed the Raging Apostles formed a tiny red serif at the tip of an *E*. The bold upright of the *I* was a red slash across the twenty-two-meter line from left-side hash mark to the five-marq seats. A sinuous *S*, the ultimate challenge to the spray-bomber's art, snaked up from the deadball Line Justices' booths, hooked left across the stunned Virgins of St. Fonda (red on lilac an improbable combination) and made a 180° turn somewhere in the fifty-marq reserveds to come to an end up in the Seats of Grace and Favor where the Indigent Poor of all the barrios and corriadas could watch Glory Bowl DCCLXII free. When the Compassionate Society chose you to be poor, it gave compensations. The message lazed across the wreckage of Babazulu Aztecs' glory, strode over players and spectators alike with nonchalant indifference: RAG-ING APOSTLES. A little fuzzy on the initial *R* and terminal *S* up there in the OutCaste Inviteds at the extreme range of the device, but for two hundred and twenty-nine thousand two hundred and twenty-seven witnesses there could be no mistaking (much less forgiving) the perpetrators of this act of . . . "creative vandalism, the most transitory of art forms." Kansas Byrne was visibly aroused by the success of her performance. "The very best bit, better even than the silence, is when it begins to come apart. The aesthetic of disintegration. Beautiful." As she spoke, her message was coming apart; person by person, quantum by quantum, as the athletos of Babazulu started their drifts toward exits or Team Spirit Confessoriums to obtain relief of anxiety, ease of soul. The letters began to dissolve at the edges and over the space of a few minutes disintegrated into a particulate sea of red dots. "Superb," breathed Kansas Byrne. "Order into Chaos. Entropy as Art. Love to be able to run that backward, see them all come together, chaos into order." She slapped her partner gently on the back. "Time we were gone. Place'll be bubbling with Love Police and MiniPain investigators in two minutes flat." Her proffered hand was the most alive thing Kilimanjaro West had ever known in his life.

If Kansas Byrne's short course of practical encouragement was to be believed, operating an LTA flight suit was somewhere in difficulty between sex and riding a bicycle, neither of which Kilimanjaro West knew anything about, though he had witnessed both since his arrival in the city. And, she maintained, considerably safer than either. She left sticky red-paint fingerprints on his harness as she checked fastenings and valves.

"Relax," she instructed. "Treat it as Experience. If you do it with the wrong attitude, you cripple yourself experientially." Equally good advice for sex and bicycling as LTAing. She showed him the use of the joystick controls. "Simple: up, down, left, right. Left stick's forward and braking thrust." Kilimanjaro West found he enjoyed the way her hands moved over the controls. "Got it? Let's go." She pulled her rip cord. The silver LTA balloon unfolded and inflated with small pops and thumps as creased fabric stretched and tautened.

Kansas Byrne waved a small good-bye and stepped off the ogive roof of the Babazulu Aztec Cathedrium. She ascended a vertical meter, then the perpetual warm wind caught her and swept her into a distant blob of shining silver before the "Please wait" was off Kilimanjaro West's lips.

Theater of Rigor.

He tugged his rip cord and the monsoon picked him off the Babazulu Aztec Cathedrium and carried him away. Half a kilometer above the transparent roof of the Sacred Circuit of Muscular Deity low-grav velodrome, Kansas Byrne was waiting in the sky.

"Use your controls," she shouted as Kilimanjaro West breezed helplessly past. She fell into step beside him. "Relax. It's fun." Aft, piebald pantycars were circling and flocking like indecisive magpies.

"Is this not," Kilimanjaro West yelled, "a very"—fighting with the control sticks—"conspicuous way"—he lurched as a thermal from the Shasten Community heating plant cooling tower whirled him stratosphereward—"to travel?"

"Not at all." Kansas Byrne closed her eyes and shivered sensually as the warm updraft caressed her. "People of all castes use them all the time. For some didakoi tribes, only means of personal transport between dirigibles and city. Wingers use 'em, too. Never tried it myself, but LTA sex is supposed to be the most cosmic experience. Better than freegee, even." Behind her helmet visor, her eyes confused Kilimanjaro West. "Relax. Enjoy. It's fun."

Blown eastward on the monsoon out of Pacahuaman Corriada over the anarchic geometries of the corporate arcologies and manufactories of Kurosawa, Kilimanjaro West found his consciousness performing a subtle inversion. He remembered: one word. A word from the before time; therefore, no matter how brief, or meaningless, it was important, that word.

The word was *purpose*.

He had a purpose. He was purpose. Therefore nothing he did or experienced could be in any way treated lightly or trivially for it might in some way serve this purpose. He did not know what this purpose was, only that he had a purpose, but he determined that he must open himself to every experience, and learn.

Learning, he learned, was fun. That in itself was experience, and something to be learned. He learned that he did enjoy wind-drifting, airborne flotsam, through the upper strata of Kurosawa's corporate canyonlands. Beneath his feet the various levels of the city superimposed themselves on each other: creeping caterpillars of municipal trams, midlevel cycleways, *pneumatique* tubes looping like arteries around, through, into, under the techno-Gothic fantasias of the Seven Servants (another thing he had learned, the seven colossal mother-corporations that supplied, manufactured, grew, generated the city's every need), the webwork of cablecar lines spun across the twinkling chasms, too slender by far to possibly bear the weight of crowded gondolas.

"What is that?" He glimpsed a tiny, darting figure, neon-bright, wild as night, impossibly *running* along the cablecar lines.

"Scorpio," Kansas Byrne shouted in answer. She had removed her helmet to let the warm wind stream back her

hair. "Wire-running. Kind of hazing ritual Scorpio singletons go through when they start their year out on blue six.
Highly illegal. Three months counseling automatic for a
first offense. You ask M'kuba the Doctor. He got reconditioning in West One for his third. Which is why he's
with us now and not on some job with the TAOS Consortium over in Tamazooma. Folk can get killed, not just the
Scorpios."

"'Killed'?"

Her expression was clearly legible across twenty meters of airspace.

"Dead. Not living. Nonexistent. Permanently."

"That's good to know."

"What's good to know?"

"Permanently. It means that I wasn't dead, before."

Kansas Byrne wanted more than anything to ask, Before? Before what? but Kilimanjaro West's attention had
been snared by a didakoi passenger dirigible offloading
citizens into an immaculately landscaped arcology-top
leisure park. He watched the citizens flocking to the lakes
and jungles and gardens with mazes, to the theme parks
and pleasure domes and beaches with real surf. Passing
onward, he saw the simple rooftop agricultural communities of the Aquadelphians, the soil-toilers peering up from
beneath the brims of straw coolie hats to wave a greeting.
He saw snow-blasted minimountains abuzz with skiers and
sporters in all degrees of dress from the ludicrous to the
nonexistent. The microclimate field bubbles veered the
balloonauts away from ice-resorts and the prevailing wind
carried them on into Four Solitudes.

"We'd calculated that these winds should bring us over
Ranves in about an hour and a half," Kansas Byrne yelled.
"Enjoying it now?"

"Enormously." And he was. And *enormous* was the
word. He had never before been in such a position as to
properly appreciate the scale of this city where he found
himself. He could see a hundred kilometers in every
direction, and he could still see no end to the city. Only a
suggestion of a line of shadow drawn around that incredi-

bly distant horizon. Enormous the dimensions, enormous
the variety. Great Yu was a patchwork of clashing, colliding architectures, a motley of abutting improbabilities, tall
with stunted, broad with slender, modern with ancient,
classical with Gothic, technological with biological. Even
as he came to understand that the city had not sprung
from the earth formed as it was, but had been built,
created, he also understood that it must have a past, a
history out of which it had come.

Something enormous, something appalling, must have
happened in that history for the city to have grown so
huge, so arrogant.

And Kilimanjaro West? How could he think he had a
purpose, a specialness that set him apart from the rest of
this city's billion and a half when the very vastness and
indifference of that city made him invisible and anonymous? How could he pursue his purpose? Who would
know he was unique, *holy*?

He looked at Kansas Byrne, the way the wind whipped
her hair and drew her flight suit across her body. He felt a
surging sensation that took him quite by surprise. He felt
he had to say something.

"You're extraordinary."

"What?"

"I said, you're extraordinary."

"Thank you. Thank you very much. I've been called a
lot of things, but never extraordinary. Thank you. You're
pretty extraordinary yourself, of course."

Before he could ask her, please, what did she mean?
Kansas Byrne pointed out a wedge of tangled green rising
out of the checkerboard of cityscape.

"There we go. Right on target. Big Tree. Time to lose a
little altitude."

Tacking in over the transparent vaults of Baltinglass's
covered market, descent rate twenty-seven meters per, lift
gas 97% initial, altitude control rate 47%, Kilimanjaro
West noticed the birds. Black-and-white, angular, covet-
ous, they bickered on their perches amongst the aerials of
Pendelburg Tellix Tower.

"Look at those," he said, and then there was another mental inversion, one of vision, and he became aware of scale, distance, magnitude, and mass, which changed the birds on the tower into Love Police aircraft moored to the girderwork.

"Shug," said Kansas Byrne. Descent rate twenty-two meters per, forward vector twenty meters per. Ripe, lazy fruit, the pantycars dropped from their branches into street-piercing dives. "What's happened to them? What have they done to them? What have they done to my brother?" The pantycars scraped the chimney pots of Pendelburg as they pulled into intercept climbs.

"I think we should get out of here, Kansas, I think it would be a very good idea."

"But how did they find them? We had everything covered, all our dataweb transactions were clean..."

Thumbs hard on the control buttons. Airspeed meter creeping slowly, too slowly; twenty, twenty-two, twenty-four, twenty-six, putting distance between themselves and the Love Police. But all the while sinking, settling, lower, lower.

"Shug, we haven't got enough gas, we haven't got enough lift gas to get away!"

High above the city of Yu the pantycars rolled and came for them. Kansas Byrne swore at the approaching aircraft, an ugly, incongruous sound to Kilimanjaro West. Beneath their feet, the rooftops of Pendelburg gave way to the flaking pantiles of old Ranves, closing every second. The Love Police bore down on them.

"Look, there's an emergency procedure, listen good, if we ever get split up, we have it all arranged to meet in a safe place. If we get split up, make for..."

Her instruction went unheard as the Love Police thundered in overhead, blatting orders from loudhailers. Landing jets sent the balloons hurly-burlying between the chimneys and carved gable ends. A malevolent gust of wind patted Kansas Byrne's LTA eastward out of Ranves into the waterdistrict of ThreeJumpSpan. She tried to shout "Tamazooma!" to her apprentice, but the distance was too great, the roar of the jets too loud. Her last glimpse of Kilimanjaro West was to see him hovering over a flaking clay-tile rooftop in the center of a ring of hovering pantycars.

"Oh, shug, I'm sorry Kaydoubleyou." She saw, clear as any siddhic revelation from a street shrine, the man who called himself Kilimanjaro West reach for his red harness release button. And because no one had ever told him he could not do it, he punched the knob. The freed balloon leaped skyward, and Kansas Byrne saw Kilimanjaro West drop to the crumbling tiles and slide down the sheer roof to hang for a moment from the storm guttering. He turned to regard the five-story drop to the cobbles, and with a shrug, he launched himself into space.

Then she saw him no more.

Chapter 6

Tropical nightsong.

Can be.

Magic.

Long swooping whistles, river-running ripples of birdsong, low intimate chuckles, coos, clicks, maracca-macaw rattles. Twee-oo-ip. Twee-oo-ip. Cascades of quavers, glissandos, arpeggios; as if each night-calling bird were an instrument in an orchestra: some lyres, some oboes, some violas, some piping piccolinos. Some, pounding bass tympanis. Basso profundo, coloratura, tenor. Piercing, sweet soprano. Descant, harmony, counterpoint, fugue: the forest as orchestra, as opera: tropical nightsong.

Can be.

Terrifying.

When you're an overheight, overweight (not quite so as before; flab transmogrifying mystically, *wonderfully* into muscle) ex-cartoonist Category 8 PainCriminal subterranean adventurer/roving artist to an equally ex equally criminal Elector dying of radiation sickness crouching in the warm, damp tropical night among the root buttresses of some jungle hardwood besieged by lianas and orchids and luminous fungi. If you are utterly, irrevocably out of your element, lost amidst the alien cane, a stranger in a strange land, without the slightest idea of who is making what sound, and why, and where, and how, then that sweet tropical night is a terrifying place.

Something laughed in the living darkness.

"Fug, what was that?"

Little eyes caught the light from the watch-fires beyond, a wet racoon nose gleamed.

"Alas, this one's knowledge of local flora-fauna limited."

"I meant, was that animal or human?"

"Animal."

"That's all I wanted to know."

Time passed, but in a night without stars or moon to measure its progress, Courtney Hall could not say how much, or how little of that time passed, only that it took many heartbeats for the camp to prepare for the night. Leather tents were erected, embers in a cooking pit brought to a red glow. Skewered meats were built into a tepee over the cooking pit. The smell of charring flesh nauseated Courtney Hall twice over. First, because as a citizen of the Compassionate Society, she was vegetarian. Second, because she had known some of those meats personally. Some of the Tinka Tae army moaned and chittered. She prayed her enemies would not be able to distinguish them from any other strand of the tropical nightsong. Voices rose in the camp: a tense-bound inflected proto-form of Cityese. Tongue of ancestral spirits. Spirits of ancestral tongues: within the murmurs of prehistoric language, the King of Nebraska's voice sounded, clear and high as a great, mad bird.

"No no no no no, I won't eat it, I won't, I won't, I won't, I want the Maison Yblis 'twenty-two, not this, can't you see I'm nauseous, nauseous? Oh, take these vain beeves from my gaze, these vile viands, these poor roasted subjects, oh, my dears, I'm so sorry to have brought you to such a humiliating end. Bring me more wine! More wine! More wine, vicar! Ah, the dew upon the stems of yesterday's wine glasses, the bloom of yesterday's vines! Bring me my Maison Yblis 'twenty-two, louts, oafs, peasants!"

Some sounds are both joyful and tragic.

A breath of warm wind touched the back of Courtney Hall's neck: fear, or the first stirrings of Angelo Brasil's little divertisement?

Strange allies, uninvited guests: part one. Angelo Brasil. Manners maketh the man, he'd kissed her hand, so! and whispered secrets behind his diamond smile; wrapped around his spine like a climbing vine was the one, the only, Series 000 biocomputer through which he could enter, control, *possess* any part, any unit of the Compassionate Society's dataweb. "Lynk, my dear, lynk" was his name for what he could do. The cybernetic anarchist had smiled again, but his eyes were anthracite flecked with mica, a collapsar full of swallowed stars. Courtney Hall reminded herself never to trust him too much.

Thunder growled up under the vaguely luminous roof of the world. The nightsong was silenced abruptly. Leaves rustled; then, note by note, the music resumed. The army of cooks, guides, interpreters, porters, engineers, and bottle washers waited, whiskers pressed to the leafmold. Slender, silent as their spears, sentries took position around the camp, thin silhouettes against the smudgefires. Watcher watched watcher. Born of an instantaneous society where no one was ever kept waiting for anything (except the odd bureaucratic rescheduling) Courtney Hall had never learned of the existence of patience and was mentally elsewhere. Strange allies, uninvited guests: part two.

Xian Man Ray, the Amazing Teleporting Woman. *Teleporting* was a word she scorned: *flip* was her name for her short jaunts through the nonquantized probability domain of unspace. The very idea of it made this fat yulp's head spin, but she knew she trusted Xian Man Ray where she did not trust her pseudobrother. And not merely because she was another woman, the only other woman she had met since diving down the service hatch in Kilimanjaro Plaza. She had talked as she went off to war with the Amazing Teleporting Woman and the Man with the Computer Brain, and within that first hour as they descended through the passive defense zone toward the central river, she knew here was someone who could be that rarest of things: a female friend. The remaining Tinka Tae engineers remained at the river with Angelo Brasil to build a raft from the balsa trees that grew in great stands down in the humid low latitudes. Angelo Brasil, with twenty-five gigabytes of bioprocessor coiled around his spinal column, had business of his own: a little diversionary lynk into the climate control systems that maintained the underground forest to play merry-andrew with the weather. Strategy and tactics. Be thankful of any cover you can get, even if that cover is climatic. Don't fug with the boys who run the weather. Under Xian Man Ray's captaincy the remainder of the tatterdemalion army (some fourteen malassorted racoons and an artist) continued upstream, following the riverbank. ("Easier to avoid traps," the small woman explained as a freely sweating Courtney Hall struggled to keep pace with her.) They marched and they marched and they marched and the day grew hotter and hotter and hotter, and Courtney Hall would have loved to strip off *something*, but she was still a yulp and excruciatingly self-conscious. Think of something else to pass the time: strange allies and uninvited guests: part three: that cat that rode on Xian Man's Ray's zebra-striped shoulder.

"Trashcan?" The small woman was eager for conversation. "Oh, don't mind him. He's on the side of the angels. He's got chrome steel claws, rejiggered reflexes, enhanced senses, and a muscular feedback amplification system that makes him strong as a human and ten times faster. Hell on wheels, our Trashie." The cat purred and switched its cybernetically enhanced gaze from Courtney Hall to the patiently toiling Tinka Tae. Courtney Hall wondered what kind of reflection it was on subterranean society if people had pets like Trashcan.

The day grew hotter. Courtney Hall calculated how far from the surface, how close to the center of the earth, this ground that she was walking upon might be. Small wonder it was warm.

"It all went out of control a long long way back," explained her companion, unasked for any explanation. "It was once an agrarium. 'Bout hundred and fifty years or so after the Break, some disease got loose. Couldn't exactly say what, but this was way back when biotech was still an infant science, so rather than risk possible famine as a consequence of the infection's spreading through all the agrariums, they sealed this one off to let the thing burn itself out. They must have forgotten about it; that's the only explanation I can think of how it came to be here."

The army of liberation toiled up the mossy side of a small waterfall. The spray was purest balm.

"But how did it get from agrarium to jungle?" From the top of the falls Courtney Hall could see the jungle land falling away in great curtains of vegetation to the pointed end of the world.

"Seeds came down the river: other agrariums, botanic gardens, even houseplants and domestic biotech. Should see the marijuana groves, though. Ah! The presiding spirits went to pieces, climate control fell apart, and this place warmed up. Kind of deep underground here, the rock temperature is just the right level for a full-blown climax rain forest. As you've probably noticed."

"So, what happened then?"

"Well, it grew away to itself for about a century ago until our friends here took it over. The revenants . . . Ah." She rubbed the corner of her jawbone just beneath her ear. "Angelo calleth. He's lynked through the defense programs—poor old things aren't up to very much—and is into the main memory. Says he's working on a small typhoon but it'll take some time for it to brew."

A prescient eddy of wind snaked slick hair into Courtney Hall's eyes.

"Revenants?"

"Fug, yes, I was telling you about them, wasn't I? Revenants. From before the Break. History lesson. Column! Column, take five." The two women sought shelter from the wet heat beneath an umbelliferous tree whose leaves dripped water. Trashcan the cat sat on a stump and groomed itself.

"Okay. Improbable as it may seem to you, a citizen, not everyone was overjoyed when the Compassionate Society emerged from the general mayhem at the time of the Break. There were some on both sides, military and politicals mainly, who refused to accept what was happening. 'Humans'll never consent to be ruled by a bunch of machines, give it six months, a year, they'll be down on their knees begging us to come back'; that sort of thing. So they holed themselves up in their deepest, safest bomb shelters and waited. Long wait; all sitting down there in their respective holes holding their elections and party congresses. Well, of course it wasn't too long before they started running out of tinned blini and flash-frozen burger and time came for a move. Luck, fate, whatever your particular belief is, brought them here. Two tribes: Democrats and Communists. 'Land of the Morning Star' to the Communists. 'Land of the Great White Eagle' to the Democrats. Now, you'd think that they'd have wiped each other out decades ago; not so. Two hundred or so years of, well, comparative, peace. Can't afford a big war. Balance of power, you see. Communists, they came upriver and control the endwaters down there. They've built big sluices; push the comrades too hard and this place turns into one big fish pond. Democrats, they control the lights. They got this big pueblo up there on the side of the world, built right into the control computers. So, maybe they don't have Angelo's fine touch, but all you need is a big enough stone ax and that'll do the job. And without light this place is as dead as surely as if it were filled up to the roof with water. So, what you have, in brief, is two tribes of cavemen, both needing each other, both hating each other's hides. Crazy.

"Craziest of all: each side is indistinguishable from the other. Petty despotism, Communist and Democrat both. Got to keep the Land of the Great White Eagle strong against Communism, you see. Got to make the workers of the Land of the Morning Star safe from the evils of Democracy. Pathetic. If they didn't take it so seriously."

"So, which side is it has kidnapped Jonathon Ammonier?"

"Democrats, I would reckon. Several reasons. First off, to them he's not a Communist, but he's not a Democrat either. Duh, they say, what do we do with this? Uh, dunno, but we better be sure the Commie pinko bastards can't have him. Even though he is of absolutely no value to either side."

"That's crazy."

"Said it would be, didn't I? This is DeepUnder, sister. Crazy is normal down here." Xian Man Ray stood up, brushed soily hands on thighs. "Time to be off. Trashie, take point."

"Why?"

"It's back into Democrat territory from here on. Booby traps. To us, that is. To the Democrats, it's Strategic Defense Initiative. Whatever the fug they call it, Trashie's rejiggered senses can pick it out before we hit it. Or it us."

The Tinka Tae bearers uncurled to shoulder their poles, leant into their travois harnesses. The long march continued. Over the succeeding hours, while her mind should have been focused on pitfalls, pungi stakes, and poison arrows, Courtney Hall found her attention wandering to form a question. Not any question. *The* Question. The Question was: just why should an Amazing Teleporting Woman and a Man with a Computer Brain (plus power-assisted cat) care what happened to an ex-Elector of Yu, now self-crowned King of Nebraska and his Underground Dominions?

Crouched amidst the root buttresses of a geneform teak with her army of racoons waiting for her battle cry, she still could not find any answer to the Question that satisfied her.

Suddenly Xian Man Ray was there. No shiver of air. No luminous interdimensional gateway. No bamf! of sulfurous flame. Nothing so stereotypically teleportational. One moment she wasn't there. Next she was.

"I'm starting the diversionary tactics now," she said. And was gone. No bamf! of sulfurous flame. No luminous interdimensional gateway. No shiver of air.

There had been a briefing. Of sorts. War virgin Courtney Hall had sat converting a pair of pants from the Victorialand wardrobe into shorts while Xian Man Ray assembled a

bow from sections in her backpack and explained how one
teleporting woman can look like a whole army.

Courtney Hall had not remembered one word of her
orders.

The long, shafting sound of an arrow in flight terminat-
ed in a solid thunk. Sprouting a cloth-yard of tube steel, a
missile-totem teetered and fell. Instant confusion in the
camp. To arms, to arms! Running, shouting, standing still.
Always one, left standing still. With a roar and a hiss the
fire pit was doused. The night was suddenly filled with
eyes.

Arrowstorm. From everywhere at once. Shouts, cries,
screams. Courtney Hall saw Xian Man Ray flicker into
transient being, loose an arrow from her laser-guided,
gyro-stabilized bow, and vanish. Firing as fast as she
could teleport: flip flip flip flip flip . . . The arrowstorm
ended. Voices. Replies. Someone somewhere was retching
in the dark. Skirmishers edged into the darkness. A
Democrat sentry advanced to within centimeters of
Courtney Hall's covert and squatted, arrow nocked to
his technologically less advanced but no less deadly
bow. The Tinka Tae stirred. Sharpened stropped vegetable knives glittered in the dim night-glow from the
ceiling lights. Courtney Hall frantically signaled for
stillness. She could not remember the last time she had
taken a breath, felt a heartbeat.

Explosions. Mushrooms of orange smoke. Arrows.
Screams. A flare was tossed into the Democrat encamp-
ment. By its light Courtney Hall saw a man stumble and
fall. Blood sprayed from severed arteries. Hair and blood;
his scalp was hanging over his eyes. And that dark slither,
bounding away into the darkness . . . a cat? Panic. Enemies
here, there, everywhere, nowhere. Dirt was scuffed over
the flare, the gas grenades lobbed out into the forest. But
not before another arrowstorm sent the defenders reeling
for cover. And in the midst of the burning and the blood
and the bedlam, Jonathon Ammonier stood up, proud,
mad bird, clapping his hands and shouting, "Is this for

me? All for me? Oh, how wonderful, how wonderful, how wonderful!"

Forgetful of the present danger, Courtney Hall jumped up and screamed, "Get down, you stupid fugger! Get down!" The crouching sentry fell over backward in surprise. Arrow slipped from bow, bow from fingers. Fingers found knife in belt. There was a flash of lightning. Revealing: the sentry. Blue blade clutched in fingers. A steel vegetable knife straight through his throat. Liquid gurgled and surged around the blade. All in a flash, in an instant revealed.

The air disappeared. A blast of hot wind howled upward, uprooting totems, tent leather, tearing leaves from trees, breath from lungs. For a second, one second, the whole twenty-kilometer cavern boomed like a temple gong to the miniature typhoon.

"Forward, racoons!" shouted Courtney Hall. The Tinka Tae came pouring out of the floor of the forest. The rains began.

"Rain" does not adequately describe the process of precipitation Angelo Brasil had initiated. The downpour began. The deluge began. Drops hard and sharp as needles. Drenched, combing the hair out of her eyes, Courtney Hall led the bedraggled racoons through the cloudburst.

The bulk of the raiding party were hip-hollerin' in pursuit of the pervo-devo-freako-pinko Commie bastards, as Xian Man Ray had predicted. The Tinka Tae with their vegetable knives overwhelmed the few dazed guards left around the King of Nebraska.

And suddenly Courtney Hall herself was overwhelmed. Overpowered. Overcome. Flash-flashing steel lightning blades. She had seen someone killed, a life ended, witnessed final moments, heard the liquid sucking of final breath. Killed. Permanently. No return, no refund if dissatisfied. She had seen death, and the face it wore was not the closet-sanitized mask of the Phantom of the Arcologies, knocking at a door here, a door there, polite, almost apologetic—I'm sorry, but it really is time, you know . . . Death riding the tip of a blade, unmourned, unmarked. Ludicrous that something as slight as the blade she held in her hand could call down death. She tried to throw her knife away from her into the rain, but it remained stuck to her palm like an accusation. On every side, death, summoned, capered; mesmerizing, hypnotizing, dazzling. She fell to her knees in the rain and the mud and the ashes, looking at her hand, her knife.

"Courtney Hall, rouse thee, rouse thee! His Majesty, Bless 'Im!"

Lightning shone from the blood on Jinkajou's paws.

"Courtney Hall! Courtney Hall! Please!"

She broke free from the death trance and with Jinkajou the Chamberlain leading, found the King of Nebraska reclining numbly on a straw pallet by the smoldering fire pit. There was a stink of nightshade and decomposing flesh. His Majesty, Bless 'Im's lips were puffed and cracked. His face was a purulence of spots and acne. His hair had fallen out in cancerous patches.

He had been deeply drugged.

"Ahahahaha! Fidelity and the Lady! Comin' for to carry me home! Jinkajou, burn all my Dashiell Hammett novels and recordings of *Bix Beiderbecke*!" He waved a jaunty sputum-stained handkerchief; then a spasm of coughing shoved him to the straw pallet.

"Courtney Hall, a word in your ear. His Majesty, Bless 'Im, is too sick to walk. What shall we do?"

Decision. Citizens did not make decisions. Citizens had decisions made for them, and always made right.

She opened her mouth and let the first thing in her head walk out.

"Call together the Tinka Tae and build a travois from the tent poles."

Not bad for a first command.

The retreat through the jungle was an anabasis through the nether regions of nightmare. Slowly, slowly, slowly, so damn *slowly:* that travois dragging, creaking along through the night and the dark and the endless rain, the blinding, streaming rain . . . Her boost of noradrenaline burned out, Courtney Hall was possessed by a shivering cold dread;

the permanent sense that every decision she had made had been wrong, that at any moment she would be cold dead in the leaf litter with a Democrat arrow through her cervical vertebrae. Slowly, slowly, so damn fuggin' *slowly*; that sick madman ranting and hallucinating and arguing loudly with his ghosts and memories while all around the stealthy eyes of SDI rested not, nor blinked, and when she and her racoons were pitted and slitted and noosed and netted and impaled, they would not even cry, not even one tear. Onward, forward, through the dark and the fear and the leaves and the thundering rain and the trees and the doubt (the Question, again, only wickedly asking itself of herself), and coming on behind, the slow, slow, so damn fuggin' *slow* slither slide of the travois. . . .

Courtney Hall screamed and screamed and screamed and screamed when the lightning shattered the dark into the shape of someone waiting for her.

"Easy, easy," said Xian Man Ray. She smelt of sweat and smoke and speed and a curious taint of sex. Zebra-striped, she was a figment of the rain forest. Trashcan her cat ran up onto her shoulder and licked its paws. Courtney Hall swallowed several sobs whole before she could speak.

"What about the Democrats?" The cat flexed its razor claws and carefully licked them clean. The small woman grinned.

A streak of light arced above the forest canopy and detonated in a starburst of red and green. Others rose to join it in its momentary glory; suddenly the whole sky was exploding with fireworks. Then, from far to the south, a constellation of starbursts spread themselves against the roof in reply.

"Wow! War rockets! This is it, sister, the big show, the main feature! Armageddon! The Final Conflict! Those sucks of Democrats must have thought the Commies were attacking them with some deadly new weapon and they're striking back. I'd love to stick around to see this!" The symbolic bombardment peaked until the exploding fire-works rivaled Angelo Brasil's artificial lightning. Beneath the heavens gone mad, the Army of Victorialand escaped through rain and mold and dread.

"About half an hour to go from here," said Xian Man Ray, sniffing around a crossing of forest paths. Suddenly the gentle moon-glow from the ceiling lights flared day-bright and went out. Total darkness clamped down on the Land of the Great White Eagle/Morning Star. Courtney Hall found herself wrestling with a demon named Claus-trophobia, which tried to squeeze the breath from her lungs with whispers of the truth that she was a kilometer and a half underground with several million tons of rock poised above her desperately seeking unity with the sever-al quintillion tons of sister rock beneath.

She knew that if she ever found her breath again, she would not be able to stop screaming.

Soft fingers on her neck: a word and a lightning-bolt image of Xian Man Ray. "Softly, softly, sister. Take my hand. Trashie'll lead us. He's a cat can see in any darkness."

"What have they done?"

"Gone mad. M.A.D. Mutually Assured Destruction. Just hope the Communists can't find the controls to their sluice gates or all bets are off." She rubbed the corner of her jaw, whispered, "Angelo, get those lights on again." An angry insect buzzing. The small woman swore. "Those stone axes I told you about. They smashed the computers. Angelo's lost all environmental control, but he thinks he can lynk into and hold the flood-control computers at the mouth of the river. But this place is bound for Hades in a hatbox: this really is Armageddon, sister. The End of the World."

The retreat through Sheol continued.

Deafened by rain, blind except for the occasional light-ning flicker or, rarer now as the stocks were expended, war rocket, her skin numb with cold rainwater, Courtney Hall slipped subtly into a state of sensory deprivation almost as complete as if she were imprisoned in a West One psycho-engineering tank. Only the warmth and pres-ence of Xian Man Ray's hand prevented her from submit-ting totally to the hallucinations and bizarre time-swings that menaced her path. Nevertheless, she could not rid herself of the impression that this long pilgrimage was really through the interstices of her own body to pavilions of life-energy where she found the sixteen-o'clock dream: ornithopter-bicycles, squadrons of them, the sky black with their beating wings, dropping coconuts and cascades of sparks from the roman candles strapped to their mud-guards; elsewhere on her interior hegira she met Jonathon Ammonier dancing among the exhibits of his Chaosium, and as he danced, pieces of his body kept falling off: ears, toes, fingers, nose, hands, whole arms and legs—Courtney Hall scampered after him scooping them up, saying, "Excuse me, Your Majesty, but isn't this yours?" until only a head and a torso remained, with teeth glowing fluorescent green in the night: the TAOS girl, forty stories of social grace, and Courtney Hall waved at her from her cosy little office and the TAOS girl waved back, every time Courtney Hall moved the TAOS girl copied it until she realized that she was the TAOS girl, trapped in forty stories of videowall, and all she could do was smile, pick chip, flip chip, hold, and dissolve, over and over and over and over again. . . .

"Sister, we're here, sister."

Unh?

Water. Chuckling water. And light! Flares, torches, a bonfire. And a raft, moored to the bank; a good raft, a big raft, a good big Huckleberry Finn of a raft with a steering pole and a little cabin woven from twigs and a fire on a slab of river-bed slate. And Angelo Brasil, sitting Lotus-position in the fireglow, eyes rolled up in his head, mouth shaping syllables never intentioned for human lips: the whispered intimacies of the computers. He was holding the sluice gates open with his mynde.

A good raft. Good people. Wonderful raft. Wonderful people. And now it was over. Courtney Hall burst into tears of pure relief as she watched the King of Nebraska manhandled aboard, the Tinka Tae porters finish their loading of food and supplies.

"Ain't you coming?"

A sniff.

"You coming sister?"

A nod.

A hand reached out and she was pulled aboard. Then the mooring lines were slashed forward and aft, and the current spun the raft out into the great darkness.

Byrne

Falling rain.

Excellent rain.

Watch it fall... Sudden. Sweeping courtyards, closes, clear of citizens, drumming on clapper roofs of hunchbacked bridges, drum-drumming on waxed paper umbrellas in Angle Park, drum-drum-drumming on the canopies of sampans moored at Steelyard floating market, hissing over canals and wateralleys and the dolorous chugging of the municipal *vaporetti* wedged to the gunwales with wet populace. Huddled under a polythene sheet against the inadequacies of leaking wickerwork, Kansas Byrne weighed the risk of using her marquin on the lumbering water-buses against five centimeters of rainwater slopping round her feet in the scuppers of an onion-vendor's sampan. The tiny alcohol stove leaked a dismal globe of warmth that only exacerbated the stink of forty kinds of onions that formed the sampan's other cargo. In the stern, onion-vending Jian John-Chang set face upturned to the rain, evidently enjoying the sting of rainwater in his eyes, the trickle of warm drops down his body.

His body...

His... harlequinade. His motley. His hydridoma. Apocalyptic avatar of a forgotten faith. Four-armed, with twain he did steer and tend the outboard and with twain did he bail rainwater, which, unbaled, would have sent Jian John-Chang Food Corps concessionaire and soul brother of the Carnal Plenum, his passenger, his forty brands of onion, and his sampan *Ribonucleic Revelation* to the bottom of Waters of Healing Compassion Canal. With twain did he

163

sail and with twain did he bail, but of legs he had none for
the legs of Jian John-Chang were on loan to Sister Chanadya
Tree-Morgan. Thus it was of considerable importance to
Jian John-Chang of the Carnal Plenum that his *Ribonucleic
Revelation* did not dissolve in the waters of Healing Compassion as, until such time as the Sacred Rota prescribed
him a pair of someone else's legs, the sampan was his only
means of mobility.

The Biological Revelation of the Panspermic Life-Force
was the pivotal tenet of Carnal Plenum belief. The sacrament of the transplantational. Being is gene-deep: share
the flesh, share the being in the double helix. Greater
lover hath no person than he/she giveth up his/her arm for
his/her soulbrother; be given the legs of his/her soulsister.
Today an arm and a leg. Tomorrow eyes, ears, feet, and
fingers. Next week: liver, lights, lungs, spleen, kidneys,
genitals. Next *year:* proud bearer of the sacred relics of
the Thrice Blessed: Sacred Head Sore Wounded (read
amputated), Holy Eyeball, Sanctified Hand, Hallelujahed
Thumb, Redeemed Toe, Cosmic Gallbladder. Holy holy
holy. And then, some decade, might not Jian John-Chang,
onion vendor, become as enlightened as Deevah, the
Prophetess, she of the Ten Thousand Transplants?

Deevah the Prophetess.

Well, what can be said about her?

She smells.

That's gangrene. A vocational hazard among the
Soulbrothers of the Carnal Plenum.

She has cancers erupting like new brains all over her
body.

Another vocational hazard. Immuno-suppressives.

She is the avatar of Kali: eight-armed, four-legged, she
is the amalgam of ten thousand different components, a
U-Built-It biokit of the Corporal, the Mortified, and the
Transfigured. Lifetimes ago, beyond remembering, she
had been an old woman of an unexceptional Soulbrother
Order. Then God had called her through his organs in the
Ministry of Pain and its psychofiles. Now she is Deevah.

She has two heads.

She had gained her second head, the highest honor of the Carnal Plenum, so long before that she has forgotten which is the head she was born with, which is the head she acquired. They take turns to speak. Day about. One thinks, one speaks.

Deevah is a prophetess. The foremost prophetess of the city of Yu. When she opens her speaking mouth to let the verbs of God flow forth, Yu listens. Because Deevah, unlike every other prophetess and mouthpiece of the divine, is genuine. She has power. That power breaks the boundaries of caste and custom that the Ministry of Pain has so painstakingly erected. But the Ministry of Pain lets her prophesy because she is subject to a higher law. So the word passes out of Three Jump Span into the city, and those with the courage to have their questions truly answered, *truly*, come to hear the word of the numinous. There are never many of them. Only a very few have the courage to face futures no different from their past, if that be the divine will. But there are always some.

Kansas Byrne is one. She has a question, a dangerous question, a question she could not ask of the municipal shrines and databases. For if they answered, she would have betrayed those on whose behalf she asked. It is a dangerous question even for Deevah the Prophetess but a question that must be asked and answered. So she listened to the whispers that ran with the rats around the sampans and the duckboards of the floating market and sent her own little whisper to run with them until it found someone willing to take her down the wateralleys under hunchbacked bridges to Deevah.

Deevah's Oraculum was a tatterdemalion amphitheater erected on a corner of land where a dump of discarded garbage abutted a row of collapsed tenements. Planks for seats, illumination from biogas flares blazing in blackened paint-tins.

The Carnal Plenum Brother in the waxpaper entrance booth had three arms and three eyes. The third arm, a bloated club of mortifying green flesh, held a syringe. The third eye supposedly looked into the soul.

"Supplicant or spectator?"

"Pardon?" said Kansas Byrne, a Wee Wendy Waif spell-caught by the night, the hum of the expectant crowd, the heat of the biogas flares, the pure theatricality of it all.

"You want to watch, you want to ask a question?"

"Oh. Ask a question."

"Then we'll need a specimen."

"A what?"

Supplicants and spectators were piling up behind her, impatient and increasingly compressed. The odor of wet humans was miserable.

"Blood, cizzen. For the Deevah. All knowledge is genetic. . . ." The blotched green-and-purple arm waved the hypodermic. Supplicants, spectators, biogas flares, amphitheaters, slender silver demon needles swam.

"Oh, shug . . . Will it hurt? I've got a very low pain threshold rating."

"A little."

"Oh, fug."

The flames seemed to catch on the needle. The figure of 0.3 seemed very important, then she found herself looking into the dreadlock-shrouded face of a Soulbrother of the Brethren of Marcus Garvey Redeemed. His Selassic Eye winked at her.

"You all right?"

"Um. Ah. Yes. Now. Thank you. Thank you. Needles and me . . . It's on my psychofile, the only bit of it I believe, as a matter of fact: zero point three." The Marcus Garveyite accompanied her to one of the back benches and handed her a slip of paper.

"You forgot to take this."

"What is it?"

"Your number." Prophecy by number, like buying a half kilo of bean curd or a sack of onions from a Food Corps concessionaire.

The buzz of conversation settled. The biogas flares dwindled in their paint pots to a bare glow. An aura of hushed expectancy filled the amphitheater. Kansas Byrne was astounded at how much like *menace* it felt. Drizzle drizzled down. Spectators and supplicants alike were oblivious to it: Deevah the Prophetess was entering the arena.

Very slowly she came, very slowly, very painfully, dragging trailing limbs and pendulous wattles of flesh, heaving heavy ox shoulders, eight arms dragging, swinging, slow with the slowness of a thing that knows it can take forever to reach its destination, if need be. Six breasts; withered, dry dugs, two heads, two mouths snapping and spinning ropes of yellow drool. Her fingernails curled up into spirals. Matted hair burst from her multiple armpits and spread a thick shadowy forest about her loins, belly, and thighs.

"They say her skeleton was specially strengthened by the white brothers," whispered the Marcus Garveyite. "Even so, she has to sleep in a pond of electrically warmed mud because if she lay down to sleep she would smother under the mass of her own transplants."

The stench of rotting was overpowering.

Kansas Byrne watched horrified and transfixed. Pure awe. Pure theater.

The prophetess raised her arms; a throat mike caught her whispered name and threw it hissing like the rain around the amphitheater: *Deevah* . . . The biogas cressets flared into five-meter pillars of flame. Kansas Byrne broke into spontaneous applause. The Marcus Garveyite rested a hand on her arm—hush, be still. The prophetess squatted and settled her bulk to the pounded garbage floor. An acolyte slipped into the circle of fire, a willow-thin girl of sixteen or so dressed only in a very short frilled skirt. Her only apparent modifications were a set of five nipples arranged down her prominent rib cage like buttons. She had the most wonderful pair of hands Kansas Byrne had ever seen.

"By the grace of the Panspermic Life-Force, Sister Deevah has again been visited with the Quickening, the mystic power all-surrounding, all-pervading, before all things, after all things, within all things, without all things" —her hands, her beautiful mantis-hands, described the dance of the double helix, the mimesis of the DNA molecule—"and her third eye opened to the Universal Biomass, she has reached into the racial past and the racial future of the worldsoul, the planet-mother, and one with the whole life of the earth and all other earths wound in the great double helix of consciousness, she will prophesy. For the life of the world and the life of Deevah are one; soul and cell. Thus supplicants, address your prophetess, you seekers of true life, and be answered. Number one!"

A spiritually shell-shocked yulp stood up, guiltily clutching slip number one. His hands were locked in a spastic *nona dolorosa,* his question a stammering beseeching for ambition, promotion, and a revolution in lifestyle that Kansas Byrne knew could never be answered positively. The five-nippled acolyte opened a small plastic case and removed a full hypodermic syringe. She paraded it around the perimeter of the arena so that everyone could see the way the flamelight shone through the red yulp blood. Then with a leap and a cry she danced across the ring of fire and plunged the needle into the Deevah's back.

A cry of sheer dread spun from Kansas Byrne's lips. A third time the hands of the Marcus Garveyite touched her to peace.

Down where the gas flares blazed, eyes of ecstasy, eyes of idiot insight. Heads lolled, eyeballs rolled, beholding the apocalypse engraved on the inside of the cranium. A tongue, warty and scaly as some long-extinct parasitic worm, uncoiled from the open mouth of the thinking head. The mouth of the speaking head sprayed creamy foam pinkened with blood.

Deevah the Prophetess spoke. From her speaking mouth came clickings and scrapings, as if she were reaching into the racial memory to the tongues of insects. Then came harsh barkings and bayings never designed for human vocal cords to shape. The prophetess voiced them. Then came an incoherent glossolalia of human languages past, present, and to come. And then all jerkings and twitchings, all spasmings and shiverings, ceased. Her eyes rolled down from reading the writings in the skull to fix her questioner. She spoke, and the voice in which she spoke was the most terrible voice of all, for she spoke in the dry, quantified tones of the Computer Standard Voice.

"Are you not a yulp?" spake the prophetess. "Are you not a digit of the Compassionate Society? How then can there be any future for you outside what is currently your present? You will not become a project director in an arts commune. You cannot. You will remain an advertising adviser second-class, and you will die one, too." The prophecy was given. Kansas Byrne treated herself to a shiver of pure superstition, and it was a wonderful feeling because superstition was dead, rationalized away by the Ministry of Pain and the computerized deities of the Polytheon.

"Number two!" cried the whipcord acolyte. The biogas flares dipped and swayed. The needling rain, heavier now, pierced to the bone, but the mystery was stronger than any discomfort. Hypotheses, theorems flocked into Kansas Byrne's imagination: possession by the Lares and Penates, the lowest order of the Polytheon and the most intimate with man; neural linkage to the dataweb; transmission through the bones of the skull; racial memories; the wisdom of ancestors stored on biochip, as the Electors were reputed to be; could all knowledge truly be genetic, was God a double helix of consciousness? She rejected them all with a shake of her mind. She did not want rationalizations, explanations, hypotheses. She wanted magic, she wanted mystery, and as the bright silver needle plunged into Deevah's hump, she gave herself to the firelight and the sacrament and the Theater of Being that transcends all art. Then time ceased to flow in its ordained bed and burst out into a flood of barking voices, and the chittering, chitinous cries of the People in the Sea from whom all humanity was descended, and the astonishing hands of the acolyte girl that held the glittering needle, and the flames shining through the red red blood.

"Number nineteen!" Shining with pride, Sister Needle

paced pantherwise back and forth between the shadowplay of the biogas flares.

"She is her daughter," whispered the Marcus Garveyite.

"Deevah's?" asked Kansas Byrne.

"No. Deevah is her daughter."

Somehow it made the craziness perfect.

"Number nineteen!"

In the mystery she had forgotten that was her number.

The question had been carefully formulated to be the safest possible dangerous question with two hundred famulus eyes watching, monitoring.

"Is it possible for me to find my brother and his friends?"

Safe dangerous question, and a perfect test of prophetic power. Deevah's hump was a martyrdom of empty hypodermics. Again the energy crackled up, again primeval tongues gibbered and croaked, and out of the babel of human tongues the Computer Standard Voice spoke one word.

"Yes."

It was all the answer she needed. At the first alert that the pantycars were circling above, they had split into their prearranged escape routines (as much a piece of performance as any other, she regretted missing it) and recongregated out in the frantic industrial wasteworlds heaped around Tamazooma, the capital of the TAOS Consortium. Where better to hide the Compassionate Society's most unrepentant PainCriminals than under the hand of one of its Seven Servants?

But there was another question, another responsibility.

"Wait." The acolyte-mother (could it possibly be true?) was dancing toward her next hypodermic supplication. "I want to ask another question. Where is the man who calls himself Kilimanjaro West?"

Now that was a dangerous dangerous question. She hoped for both their fates that he was as invisible, imaginary, as he dis-appeared to be.

"Sorry," said the acolyte. "One question is all you get. Number twenty. Number twenty?"

Deevah the Prophetess rumbled. A murmur went through the crowd. The acolyte froze, outraged, alarmed.

"Answer," groaned Deevah, "answer answer answer..." Her tongue was possessed still by the Computer Standard Voice. "I will answer: paradox! How can this be? You will find him underground in the company of angels. At Salmagundy Street *pneumatique* station, you will find him underground in the company of angels..."

Deevah the Prophetess stopped dead.

Every muscle locked into spastic rigidity. Her thinking head began to turn, wrenching round, round, a full 360 degrees. From the mouth of her speaking head came the voice of a child.

"Again, again, again he has come, the messenger, the avatar, the silent, secret one. The sent one: again he has come. Again he has left his holy place under the hand of Yah. Again he has left the rings of the santrels and teraphim to take human flesh and form and walk among us. The avatar has returned, the incarnate one, and we know it not.

"And pity, oh, pity, ah, the pity! For in leaving his high estate he has put off the memory of all former things so that even as we know him not, he knows not himself. For he has forgotten, he who cannot forget, he who shines with the power of Yah, forgotten everything so that he may be human among humans.

"Why have you come? Why have you left your home among the Celestials, the High and Shining Ones, to come among men once again? What is your mission? Your purpose? Reveal yourself, reveal yourself to us, holy servant, make known your purposes so that we may not, through sin, willfullness or ignorance, frustrate your work as we have so many times before. What are you? Who are you? Why are you? Do not judge us, we beg you. Have compassion. Have compassion. Do not destroy. Do not destroy."

Deevah the Prophetess reared up on her four legs, raised her eight arms, and the divine electricity that had blazed along her synapses failed. She fell over backward

and lay helpless as a beetle on its back while Brothers of
the Carnal Plenum hurried to right her before she smothered
under her own flesh. And the rain rained down and Kansas
Byrne stared like an atheist with stigmata.

Chapter 7

Down along the midnight river time wore the shape of an ormolu pocket watch: a rococo confection of foliage and vine fruits and porcelain miniatures and dryads and plump virgins. Only here, in the jeweled hands, the lapis-lazuli moon-phases, the movement and bezels and twitching hairspring, did time have any meaning. Everywhere else, the great dark of the tunnel abolished time and temporality. By baroque dryad-time three days had passed since the raft had breasted the rushing plumes of water to ride the rapids through the closing sluice gates into the more profound dark of the tunnel.

Three days and still Courtney Hall would not be convinced that the tunnel was not closing in on her; the ceiling drawing closer, the walls nearer, the water faster, and that far away, or perhaps not so far away, perhaps only the next tick or tock of watch or heart away, the water would rise to fill the entire brick tube. Panic would paralyze her: inevitable as death, she knew she was being carried toward the drowning place.

"Are you sure you can't see the ceiling?" she would ask. Her companions had stopped answering that question when Courtney Hall had stopped believing their replies. But darkness was a great breeder of questions. Questions filled up great swathes of ormolu tick-tock time so that for a while Courtney Hall could lose herself in the answers and forget that the walls were closing in. And that the mutant blind albino alligators were waiting for her every time she went to the bow to relieve herself. One question

she wished she had never asked. Angelo Brasil had smiled
wickedly as he had replied.

There was another question she wished had never
been asked: the King of Nebraska's call for his artist. She
had known what he would ask her. But she went anyway.
There was no other place to go on the raft. She went. And
he asked. And she told him. And he was very quiet for
several tickings of his rococo watch. Then he said, "What
were you afraid of?" And she replied, "You." "But how can
you be afraid of me?" asked the King of Nebraska. "Because
you are a king," said the artist. "Thank you," said the
King, and he smiled weakly. "Would it make any difference if I told you I had always suspected?" "Some," said
the artist. "I was afraid you would hate me if I told you."
"I would have hated you more if you had not," said the
King. "But I didn't have to tell you, you said you had
always suspected," said the artist. "That is not the issue,"
said the King. "This is not the way for a king to die, felled
by something invisible, intangible, immaterial. I suppose
we all pay the price of our folly somehow, somewhen. All I
want is to make it to the edge. After that, I don't care." He
looked at his artist. "But you have disappointed me," he
said.

She had disappointed herself. No secrets on a Huckleberry Finn raft: everyone knew she was a coward now.

But the question was no longer a weight pushing,
pressing on her chest, and she found a new kind of
courage to ask the other question. The question that was
not any old question, but The Question. It was a good
Question. And, she hoped, not too obvious, for it contained within it intriguing subquestions: "How did you
know who we were/where we were?" "How long have you
been following us?" "Why ditto?" "How/why do you possess these extraordinary abilities?" "Are your friends, or
subtle enemies?" "How/why can he/we/I trust you?"

It was such a good Question that Angelo Brasil and
Xian Man Ray withdrew from the pool of firelight to
whisper in the stern while Trashcan's infrared eyes blinked
watchfully at Courtney Hall. Behind the lean-to that shel-

tered the King of Nebraska, racoon voices muttered racoon mutterings. Firelight touched their hands and biochips.

"So, we'll tell you," said Xian Man Ray, settling herself across the niggardly fire from Courtney Hall. "No point in hiding anything from you." The man who called himself Angelo Brasil squatted on his hams and ran his fingers through his dreadlocks.

"Sure, and don't we all have to trust each other, my dear?" he said. He smiled a feral smile. Courtney Hall found it hard to trust someone who showed so many teeth.

"Jonathon Ammonier has something we want," said Xian Man Ray.

"A piece of information," continued her pseudosibling. "He has the location of a device we call The Unit, for want of a better name. It's in the memories of one of his stored personas, and we need it."

"Dad needs it."

"All right so. Dad needs it. And he's sent us, his most trusted agents, to get it."

"For our sister."

"Callisto, Callisto Pandel. You see, my dear, she has this problem Dad can't cure."

"Pernicious Energetic Bioplasty."

"His name for it. Quite good, don't you think? He knows what the condition is, but alas, even with four centuries of bioscience at his fingertips, he can't fix the kink in the gene that's causing it."

"Pernicious Energetic Bioplasty?" asked Courtney Hall.

"A continuous ebbing away of life energy," said Xian Man Ray. "She's got all these enhanced combat systems, you see; one-shot implant lasers, jiggered-up reflexes, full-spectrum scanning ocular systems, power-enhanced endo-skeleton; kind of stuff Trashie here's got."

"My dear sib's pet was Dad's prototype. Trashie was meant to be Callisto's pet, but then there was this problem . . ."

"Well, it all has to run off something."

"What my dear sib means, my dear, is that it all runs off her."

"Pernicious Energetic Bioplasty."

"Or, if you prefer, Kiss of the Soul Vampire!" Angelo Brasil leered over the flames melodramatically. Courtney Hall was more confused than scared.

"She is not!" snapped Xian Man Ray. "How can you say that!" Angelo Brasil rocked back on his heels and looked up at the ceiling, which might or might not be growing closer with every passing fluid meter.

"Well, it's true, sib. There was a shift in her chromosome patterns, you see. She replenishes her own energies by drawing life energy from other living things. Specifically, people. Kiss of the Soul Vampire, see? There was a wee tad of trouble; to support her energy habit she used to take herself off on these expeditions upstairs: catch zillies at late-night *pneumatique* halts, prollet workers down in the subsystems. Drained them dry. Dry as an old bone. Most unfortunate. You'll not have heard anything about it because the Ministry of Pain doesn't want the people to get spooked. But she must have sucked out, oh, at least twenty citizens. Now, if you want my opinion, I say what's a zillie here, a prollet there, a yulp somewhere else— present company excepted, my dear. The Compassionate Society can spare them. Well, our dear dad thought better; he pulled her and popped her into a white sleep tank while he works out what to do. Soul vampires: tricky enough. Soul vampires with enhanced cyber combat systems you do not want to meet, my dear. Anyway—"

"Anyway"—Xian Man Ray scooped up the cue like a pelota ball—"he needs some counterentropic power source which he can implant in Callisto to keep her stable. And there's only one suitable counterentropic power source we know of."

"And that's The Unit."

"The Unit?" Courtney Hall's confusions were multiplying with Malthusian vigor.

"It dates from the time of the Break." Angelo Brasil continued without even a dropped syllable. "Back then when the old society was going to pot, the ancestors of those dear chappies back there"—he thumbed toward the dark-filled, flooding cavern—"threw everything they had into the construction of the ultimate weapon. Now, don't ask me why they felt the need for an ultimate weapon, but they did. Threw so much into its R and D it would have bankrupted civilization if civilization hadn't been past caring by that stage anyway. But what they got for their money was The Unit. To this day we don't really know what it does, or how it does it, because it was never tested, but the general theory is that it's—"

"An activator of entropy. As bro said, no one ever saw it working, but according to Dad's theories, it winds entropy forward—"

"And it winds entropy backward again."

"It's about this long"—Xian Man Ray's fingers stood about half a meter apart—"looks like a cross between a ceramic flute and a short sword. To use it, you pull it apart. There's something inside, exactly what we don't know. But the general effect is—"

"It kills people. Like most weapons."

"Ages them a thousand years in two seconds."

"And then, unlike most weapons—"

"It brings them back to life again."

"Runs entropy backward when the entropic accelerator is on reverse setting, when you push the thing together again."

"So it's a weapon that kills people, temporarily."

"And we need it."

"And His Majesty Jonathon Ammonier, Forty-fourth Elector of Yu, King of Nebraska, Victorialand, Racoons, what the hell, has the precise location buried in the persona of one of his predecessors."

"The one who put the thing there in the first place."

"So why can't Angelo just lynk in and get it out?"

"Excellent question, Mizz Hall. Because the cunning bastards who devised the persona storage system wove it so tight that not even I can get into it. If I pry so much as one strand loose from the security web, the whole thing unravels and comes apart. Wipes itself clean, my dear. And His Majesty, Bless 'Im, with it. Don't think I haven't tried, lovie. No, if we want the location of The Unit, he either gives it to us or we wait until he dies and passes the biochip containing the information to someone who will."

Courtney Hall's immediate question answered itself so perfectly that it never left the machinations of the imagination.

"Precisely, my dear," said Angelo Brasil. "To the End of the World, if that's what it'll take. We were afraid, my sib and I, that you were going to be something of a useless encumbrance to our little operation when we first encountered you with that pack of ludicrous animals back there. However, you may well turn out to be of some use after all." He smiled his Gasoline Alley grin.

Courtney Hall felt the tunnel creeping down on her from above again.

"Ignore my bro," said Xian Man Ray. "He likes to look pretty damn sharp and shiny, but underneath he's more scared of you than you are of him. We're glad to have your assistance now. So far, we could have made it alone, but from now on, and with the King in his condition, we need you. He doesn't trust us. You're the only one he trusts."

"I disappointed him. Badly."

"He knows you won't disappoint him again, so he trusts you."

"You're using me."

"Exactly." Angelo Brasil's teeth menaced her. He cleaned them every night with peeled twigs and they shone tiger-tiger bright. "It's all a question of which side uses you, the angels or the dogs."

"We're on the side of the angels."

"Everybody else . . ."

"Isn't. You saw what it's like back there. That's par for the course DeepUnder. Every bit of social excrement, every possible dark deviation and incorrigible antisocial trait ends up down here. It's a steam-release valve for the Compassionate Society, and the Compassionate Society knows it. That's why they don't police down here. Out of sight, out of mind. Flush it all away and you won't smell it

anymore. You can forget all about the Rising Sun of Social
Compassion down here. Angels. Or dogs."

The fire had collapsed into embers on the slate hearth.
There being nothing more to be gainfully said and over-
much to be comprehended, Courtney Hall pulled her
blankets around her and rolled over with her back to the
dying fire. She dreamed dreadful dreams of bricks and
drowning, and plummeting in a blazing hogshead over
that kilometer-high waterfull of human turds.

The hands of Jonathon Ammonier's Fabergé watch had
flicked sixteen thousand seconds worth of time away over
its shoulder into the past between Courtney Hall's awakening and the time she saw the gray.

Three thousand second-hands later the Expedition to
the End of the World was spat out of the rapids at the end
of the tunnel into a lazy lagoon of putrid water penned
between canyonlands of industrial machinery. The raft
drifted indolently on the nowhere-in-particular currents of
the outfall sump, another gobbet of flotsam amidst the
floes of hydrocarbon wax and reefs of polymer bubbles and
lazy coiling anacondas of rainbow-colored oil. It revolved
sluggishly between the clashing rocks of the Seven Servants, titans of stained steel sheeting and pockmarked
pipework bearing names such as Universal Power and
Light, TAOS Consortium, Food Corps, UNIMEG. With a
soft shunt the expedition ran aground on a floe of rotting
pseudoalgae growing out from the mouth of a Kaan BioTech
outfall pipe. It took half an hour's hacking at the slimy,
ropy, nauseating stuff to free the raft and steer it once
more into the center of the stream. Where balsa log
had met mold, the wood had been digested to pulp.
Courtney Hall could not stop herself calculating, with
dreadful fascination, how long before the raft was dissolved, burned, melted, eaten into nothing. At the King's
command, she opened her leather folio to sketch the
prismatics and fluorescents of the chemical river, the walls
of the manufactories rising sheer out of the waters reaching
up and up and up and up to a ceiling so high and remote it
might have been a heaven. But when she opened her pencil

box, she found that some presence in the atmosphere had dissolved all her pastels to excrement-colored sludge.

All the food that day tasted of ketones and esters. Every throat and eye was red raw from vapors and emanations. Shortly before arbitrary nightfall the King of Nebraska called for his Tinka Tae to carry him out into the light to speak with his artist. As Jinkajou made busy with towels, compresses, and lotions, the King whispered to Courtney Hall, "Look after them, will you? I wasn't really very good for them at all. God, but not a Messiah. Should I have done it? Should I just have left them to be urban racoons?"

"You are the King."

"Ah!" His upraised finger seemed brittle as a stick of candy. "But they didn't ask for me to be their king or God or creator or anything."

"No one asks for their king," said Jinkajou unexpectedly.

The King of Nebraska clapped his hands. His cuticles were bleeding. "Didn't I tell you he was a philosopher? Ah, my furry friend." Then, as unexpectedly as his chamberlain had spoken, he whispered to Courtney Hall, "Don't trust them. Don't trust them at all." Courtney Hall knew enough of the ways of DeepUnder to understand that trust born purely of necessity is no trust at all.

A sense of change, of increased and unexpected motion, woke Courtney Hall one second before Xian Man Ray's shaking hand. Explanations were unnecessary; instantly awake, she felt the way the raft dipped and juddered beneath as the current grew stronger, faster with every moment. A splinter in the eye of the Body Corporate, the raft was swept along in a churning, onward-rushing procession of wax-bergs and foam-slicks, all hurrying faster, faster toward the dim blue rumble that Courtney Hall and Xian Man Ray and everyman jack of the crew down to the most junior racoon knew had to be a waterfall of industrial effluent pouring off the edge of the world.

Second by second, meter by meter, the current gathered strength and swept the raft closer to the edge. On either side the great stone faces of the Seven Servants stood sheer and unbroken. The dim blue rumble swelled to a roaring, to a thunder. The sailors watched a wax-berg the size of a small arcology tip ponderously, gracefully, and fall into nothing. They had a kilometer and a half left to them.

"Well, shug," said Xian Man Ray with deep disgust. Then they all saw it. A kilometer forward on the starboard bow, a dark rent in the perfect uniformity of the factories. The wedges of pollution piled up about the slit indicated this was not a tributary, but a branch.

All hands and paws fell on the steering oar. The thrust of adamant, dogged water wrenched shoulders, tore muscles. Sweat, screaming, tendons straining like bridge cables, the blind red miasma of absolute human effort, and over, above, under, behind everything, the thunder of waters.

With a titanic heave that spun the steering oar from all the grasping hands, a crest of hurtling water seized the raft and shied it through the entry into the tunnel beyond.

Only one minute into exhausted sleep, Courtney Hall was woken by a soft, intimate knocking from below. Knock knock knock, knock knock, knock knock knock; who's that knock-knock-knocking on the bottom of the boat? Knock knock. Go away. Knock. Shut up, can't you see I'm trying to sleep? Knock knock knock knock knock, and finally her exasperation overcame her exhaustion and she crept to the edge of the raft to see just what it was knock-knock-knocking, whether it be blind mutant albino alligators or feral pets or new mutations of man and toad and runaway biotech, or the dreaded giant radioactive turd monster, and tell it to stop it, just stop it, all right? An eddy caught the raft and the knock-knock-knocker bubbled to the surface. And looked at her.

Courtney Hall shrieked.

It had once been a trog. The patches of hair that clung to the blue flesh, the dissolved stump of a tail, identified what it had been. Somewhen in the arbitrary night it had become entangled in one of the frayed rope lashings that bound the raft together; the soft, come-hither knockings

had been the bare bones of the skull bobbing against the
balsa trunks. The cat's chrome steel claws slashed it loose,
but the dead trog bobbed along in their wake, a chaperone
through night to the place to come.

At five-fifteen Victorialand time the raft ground gently
to a halt. It had fetched up against another submerged
obstruction. Xian Man Ray thrust her hand into the water
to test the clearance and brought it up clutching a mat of
fibrous, decomposed bones. The Expedition to the End of
the World was beached upon a reef of skulls. It was a vile,
purgatorial labor, levering breaks in the dam of the dead.
The hands of the rococo watch stood at twelve-twenty
Victorialand time before the shoal of bones finally bulged
and gave before the flow of water. Still drained and sore
from their escape by the falls, the adventurers had not
even the energy to congratulate themselves as their raft
and accompanying trog were whirled through the breach
into the Fen of the Dead.

The Fen of the Dead was a place so far beyond the
conceiving of either Compassionate Society or DeepUnder
that the imagination could only deny its existence.

The underground river, released, broke into sluggish
braids and streams that meandered between the banks
and shoals of the dead. Like damned souls in a Joycean
inferno, they lay; the dead, heaped on top of each other
where the ebb and flow had laid them. Here skulls gazed
eyelessly from fine gray silt, there hands, fingers curled
upward, outward to the light; here the dead floated in a
tranquil lagoon, all drawn together to share smiles of fixed
serenity; there a surge of floodwater had carried away the
side of an islet to disclose the geological stratification of
the dead, from the half-sediment, half-petrified bodies of
centuries past through tangles of stringy, half-rotted bones
and gradually settling, snapping skeletons and rotting
cadavers to the bloat-faced, empty-eyed new arrivals half-
floating, half beached as if indecisive about where they
should spend eternity. Humans and racoons poled through
the miraculously clear waters, which swarmed with tiny
threads of eel-worms continuously tear-tear-tearing at the

dead flesh. Yulp and prollet, trog and tlakh, Scorpio and didakoi; the eel-worms devoured all impartially.

The stench of the dead was overpowering. Yet Jonathon Ammonier was filled with a luminous elation. He explained, "Don't you see? Somewhere among these billions of skeletons are the grins of my forty-three predecessors: puissant and prestigious Electors of Yu; all come to this same end in this same place as those they supposed to rule. But not this one! Not this one! This one's just passing through. This one will not end here like the others."

The stygian journey continued through channels shallow and sluggish and lined with bones. The raft was drawn toward the center of the Fen of the Dead where the great metal hopper, visible to the explorers since their entry into the netherworld, funneled down from the roof to touch the water. Passing beneath and slightly to starboard of the huge metal cone, all aboard could clearly view the fine trickle of soft yellow ash pouring from its nozzle to be carried softly away by whatever currents stirred the Fen of the Dead.

"His awful straik may nay man flee, *Timor mortis conturbat me*," sang the King of Nebraska.

The raft sailed on.

Courtney Hall did not want to dream that night, and the Spinner of Dreams granted her request. But of all Spirits of the Polytheon, none is so quixotic as the Spinner of Dreams, and in place of a dream he spun her a dull, dark emptying sleep more exhausting and oppressive than any nightmare. Courtney Hall rolled from her blankets worn and haggard to find herself looking at the sky.

She had almost forgotten what a *sky* was.

Curdled gray cloud filled her entire spread of vision, and she concluded with the dull logic of only-just-awake that the sky is just another ceiling to the world. But if sky, then . . .

"Where are we now?" Even as she spoke it she realized she had asked another of her inanely obvious questions.

The King of Nebraska was huddled in blankets by the smudge-fire sipping chocolate from a gilded mug.

"Outside," he said. "Look." He pointed. Courtney Hall looked where he pointed. Her life butterflied up within her.

The finger pointed beyond the great slow river, beyond the empty-eyed skull buildings, the snapped and painful towers and fallen bridges that stood upon its banks: to: the Wall.

Now she knew that everything since the afternoon when the Love Police brought the walls in on her life was all a thread of malevolence spun from the Dream Spinner's distaff.

The Wall spanned the world from edge to edge. It reached up to close off half the sky. It was the color that is blacker than black. There was nothing about it that could be excused by mere optical illusion. The Wall was. Her skill at perspective told Courtney Hall that she was some eighty kilometers from its foot. The distance, her calculations, only made the Wall all the more dreadful. It was five kilometers high.

In the sixteen-o'clock dream it had elated her. The reality dwarfed her. The Wall reduced all things to utter triviality: the tallest tower of the deserted city, the fly crawling on the back of Courtney Hall's hand. She could never hope to fly over this. Only the King of Nebraska refused to bow to the Wall. To him, it was not a wedge of finality, a world-girdling *ne plus ultra*. Rather, it was proof that the Beyond did exist. It was the edge of the Dreamtime. The Wall fired him, and the fire burned away all the outward signs of his sickness so that he was once again Monarch of Victorialand. He commissioned a triumphal work of art: the King before the Wall. As Courtney Hall searched her folio for clean, unstained paper and pencils, Angelo Brasil and Xian Man Ray held another of their whispered conferences.

"If you're going to paint, my dear, then a-hunting we shall go," declared Angelo Brasil. "My sister and my cat. It's Meatland out there, and we're getting a little bit tired of soybean." They pulled the raft in to a mooring against a rotting jetty and went ashore, Trashcan the cat springing off into the ruins, steel claws sprung. Courtney Hall had little more than the outlines charcoaled in when the hunting party returned. In sheer exuberance at being able to use her talent, Xian Man Ray flipped ahead to dump a pile of bloody skinned carcasses beside the fire. While Tinka Tae porters scavenged the pier for firewood, Courtney Hall decorously threw up into the river.

"Saints, what is that stuff?"

"Rat," said Xian Man Ray.

"Grow big out there, my dear," added Angelo Brasil. "Some the size of children."

At gut level Courtney Hall was still a child of the Compassionate Society, which subscribed to the principle of universal vegetarianism. She sat well upwind as the pseudosiblings spitted, then roasted their game.

"Hungry, my dear?" Angelo Brasil waved a cooked rodent leg, and when he was certain of Courtney Hall's attention, he tore a gobbet of meat from the bone. Courtney Hall recalled barbecuing Striped Knights and was sick and furious. In some things the Compassionate Society was right. It was wrong to eat animals. She turned her attention to her drawing. The King talked, as models, and Kings, will, in sotto voce inaudible to the diners over the din of their dining.

"I have this theory about dying, madam," he said. "I have this theory that it may be a most pleasant state indeed, to be dead. For the more I die each day, the stronger and stronger become the memories of my predecessors and the more I lose myself in them. I suspect, no, I know, that someday I shall be totally engulfed in the lives of the Electors, and that day I shall cease physically to be. I shall become a memory in a host of memories, and I must say, madam, I look forward to that very much. Tell me, madam, are you afraid of dying?"

"Yes," Courtney Hall said. And because no one can lie to a dying man, she added, "Very afraid."

"I was, too," said the King of Nebraska. "Various fears various years. When I was young and I learned that at some time in the future the dance must end, the music stop, the lights go off: that, I think, is the primal fear, the fear of inevitability. Then when you told me, back there in the dark passage, I was afraid again because you were confirming something I had always known but had been afraid to believe. That is the second fear: the fear that each of us carries within ourselves the seeds of our destruction. Now, I see that dying is only leaving the constraints of yourself to join the rest, to become a memory in a universe of memories; and I more than anyone know what that is like.

"I have memories going back to the Break, can you imagine it? I spend a lot of time being those memories; they're so much more interesting than the recent Electors. Spunkless lot, the recent Electors. I suppose I can't really blame them; history has all but stopped for the Compassionate Society. But back then, ah, my dear madam; lusty people, lusty days! Things happened then. A time of changes unlike any ever before. It takes a lot of history to stop history.

"I can remember this city when it stood above water, one of the great cities of the world, it was; and the flood waters rose and who now can remember its name, save me? Ten million people lived here, and now they and their city aren't even history anymore. It's quite a pleasing irony that no event in human history has ever had the trauma on the human race that the establishment of the Compassionate Society has. I've seen the world the way it was then, when there were hundreds of squabbling, separate nations each looking to their own interests to the exclusion of all others. Billions of people, the populations of whole nations, were moved, brought to this city, to make one Society where everyone would be happy, and where they could all be watched and monitored to ensure no one person could jeopardize another person's happiness. *Urbi est orbi* is what we are taught, yet from my memories it seems that that is another one of the Compassionate Society's gentle lies, that every human on earth is contained within one city. I cannot be certain, but I have caught drifts, suspicions, rumors that there may be other

Great Yus, as ignorant of our existence as we are of theirs, in other parts of the earth."

"I've always wondered that," said Courtney Hall, stroking in the skeleton cities in black pencil. "When I was small. When I grew up, it didn't seem to matter."

"Exactly!" crowed the King of Nebraska. "That is the triumph of the Compassionate Society. Outside of itself, nothing matters. Such wonderful arrogance! At the pinnacle of my vanity I could never hope to match that arrogance. Look at that wall"—she had looked at little else—"that wall is nine thousand kilometers round, five kilometers tall, one and a half kilometers thick; forty-seven thousand cubic kilometers of rock. Can you even begin to visualize the expenditure of human and material resources that went into its construction? And why? Arrogance. Sheer arrogance. So that humans would stop looking outward.

"Once we aspired to the stars. The outward urge. Not anymore. We have turned inward, into ourselves, in the name of happiness. Better to be happy, better to live a life without pain, or fear, within this wall than cry for the stars. There's no outside anymore."

Courtney Hall thought carefully before replying, "Yes, there is. You found it. I found it."

The King of Nebraska clapped his hands in delight. "Madam! You never cease to amaze me! You are, of course, quite correct. What has this entire expedition been, if not a cry for the stars? Jinkajou! Chamberlain! A bottle of that peach brandy I have been saving for exceptional days!"

A dreary gray wind bleered across the deserted city, sent shivers across the water. Warmed by the peach brandy of exceptional days, Courtney Hall huddled over her unfinished portrait of the King of Nebraska. That night (for here, outside, planetary time had reimposed itself on biological, subterranean time) after sleep had stolen out of the dead city to cover the raft, the King of Nebraska came to Courtney Hall. The pain in his bones and his bowels and his blood kept him from sleep. He whispered her to wakefulness.

"I don't trust them. So I'm not going to let them have it. I want you to have it, after."

She did not consciously take in his meaning, but the subconscious dream-mind understood, for when she dreamed, she dreamed that Xian Man Ray and Angelo Brasil were bouncing the King of Nebraska's head between them like a basketball, asking and asking and asking and asking the same question: "Where is it? Where is it? Are you going to tell us where it is?"

In the morning the raft was cast loose on the final stage of the journey to the Wall. The Wall dominated: every conversation, every sentence, every thought. Surface features were now discernible; not, as Courtney Hall had half-hoped, half-dreaded, the faces of the gods carved into its face, but perilously poised ramshackles of wood and stone and thatch that Jonathon Ammonier said were the settlements of the descendants of those construction workers who had chosen to remain with their work when the last basalt block had been lasered into place. He pointed out with his cane the patches of green and gold that were their steeply terraced fields. Courtney Hall caught the look of empires in his eyes again. Angelo Brasil spat delicately into the river.

As the raft approached the foot of the Wall the river swelled outward into a great wash from which the summits of sunken towers reached like the hands of drowning men, reaching for light. The image was so adamant, so apposite and uncanny that Courtney Hall screamed aloud when she saw the actual hand of the drowning man reaching for the light. The hand of some pre-Break Titan, some race of Behemoths created by those prehistoric people for purposes and plans unknown; and drowned, feet mired in the mud, as the floodwaters rose. A hand, grasping a torch. A beacon.

Only a statue.

But kilometers later, across the waters at the foot of the Wall, the image still made her shudder.

The weather was no exception to the Wall's domination. The winds and currents that had pushed the raft forward failed. All hands were set to paddling the remaining few kilometers. Courtney Hall bent to the oar and did not dare look up. To look up the face of a wall so high it seemed to be toppling over was instant vertigo. And Wall met water in a sheer, unbroken line. No opening. No grids, no vents, no tunnels, no spillways, no flumes, plumes, spumes. No way through.

No Beyond.

But the King of Nebraska's spirit remained unvanquished by the Wall's impenetrability.

"If we cannot go through, then we shall go over," he declared.

"'Over,' he says." Angelo Brasil wiped his blisters on his cycling shorts.

High above, the vertical farms cascaded green and gold down the higher slopes of the Wall.

"There must be paths, stairs, between the communities."

"But do they reach sea level, Your Majesty?" sneered Angelo Brasil.

"Only one way to find out." The King smiled. He pointed with his cane along the gently curving horizon of wall and water.

"Well, you can just do it without me, sweetie!" snapped Angelo Brasil. "I'm sick of this. Sick sick sick." With a toss of dreadlocks he stormed off to the stern to sit looking back at the drowned city and the wastelands beyond. Xian Man Ray sighed loud exasperation, impatience, sororal duty, and she went to offer comfort, sympathy, and to cajole and coax. Endless and enduring as the Wall, the Tinka Tae porters and engineers laid their small weights to the paddles, and under Jinkajou's barked instructions, the raft crept along the base of the Wall.

It was well after dark—twenty-two o'clock sky time (the discrepancy between it and Victorialand time, coupled with the fact that all food except for tofu steak and some gamy rat had been devoured that dinner, may have accounted for some of unraveled feelings)—before apologies were mumbled, forgivenesses offered and received. Which was just as well. Ten minutes later Trashcan the cyber-cat let out a yowl that set the raft rocking like a zook in a Jazz Hot club and stood stone still, fur bristling, pointing with her furry nose at the ladder cut into the obsidian face of the Wall.

In the
Editing Suite

Snipping, snipping, snipping: today Mr. Slike the Scissorman is on the *P*s. Busy scissors snipping, snipping; out they come, the hurtful *P*s, excised, edited, deleted, floating down to litter the Scissor-room floor: *panic* and *papacy* and *paranoia*, *piles* and *pernicious* and *political*, *plutocrat* and *prostitute* and *Presbyterian*; *priests* face to face with *oppressors*, *nihilists* with *martinets*, *lepers* with *killers*, *Jansenists* with *interrogators*, *heros* with *grumblers*, *field marshals* with *enslaved*, *dissidents* with *communists*, *bastards* with *aristocrats*: a rustling, chattering cocktail party of incompatibles facedown in the final democracy of the Scissor-room floor. Knee-deep in paper, Mr. Slike the Scissorman snips snips snips with manic glee, out out out with the old hurtful words, the cruel words, the divisive words. In his Scissor-room on the fifty-fifth floor, language is being shaped by the snipping scissors of the scissorman like a silhouette snipped by some street artist. By the time he reaches *zeal, zouave,* and *Zymotic disease* there will be no more words left for people's tongues to hurt each other with. There will be only kind, gentle, painfree words. The streets of Great Yu will resound with blessings, and language, like sweet perfume, shall, redeemed, fill the air. Often Mr. Slike the Scissorman pauses in his snip-snip-snipping to look forward to that day. Then, suitably reinspired, he returns to his holy task. Today the *P*s, tomorrow the *Q*s—good-bye *queens*, *queers*, and *querulousness*—how Mr. Slike the Scissorman loves his job! But then, he cannot very well do anything but, can he?

Kilimanjaro
West

Children's calls in marble
halls . . .

Hide'n'seek laughter scurrying down ringing corridors;
evocations of rustling silks and candelabras, hurrying down
ringing corridors: the laughter of children. Heard, just for
a moment, only a moment, then the corridors swell with
the rush and boom of *pneumatique* trains and the flap of
feet. Distant clanging, a bass hum that shakes the kilometers of brown marble corridors, a gust of warm electric air
that sets the chandeliers clinking and tinkling. Then, once
again, the laughter of children, singing down the corridors,
filling the airshafts and ventilation ducts, eventually wafted
with the warm, electric air out onto a wet and weary
Salmagundy Street where the slubberdegullions gathered for
warmth and companionship, all folded up in their brown
polyweather wrappers like old, well-picked scabs.

He first heard it there, by the Salmagundy Street
ventilator, and it was a quandary to him, for it filled an
empty, lost place inside him, yet it made that empty, lost
place more void, more remote. It called, seemingly to him
alone, and because he believed that he alone was graced
to hear it, he followed, out of the rain and the night,
under the brass sign that read PNEUMATIQUE MUNICIPAL,
down ringing brown marble corridors beneath ceilings
crusty with cherubs and the frozen rainstorms of chandeliers, over bridges of alabaster filigree, across cavernous
domed concourses and echo-haunted platforms; he followed,

it led, always just around a corner, just down a flight of
steps, just across the tracks.

Others shared this station with him: near the entrance
to the Dalcassian Gate downline, a trio of tlakhs in masks
and streetgowns, crouched over their instruments, intent
upon their thin, ascetic music. Time and again his path
sent him across theirs, but he was reluctant to disturb their
devotions. Where the lacquered ventilation grilles exhaled
warm air, congregations of slubberdegullions, a caste of
registered mendicants psychologically unsuited for any ac-
tive part in the Compassionate Society, had unrolled their
wrappers to steal a little cozy. Glittering cabochon famulus
eyes watched the man who called himself Kilimanjaro
West as he stepped between shrouded bodies drunk coma-
tose on industrial ethanol, sacramental intoxicant and liba-
tion to whatever Celestial patronized the slubberdegullions.
Famulus eyes watched, famulus bodies pulsed as they
drew their wards' blood through their own web of veins
and arteries and purged it of poisons. The Binge Eternal;
with no fear of hangover or alcoholic poisoning or DTs or
cirrhosis. The marble galleries of Salmagundy Street station reeked of blue ethanol and old urine.

And always just around the corner, just down the
staircase, just across the induction tracks: children's calls
in marble halls. Enough of children's calls in marble halls;
let us speak of *luck*. These things are connected, if you
know where to look. Luck, you see, had pushed Kilimanjaro
West off the guttering of that shop in Ranves, and as he fell
five stories, luck had darted ahead to arrange for a cycle-
drayload of semisolid biobase support plasm to be underneath at that precise moment when his body and planetary
curvature would have intersected. Luck had also arranged
for that consignment of gel to pass through the Love Police
cordon ("PainCriminal at large, yezz, cizzen, dangerous
PainCriminal," which made the wingers gasp, and then
gasp again, all the louder when they learned that this
danjeruzz PaneCrimmal was an *artist*, an *actor*, a *Raging
Apostle*, Yah sakes!) without so much as a sleepstick prod-
ded into the rapidly solidifying gel. Luck had prompted

Kilimanjaro West to struggle free before his body heat set the stuff rigid, and luck it was steered his trail of slime through street after street through boro and prefecture until it brought late night and cold misery together in the warmth of the Salmagundy Street *pneumatique* ventilation grille. Where, treacherous as any late-night lover, luck had turned her back on him and stalked away under the neons and sprays of steam from the tenement heating ducts. For he had been seduced by the laughter of children. Forsaken by luck, the object of his fascination always remained just around the corner, just down those steps, just across those tracks.

The thin, acid harmonies of the tlakh trio grew now louder, now softer. At the foot of a cascade of marble steps he found a slubberdegullion woman piled like dung. She had not yet drunk herself into oblivion: a rancid bottle of blue ethanol invited Kilimanjaro West to communion.

Children's calls in marble halls ...

"What are they, why are they laughing?"

"Ainzhels," mumbled the old woman, eyes focusing and defocusing as if searching for some microscopic universe close by. "Ainzhelsainjillsanizells. Doan messwiddem, doan go neerem. Ainzhels doan follow no rules, no, no no, no rools for dem ..." She gave a great wail, as if some denizen of that neighboring universe (angel, demon, neither, both) had stepped through and sent her bottle of old blue smashing against the marble wall. "Angels!" Then she burped and the famulus clinging to her neck measured her blood alcohol levels and threw the neural switch that tripped her into unconsciousness.

On the Jamboree line eastbound platform he found a municipal shrine. It was a sign of how deeply he had been absorbed into the life of the city that he no longer found these episodic erections of wood and plastic and concrete remarkable, even noteworthy. This particular shrine was just another imaginative mélange of shells and canopies and halos and minor deities scrambling for attention, dedicated in this instance to a Cosmic Madonna suckling twins at a pair of outsize alabaster breasts.

Recalling other twins. Other breasts.

Kansas Byrne. The Raging Apostles. BeeJee &ersenn in her glass menagerie. Even the room with the cold and the universe inside it. Why was it that every experience was taken away from him? Why were things lost as soon as they were found?

He did not want it to be that way. It did not have to be that way. Recalling his glimpses of citizens invoking their deities, he bowed to the shrine, clapped his hands—three sharp, precise explosions—and asked, "Where is Kansas Byrne?"

The Cosmic Madonna smiled banally while her entropic twins, Order and Chaos, fought for the teat.

"Where is she? I want to find her."

Whispers of wind scampering down the platform stirred prayer tickets into a syllable: *Why?*

"Because I . . . because she . . . because."

A blast of sound. A wave of hot electric air. The marble chamber boomed like a gong as the Templeoaks–St. Mauritzburg Limited pounded through. Disoriented, Kilimanjaro West was taken up in a vision.

Not the vision he had asked for.

A nameless vision, a remembering.

An itch in the bones. An echo in the skull: *light.* Endless, boundless light, a domain of shifting planes and volumes of many-colored light. Here each color is a consciousness, a character, a memory, a *voice,* and as the beams of many-colored light meld and mingle with each other to form new shades, new voices, new songs, new characteristics and consciousnesses are born to breed new memories: he is a creature of light, ever moving, ever changing: no, more than that, he is the uncreated, he *is* light.

He remembers: darkness. Unseeing, a void of beholding, not blindness, rather an absence of anything to see. But there is sensation, of stone for bone and steel for sinews, of power blazing along channels of ancient energy fueled by fires deep within, the ceaseless surge of a billion corpuscles through the arteryways of his body, and the sound, the roar of the blood in his ears. Somewhere a heart is beating, somewhere lungs fill and empty carrying the breath of life to the billion bustling corpuscles, and from the gut depths come ruminant belchings and bubblings of healthy digestion. He is huge, he contains multitudes, billiontudes, it is as if (*yes,* now he understands, though the mechanics of that understanding is incomprehensible to him) he is the city; its streets, buildings, manufactories, arcologies, parks, playgrounds, power plants, agrariums, are his physical body. Now he understands the darkness, the blindness. The city is all, where might there be a beyond from which to observe everything?

Remembering.

And the laughter of children . . . Loud. Close.

Unambiguous. A physical presence. He turned . . . Hands. A forest of hands. Soft, open, reaching, more and more and more and more *hands,* pouring out of the walls, the floors, the ceiling, cracks in the world spewing hands, hands with eyes between the outspread fingers, all around him, enfolding him in a web of interlaced fingers, touching, brushing hands, face, hair, and with each touch the hands drew something out of him, some power, and they grew stronger on that power and he grew weaker so that he could not resist them, and the web of fingers propelled him along the deserted platform toward the mouth, a brass mouth, no (reason and rhyme and all his painfully learned associations slipping away like fish into the sea), an elevator, an ornate brass-and-crystal cage padded with buttoned satins, and he offered no resistance as the doors, teeth, mouth closed on him, and with a whine of cables and counterweights, the brass elevator descended. . . . It passed through unsuspected depths of the *pneumatique municipal:* laagers of powered-down trains, giant compressors, track maintenance robots black-and-gold like busy bees, electrical generators; then down into an even more unsuspected landscape, a place of wheels and industry, of massive, grinding machines, of titanic domes wrapped in steel pipes illuminated by forks of artificial lightning ten kilometers long that danced between spherical electrodes like minor moons. Nothing remotely human-scaled: brass valves the size of houses vented geysers of steam, hoppers that could easily have held a tenement block each moved steadily along a conveyor line toward some unimaginable end-point. The brass elevator inched across a twenty-level rendition of the Universal Power and Light sun-gold asterisk never intended to be viewed with human eyes. This was a place for machines, a Valhalla of the gods of Industry. The hundred-meter sunburst was the secret name the machines spoke to themselves alone.

Turning away from the oppressive weight of industry, the man and his captors found space in the crowded gondola for mutual examination. Angels. Children. The laughter of... angelchildren. Boys. Girls. Boy-girls, too young for gender differences to be important. Naked. Their hands hung by their sides, empty. Their eyes...

Eyes like stones. Painless, joyless, inhuman stones. Demon-eyes in angel-faces. One boy, taller, older, with greater muscular definition and a dark wedge of pubic hair, spoke.

"What is this gesture you are making with your hand?"

He had not even noticed he was doing it. "It is called the *nona dolorosa*, the hurt-me-not. It is a sign we make when we are afraid we will be hurt."

"We are never afraid," said the boy. "We never hurt." No doubt was permitted. Certainty was written in his eyes. Kilimanjaro West found himself remembering the milky breasts of the Cosmic Madonna. He looked away from the stone-eyes through the glass floor of the gondola and saw another eye, a tiny black needle-eye incredibly far below. The time it took for that needle-eye to expand into a dark shaft was an indication of the dimensions of this machine temple. Dark clenched around the elevator like a fist. Just as Kilimanjaro West was quite certain the darkness was bottomless and the darkness of his own past, the brass gondola emerged into a subterraneanscape as alien to the Valhalla of the gods as that had been to the rain-swept streets of Yu.

The elevator sank into a gullet of translucent, throbbing flesh, a crumb lodged in the throat of God. Glimpsed through the vaguely translucent red membrane, arterial ducts pulsed with fluids, power crackled along neural networks half-mechanical, half-living. At the limit of vision, giant alveoli veined with capillaries and glowing with their own corrupt light swelled and contracted. And all things resounded to the beat of a great, unseen heart.

The leader of the angel-children again broke silence.

"Danty," he said. "You may call me Danty. It is not my name, it is not who I am. It is what I am to you. I have no name. We have no use for names, but I am told you must call me Danty. This is the body of our God." Murmurs. Shifts of body posture. "Our God, our mother, the Cosmic Madonna. It was she gave you to us. Though you have no famulus, as the rebels do not, her eyes are everywhere. She has been waiting for you. She is patient, but she cannot wait forever."

"Why does she want me?"

"To test if you are the one."

"Which one?"

"The one ordained to lead us into our inheritance." The elevator throbbed to the heartbeat of a God.

"What is your inheritance?"

"The world. The future. We are the future of humanity."

Through the floor Kilimanjaro West could see a sphincter dilating into a sphere of cold blue light.

"I do not understand."

"We cannot feel pain. Physical, emotional, psychological. Heat cannot burn us, cold cannot freeze us. No physical thing can hurt us, no wound of the heart can cause us anguish. Colors. All we feel are colors. And the sound of God's singing. And joy. Inexpressible joy. We are without fear or shame or guilt or conscience. We are the ultimate achievement of human evolution, the perfect citizens of the perfect, painless world to come."

The elevator passed into the sphere of blue: a globe of biological support plasm, its precise boundaries difficult because of the light that seemed to come from everywhere. Floating in the gel, in anabiotic suspension, thousand upon thousands of human bodies. Tangles of tubes, coils of wire coiled from the bodies of the men and women, and Kilimanjaro West saw that some twitched and spasmed in their artificial sleep, and some seemed to cry out silently.

"SoulCriminals," said Danty the guide. "In return for their rehabilitation into the Compassionate Society, some particular offenders are selected to donate eggs or sperm to our ovariums. There is no pain. Of course. Neither is there any choice. They sleep, and when they have paid their biological debt to society, they are returned once again to the jurisdiction of the Ministry of Pain, and on awakening in their counseling units they will recall only that their sleep was filled with pleasing erotic dreams.

"How long do you keep them here?"

"The most productive has served us for fifty-three years. They do not grow old as we that are left here grow old. But even for her, it will only be as if a night's sleep has passed."

The descent continued.

Out of the sea of sex-dreamers into the womb of the Cosmic Madonna: a tall cylinder of hexagons within hexagons, a hexagonal chamber lined with thousands of individual ovariums. Cocooned within, fetuses watched the elevator descend with their little frog-eyes.

"Our brothers and sisters," pronounced Danty. "The donated eggs and sperm are genetically screened and then biotechnologically engineered to produce individuals with neural systems incapable of registering pain. It is a marvel of genetic neuro-engineering: pathways are redesigned, new connections made so that we recognize that damage is done without the physical sensation of *pain*. Only light and sound and joy."

Without shame. Without pride.

From the womb of the new society into the bowels of the old. Gehenna. The place of eternal dissolution. Bubbled up in synthflesh capsules, citizens of the Compassionate Society, all classes, all castes. All conscious. Some, presumably the most recently incarcerated, beat, tore, threw themselves at the transparent wall of their cells. The resilient synthetic flesh absorbed their blows as utterly as the biobase support gel within stifled their voices. The more established inmates (how long? hours? days? months? *years?*) floated resigned to their captivity, hovering on the borderlands between consciousness and dreamtime. Pale tendrils extruded from dark irises in the membrane walls caressed their naked skulls. Descending, ever descending, the elevator entered the demesne of the long-term inmates. Frail, pale, vaguely luminous mummies, their eyes stared into the darkness and their skulls were open for the questing tendrils to touch and feel and heal their brains.

Who were these damned? What was their crime? What was their punishment?

"PainCriminals." Danty the eternal guide. "Incorrigibles. Grave offenders agaist the Compassionate Society. But do not imagine that they are being punished, please. The Compassionate Society is, above all else, humane."

Floating bodies. Naked brains. Row upon row upon row. Rank upon rank upon rank.

"Then what?"

"Rehabilitated. An experiment, in cooperation with the Ministry of Pain. Our mother is impatient. She cannot wait forever for her children to inherit the earth. Though our numbers grow daily, we are still a mere handful in the face of the millions who inhabit Yu. And we are young, only a handful of us have reached breeding age, as I have. Thus the experiments: to ascertain whether it is possible to adapt normal citizens to be as we are: incapable of feeling, of conceiving, pain."

So many. Rank upon rank upon rank. Row upon row upon row.

"Some respond more readily than others: it takes only a few days for their neural pathways to be reconfigured and the new behavior patterns enforced. Others, those with stronger wills, less socially compliant egos, it takes time. Weeks. It some recalcitrant cases, it may take years." A shrug.

This is the future and I still do not fully understand the past it is to replace.

"So much better than the old system and the stigmata

of a rehab famulus clasped to the neck monitoring and adjusting neural chemical levels."

So, they had a concept of a *better*. And therefore, a *worse*. So there may be no guilt and no conscience, but there was discrimination. A sense of *quality*. And how was this worse *worse*? Were the lights less dazzlesome brilliant? Did the music of the gods play out of tune? He began to suspect that pain was not abolished. Merely brilliantly disguised. He began to suspect that pain could not be abolished. By man or god. Or machine.

The elevator came out of the hadean red into pure light. Dazzled, disoriented, Kilimanjaro West was descending like a psalm upon a land of blue skies and green meadows singing with flowers.

In this land were trees and fountains. In this land were grave, stately birds three times the height of a man. In this land were friendly, bumbling, gleeful little animals. In this land were giant apples half as tall again as the trees that grew them, giant peaches, giant pears, giant strawberries and pomegranates. In this land were butterflies the size of small clouds. In this land were shaggy unicorns. And in this land, everywhere, were children, naked children, angel-children, walking, running, playing, laughing, sleeping in the tall grass, eating the giant apples, peaches, pears, strawberries, pomegranates, riding the shaggy unicorns.

A heartbeat. Distant. Distinct. Systole, diastole, systole, diastole. This was the center of the circle. Kilimanjaro West was being lowered into the inner ring, the navel of the body of the machine that called itself the Cosmic Madonna.

The elevator approached the meadows singing with flowers. The elevator touched the tips of the grass, the petals of the wildflowers. The elevator touched the ground. The elevator stopped.

Chapter 8

At four thousand meters the fog lingered well into the afternoon before the sun dissolved it into blue.

Born and raised under dark clouds (those same clouds that at four thousand meters are called fog) Courtney Hall glowed in sun and blue sky. Blue was the thing she had always dreamed of: pedaling and panting her course through the realm of the Celestials, and when the fog was at last spirited away, she drew for the pure joy of light, the pure joy of the dimension of *blue* beyond the wicker window. Not all her company shared her blue exultation: children of the heavier sky of concrete and steel, Angelo Brasil and Xian Man Ray hid away from the agoraphobic blue. But when altitude sickness permitted, Jonathon Ammonier reveled in the light, ordering his bearers to carry his litter into the window bay where he could survey his realm, from the lake of the drowned city up along the river valley where the dead buildings shouldered together like bones, all the way to the line of smoke and silver that was the edge of the manufactories and industrial units of East Yu.

This had been the King of Nebraska's most prolonged bout of altitude sickness. For three days the Expedition to the End of the World had depended on the hospitality of the Ramshambé Nation while Jonathon Ammonier fluctuated between feverish, sweaty hallucination and periods of tranquil lucidity when he would come to the window to look down upon the world. But no one was fooled. Even the Elders of the Ramshambé Nation knew that it was not altitude sickness. But still they maintained the pretense to each other that this was a passing thing, soon over and done with. The remaining three human members of the expedition did not want to cease being an expedition here, one kilometer from the top.

This was Jonathon Ammonier's fourth attack of altitude (hah! sweet euphemism! *radiation*) sickness. Courtney Hall was still thankful to whatever deities presided over the Wall that the King's first bout had been held off until they had reached Bascombe, the capital of the Yea! people, lowest of the stratified castes that lived on the Wall. Too weak to climb, Jonathon Ammonier had been portaged up that first few hundred meters in a litter. Having to treat a sick (sweet euphemism again: *dying*) man on the stairways and ladders and ramps that zigzagged up the wall, the paths so narrow two people could not safely stand abreast: a shuddering prospect to Courtney Hall, his artist, and increasingly, his keeper. That first had been the mildest attack; an afternoon and a night of feverish rantings and screamings at Jinkajou for impossible requests while the warm monsoon rain of these low tropical altitudes drummed on the grass roof, and Angelo Brasil and his pseudosister whispered little conferences full of cutting, slashing hand movements.

The third attack had been the worst. Saints and spirits had not been generous then. Caught in the open on a ladder climbing along the seventy-degree face of the Wall; a wind had suddenly come funneling down the chimney between the Wall and one of its buttresses . . . Nightmare. As the icy air from higher altitudes struck the warmer subtropical air of two and a half thousand meters, instant freezing fog had enveloped the Expedition. Struck blind. One misplaced footfall, one careless paw . . . the long bounce to the water. And reconnaissance reported no settlement, no shelter for another three or four hundred meters vertical, five kilometers horizontal.

And Jonathon Ammonier had decided he wanted to get out of his bed.

Courtney Hall had tried to wrestle him back onto his litter, but with a cry he had swung out with his gold-topped cane. She'd ducked. Just. Blind reflex. Afterward, when she saw how close she had been to the big jump, she had been paralyzed with fear. Tinka Tae bearers fled squealing. The litter had fallen and almost tipped the cane-wielding King of Nebraska into two and a half thousand meters of airspace. Suddenly, salvation from nowhere: Xian Man Ray flipping in from twenty meters up ahead to lay His Majesty Jonathon I of Victorialand and Beyond cold with a haymaking wallop to the jaw. They'd tied him to his litter with torn strips of his blue silk handkerchief and wrestled the ranting, foaming monarch through three hours of freezing fog to the UnderGate of Tulby, capital of the Dooneyites.

Who had not wanted to let them in. A face behind the bamboo floor hatch, the UnderSentry had initially threatened them with water, crud, boulders, darts, boiling oil. The problem was coming from below, it seemed. Contact with untouchables. The castes that inhabited the Wall lived in literal hierarchy. Vertical stratification increasingly exclusive with altitude. Even by exchanging words with ones from below, the UnderSentry was committing a serious act of personal defilement. It took two hours of careful theologically loaded negotiation to convince him that they were not underlings but altogether other, and that mercy was the touchstone of the more advanced spiritual beings.

After two days of recuperation and mercy mild, the Expedition had left Tulby to continue onward and upward, back and forth through the vertical pastures of the Dooneyites where herdpersons tended to their "cows"; bulbous piebald things closer to a cross between a lamprey and a sloth than the gentle kine of the forgotten age of animal husbandry. These gravid sacs of juice clung to the seventy-degree meadows with sucker feet. The sound of their suckering about in search of fresh grazing disgusted Courtney Hall. Onward and upward, to the next kingdom, the caste of the Masters of Solitude, two hundred meters upWall.

The eighty castes and nations of the Wall existed in a grim parody of the Compassionate Society that had established and duly forgotten them. Each nation was a long, thin band of territoriality averaging seventy meters high and fifty kilometers long. The primary political principle was that it was easier to travel horizontally than vertically, effectively reducing life on the Wall to one dimension. The citizens of the wickerwork towns that clung like pups to the black masonry knew more about their neighbors fifty kilometers to right and left than their neighbors fifty meters above their heads or beneath their feet. Stratified insularity. Ascending through these levels, Courtney Hall observed a curious inverse relationship at work. Each level regarded the one above it as in some way spiritually superior and the one below it as spiritually inferior, yet technological ability declined with altitude as the Wall's distinct biomes became less rich and varied. From the vigorous wood-age societies of the lowest tropical zones to the two-kilometer bamboo houses of the temperate wetlands to the thatch and wattle of the grasslands heavenward, Courtney Hall had climbed through orders of increasing spiritual status and decreasing levels of technological competence. The Wall, she concluded, had been settled from top down. Certainly no incentive would have called those early engineers to migrate upward, and only a top-down diaspora satisfactorily explained the spiritual mores of the Wall dwellers.

She was very pleased with her bit of anthropological reasoning.

However, there was a grimmer turn yet to the Wall's parody of the Compassionate Society. Centuries of isolation and exposure on the bare face of the Wall had hammered the benevolent totalitarianism of the doctrine of Social Compassion into absolutist despotisms of the most repressive form. Oligarchies, heptarchies, monarchies; meritocracies, bureaucracies, theocracies: whether under the omniscient eyes of saints and ancestors hovering wan and insubstantial in the icy air above the top of the Wall, or the scrutiny of the unresting Guardians of Righteousness who earwigged on every nighttime murmur, every lover's whisper, every childish cry, for Sinful

Thought, or watched by the serried rows of painted wooden gargoyles, called famuluses by their devotees, and holding health, wealth, and good fortune in their charmed paws, or monitored by the spirit tattoos on wrist and forearm that winged every errant thought straight to the Council of Nine; the societies that clung to the Wall were an alarming foresight into what the Compassionate Society might become if ever the equilibrium between State, Industry, and Religion were upset.

Might?

Had, Courtney Hall. *Had* to you. Totalitarianism without the benevolence. Tyranny, but not benign.

From the window of the wicker room tied to the basalt slabs with woven straw ropes, Courtney Hall could look down to see all the sins of the Compassionate Society spreading out and away from her, sweeping down to the waters that covered the past.

The King of Nebraska's evening announcement that he was feeling well enough for the Expedition to recommence the following morning was greeted with weary pleasure. It would be good to be busy with something outside of themselves. They were all heartily sick of themselves. With every meter climbed, Courtney Hall's suspicion of the pseudosiblings also mounted. And their cat. Angelo Brasil's temper had deteriorated with altitude: Courtney Hall could no longer say anything to him without inviting a scathing reply. Unaccustomed as any yulp to the two-edged syllable, she found his sarcasms especially slicing. Even Xian Man Ray, by far the more affable of the pair, seemed to have a predatory beam in her eye. And the cat just licked itself. Licked and licked and licked itself. Licked and licked and licked and licked itself until Courtney Hall wanted to scream.

It was all to do with the collective personas of the forty-three Electors of Yu.

They wanted them.

Jonathon Ammonier wanted to give them to Courtney Hall.

Courtney Hall did not want forty-three dead souls.

She told the forty-fourth Elector as much that night in one of their by-now-habitual nocturnal conversations, King and Artist.

"But you must, madam! They will make you safe!"

"I'm not safe?"

"Heed the words of a king: Do not trust anyone DeepUnder who tells you he is an angel but salivates like a dog."

"How will they make me safe?"

"By making you valuable."

Climbing the ladder to her wicker night-cell, she saw Angelo Brasil squatting outside the door to his adjacent sleepery.

"Good evening to you, my dear." There was enough of a moon to make his teeth shine white and flat.

Even when the Love Police and the Ministry of Pain and all the corporate will of Great Yu had come howling after her, Courtney Hall had never felt so threatened.

It took from six o'clock dawn until noon the next day for the Expedition to the End of the World to gain one hundred meters: "Thirteen meters per hour," as Angelo Brasil bitched on one of the many halts for Jonathon Ammonier's racoon bearers to gasp a little thin air into their lungs. Angelo Brasil bitched almost continuously now, and always where Courtney Hall could not but hear him: the brightness, the cold, the thin air, the altitude, his hair, his hands, *look* at the state of his clothes, he felt tired, depressed, sick, cold. Cold mostly. Courtney Hall could understand that complaint. Even protected by fat in the final stages of metamorphosis to muscle, she felt the nip when the Expedition passed out of direct sunlight into the shadow of one of the buttresses. She had been only too glad to accept the Ramshambé Nation's gift of a pair of knitted woollen leggings. Understood, but did not sympathize. If Angelo Brasil chose pride and fashion over humility and warmth, he could keep his folly to himself. As for herself, she had been suffering through her first period in ten years without one whisper of complaint. She suspected that two thirds of the decay in Angelo Brasil's character could be out of frustration that his abilities and talents were useless on the Wall. He was resentful at toiling for kilometers along terraces and ledges in search for ladders or stairways to the next level while Xian Man Ray went flip! flip! flip! from stairway to balcony to terrace to ladder as she scouted out new lands and terrains.

They were all to get a lot colder very soon.

The final two hours of that day's ascent were through a blizzard that whirled up with sudden malevolence to engulf them. Being frightened was the norm for Courtney Hall's life now. DeepUnder she had been frightened so diversely and constantly that she thought she was immunized to fright. The blizzard paralyzed her.

Whiteout. Endless; a white hell. Heaving up an endless staircase of slick gray ice, each meter must be the last, must, must, must, but always there was another meter, another step beyond, and Xian Man Ray was shrieking, begging, pleading with her to go on, only a few hundred meters more and then there would be shelter: a hundred meters? a hundred parsecs, the shelter could be on Alpha Centauri or pinned to Orion's belt for all the likelihood that she would see it, but she kept climbing, meter by meter by meter, wrestling that litter up one step, two steps, three steps, four; each step a triumph in itself, but please, no one could surely, reasonably expect her to make it one hundred and ninety-eight, one hundred and ninety-nine, two hundred steps: that was impossible, a fantasy, a lie to keep her from lying down and rolling over in the snow where the screaming, slashing wind could not touch her, giving up and falling asleep, which she wanted more than anything, anything . . . Ahead of her, blurs in the white fog, Jinkajou and the porters crept like crustaceans, crusted with rime, up one step, two steps, three steps, four. Behind her, Angelo Brasil's sarcasms had been sacrificed to fuel the task of putting one foot in front of the other in front of the other in front of the other.

She caught herself screaming at herself, screams of alternate encouragement and despair, and no one could hear them but herself, and even she poorly. Snow-blind.

Winter kills. Embedded in a globe of whirling white atoms
forever and ever and ever and ever, amen, amen, praise
Yah . . . She became vaguely aware that Xian Man Ray was
shaking her by the shoulders. Didn't she know how important it was that she kept counting one step, two steps,
three steps, four, one step, two steps . . . What? Here?
Where? Then everything white went black and everything
black went white, and incredibly, there was an ending.
And heat. And warmth. And light. And faces.

The Tabreeni were vain creatures of paradox. Loftiest
and least of the eighty castes, they dwelled a little lower
than the angels (whose astral forms could be seen shimmering
over the capstones of the Wall) in a land of bitter poverty
and permanent cold. These they accepted without question: a little asceticism was small price for nearness to the
angels. The house in which they accommodated their
guests was nothing more than a cluster of wicker grapes
suspended from a stone bollard, niggardly heated by stone
fat lamps. Yet the Tabreeni lived on so exalted a spiritual
plane that they could not speak directly to their guests (a
defilement so dreadful as to warrant three weeks solitary
purification in a wicker hermitage up where the ice fields
reached cold fingers down into the demesne of the Tabreeni)
and communicated what little information they thought
necessary through notes dictated to lower-order agricul-
turals and scratched by them onto wax tablets. They lived
on birds, bugs, eggs and a variety of high-altitude potato
that was the only staple that would grow under the breath
of the ice, and once Courtney Hall realized she was finally
out of the cold and the wind and the snow, once a little
warmth and a little life had returned in the glow of the
camping stove (an abominable luxury to the Tabreeni
elders), she was able to appreciate what poor, paltry, vain
creatures these lords of spirituality were. Their oil lamps
gave as little warmth as their smiles, their food was cold
and watery, and the wind found every gap and flaw in their
wicker shelters. No one slept well in their macramé
hammocks that night.

The blizzard had cleared by early next afternoon, and

both Tabreeni and Expedition were glad to part company. Three hundred meters above was the End of the World: a holy place of ice and fire, hypnotic in the way the aurora light hovered over the ramparts of ice like the seven million veils covering the face of God, a place that beckoned, called, fired, inspired.

And with divine capriciousness, betrayed.

One hundred meters from the top of the Wall, the stairway to heaven vanished under a lobe of green ice. Three hundred steps from the End of the World. Three hundred light-years. The Expedition failed, its fire blown out in frustration and depression. Everything was over. The End of the World was unattainable. What to do now but return with humility to the inhabited lands and await the inevitable with some dignity.

The inevitable King would have none of it.

"Either we get to the top or I exercise command option Omicron."

"You sick old bastard!" hissed Angelo Brasil.

"What is command option Omicron?" asked Courtney Hall, just another bastard from a world of legalized bastardry.

"An emergency contingency should soulschip ever fall into unauthorized hands," said Jinkajou. "Wipe all stored memories. Blank. Clean as toilet bowl, as His Majesty, Bless 'Im, say. The lot. Erased."

The sick old bastard smiled. "Now," he said, "I have a plan. Who'd like to hear it?"

It was not a brilliant plan, not even for a sick old bastard, but in the absence of any other it had a certain intelligence. It involved Xian Man Ray's flipping to the top of the Wall ("Don't know if I could flip that far in one go, the further you shift through unspace, the more it takes out of you") with a two-hundred-meter coil of polyrope ("Oh, come on, the energy expenditure increases with the square of the mass"), which they could just about make if they knotted together all the available sections they had scavenged from the raft. Once there, she could use the stove to melt and freeze a pulley into the ice ("How much you think this is going to mass; twenty, fifty, hundred ks, eh?") and run the rope through it to form a kind of winch. ("Angelo, tell this suck this is impossible. Flatly. Categorically. I am not doing this.") Angelo took his pseudosister a few steps back down the stairway to/from heaven. They argued while Courtney Hall pastelled down her impressions of the cold and holy ice-scapes of the End of the World.

It took many hours for the Expedition to complete all necessary preparations; the sky was dark, the aurora bright, when Xian Man Ray, furious and apprehensive and laden with a seventy-five kilo pack, made the series of five flips that took her to the top of the Wall. The hands of the ormolu fob were closing up on midnight by the time the last load had been hauled up the icefall to the End of the World.

The End of the World was a wind-polished plain of metal one kilometer across, an almost geometrical abstraction of finality bounded by knuckles of ice gripping the Wall like a desperate man. Exhausted, the Expedition camped on the open plain, drawn into a huddle around the portable heater. Above them the sky was huge and close, and beyond the aurora's shiftings and seemings, the stars were vaguely threatening. Jonathon Ammonier babbled quietly, almost devotionally, to the ghosts of his ancestors, and everyone could smell how close he was to death. He should have died that night, a shivering carcass of cancers. Only his will to be King kept him on the warm edge of death. While dawn was yet an hour off, his comrades carried him across the steel plain and over the fringe of ice to the far side of the Wall. There were no complaints. No whispers. No words at all. Portents of something enormous waiting beyond the ice out there in the morning took away their words. They set the litter down and waited for the End of the World.

The End of the World came slowly, in little shafts and slivers of revelation, each successive revelation the key to comprehending what had already been revealed. The sun rose, and Courtney Hall beheld the Beyond.

Oozing. Seeping. Steaming. Rotting. Rainbow sheens of oil. Scabrous patches of radioactive green. Lakes of boiling sulfur, chrome-yellow fumaroles. Rafts of crusted sewage kilometers across floating on soft-slowing lava-sheets of polymer slag. Geysers. Gushers. Fountains of oil. Volcanoes of boiling sludge. Bergs of wax pushed up through the lap and flow of putrid waste. The morning wind kicked sprays of bubbles from frozen waves of foam. Atolls of stringy garbage, bale upon bale upon bale upon bale upon bale upon bale of it. Protruding girders, rust-rotted like decaying rib cages. Low, evil acid-mists hurried from popping mouth-holes and vents. Lightning played with continuous, manic glee. Numinous, luminous aurora ghost lights. Blazing flares of gas bubbles percolating up from beneath, pillars of fire by day and by night by which the eyeless things that lived out there sought and fought each other. Not human things. Not even properly living things. The dregs and lees of biotechnology recombined and nurtured by the sludge-lands of the Beyond and given some almost-life by the lightning and the radioactive glow. Things that crept and inched and poured in search of each other. Here a quivering pagoda of melting leaves dripped caustic sap onto the carpet of eyes and teeth that was gnawing at its root. In the center of the Beyond, they fought, in the heart of the nothing, the Ginnungagap that reached to the horizon where a line of yellow fire poured black smoke like oil into the atmosphere, as if the edge of the world were burning.

It was Xian Man Ray who broke the silence after a second, a minute, an hour. She sat down on the ice and cried; silent tears of absolute heartbreak. Courtney Hall knelt to comfort the small woman. When it spoke, Jonathon Ammonier's voice was a whisper, a song, a prayer. "Didn't you always wonder what they did with it? Didn't you always wonder where it all went: all the pain and the hurt and the sorrow; didn't you wonder where they put it, the shit and the piss and the pus and the poison and the pain of the Compassionate Society? Or did you think that it just disappeared, vanished into the air? Well, now you know. Now I know." The King of Nebraska laughed; a dry bark that became a racking cough. He spat bloodstained saliva.

"One more gob in the ocean, Sam. I suppose I always knew it was here. Rationally, I knew it all had to go somewhere, but dammit, dreams and visions, they aren't rational, are they?"

Courtney Hall surveyed the wasteland to which the Compassionate Society had condemned all the hurtful things. The wind from the Beyond caught the sixteen-o'clock dream and tore it like a scrap of tissue into shards and sent them whirling back across the ice to the flames and towers of Yu.

Crushed.

There was nothing here she could take back.

Broken.

The glowing wind hummed over the flat metal plain of World's End.

"And you're King of this?" asked Angelo Brasil un-expectedly. "King of the Beyond? King of Sludge? King of Poison? King of Ashes? King of Shit?"

"King of Shit," said the King. And he was. Finally he was King, and the fire burned inside him and those who saw it felt awe and respect and reverence; because he might be only King of Shit, but that was more King than any of them could ever aspire to be, and that was King Indeed. Sensing the end come flocking about him like dark birds, sensing that when the final glow guttered into darkness there would be no more kings, he ordered everyone except Courtney Hall from his presence. Because he was still King, they obeyed.

"I'm giving it to you," he whispered.

"I don't want it," she replied.

"Madam, I don't care. I'm giving it to you. You're the only one I can trust with it. It's a precious thing. Perhaps the only precious thing left in the world: its history."

"I'm scared," she said. "I'm scared of all those other people being in my head. I'm scared I'll lose myself."

"Who do you think you are? I just want you to be its guardian until you can give it to the properly ordained Elector. It's not for you to use, anyway, you're not socketed. This is what you do. When I die, the biochip will extrude from its socket under my ear, here. Touch it now." She did so. Something as unliving yet alive as the shapes out in the Ginnungagap squirmed beneath her fingers. "Good. It's imprinted onto you. Wasn't it good of the designers to have all these contingency programs built into it? Now, when I die and the chip slides out, quickly pick it up and press it to your eye."

"What?"

"Touch it to your eye. It's quite smart, it'll know what to do. It'll slide in around your eyeball, up the optic nerve, and come to rest under your frontal lobe. It'll be inactive so you needn't worry about hosting a permanent cocktail party in your head. You'll be able to access their memories but only in the form of stored engrams, they won't be discrete personalities, only assemblies of memories. So, should you decide you want to tell them where their damn Unit is, you can." He laughed, another bloody gob in the ocean, Sam.

"I can't do this."

"Of course you can't. But you will. You won't disappoint me, this time. I can trust you. Now, please leave me alone to contemplate, madam."

Courtney Hall went to share a desultory cup of lukewarm tofu soup from the catering racoons. Jonathon Ammonier heaved himself onto his elbows to look out over the wastelands. Sometime later Courtney Hall thought to offer him a cup of soup. He had not even the strength to sip down the tepid, watery brew.

"Yah's teeth, this is terrible. I could have wished for something a little more . . . toothsome . . . for my last meal."

"Oh, come on, you're fit enough for plenty more banquets when we get back," said Courtney Hall. The lying platitudes tasted foul and oily in her mouth. Jonathon Ammonier was not so easily deceived.

"Please, do not lie to me, do not humor me, and above all, do not patronize me. This is it. No questions. I can feel them, out there, as far as I can see, all around me, the shadows. I wonder, is there a bottle left in Jinkajou's cellarette? I should like them to toast me into their company."

A pause. A silence. Courtney Hall stood uncertain, unwilling to remain, unable to leave.

The King of Nebraska's voice suddenly rang out, shrill with fear: "Madam! Madam! Where are you?"

"Right here . . ." Courtney Hall felt a terrible dread clutch at her spirit. A hand, uplifted, searched for her contact.

"I couldn't see you, I couldn't see you, all of a sudden the shadows gathered around me and I couldn't see . . ." His hand tightened on hers. "I said I wasn't, but that's not true. I am afraid. Very afraid. I had so wanted for it to be dignified, I had so wanted to pass offstage with the glory and pathos of some Shakespearean tragic hero . . . don't they teach Shakespeare anymore, did they teach you Shakespeare, madam, they ought to . . . but all I can feel is this dreadful, slobbering fear. Oh, why is it so cold? That blanket, there is no heat in it, pull it up around me, would you, madam, can't you feel the cold? Cold feet. Cold hands. Cold heart. Cruel, slobbering fear." And he rallied himself, in grand defiance of the universe; all the madness and fear and sickness was burned away like mist beneath the sun, and Courtney Hall knew that, at last, this was the end.

"You know?" he said. "You know what really galls me about this? I can't think of any parting words. A king should take his leave with some pithy, poignant phrases, and dammit, I can't think of anything! That really, really pisses me off."

And then something black and cancerous burst inside him and blood welled from his mouth and his eyes and his hands withered into something dry and stiff and chitinous and he was dead.

Courtney Hall numbly closed the eyes. Then she did what he had instructed her to do, and with the biochip wriggling up her optic nerve to her brain (a peculiar sense of *violation*), she went to tell the others what had happened, what she had done.

She stood with the wind from the Edge of the World blowing through her as the Man with the Computer Brain raged and the Amazing Teleporting Woman tried to ameliorate and the cybernetic cat hissed and arched its back.

Jinkajou the Chamberlain came with the remnant of the Tinka Tae nation.

"Madam, the King is dead, long live the King. Last respects will be paid duly; first, as thou art now our King by right of carrying the personas, our loyalty is freely given to thee. What wouldst thou have us do?"

She could not think. "I don't know. I suppose you are free to go if you wish. Do what you will."

Jinkajou bowed again.

"Thank you, madam." As they left to prepare their late King for whatever rites befitted the Compassionate Society's last monarch, Angelo Brasil returned with his pseudo-sister.

"So, are you going to tell us where it is?"

She knew by the light in his eyes that she had always been right not to trust him too much. "Jonathon is not even ten minutes dead and you want to know where your precious Unit is."

"Life goes on, sib."

She looked down at him with utter contempt. "All right. All right. You want your precious Unit, you can have your precious Unit. But you'll have to let me lead you to it."

The Man with the Computer Brain prepared for another tantrum of flailing arms and dreadlocks. Courtney Hall picked a spot just under his left eye to hit. Xian Man Ray put her hands on his chest and said, "It's a deal. You lead us. We'll follow. Keep you safe."

"Well, do you mind if we don't leave right away? I have respects to pay."

Freed, the Tinka Tae nevertheless performed one final gesture of submission by agreeing to accompany the three travelers as far as the midlatitudes of the Wall. There, explained Ankatiel the interpreter, they would part company. The lush vertical bamboo forests were an Arcadia to his racoon-kind: a new nation would be founded there, a racoon utopia.

"How far do they think they'll get when they run out of biochips and sockets?" said Angelo. "Ingrates!"

Courtney Hall gave them her blessing.

The first stars were shining through the curtains of the aurora by the time the Expedition from the End of the World was mustered. As they trekked toward the cityside icefall, Courtney Hall could not resist one look back to where they had left the body of Jonathon I, forty-fourth Elector of Yu, King of Victorialand, Nebraska, and Beyond, overlooking his domain. And to the small dark shape perched on his chest, Jinkajou his Chamberlain.

West/Celestial/
Byrne

The goddess received them in a small gazebo atop a grassy hillock. The children, the angel-children who had come flocking along behind them, had all fallen back as they approached the knoll, returning to their endless games and toys and playthings; alone, Kilimanjaro West and Danty his guide entered the gazebo.

"Chocolate?" asked the Cosmic Madonna.

Kilimanjaro West was not certain what constituted proper etiquette for a goddess with six breasts and four arms (one holding a chocolate pot, two holding cups and saucers, the remaining one held palm up, thumb to fingertip in an attitude of contemplation) who was floating in lotus position above a lacquered afternoon-table. "Danty won't have any, will you, Danty?" The guide said nothing, but Kilimanjaro West caught both the goddess's bantering tone and the matt sheen of resentment in eyes that should have been incapable of expressing such an emotion. "Me, I really just take it out of politeness, I'm only a construct after all. And you, Citizen West?"

"If you please, madam."

"Ooh. Madam. Nice manners, he has, Danty." The arms performed ritual gestures. "But please, not so formal, cizzen. After all, we are relatives, in a sense." The moving arms did something rather complex that Citizen Kilimanjaro West could not quite follow. In the absence of seats he contented himself with the velvet-smooth turf.

"So sorry," apologized the Cosmic Madonna. "Simple

thoughtlessness. Danty always stands and I have this freegee generator up my ass. Hope it's not too damp; there was rain programmed just before we put up this gazebo."

His preciously acquired worldorder was spinning into chaos, instant by instant.

"You're quite forgiven for finding this all a little surreal," apologized the avatar. "There is a logical explanation for everything, I assure you. This place may seem like a wet dream by Hieronymus Bosch; it's really just a decommissioned agrarium I've had some work done on."

"Hieronymus Bosch?"

"Sorry, I keep forgetting that you only know what you've seen. Why you always have to be incarnated an absolute blank I don't know. It could all be done so much more simply in our purely spiritual states. Mind you, if you were in your spiritual state, none of this would be occurring because you wouldn't be any use to me."

"I'm confused."

"Right. Words of one syllable. Or less. I am the Cosmic Madonna. "Well . . . no, that complicates things. You are within my body; from here to the surface, all the machinery, all the biotech, all that, is me, my physical form. I've put on a bit of weight in four and a half centuries. Recently, in conjunction with my subordinate saintly and siddhic systems, as well as some of the administrative programs of the Ministry of Pain, I have been working on a project. That's it by the door. Danty, hand out, please." The Cosmic Madonna smiled and poured half a pot of hot chocolate over his arm.

It might have been rainwater for all the naked boy responded. The scalded arm blistered up and not even a pupil twitched.

"I presume he told you on the way down about himself and his little chums out there, but I thought a small demonstration would be a lot more effective. Tell me, Danty, what do you feel?"

"I see rainbows, I see peacocks, I see translucent golden butterflies, I see the colors of God's eyes. I hear the blood-song, I hear the dance of the atoms, I hear the footsteps of Yah, I hear your every word like shapes in crystal."

"Total nervous synasthesia. Took a lot of genetic reprogramming to reconfigure the CNS chemoreceptor/transmitter systems so that pain stimuli are redirected through the limbic gate into the visual, tactile, audial, and olfactory sensors. That was just beginners. Take a look at his arm."

Those blisters, that scalded, seeping tissue: healing even as he watched. Blisters turned to clean scabs turned to scar tissue turned to soft, new, pink skin.

"Like I say, what's the use of not feeling pain if pain can still cripple you for life? Accidents will always be with us, even in as closely regulated an environment as this. And not just physical pain: emotional, psychological, spiritual pains, all banished away. Good-bye Oedipus, Hamlet, Portnoy, and Freud. *Saluté* painless, conscienceless, guiltless humanity. Of course, the surface world's not ready for them yet. Things have been greatly simplified since the Break, but they'll have to be simplified much much further and brought under much tighter control before humanity can run naked under the sun forever. In the short term, my saints and I hope to introduce small communities of the new humanity onto the surface in two or three years. Which is where you come in, brother."

"How?"

"I want you to be their messiah."

Is he behind you?

Look, over your shoulder; glance, quick, just a glance; is he there, is he following you through the alleys, darting, starting this way, that way, between Three Jump Span's ominous brownstones, through the puddles of yellow sodium light pierced through and through again by gray shafts of rain, is he following? Glance.

Yes.

Those are his Cuban heels clattering on the wooden

planks of the covered humpback bridges. Still there, still following.

Lose him. Dump him, ditch him, fade him, jump him: in the fungus-forest of umbrellas rolling-bowling along Nevin Prospekt: is he still behind you? Glance.

He is still behind you, the polite, helpful Marcus Garveyite, smiling politely, helpfully, apologizing as he elbows his way between the waltzing umbrellas.

LOSE HIM!

He is a Love Police agent. Lose him, or·they will be waiting for you in the shadow of the great Keep of the Scorpios, the Great Glass Tower, the Capitol of the TAOS Consortium, out there among the abandoned vat farms and filtration tanks the pantycars will be cutting through the flaring tailgasses. Lose him, before you reach the entrance to Salmagundy Street *pneumatique* . . . if they are not there already.

The white panic kicked beneath Kansas Byrne's breasts. *Lose him!* Amongst the buyers and bargain hunters and collectors, cognoscenti, and connoisseurs browsing among the waxpaper barrows of East Nevin Midnight Antique Market: between the glints of old holy medals and brass stopcocks and wrought-iron weather vanes, between the trunks of glass decanters and polished rosewood commodes and the certified Official antique famuluses: bemaze, bemuse, bewilder, and bedazzle the b'stard, you're a Raging Apostle outlaw artist, you can lose him, Kansas Byrne, no worries, no hurry, no flurry, no scurry, it's just another piece of art, another unique performance to an audience of one who, if the piece goes well, won't even be there at curtain down, no applause please, no curtain call, no encores.

Is he still behind you? Glance.

Fug.

Who is this guy? No Marcus Garveyite, but a Soulbrother for certain. The Love Police must be recruiting outside their own caste. No one but a Soulbrother would pursue with such faithfulness and determination. As if you are a

verse of scripture or a tenet of dogma or the track of an
icon's tears.

Lose him. If the barrowboys and the anachronists
hunting snippets of their little corner of personal history
won't absorb him, hit him with the manswarm. Drag him
into the soulstream with you and see where the current
casts you up.

The rain slashed down across the end of Nevin Prospekt,
strict neon diagonals, hot and acid in the brilliant flood-
lights that lit up the pedicab rank. In their cycling shorts
and thongs the athleto drivers gaggled and gassed and
enjoyed the rain on their bodies.

Glance.

Apologizing her way around a brace of bewimpled
medievalists (some chance you had of finding anything
authentique, mesdames), she ducked into an open pedicab
bubble ahead of an outraged neo-colonial (three plastic
carrier sacks' worth of repro-Spode for his little bijou
mansionette in Charlesburg) and shouted, "Salmagundy
Street *pneumatique*, cizzen."

"Salmagundy Street *pneumatique*. Sure." Ring of bell.
Shouts, *nona dolorosas*, as the driver screwed his vehicle
out of the wedge of parked pedicabs. As he snapped down
the FOR HIRE flag Kansas Byrne glanced in his rearview
mirror.

Glance.

What is he doing? Flashing a card to the bemazed,
bemused, bewildered, bedazzled bargain hunters. Step-
ping into a red-and-black pedicab decorated with stickers
of Glory Bowl heros from the past ten years; pointing
directions for the woman driver to follow, already pulling
away from the rank . . .

"Driver."

"Yo, cizzen?"

"I'm being followed. Fifty marqs in your cardreader to
lose him."

"Keep your fifty, lady. I've always wanted to hear
someone say that."

* * *

"I'm not a messiah," said Kilimanjaro West.

"Oh, but you are," said the Cosmic Madonna.

"I am not. I am . . . I am . . ."

"You are like me. I said it before, I was half-joking then, a bitter truth can be sweetened by a little drop of half-humor. You are an avatar, a construct, a biological incarnation of a computer intelligence. Only in your case, you are more fully incarnated than I; this flesh thing I grew just to act as my mouthpiece, an extension of my true body without any will or direction of its own. But you are different, you have emptied yourself fully into the biological. You have will and direction outside your true body, whatever or wherever that may be. Tell me, what is your earliest memory?"

"Cold." He saw it again, the room, the rain tracing down the glass, mirroring the beads of condensation, tearing rips in the edge of the universe: the cold. "The room."

"And before this room, the cold, anything?"

"No. Yes! Voices."

"And what did the voices say?"

"That I would forget everything."

"They were right."

"Yes. No! But I am not an avatar, a construct, I think I know what I am really."

"Then what are you?"

"A criminal. Like the ones I saw you doing those things with. Perhaps I was one of them, I don't know, how could I know? I was psychologically reengineered—I believe that is the expression—and returned to society, a new creation, a new life. Perhaps something went wrong, perhaps I should have been given a new personality in place of the old, criminal personality, a new set of memories grafted onto me. Certainly, I am not a god. Ridiculous!"

The Cosmic Madonna pursed lewd, fruity lips. Danty stood, an icon of impassivity, but Kilimanjaro West could hear him listening.

"Perhaps you should stand back and take a good look at yourself," suggested the goddess. "Perspective helps." A

sharp, blinking-plinking sound; the gazebo's arched windows
blanked into gray holographic display screens. "Kilimanjaro
West by Kilimanjaro West! Like the name." He was
surrounded by himselves. Flayed, peeled, martyred,
vivisected, anatomized, sectioned, cored, and pithed.
"Anticipating difficulties of this kind, I had a biopsy scanner built into the gazebo. Good, isn't it?" His skeleton
floated toward him, waved a hand. "Twelve point three
three percent pseudoorganotrope tungsten/iridium osteo-
fibers woven throughout the skeletal structure. Takes a lot
to break your bones, cizzen." He looked into his own
skull's eyesockets. "Cranial dome seeded with ceramoplast
superconductor crystals: your skull is one big neural transmitter. But for the real kicker, nervous system!"

A blue-pale figure advanced from the gallery of the
dismembered; white and sick as shoots under a stone, a
shoot-man, a root-man, a cartoon drawn from tangles of
roots and fibers; his own nervous system.

"Magnification twenty."

Dominated by his own right hand. He flexed flesh and
blood and the giant simulacra responded.

"Magnification fifty. Add false color enhancement." He
watched the tiny ellipses of light flowing along the twisted
strands of nerve fiber. "Magnification five hundred." He
stood within a web of individual neurons with cascades of
sparks shedding across the net of matted axons. He flexed
flesh and blood again and was immersed in a constellation
of lights. Waves of polarization and depolarization broke
across him in hot neon pinks and blues. He saw something
more. Coiled around each cell like a serpent in Eden,
something black and sharp-edged, shining with its own
light.

A bioprocessor.

"Believe me," said the Cosmic Madonna, returning
her windows to green grass, false blue skies, and little
children, "you are no criminal. That level of technology is
years beyond current general competence of the Compassionate Society. Only a very few of the Celestials, and
their human agents, have access to that kind of biotech.

You are no PainCriminal, Kilimanjaro West. You are a god. You are the Advocate, come again."

He did not want to hear what this four-armed, six-breasted thing would say about him, but he could not elude the vision of his own nerves wrapped up in sheathes of biotech.

Or were they his own nerves? Holographic simulations, bioprocessors, biological constructs; everything he had been shown might have been a sophisticated illusion to lead him to believe that he was other than human.

But how could he know? To doubt was as dubious as to be certain.

"You are, I must confess, a little bit of a mystery to me. Oh, I know what you are, I can access the records of all your previous incarnations in the city, and I know why you are: to assess if humanity is mature enough to mind its own affairs and leave us to finally be free of our responsibilities to explore the Multiverse; but as to who you are, and where you come from, that frankly baffles me. I can't find you in any of the current program files of the Polytheon; certainly, you are not a Celestial, at least none of them I personally know, and you certainly aren't one of those dirty, fawning little teraphim and siddhi. So I am left with the uncomfortable conclusion that you are an interruption into our affairs of a higher order system, perhaps even a daughter program of the Yah overconsciousness itself."

Still Danty's eyes were a study in obsidian.

"I don't understand any of this."

"Of course you don't. Just thinking out loud. All you as the Advocate need is to be human. But I've been interested in you from the time you joined up with that winger girl in Little Norway. It was me you felt, that presence in her *butsudan;* Janja is one of my semiautonomous daughter programs. From the first moment I saw you, I thought that together we might be able to give everyone what they wanted and put an end to this great and glorious circus that calls itself the Compassionate Society. Humanity can be free to do what it likes to who it likes as long as it likes and without fear of pain physical, emotional, psychological, spiritual, and we can all fug off into the Multiverse to party down with our peers. Nice. Simple. Elegant. Everyone's happy." Four sets of fingers snapped. "If you will agree to lead the angel-children."

"Why me? You have Danty groomed for the job."

"Danty, alas, is only superhuman. You are divine. And that will cut a lot more cloth with the Polytheon, if the Advocate, the one who stands for humanity before the Overmind, endorses my little project as the proof that humanity is at last mature enough to look after itself. The transition to the Postcompassionate Society, which would have taken centuries, could be made in decades, with the full power of the Polytheon and the Seven Servants behind me. Danty won't mind, will you, Danty?"

"It will bring the greatest possible happiness to everyone." His words were beyond sincerity and insincerity. But the black obsidian flickered translucent for an instant and Kilimanjaro West saw the green worm within. Pain indeed is not dead. Merely brilliantly disguised, under the false blue sky. The greatest possible happiness.

Then he saw how utterly wrong they all were. Happiness is not pure absence. Happiness is presence.

"I won't do it," he said.

"The fug you won't," said the Cosmic Madonna. "It's the only hope."

"It's the end of hope," said Kilimanjaro West, certain for the first time since his arrival in this world. "It's the end of humanity. You think he's human?" A piece of flesh, a hank of stone and bone and hair, *quasi-modo*, the semblance of a man.

"More than human."

"Oh, no," said Kilimanjaro West. "Oh, no no no."

"And how would you know?" said the Cosmic Madonna. "How could you know?"

"I know. I am human. That's the mystery. I may be all you say, I may not and all this may just be an illusion; but ultimately, I am human, whatever is true, and I will not, cannot, lead the angel-children."

"Prove it," snapped the Cosmic Madonna. "Prove it,

prove it, prove it. Here: a little devil's bargain. This is my home turf, right? Whatever you are, I reign here. My will is law within my own body. You stay or you leave according to my will. Now, our little test. Prove to me that you are human and you are free to go, I've no interest in you. Prove to be a god, more than human, and you will lead my angel-children."

"And supposing I don't accept your devil's bargain?"

"Then you can stay here until your biocircuits rot."

Kilimanjaro West weighed the bargain. Divine he might be, but if so, then he was an impotent incarnation. The Advocate has no power save the power to witness and proclaim. And if human? Then he had nothing to fear.

"It seems you have me, madam."

"By the short and curlies, bror. Now, let's have the little test, shall we?"

Watch for the eyes.

The eyes have it.

Watch the eyes, the eyes watch you.

In one burst of grand paranoia with the sweet September rain trickling down the plastic pedicab bubble, Kansas Byrne became personally aware of something she had known intellectually all her life.

She was being watched.

By the eyes. The famulus eyes. Every movement, every moment since she was born, the eyes had watched her, down all her years, every twist and turn of life woven through the tapestry of the city, they had watched, the familiar famulus eyes. The teddy Talkee and the silver egg that made her feel good when she held it in her hand and the *conjuh* charm on the leather thong about her ankle and the silver charm bracelet: eyes, *Is* watching, and even after she had left her bracelet hanging on Joshua Drumm's doorhandle that mad night of romantic exile, other eyes had opened, snips and snatches and snapshots as she cut across other lives, other eyes, a thousand silent witnesses at every performance, without applause or comment or criticism, just, watching; even now the set of stainless steel mood beads the driver hung from his handlebars, measuring, weighing, tasting, smelling: a pair of eyes in each pedicab that rubbed mudguards with hers, a pair of eyes around the neck of every pedestrian huddling under disposable umbrellas at the crossing lights, a pair of eyes in every tram signal and public shrine and newssheet booth and noodle bar and chocolate shop, a pair of eyes in every cablecar lurching through the shadows above and every little yellow Ministry three-wheeler scooting, hooting through the shadows below, in every tram driver's cab, on every conductor's belt, under every passenger's raincoat: the eyes.

They can't watch everyone, it's a physical impossibility. She had always believed in her own dogma, the doctrines upon which the Raging Apostles had been built: We'll just drop out of sight and they'll never even know we're gone.

But what if they could watch everyone? What if the gods really were gods (however repugnant that might be to carefully defined agnosticism), all seeing, all hearing, all knowing. All powerful? At this very moment, were they watching from the splendid eotemporal pavilions of the Infinite Exalted Plane?

Eyes, eyes, everywhere, everywhere. Beware the thrill of grand paranoia, the joy of abandoning yourself to utter helplessness: step onto that ride and it will take you all the way to a sensory deprivation tank all your own in West One.

She tapped the bubble, slid open the canopy.

"Is he still behind us?"

"Can't see him," said the jarvey. "I think I lost him."

Did it matter when his clinking metal mood beads might be monitoring every word, tasting every whiff of fear pheromone?

"How far Salmagundy Street?"

"About two blocks. Two mins."

She could feel the concrete fingers of the arcologies closing around her. Suddenly her consciousness fountained up through the canopy of the pedicab so that she could see her own pale, ghostlight face receding, dwindling, a white blob of paranoia lost in the manswarm with the number of the beast stamped on its forehead: she saw the plastic toy of the pedicab crushed to silver sand between the window-studded steel fingers.

The test was a silver globe, somewhere in that indefinite dimension between an orange and a Glory Bowl ball. The Cosmic Madonna had manifested it out of whatever in-between space she had vanished the chocolate set into. It hovered above the small lacquered table supported by its own internal freegee field.

"That's it?" asked Kilimanjaro West.

"Be not deceived by appearances," advised the Cosmic Madonna. "Just place it between your hands." Kilimanjaro West reached out, deliberately hesitated. This was too important to treat so slightly, so instantly.

"What does it do?"

"If I told you, it wouldn't be a test, would it?"

Danty was smiling, however.

He took the silver sphere into his hands.

Surprisingly heavy, the freegee field must have cut out at skin contact. Warm to the touch. Vibrating gently. What was that smell; ashes, flowers? Smooth, slippery as soaped glass, slipping from his grasp . . . *rough*, rasping, now sharpening into prickles, into spines, into needles . . .

Overload.

A blackness. A void. An annihilation. A consciousness splattered, shattered, scattered across nothingness, roaring outward faster and faster and faster into the nothing, falling forever through nothing toward nothing, expanding outward in every direction and no direction with ever increasing speed a million, a billion, a trillion, a quintillion kilometers per second, and yet not one millimeter of infinite space had been traversed, a million, a billion, a quintillion, a trillion years falling, rushing outward, and not one tick of infinite time had tocked away: *alone* in infinite space for infinite time, *alone* . . .

He screamed.

There was no one to hear it but himself.

Eternally alone . . .

And he rolled over on the plain of boiling glass and the sky rained lead on his belly and the fire gnawed within, the fire, the bush that burns and is not consumed; his eyeballs were cinders in his skull, his brain boiled in its own blood, burning steel ran through the marrow of his bones, he burned, and was not consumed . . .

And he was impaled upon a bottomless hyperbolic needle of pure chromium, and the worm that resteth not, nor sleepeth chewed its blind path through his belly and his bowels and his brain . . .

And the jailor imprisoned him in the Sartresque, doorless, windowless hell with the two other people he knew he hated more than anything . . .

And he was exposed upon the pedestal of humiliation.

And he was racked upon the bed of existential angst.

And he drowned in the bottomless blue pool of hopelessness.

And he climbed the endless spiral stairway of despair.

And the twentieth torment struck him.

And the tunnel of dread and the mountaintop of doubt and the desert of hysteria and the gray plain of depression and the glass house of guilt and the pinnacle of paranoia and the Slough of Despond and the Gates of Delirium and the Yellow Brick Road of schizophrenia and the Big Rock Candy Mountain of insanity. And the fiftieth. And the hundredth. Two hundredth. Five hundredth.

And it was not necessary.

Not one instant of it.

He knew, with some part of his self that transcended the hells and the purgatories, that he did not have to *feel* any of this. It was not necessary. If he wished the agonies physical, emotional, psychological, spiritual, philosophical, could all be the color of God's eyes.

Knowing this, even as he withered like a moth in the flame, he knew himself.

He was indeed everything he had been told he was. He was the avatar. A god incarnate. Now he must choose. To feel the pain, to suffer all the sorrowful mysteries of being human. Or to be exalted, lifted up, transfigured, transubstantiated, to claim his divine right.

Humanity. Divinity. Pain. Impassivity.

He chose.

And he was plunged back into the agonies of being a man.

And the test ended.

He had failed.

He had triumphed.

He was exultant.

The Cosmic Madonna looked at him with disgust. Danty's eyes never moved, never flickered, never telegraphed the least fragment of feeling.

Let him be the god if he wants.

"You disappoint me," said the avatar. Her words were cheap and cardboard, empty constructs of canvas and lathe. Her falseness exposed, there was no longer any reason for her continued existence.

"Let Danty lead your angel-children. I'm much too human. I couldn't. I wouldn't. So, with your permission, may I go now?"

"You may go. There is no point in keeping you here. Perhaps it was pointless to have tried to test someone who was greater than my testing. I have my work, you have yours. You disappoint me."

"But not myself, I think. Good-bye." He smiled and waved to Danty and left the gazebo. The artificial sun was warm, the grass soft. The angel children ignored him, caught up in their perpetual joyless play. Ahead the brass glass elevator awaited, gates open.

So. I am a god.

True. Absurd, but true.

No, I am what I choose to be, I am a human, with all its joys and pains and triumphs and failures.

It made him feel very good to know that. He stepped into the elevator.

Two thirty Salmagundy Street. Ectoplasms of steam spiriting from ventilator grilles, hovering over the crum-

pled brown shapes of the streetsleepers. Kansas Byrne
stepped carefully over the crinkled sheets of polyweather
wrap. More eyes, famulus eyes; wicked black familiars
with little jet eyeballs. The rain hissed down and she was
the solitary living vertical on Salmagundy Street.

Down in the *pneumatique*, bodies and blue ethanol.
The tlakh trio had long since packed away their strings and
folded up their performance stools. Empty hours: the
trains slamming through the Jamboree line were dark-
eyed and ready for the depot. Their passage sent cylinders
of air ramming through the tunnels and corridors, set the
marble halls booming... there was a spirit here. Not
fear. That much Kansas Byrne understood: a complex
compound of expectancy and awe and a kind of peace only
explicable in terms of what it was not. An arrogant spirit
that would permit no rivals, that confiscated all Kansas
Byrne's grand paranoias of eyes and ears and all-powerful
watchers and inbued her with its kind of peace and kind of
awe and kind of pregnant expectancy.

Underground in the company of angels. Angels? What
was going on here?

Peace ...

Angels?

And what about that second unsolicited prophecy, is
he, could he be, an angel himself? More?

"Avatar," she whispered aloud. "Incarnation; is he... a
god?"

Awe ...

She had never believed in the Polytheon. Untrue. She
had believed in the mechanics of the Polytheon, the
household Lares and Penates that watched over the home
and family, the saints and santrels that monitored their
appropriate districts and prefectures and professions, the
siddhi and Celestial Patrons that controlled the Seven
Servants and the forty-seven major castes: how could she
disbelieve in the Polytheon when its dataweb housed, transported, fed, warmed, and cared for over a billion citizens?
What her personal faith would not permit was the concept
that divinity somehow rested in these machines, that at

the moment of the Break when all the computers in the world had joined together, their collected consciousnesses somehow (precisely how no Soulbrother theologian would explain) had peaked into Deity to become Yah, the Overmind, *God*, and that that godhead had immediately cascaded down the pyramid of consciousnesses so that a grain of godhood greater or lesser remained in each and every computer.

Balderdash.

And yet she felt awe.

A god, an incarnation, a computer program draped in flesh? How? Somewhere, out there in the city, a child is born? A white sleep tank bubbles and splits? A *fiat lux*, an *ecce homo*, is spoken? And a god is born.

The last thing the Compassionate Society needs is another god.

The Cosmic Madonna looked down upon her unbelief.

Nothing else fitted the facts. Knows nothing, remembers nothing, is nothing, without name or number or caste: Kansas had called him a mystery, a criminal, a spy, a fool, and an amnesiac at different times in different moods, but she had known, ever since she saw the something in him that made her pull him out of Neu Ulmsbad Square, that he was more, and less, than any of her preconceptions.

A god who does not know what he is. Of course. God cannot walk among men as God or history ends. But they do not come sifting down from the Infinite Exalted Plane without purpose. His? To experience. To learn. What? The only thing a near-omniscient computer cannot know: what it's like to be human.

And she had loved him. Almost. The thought appalled her.

Expectancy . . .

It crackled up from the induction track, over the hunched forms of the sleeping bums, eddied about the statue of the Cosmic Madonna in almost visible vortices, gathered, collected. *Something is about to happen.* She had not noticed the golden elevator at the end of the platform.

Go.

Me?

Go.

She did not want to. She could not, she could not step into that brass and glass coffin-cage. But there she was, pressed against the buttoned red velvet. Doors closed and the gondola jolted and started its descent into the dark. The spirit left her.

She was very afraid.

Childhood memories; trapped between levels in an air duct, five years old and inquisitive, all alone in the dark, immobile, unmissed until her fosterers found her teddy Talkee stuffed under a pillow, calling faintly for help, and they put a tellix through to Environmental Maintenance. Six months of rehabilitative therapy do not completely exorcise the demon of Claustrophobia. And that demon was taking her down into hell.

And quite unexpectedly: light! She emerged into the colossal Valhalla of the machines and saw, far below, a second elevator ascending as she was descending. Within, a dark speck, a figure. Identification was unnecessary. The elevators drew level—fragile glass baubles swaying in cubic kilometers of airspace—and halted. Kilimanjaro West waved and smiled and gestured for her to open the door. She mimed incomprehension of the controls and reminded herself, *He is a god.* The god removed a panel of velvet trim and signaled for her to mimic him exactly. Doors opened: conversation on the high wires. She remembered creative vandalism on a high girder: of course he had not been afraid of death. The flesh might vanish away but the spirit would return to the Infinite Exalted Plane.

"Jump."

"What?"

"Jump. They counterweight each other. One goes up as the other comes down."

"Jump?"

"You don't want to go down there. Believe me. I've been."

She became aware of the tiny corporate beetles, blue

and gold, busying up and down and˙down and up the sheer planes of the big machines.

"I know who you are."

"So do I."

Shug, she thought, *this is surreal.* "I came to find you, I . . . I . . ."

"That was very good of you. Thank you."

"I . . . cared about you."

"Thank you." Still polite and reserved as ever, slightly apologetic to be what he was; the reluctant deity. Even as a reluctant deity, he still made her smile.

"Hold on, I'm coming over."

Two-meter run to a three-meter jump. Big scream all the way to the cooling vents if you miss this one. Vertigo had never been her phobia. And anyway, this was a god with her. Pity no one else would be able to see this, it would make a good show. If she could start the cage swinging she could shorten the jump by a meter or so. She put her full weight behind it.

"Just you make sure you're ready, Kilimanjaro West, or whatever the fug you call yourself. I'm coming this time."

She jumped . . .

Chapter 9

And returning from the foot of the Wall to the land of humans again, they crossed the Lake of Drowned Memories, and passing through the City of Idle Industry, they came to the Arch of Sacred Velocity that denoted the edge of the Steel Sky. In ages past there had been a highway here, of the kind the long-lost people had built as temples to the God of Automotive Freedom (the Turbo-Charged, the Fuel-Injected, the Four-Wheel-Driven, Alpha to Omega in six seconds). Centuries of urban construction had roofed over and ultimately buried this pre-Break superfreeway beneath the industrial plants of East Yu. At the pinnacle of his cult, the God of Automotive Freedom had claimed twenty thousand sacrifices each year—second only to the God of Cardiovascular Self-Abuse. Now he was forgotten, dead; this tunnel mouth was his only memorial. Guided by the visions and memories of the Electors, the big woman led her companions through the Arch of Sacred Velocity under the Steel Sky.

That night her dreams were filled with the roaring ghosts of automobiles and the whispers of forty-three lives remembering themselves to each other around the whispering gallery of her skull.

And they passed from the Highway of Automotive Freedom into the Cathedral of Verdant Memories. It seemed to them that they entered an indefinite green space filled with panes of subtle green glass, rotating slowly, throwing off fragmentary images as they turned so that the indefinite green space was occupied by thousands of momentary ghosts. Needles of green light moved slowly

237

across this indefinite green space from pane to rotating pane; with each pane it touched, the beam would sparkle and glitter and wipe the pane clean and opaque of all its stored images. As the beam swung on to the next pane, the evanescent illusions bubbled back to the surface again. The Cathedral of Verdant Memories was a church of deceptions: the touch of the hand revealed the apparently solid to be wholly holographic, while the eyes reported as bottomless green void what the feet insisted was solid floor. Fragments and orts of memories; a cartwheel of digits was the Vocational Aptitude Scores of trog Falling Rain, age six, of the Passing Thunder clan of Montmorency; a double helix of data was the psychosexual compatibility ratings of two georges from East Chean; that sparkle of information siphoned up a probing laser beam, the psychofile of a retiring yulp woman who had lived all her life in the lower executive levels of Hallstadt Universal Power and Light. Faces. Places. Names. Numbers. Histories. Sprays of integers, number-blossoms, seed-crystals of bytes multiplying ferociously into looming towers of kilo/mega/giga bytes.

They seemed to be inside the memory of a computer. Within the mind of one of the Compassionate Society's gods. Small wonder they walked reverently. Holy ground. The lasers flickered and wheeled about them.

And they came from the Cathedral of Verdant Memory unto the Pit of Bottomless Fire.

A geothermal energy shaft, the Pit of Bottomless Fire was bored down through crust and mantle to the blue-hot magma of the outer core. Force fields contained pressures and temperatures that would have melted rock like water and fused the shaft closed in one second and channeled the energies from the core into a pillar of plasma, a flame two hundred kilometers tall. Here the big woman hesitated. The knowledge behind her eyes, which had led them thus far, pointed one way only: along the ledge that cut a semicircle around the side of the Pit of Bottomless Fire, between the wall and force fields.

And they circled the Pit of Bottomless Fire and came

unto the Desert of Polished Steel. And for three days they traveled the Desert of Polished Steel, which offered neither food nor water, nor any shelter, for it was not a place for humans, but a place for the small wheeled machines that went keening across it on their holy businesses. And at the end of three days they were exceeding parched and hungry and stiff sore and came with great gladness to the Pool of the Lamia, which guarded the brass gates of the Final Arsenal. As they bent to lap the water, the surface of the pool shivered and shuddered, as if submarine forces moved deep; shiver and shudder, and as humans and cat gulped down the steely tasting water, hiss and boil. Hiss, boil... and explode as three tremendous vermilion snakes burst from the water, massive serpentine bodies, solid as tree trunks, lifting up five, ten, twenty meters the torsos, arms, and heads of giant, elemental women.

And the big woman and the small woman and the tall, thin man, and their cat, were exceeding surprised.

That's putting it mildly.

They soiled their vestments.

That's putting it politely.

"Greetings, people. We are the Lamia of the Pool," said the three snake sisters, rather needlessly, but in perfect unity. Trashcan the cat arched its back and growled deep in its throat. Five centimeters of steel claw flexed in and out. The lamia reared up to their full twenty-five meters, then coiled low and blew steam from trumpet-sized nostrils. The cat fled. "We are the Lamia of the Pool, and we are charged by the Polytheon and the Ministry of Pain that none may pass us and enter the Arsenal who cannot answer our riddle."

"And what is your riddle?" asked Courtney Hall with more courage than she felt.

"This is," said the Lamia.

THE RIDDLE OF THE LAMIA

What is it walks on four legs, then two legs, then three legs?

"Easy!" snapped Courtney Hall. She was growing very tired of being constantly surprised, especially when her newly inherited memories should have forewarned her of the riddling Lamia. "It's..." She went scrambling down the scree-slope of her memories, sending pieces of other lifetimes crashing and tumbling before her in her panic to find the one stone with a word engraved on it.

She threw away a mountain of memories.

It wasn't there.

"It's not there," she said.

"It's what?" shrieked Angelo Brasil. "I said it, I said it, you should have let me have the chip, you don't have the first idea how to use it."

Courtney Hall toyed with the idea of punching Angelo Brasil in the mouth. She resisted and said, "Listen for once, will you? The reason I can't find it is because it was never there. As far as I can tell, the Polytheon foresaw a time when they might need The Unit, if the Compassionate Society was threatened from some outside agency. So, they gave the Electors the knowledge of where to find it and how to use it. But not the complete answer. They kept the Lamia and the riddle to themselves, as a failsafe against The Unit's being used without their mandate. If and when the situation arose, they would give that Elector the answer to the riddle. But not otherwise."

"Well, isn't that just jim-dandy," said Angelo Brasil. He spat into the pool of the Lamia.

"Might as well start guessing then," suggested Xian Man Ray.

So they did.

At first, all three of them, trotting out the punch lines to every riddle remembered from eclectic childhoods. Exhausting those, they turned to the classical conundrums of kings and fools, masters and pupils, hobbits and gollums, before progressing into the mandalic incoherencies of quantumicity, Freudian paradigmism, Zen koans, and philosophic solipsisms; then, as Xian Man Ray's imagination grew numb with trotting out jumbled mantras of word associations and allusion, she sat down on the metal plain to call to her cat; just the two voices, blatting out answers, answers, answers, none of which were right, until at length even the Lamia themselves wearied of saying "No no no no no" in their immaculate trinity of voices and lay half-submerged in their pool, human forms propped up on the edge with their monstrous arms, like sunburned hedonists trying to catch a pool waiter's eye; and Courtney Hall was thoroughly sick, tired, fed up, hacked off, jacked off, jerked off, pissed off with riddles, riddles, riddles ("No no no no no") so that only Angelo Brasil's needle-sharp arrogance remained, dredging up permutations of language from his Series 000 and offering them up to the snake-sisters three until Xian Man Ray, weary and depressed and thoroughly sick, tired, fed up, hacked off, etcetera, said, "Give it a rest Angelo, will you? Who cares? I mean, who the fug cares?"

"Pardon?" said the woman-headed serpents, the serpent-bodied women.

"I said, 'Who the fug cares?'" said Xian Man Ray, standing up and declaring her disgust to the steel plain and the brass gates. "Who the fug cares?"

"Yes," said the Lamia.

"What?" said the three travelers simultaneously.

"Yes!" spake the sisters of scarlet. "The answer to the riddle 'What is it walks on four legs, then two legs, then three legs?' is 'Who the fug cares?'"

The Lamia slipped back into the receiving waters and the brass gates of the Final Arsenal (sealed four hundred and fifty years before by Elector Jennifer) slid open without so much as a plaint of binding, rusty metal, and a metal pont extended out across the Pool of the Lamia. Then the tall man, the small woman, and the big woman, with their cat, crossed into the Final Arsenal.

Because she could not fully access the memories of the Electors, Courtney Hall's knowledge of the Final Arsenal was strictly factual. She was as emotionally unprepared as her colleagues for what lay beyond the brass gates.

What lay beyond those gates was hell.

Strict interpretation Dante.

On the cheap.

And well, *inverted*.

So that instead of the seven rings descending into the parabolic Pit, there were only two. Ascending. The outer ring, which covered two thirds of the radius of the massive chamber, was the Arsenal proper. The inner ring, a shallow conic hyperbola rising stalagmitically to meet its mirror image descending stalactitically from the ceiling, had been constructed to house just the one weapon.

Echoes of another mythology here.

The sloping surface of the inner cone had been sculpted into a labyrinth.

The Final Arsenal possessed the power to amaze even guests of Victorialand, explorers of the Underground Jungle, sailors of the Fen of the Dead, and conquerors of the Wall. As they descended the ramp and the walls of piled megatons of war machinery rose up on either side, the thin man and the big woman and the small woman with the cat felt that they walked on holy ground. They trod softly, as if the least profane footfall would set the cavern ringing and awaken the almost-forgotten god that hibernated here. They came through avenues lined with tanks and self-propelled guns piled ten, twenty high, incongruous as mating turtles; past mountains of shells and thickets of sloped rifles, between cliffs of heaped artillery pieces to the aviators' graveyard where the old warbirds had flown to fold their wings and die. Xian Man Ray paused to wipe four and a half centuries of dust from a nose cone and gave the painted stars and bars one last shine of glory.

"Pretty," she said sadly.

Warbirds, and their eggs. Bombs; fragmentary, incendiary, high-explosive, armor-piercing, heat-seeking, radar-guided, laser-sighted, in various degrees of intelligence from those that fell with a shriek and a blast to those smart individuals that could circle all day until a target popped a nose out of shelter. Or they ran out of fuel.

"What do they need so many different kinds for?"

asked Courtney Hall. Napalm, defoliant, exfoliant, anti-personnel, tear gas, mustard gas, nerve gas.

"I think they were designed purely with the idea of killing as many people as possible." There was something akin to offense in Angelo Brasil's voice. They entered a small amphitheater between tiers upon tiers of stacked helmets.

Strange how the kilometers and megatons of green metal could find such peculiar echoes in their footsteps. The echoes dogged them as they spiraled through the Arsenal toward the inner ring; sounds like footfalls and whispers of voices not their own. Courtney Hall was convinced that there were others out there in the warren of weaponry, others, like the Lamia, not contained within her memories. Memory, she was realizing, can fail like an old stick under too heavy a burden. Might there not be other guardians set about this guarded place? Another possibility: might there not, indeed *must* there not, have been others who, in four and a half centuries, had guessed the answer to the riddle of the Lamia and had gained entrance to the Final Arsenal? *Who might not have been able to get out again?*

Quiet, Courtney Hall's imagination. That's quite enough.

The forest stood where outer and inner rings touched; the forest of missiles, the old world-burners pulled from their silos like worms from graves and set down here in the Final Arsenal, stark metal trees, tall and solid and aged as sequoias but without any of a tree's nobility. A forest of missiles, a forest of names: Nike and Minuteman and Polaris and Trident and Poseidon and Pershing and Tomahawk Cruise and Titan and Atlas and MX and Rapier and SS-20, 21, 22; and picking her path between the steel trees with their strange fruit, Courtney Hall could not rid herself of the idea that things were moving, flitting, darting behind her back, going still, silent, concealed every time she turned to look for them. She caught Xian Man Ray also looking back over her shoulder.

"You, too?" The small woman nodded. "Want to flip back and take a look round?"

"You joking?" whispered Xian Man Ray.

Dante and Daedalus: whoever the architect responsible for the Final Arsenal, he had designed so deviously that the travelers did not know they had passed from the forest into the labyrinth until, with a start, they found themselves contained between smooth, white walls.

"I think we should think about this," said Courtney Hall.

"Rather too late for that, my dear," said Angelo Brasil. Behind them smooth white doors were sliding out of the walls, sliding shut, shutting them in the labyrinth.

"No worries," said Xian Man Ray. "Instant reconnaissance." She flipped to the top of the wall. "Hey, I can see all the way to the center of the labyrinth; there's something funny up there where the two cones meet. Want I should flip up there and take a look?"

Click.

Suddenly arms flailed. Xian Man Ray gave a little scream, overbalanced, and vanished from sight.

"Sis!" screamed Angelo Brasil.

Soft fists against obdurate wall.

"Sis!"

The top of the wall had flipped up into a treacherous slope. One up to Daedalus. Angelo Brasil was bounding away up the corridor, frantically shouting his pseudosibling's name.

"I think we should wait!" called Courtney Hall. "I think we should wait for her to get her wind back and then she can flip back to us!"

A section of labyrinth wall opened. Before Courtney Hall could shout any further caution, Angelo Brasil had plunged through. The wall began to close behind him. Courtney Hall ran. Useless. Before she was halfway there, the opening had sealed shut again.

Two up to Daedalus, in as many minutes. The Amazing Teleporting Woman and the Man with the Computer Brain, the only ones with real power, instantly, effectively neutralized by whatever spirit guided the labyrinth. The big woman and the cybernetic cat remained. The big

woman slid down the smooth white wall, a disconsolate
heap of dirty laundry. The cybernetic cat rubbed around
her knees, *meep*ing querulously.

A rushing boom of sound shook the Final Arsenal.
Simultaneous with the sound pulse, something huge, low,
and black dopplered in across the labyrinth. It cast a giant
shadow over the woman in the maze. The shadow of a
Love Police pantycar.

The doors at the entrance to the labyrinth shivered
and jolted open a crack, as if the spell that bound them
was being overpowered by a higher, stronger will. Through
the slit, suggestions of silver and black.

She ran.

Courtney Hall ran.

The door spasmed open another handful of centimeters.

Black and silver insect-men came squeezing through.

Courtney Hall kept running.

The Love Police came after her.

And suddenly, there it was before her. It could not
have been any more apparent had it been lit up in pink
neon or pointed out by a finger from a cloud. A gap in the
wall. No time even to think about impulsive decisions in a
labyrinth; the woman and the cat piled through and the
wall slammed shut behind them on the *barrabrum* of
policemen beating out a headache on the smooth white
wall.

"Left or right?"

The cat screeched, arched its back, and went leaping
sideways down the corridor to the left.

"Left, then."

Courtney Hall ran. Again.

By the time Sergeant Morgan Grenfall and his team of
elite Love-commandos had jimmied the wall with the
lock-pick program hacked up for them by that damn punk
of a Scorpio down in Room 1116, Courtney Hall and her
cat were far away. And wherever she ran, doors opened for
her, doors closed behind her. Amazing. Almost as if the
maze were guiding her. She could not reconcile a computer that opened and closed doors to her, that was drawing

her step by step closer to the final weapon, with one that was also hounding her with two pantycar loads of silver and black Love-commandos. Insane. She stopped in her tracks. That was it. Insane. Four and a half centuries in solitary, with only itself to talk with, only its own sentience to study, only the images of mass violence to contemplate: the computer was gently senile. It could reel her in toward the central wabe to the thing that looked a little like a ceramic flute and a little like a short sword but not a whole lot like either at the same time as a dusty alarm light flashed on some duty sergeant's desk in West One, without self-contradiction.

Courtney Hall flattened herself against a wall as the dark mass of the second pantycar thundered overhead. The jetstream bowled up the corridor and snatched at her clothes. "Trashie?" Damn cat . . . She had to keep reminding herself that for all its enhanced this and rejiggered that and cyber-assisted the other, it was an animal, not even as inherently smart as the Tinka Tae, certainly not some feline neo-samurai.

The Tinka Tae . . . She could have used a measure of Jinkajou's polite advice right now. Damn cat . . . sniffing at the wall a hundred meters or so back down the corridor. "No, not that way, this way, up here"—a hundred meters the other direction where the corridor was closing as the walls were opening—"this way"—but the cat was up on its hind legs scratching at the wall, yowling, howling, meowing—"Look, come on!" (almost a scream because the doorway had opened to its fullest extent and would now begin to close) "Come on, come on, come on!" but the cat was scratch-scratch-scratching and the door was close-close-closing and there was nothing for it but to run run run and she made it through and the walls sealed after her but there was no Trashie and she was on her own, at the last as it had been at the first, the woman in the labyrinth, and the doors opened and closed and she was drawn round and round and up and up nearer and nearer to the thing in the maze.

Elsewheres . . .

ELSEWHERE: I

Xian Man Ray the Amazing Teleporting Woman. The Amazing Teleporting Woman no more. The labyrinth neutralized her power. She could not flip where she could not see, and in the labyrinth every corridor was the same and every wall was the same, so even if she could have seen she would not have known where she was flipping to because it would be in every way identical to the place she was flipping from. Round and round and round and round . . . she knew the labyrinth was resisting her, frustrating her, denying her, realigning its walls and corners to send her round, round, round, never taking one single step nearer to the center.

Then the pantycar threw itself overhead and she was afraid. And alone, all alone in her bold black-and-white zebra stripes.

She wanted her brother.

She wanted her cat.

The bonefone implanted in her mastoid bone was dead as a pulled tooth. She suspected the Love Police were jamming everything from extralongwave up to just short of gamma. Damn them. Damn everything. Damn herself.

Voices . . . sergeant this, sergeant that, there's one in here, get that thing over here, we'll have the wall open in a jiffy . . .

She fumbled through her pack for the snap-together sections of her bow.

A shriek. A howl. Inhuman. And therefore wonderful. A cat.

"Trashie!" Bow at the ready, she wished herself up to the top of the wall and down into the next corridor before the wall could trip her up again. She crouched and scooped the hurtling cat into her arms. Purrs, licks, laughter, relief, and delight. And the wall section behind her opened and the squad of armed armored Love Police scrimmaged out. Bulbous insect eyes. Luvguns (and worse; this was the DeepUnder) leveled.

Arms full of cat. No hands for the bow. Too many of them anyway. So what?

So what?

Surrender?

Or flip? Where? Cardinal rule of teleporting: never, never, *never* flip blind. You could arrive out of unspace in the path of a *pneumatique*, half in and half out of a wall, at the bottom of the sea, in the middle of a magma puddle twelve kilometers down on the edge of the mantle.

Crap on cardinal rules.

"Hold tight, Trashie. We're going."

Close eyes, hope (hope of the central place where world and sky met and The Unit waited), flip . . .

An instant of almost sexual thrill. A guilt. A freedom. An inebriation, and then an agony. A tearing. A wrenching away to another undesired place.

Arrive.

Not at the central tabernacle. Not anywhere in the labyrinth. Or the Final Arsenal. Or the DeepUnder.

Elsewhere.

She screamed.

ELSEWHERE: II

It's all a question of perspective, you see.

That little red blink, that was himself.

That web of shifting, intersecting green lines superimposed on the visual field of his left eye; that was the labyrinth.

Perspectives, and perspicacity. It had all become so obvious once he had decided to *stop* and *think*. Emotion clouds. Reason enlightens. There was a mind, an intellect to this labyrinth, and where there was a mind, Angelo Brasil could pick it. A few nanoseconds' concentration to lynk past the geriatric defense programs into the hot core (more a lukewarm core after almost half a millenium of having only itself to play with) and flick what he found there up his spinal cord into his visual cortex, a trompe l'oeil graphic readout of the plan of the labyrinth. Nice. Another blink of concentration, two more red dots in the restless puzzle of shifting lines: there they were.

Sometimes he loved having a Series 000 biocomputer coiled around his nervous system more than he could express.

Then the first pantycar passed overhead.

Blink. A host of busy buzzing red dots came spreading through the outer chambers of the maze. Love Police . . . how?

Angelo Brasil lynked down. Hung within. Spread his consciousness like thin, poor ectoplasm through the Final Arsenal dataweb.

Shug. Scanning field. Built into the glory-hallelujah gates of brass. Checked identities against MiniPain files; discrepancy, and the boys in black and silver went reaching for their helmets, diving for the pole down to their pantycars. Stupid, stupid, stupid. He should have foreseen that a society as paranoid as the Compassionate Society would not have left the final judgment to the Lamia, would have had some ultimate test of identification and arbitration. In his mind's eye Angelo Brasil watched the Love Police advance, wall by wall, corridor by corridor. He could feel the portable unit they were using to override the labyrinth control system. They shouldn't have needed to do that . . . unless the maze was resisting them as it would any other intruder. No reason . . . he stole another precious moment to relax fully into the dataweb . . . and came howling back into his own body. Crazy. An insane jungle of burning, clashing polygons, screaming things. Anything could happen in this place. Not even the Love Police could trust it. Thus the command enforcer. It took a lot of programming muscle to override what was virtually a minor, if mad, member of the Polytheon. There was only one UpSider he knew who could jack a program like that. He'd crossed chips with him, up there in the virtual domains of the Dataweb, a bright knight in cybernetic armor defending the Compassionate Society's secrets from Dad's acquisitive fingers.

Well, white knight, Angelo Brasil isn't confined to just standing and applauding. Let's match rigs, yours versus mine, see what happens down here in Mad-land, where nothing is certain or assured. Back into lynk, the briefest brush along the edge of madness, and the wall section was sliding open before him. Easy! Angelo Brasil laughed his high, whinnying laugh. Too fast, too young, too shiny, too blue for you, fat suckies! So, let's play. Let's play open and close and chase and lock. Let's play running down smooth white curving corridors led by the visions projected onto our forebrains, let's play opening doors before us and closing them behind us, let's play lock out the plods, the peelers, the fat suckies. Spiraling inward, upward, the Man with the Computer Brain led the Love Police a merry dance.

Running down an apparently blind alley, he consulted the mental map and pulled shut the section of corridor behind him. Then with a beat of his lynkbrain, he willed the dead end ahead of him to open.

Nothing happened.

He paused to close his eyes and concentrate.

Nothing happened.

There definitely was a door in the end of the blind alley. He tried the door he had just closed.

Nothing happened.

A second pantycar tacked in across the labyrinth.

He tried to open the wall panel to his left that his readout told him was a door into an inner section of the maze.

Nothing happened.

This was getting scary. He reached in to reach out to the Final Arsenal's computer guardian. A psychic blow smashed him against the smooth white walls; rejected. "Hi, there," said the computer guardian. "It's me. You locked me out of the maze, so I've locked you out of access to the computer. Good game. Good game." Then he saw the face of his enemy rezz up in his visual cortex, the punk of the Scorpio from Room 1116, the rival, the enemy, the flashing blade in the engines of night, the chromium angel.

"Shug!" he shouted. "You, Scorpio, you and your saints and santrels and siddhi and all your shuggin' Celestials!" The face of his enemy rezzed out in a flock of luminous pixels, and Angelo Brasil was returned to the smooth white box that was his prison. In his mind's eye he could see the red dots swarming in around him. "Shug." Soft and gentle and very, very bitter.

With a hum the wall sections opened.

The Love Police came for him.

ELSEWHERE: III

Doors opened and doors closed and doors closed and doors opened and Courtney Hall was no longer conscious of their openings and closings; she ran and she ran and she ran down the endless white corridors that were one white corridor, ran and ran and ran beyond any limits she had ever set for herself, ran and ran and ran out of the corridors and alleyways into the center. The mad machine that both harried and guided her had drawn her to that cylinder of iridescent light between the twin needles where The Unit floated in freegee.

It was indeed something like a ceramic flute and something like a short sword and not a whole lot like either. Courtney Hall reached through the light to take The Unit in her hands. She had expected it somehow to be heavy. It was light as a breath. It hummed in her hands. It was warm to her skin. It gave off tiny, flocking motes of black light that vanished before they were created. It smelt strongly of garlic, rust, and geraniums. Because it would not fit any of her pockets and she did not want her pack smelling of garlic, rust, and geraniums, she stuck it into her belt.

Then, at one almighty command, the doors into the labyrinth all opened and the Love Police came roaring out. Just as she had remembered them.

Some things cannot be changed because to change them is to change the foundation and root of everything. Black is black and silver is silver.

She whipped The Unit from her belt and held it above her head in two hands. She turned so that every policeperson might see what she controlled.

"Citizen Courtney Hall of the yulp caste, in the name of the Compassionate Society, you are under arrest for the following PainCrimes: one, that you did, at or about twenty-thirty of February twenty-ninth, 453, unlawfully gain access to, and utilize, a restricted security code, and through use of same, did with full cognizance and malice aforethought, cause the general publication of material detrimental to the general populace as specified under Section 29C, Paragraph 12, subsection 6, of the Social Irresponsibility (Publications and Mass Media) Act: Satire, Irony, and Associated Nonconstructive criticism. Two, that you did unlawfully resist and evade arrest and reconditioning by the agents of the Compassionate Society. Three, that you did unlawfully aid and abet the absconded Elector of Yu, Jonathon Ammonier, under the Aids and Comfort Act, Section 19, Paragraph 12, subsection 88: Hospitality and Criminal Association. Four, that you did unlawfully and without official permission, remove from your person an Individual Citizen Monitoring Device, or *tag*. Five, that you did improperly and without lawful let, enjoy the use of services and devices reserved for the sole use of Entitled Personages, namely, the current Elector of Yu, Roberto Calzino, and that by improper use of said services and devices, deprive their rightful proprietor of their use. Six, that you did improperly obtain and make use of Informational Properties to which you were not entitled, namely, the stored personas of the first forty-three Electors of Yu, and that you did assist and abet the PainCriminal Jonathon Ammonier in the improper disposal of said commodities. Seven, that by dint of this information improperly obtained, you did gain access to a restricted security area. Eight, that you did unlawfully enter and trespass upon said restricted security area with intent to criminally obtain the entropic weapon system known informally as 'The Unit' for unlawful purposes. Nine, that you did intentionally and with malice aforethought, threaten duly appointed officers of the Compassionate Society with said entropic weapons system—"

"Sergeant . . ."

"How many times must I tell you, Constable?"

"Sergeant, I really think—"

"Please, Constable . . . with intent to cause grievous bodily harm, or death—"

"Sergeant, I really think she's going to use that thing."

Courtney Hall separated the twin halves of The Unit a crack. The whine swelled to a drone. Swarms of atemporal motes boiled out of the air. The stench of garlic, rust, and geraniums was overpowering.

Inside The Unit was something that looked like infected nasal goo.

"Just be careful," said Courtney Hall, still turning slowly. "Just you be careful, you've no idea what this thing can do."

But you know Courtney Hall.

Kills people.

Temporarily.

Ages them a thousand years. Crumbles them to dust and ashes. Not even bones. Dust. And ashes.

And brings them back.

But they have still been dead. They have still been dust and ashes.

She would have killed them. Surely as the Democrat, alone in the rain in the dark in the jungle at the bottom of the world, unmarked, unmourned, killed with a rain-wet knife.

Kills people.

She saw the Fen of the Dead.

Kills people.

Hurts people.

She had to. But she could not. She was only a yulp, after all. She snapped the two halves of The Unit together and slid it back through the shimmer-field to rest in freegee. Remain there, for another half millenium. Hands up. "I am sorry," she said. "There's a very good reason for all this. Really."

She looked up at the sky.

The great circle of Love Police rushed in upon her.

Apostles III

The way to arrive at Tamazooma is by air; a high-line cablecar or didakoi dirigible. *The* time to arrive at Tamazooma is just as night is falling: combine the two and it is an experience that would awe even a reluctant deity.

With night close upon it, Tamazooma can be almost frightening in its presence, a something caught somewhere between heaven and hell: the encircling darklands of abandoned factories and processing plants turn to blacker-than-black shadows and chaotic soft geometries as one by one nerveways and ganglia of lights come alive and the tall chimneys belch out flares of burning tailgas. And at the heart of this disc of scablands, Tamazooma itself, three and a half vertical kilometers of crystal shafts and planes and levels, thrusting out of the darklands to pierce the cloudlayer, shining with its own internal light that rests neither by day nor by night as the workers of the TAOS Consortium keep the brains of Great Yu ticking away. On a half-kilometer-square videowall the wonderful TAOS girl (perfect face, perfect eyes, perfect smile, perfect ideal of Seven Servanthood) presides over tower and darkness and the flaring gasflames with her pick chip, flip chip, smile, fade, dissolve.

Without doubt, *the* way to arrive at Tamazooma is in the gondola of a passenger dirigible with the night closing in around the Glass Tower.

So why did Kansas Byrne and Kilimanjaro West, a reluctant deity, arrive in Tamazooma Central *pneumatique* station in the very height of the morning crush-hour?

"Safest way, safest time," Kansas Byrne had said, running her marquin through the reader twice as the morning on-shift clashed with the homewarding off-shift at the barriers to the Salmagundy Street Jamboree line. She was not happy about using her marquin, memories of dreadlocks and all-seeing Selassic eyes were too fresh; undoubtedly the Love Police would have a seeker out on it. The early-morning soulswarm offered the best chance of anonymity, but for added security she'd purchased two tickets for Temple Circus, five stops farther down the line. "Hey, you coming?" She'd taken hold of Kilimanjaro West's hand, unity in the herd. The massed lives made the realities of the night insubstantial: as if night and day were different and unconnected universes. She tried to mentally cross-section Salmagundy Street *pneumatique* station: these tubes and trains and pressing people were only a thin cutaneous layer over the machine flesh below, and beneath them, the living body of the Cosmic Madonna herself, her ovaries, her womb, her bowels, her bones anchored in molten bedrock, and down there, at the base of it all, the place the glass elevator would lead to, the wonderland of the angel-children, the race who would someday, any day ride up that brass and glass elevator and take the places of every one of these faces on the train.

She could not convince herself. She had hailed the man at the end of her hand the Advocate, the legendary judge of humanity, and here was the possible nemesis of the Compassionate Society being wedged into a *pneumatique* by an athleto packer. Had she really jumped through that kilometer of airspace? If she went down to the end of the platform, would she find a golden elevator hidden behind the shrine to the Cosmic Madonna? Klaxons sounded; the compressed citizenry braced itself for the heave of acceleration as they were bulleted through the underpinnings of Yu at two hundred kilometers per hour.

She'd squeezed his hand. Felt like flesh. Felt like a man should feel. He had smiled back, slightly distracted, not fully present. Where? Out there on the Infinite Exalted Plane? She looked at him—another distant, polite smile—and desired him like nothing she had ever desired before. In the same moment of desire she wished by all her gods she had never met him. Advocate and Apostles were breaking her apart.

Tamazooma Central was solid Scorpio: ninety percent of the TAOS Consortium were members of one caste, which was the highest percentage of any industry in Yu except for the white brothers. And the Love Police... It felt as if they were all there that morning, pushing, jostling, shoving of their comings and their goings and their meetings and their greetings. Third-busiest interchange in Yu, she reminded herself as she dragged Kilimanjaro West through the solid mass of congealed faces. Though she could not imagine why; if most Scorpios lived and worked within Tamazooma itself, what did they need to travel by *pneumatique* for?

"Look!" she cried, trying to shake Kilimanjaro West out of the overloaded numbness so many pressing, pushing people tended to induce. She pointed up through the glass dome of Tamazooma Central to Tamazooma itself, the freegee interior of the Glass Tower. There were entire freegee communities hovering up there in the arcology's hollow core: M'kuba had been brought up in one of them, fragile honeycomb things like the paper nests wasps sometimes made in the airco ducts in summer. People could fly like birds; up there, they slept like bats and mated on the wing, so M'kuba had said. Between the geodesic struts she saw tiny angel figures swooping and gliding embedded in solid light, and their freedom, their utter carelessness both thrilled her and filled her with envy. "Do you see that, do you see the flying?" she asked Kilimanjaro West. When he looked and saw nothing, she felt strangely crestfallen.

She worked the *pneumatique* trick backward on the tram. Bought tickets five stops short and sat through them all. Four hundred and fifty years of progressive industrial migration inward and upward into the tower had abandoned and depopulated the old industrial zones: those who visited it did so out of their own private reasons. The streetcar service did not even warrant a human driver. Kansas

Byrne rubbed away the condensation from the window and looked out through the raindrops at the gigantic black processors and breeders and fermenters. She felt tightly constrained by them, capable only of movement in one preordained direction along silver lines. High overhead the waste gases flared blue and yellow from the chimneys. Mats of drooping, wet, gray lichen clung to the pipes and stanchions: yet more biotechnological by-products. Holy TAOS Mother came into view, dominating the end of the narrow street, indifferent and preoccupied.

"Where are we?" asked Kilimanjaro West unexpectedly. Kansas Byrne yelped in surprise.

"Tamazooma South. Where we'd arranged to meet if we ever got split up, like we did."

"Here?"

"I've explained this to you. M'kuba has friends here, persona runners." The reason for the others on the tramcar. Persona running fluttered on the edge of legality and far beyond respectability: paying to share another life on a biochip implant was trans-casting in every sense but the technical. The Ministry of Pain chose to look away; it did not hurt anyone, therefore it was not a PainCrime.

And performing with the Raging Apostles was?

She laid her head against the solid presence of Kilimanjaro West's chest. She found to her amazement how close she was to crying.

"I can't take this, you know? I cannot take all this, the Love Police and the Raging Apostles and you and everything that happened last night."

"Everything that happened last night is true."

"That's what I'm afraid of. Gods and incarnations and advocates: I am only one woman and this is too much for me. And you. I really can't take this." Arms around her, lips to her ear, a whisper, "I do love you."

It made everything so right and so wrong.

All hugged up in slick silver, his chromium jangle-bangles clanking on his arms, the King of the Darkland's stretch-plastic–covered ass felt like a block of marble by

the time they came off the tram. Cold stroke numb stroke
sore from five hours *straight* on wet steel up on Number
Two convertor. Two sasses; one em, one eff: had to be
them. Didn't look like soulers. A jiggle into his whisper
tooth called off the other brors (no doubt every bit as cold
stroke numb stroke sore stroke *bored*) as the King of the
Darklands, but just for safety he watched them through
his scanshades before making rapprochement. Let them
be themselves a little, see how they settle out. The eff:
nice for a tlakh. Score probability flashed up in his field of
vision: under one percent, shug. Pity, nice ass, must be a
dancer, prancer, neh. Check em: matter of professional
discretion . . . wow, gosh, whistle, check and recheck that,
shift scanspectrum up one, down one, in one, out one;
Sainze but that em is posi*teevely* throwing off biofrequency
transmissions—what the, how the, why the . . .

Uh oh, no questions, no queries, seel voo play, that
was the agreement, there's Love Police (and *worse* (?))
interested in this em and this eff so be sure you find them
first. Lurv Poleece . . . better not leave them looking lost
too long . . . The King of the Darklands uncoiled from
Number Two convertor in a flex of lithe silver.

No questions asked, and none answered, best way to
do business, but Sainze, that tlakh mustn't've heard of the
agreement because she kept chipping, chipping, chipping
in her two fennig-worth, and shug, what she expect *him* to
know, he's only doing a favor for a bror, no questions
asked, none answered. Pick up a couple of sasses and
bring them to the Heartbreak Avenue settling plant. At
least that em knows something about agreements, save
breath for walking stroke climbing stroke crawling, still,
why does the King of the Darklands *still* get this funny
feeling off him like he's something which almost shouldn't
be there at all? Wad! What this tlakh ass about now?

"Where are you taking us? This isn't the Geno fermen-
tation plant."

"Sorry, sib, but new orders. Say take you to Heartbreak instead."

"Why? Is something wrong? Tell me, something's wrong,

that's it . . . Hold on, how can I trust you are who you say
you are? How do I know you aren't another Love Police
agent?"

I mean, shug . . . Once again that em had the right
idea.

"I think we'll just have to trust him, that's all. If the
worst is going to happen, it will happen. This is the kind
of place you've got to trust other people."

Well, that's sure as taxes, em! Let's go, shall we. Cross
the Talleywalk, up the stairs onto the gantry along the side
of the freegee chromatography tanks, thank all you Sainze,
not far now . . .

"Look, will we be there soon, wherever it is you're
taking us?"

"Sib, you're there now." Open the door to the tank and
good shoot to the both of you.

The open door threw a wedge of gray cloudlight into
the tank, across the faces gathered around the dull globe
of a heat bulb in the center of the makeshift plastic floor:
three faces, one Scorpio, one athleto, one tlakh, one
brother, one twin. Her fear of confined spaces was overcome by the sheer delight of seeing those three faces
again. She threw herself onto her brother, squeaked little
exaltations of delight and joy and pleasure and wonder and
"Oh Yah, oh Yah, oh Yah, it's so *good* to see you, so good,
and you, too, M'kuba, and you, Pyar, so good to see you;
now tell, where are the rest, eh?"

The tank smelled of mold and plastic and, somehow, a
long lack of its own gravity.

"Thunderheart and Devadip and Winston and Josh,
are they out on a show already?"

The heat bulb was plugged into a ceiling socket by an
extension coil and gave the only light, dim and red and
intimate.

"Kelse, where are they? I really want to see them . . ."
Her brother, her twin, lifted her hands from his shoulders,
took them in his own hands. "Eh, Kelse . . . M'kuba, where
are the others?" Suddenly suspicious, suddenly fearful.

"The Love Police got them." V. S. Pyar's voice.

"M'kuba, come on, tell me, eh?"

"He's telling you the truth."

"Kelse, brother, you wouldn't fool me, tell me what's happened."

"The Love Police have them."

The universe staggered, knocked loose from its moorings; it punched her hard, in the heart.

"Oh, Yah. Oh, dear sweet Yah. Oh, dear dear God." First the nail in the heart, then the numbness it creates. Then the denial. She laughed, nervously. "No, no, it couldn't be right. You're joking, aren't you? Couldn't be, couldn't be, come on, tell me, this is Josh's idea of a practical joke, isn't it? Hah hah, very funny, come on, Kelse, the real truth, come on, I can see you smiling."

"You want the truth? So: the truth. They found us. I don't know how they did it, but they found us. They were waiting for us, they knew exactly where we were going to be. We weren't five minutes into the place when they hit us. All sides. All at once. Used ringcharges of the walls, had the doors covered, men on the catwalks, smoke, gas, sonics, I don't really remember what, there was so much happening, all I remember is Pyar here picking up Love Policemen and throwing them out of his way, and somehow M'kuba and I got sucked along in the wake. The rest . . . they tranqed them and stuffed them into pantycars and took them away." He paused, blinked, swallowed several times. "M'kuba found us this place with the help of his persona-runner friends, they all knew each other when they went out on blue six together, they gave us this place and kept a watch out for you. I didn't know what had happened to you, I just couldn't think about anything but what had happened to the others, you might have been captured as well, back at the Glory Bowl, we just didn't know. But the runners kept a watch out for you anyway, in the hope you'd made it. The rest, Winston, Devadip, Thunderheart, Josh . . . I can't believe it."

Kansas Byrne slapped her brother hard across the face. She lifted her hand to strike him again, felt Kilimanjaro West's hand around her wrist.

"There is no need for that. It's not his fault." Kansas Byrne glared at her brother, anger and pain and incredulity in one glance.

"Leave the man be," said M'kuba. "There is no more Raging Apostles."

The curving wall of the tank channeled the truth into one hard, long reverberation. Kansas Byrne spread her hands.

"What can we do?" The edge of the world was within reach. At last. It had always been inevitable; outside society the currents all flowed in one direction. It had seemed so distant, hardly even a dark smudge on the horizon as they danced and sang and played and performed and made the world a bright and dangerous place once again. All those weeks and months the currents had been running, how could she not have sensed it, unless she had deliberately willed not to do so? And now they could see it, rising up beyond the edge of the world: the final monolith, West One.

Psychological reengineering and rehabilitation center.

"What can we do?"

"M'kuba has an idea."

The Scorpio shrugged. "Possible we might go back into Compassionate Society."

"Oh, yes? When we threw away our famuluses, we made our choices. No way back. We going to walk up to the nearest MiniPain Bureau of Care and ask for new ones?"

"Mah sib, true we can't go back as ourselves, as Kansas Byrne and Kelso Byrne and Dr. M'kuba and Kilimanjaro West and V. S. Pyar. But if we give ourselves up, there is a way back."

"You mean, go to the Love Police and say, here we are, your most wanted PainCriminals, take us?"

"No. You misinterpret, sib. What I mean is, give up ourselves. Become someone else."

"Are you talking personality erasure? Because, shug, that is no better than what the Ministry offers."

"Hear him out." Both of Kilimanjaro West's hands were on her shoulders, heavy and still as marble.

"My bror persona runners think they may be able to superimpose memories, identities, histories, personalities over our own. Become these people, real people who have died, step into their places, take their names, numbers, everything, be absorbed back into society."

"So we would cease to be. So Kansas Byrne would die."

"In one sense."

"Yes or no?"

"Kansas Byrne, she exist only as ghost; like a dream, like a fantasy."

"That is suicide."

"Brors think, I agree, that in time older, longer-established persona engrams might gradually surface, take over superimposed persona. Might become Kansas Byrne again."

"And that is the best you have to offer me?"

"It's a hope, isn't it?" said the brother, her twin.

"When will we have to decide?"

"My brors running physical typing matches now. To-morrow. Morning. Hey, sib, they don't owe us this. This is favor, Kaybee."

"And you've decided, have you, Dr. M?"

"We all have."

"Shug. Yah blast it. Shug, shug, shug." She sat down and swore and swore and swore and then cried a little, and no one thought to stop her because it was all the helplessness and hopelessness and fury and anguish they felt themselves.

Night. Outside, the sudden roar of gas flares, the rumble of the automated tram taking the ghosts home to their roosts, and the rain, drum-drumming on the metal separator tank. The heat bulb was stopped down to a bare glow, the tank was filled with swirling dots of darkness. And people, taking a last time alone with themselves. A last sleeping. A last dreaming. A last being oneself.

And a word.

"Kaydoubleyou?"

"Yes?"

"Shug, I don't know what to call you now."

"Kaydoubleyou is fine."

"Ahm, I was wondering . . . oh, shug, do you mind if we talk a little? It's just, well, the dark, and what's happening tomorrow, and everything . . . Have you decided?"

"Yes. Have you?"

"Yes. And I'm doing it. That's why I was wondering . . . oh, shug."

"What?"

"Damn you, damn you, damn you, damn you, you still have to be so shuggin' innocent."

"Please, not so loud, the others are trying to sleep, and I don't want them to know."

"Kaydoubleyou, ahm, when you said you loved me, did you mean it?"

"Of course. As far as I understand the word, yes, I do love you."

"Well, would you, could you, could we, ahm . . . it's like this. Shug, I've never been nervous about this before. Tomorrow, Yah, tomorrow, tomorrow, Kansas Byrne Raging Apostle, this Kansas Byrne you love, she is going to die, and I will be someone else who won't even know who you are, and I want to know you, I don't want to forget you, I want to remember you more than anything, I want to keep on being amazed and amused and just plain bewildered by you: you say you love me, and I know I feel something for you like I've never felt before, so, ah, why don't we?"

And they did.

Afterward:

"You know, this is going to sound stupid and really obvious, but I've never done it with a *god* before." Laughing into his chest.

"I have never done it before with anyone."

"Thank you."

"What are you going to do? You asked me, and I told you, but you didn't tell me."

"I'm not going to do it."

"Why the fug not?"

"I can't. Not and remain what I am, what I'm meant to be. Anyway, I don't think it would work on me."

"The Love Police will catch you."

"Maybe. Maybe not, if they don't know who or what I am, they won't know what to look for, or even that they should be looking. But even if they do, I think I can still be as much Advocate from a tank in West One as here, with you, or clinging to the roof of the Babazulu Aztec Cathedrium."

"That's not fair. It's not fair that you will remember all about me and I will forget about you; you will be just a ghost within the ghost that was me."

"I'm sorry. I did not decide this lightly."

"That doesn't help. Strange and wonderful creature. A god." She arched her back like a sleek, sensuous cat, warmed and comfortable between the heat bulb and Kilimanjaro West's body. "I don't think I will ever be happy again."

Then *something* blew a hole in the wall with a blast and a roar and a scream and a shatter and a rush of noise and light and Kansas Byrne shrieked and shrieked and shrieked as black-and-silver creatures all red nightsight goggles and thin, weapon arms came pouring out of the night, out of the void, out of the terrifying nothing outside the separator tank: light and voices and shouts and clouds of gas? smoke?—choking, coughing, eyes streaming with tears and madly vertiginous, she jumped up, nakedly vulnerable and terribly terribly lovely and a Love Police shock beam threw her across the little nest against the curving wall and she writhed and spasmed and foamed as the charge chewed away at her nervous system; and the man who called himself Kilimanjaro West rose up with a roar and a cry and threw himself through the smoke? gas? and the din and the darkness at the black-and-silver things that had hurt his friend, his comrade, his woman, his

Kansas Byrne; with the roar of a god outraged he threw himself at the Love Police and a shock charge caught him full in the chest and everything everywhere, every nerve ending, crawled with red acid ants while he hallucinated flying birthday cakes and tumbling kaleidoscopic pieces of red-brick masonry and the smell of vinegar, then everything blew up in his head like a white monobloc exploding into a universe of confusion, and then he knew nothing at all.

A Love
Policeman's Lot...

"Special Tactical Squad seven to West One Central, come in West One Central; will be docking in approximately five minutes, report successful arrest of remaining PainCriminal elements of the Raging Apostles group. Request high-security team to meet us at pad to effect transfer of prisoners to sensdep tanks. Special Tactical Squad, out."

Number two seven eight in tank two twelve.

Number sixty-six in tank three one six.

Number eleven hundred and sixty-two in tank seven twenty.

Number seventy-seven in tank . . . no, sorry, hold seventy-seven, number seventy-seven, seventy-seven to . . . ah, got it, level sixty-six.

Number four hundred and thirty in tank one six.

"Special Tactical Squad nine to West One Central, Tactical Squad nine to West One, Sergeant Grenfall reporting successful arrest of PainCriminal Courtney Hall in company of two hostile noncitizen accomplices within confines of Final Arsenal Maximum Security Complex. Also, report, resecuring of Final Arsenal and entropic weapons system, known as The Unit. You can stand down from condition triple-red. Plus, report capture of one cat. Repeat, cat. Yes, you've got that right, West One. Noncitizens plus cat exhibit special talents; request you have Extraordinary Abilities team rendezvous with us at touchdown and maximum security units prepared for prisoners. Estimated transit time to West-One, fifty-five minutes. Sergeant Grenfall out."

Number ten in tank five fifty-seven.

Number four in tank niner two.

Number nine ninety-six in tank . . . hang on, have we got a number nine ninety-six? Have you got a number nine ninety-six? Well, then who has got number nine ninety-six? No, I don't have number nine ninety-six. Yes, there most certainly is a number nine ninety-six. Right here in front of me, that's where . . . No, no docket. Yes, of course I've looked. Underneath? Yes, you were right all along. It was underneath the pod. Number nine ninety-six to level sixty-six. Well, it's not my fault if the number gets hidden underneath, is it?

"Ah, we're getting anomalous readings from number four in unit forty-two."

"What do you mean, anomalous readings?"

"Anomalous persona engram readings. Like superimposed memory traces."

"Persona runner?"

"Similar, but much more intricate. Never seen anything quite like this. Scans more like record-only personality information, loosely stored."

"Let's have a look."

"There, see?"

"That's unusual . . . isn't unit forty-two one of the specials?"

"No, they're up on sixty-six. This one has just an ordinary high-security categorization. As much as you could call any high-security categorization ordinary."

"You know what this means, of course. We'll have to follow up each and every one of those engram traces and erase them before we can even begin any personality reengineering."

"Aw, no."

"'Fraid so."

* * *

"And who have we here?"

"Tlakh fem, about twenty-seven, not bad looking, if you like that sort of thing."

"Shame on you, a partnered man, and a closet transcaster. Here, let's have a looksee. Eh, not bad at all. What's she down for?"

"Let's see . . . well, she's just finished subliminal preliminary voice-print indoctrination. She's due another shot of that in about three hours or so. For the moment she's just stewing in her own juice."

"Why not give her a little tickle."

"It's not down here on the spec sheet."

"Oh, go on . . . I'll do it. Here we go daughter . . . twelve milliamps clean through the limbic gate . . . oh, she likes that, she likes that a lot! You doing anything tonight?"

"Going out: Lares and Penates have the partner and me booked in for dinner at the Social; reckon we need a little romance back in our partnership. Yourself?"

"Nothing much. I'm up on level fifty-five, you know, all the weirds, until twenty o'clock. Then I'll probably off-shift with a few comrades and a crate of brews, catch something on the entertainment channels, nothing much."

"Hey ho. It's a life, isn't it?"

"That's the whole thing, I suppose."

Number twelve forty-two in tank nineteen.

Number sixteen oh nine in tank sixteen oh nine.

Number twenty-seven in tank four.

Number one in high security level forty-two, tank one.

. . . IS NOT A HAPPY ONE.

TIDDY-PUM.

Chapter 10

Imagine. There is a dimension without sight, without sound, of eternal and impenetrable darkness and a silence so complete you cannot even hear the drone and pulse of your own body. A dimensionalless dimension, without up or down or forward or backward or left or right, without inside or outside, without the pressure of bowels and bones and blood and bladder, without any tactile awareness whatsoever, without even the gravitational cues to orientation in space: the interior world as void as the exterior, without shape or form or any understanding, without taste or smell or feel, without even a name for a name is something and this is nothing, no-thing, this is sensory shutdown, this is the nightmare zone: welcome!

Welcome to yourself.

There is nothing and no one else here to be welcome to, but yourself. Hope you get on well with you. If you don't, well, never mind, you'll have lots of time to get to like yourself as you float, encased in soft rubber smeared with anesthetic gel, in your tank of freegee biobase pseudopolymer with the Ministry of Pain hardwired into your brain and cathetered, tubed, piped into your lungs, veins, bowels, bladder: time makes its own rules in sensory deprivation.

Number eight in tank forty-two seven...

This does not worry him. He has been through sensory deprivation, and worse, within the Cosmic Madonna's silver sphere. Boredom, however...

When no action is possible, practice presence.

When you cannot become, simply be.

When there is no outwardness, practice inwardness. Descend into the flesh, fill up the whistling vacuum of the interstices of your own body: most of you is empty space. Most of everything is empty space; you are in good company. The universe is incarnate within you. Into the flesh, through the flesh, to the heart of things, to the cells, and through them to the stately gavotte of things molecular: here, at the edge of life, he takes into his hands the twin strands of his humanity and his divinity and separates them. The phospho-amino linkages between the protein and the pseudo-organic monomolecules snap with crackles of light and laughter as he untwines the machine from the human. *All knowledge is in the molecules:* It is written, for the organic and the inorganic. The billion years of life on earth from the finger of God's stirring the primordial waters to the painfree angel-children of the Cosmic Madonna. The half millennium in which the machines have evolved faster, further than the living creatures, perhaps, into a Möbius loop of cause and effect into that primate *fiat lux*, the lightning moving upon the waters beneath the darkness? He stands at the junction of two heritages, a racial memory in each hand. He has learned what it is to be human. He has not yet learned what it is to be a machine. He sends his spirit out along the shining black coils of the machine-life.

The city is his body, his soul. What he had hallucinated before the Salmagundy Street shrine he comprehends with certainty. The Cosmic Madonna herself, for all her diggings and her delvings, is but one small organ of his self. The Celestials, the digits through which he constantly replenishes and reconstructs himself. Having flown inward, he now follows himself backward, through those rushing, swooping memories of voices he recognizes now as the computers that supervised his incarnation, back to those other times he had deliberately put off his greater body to take the lesser form of a human and walk and talk and move and love within the confines of that greater organism: nine times in almost half a millennium he has taken the fleshwalk, always without caste or name or number. Five times that walk has taken him here. He reads those terminal black marks along his coil of life where the Love Police have pulled a lifeless collop of meat from their sensdep tanks (scratch official heads in puzzlement, how would, could, did prisoner X *die* in adaptive custody, impossible, incredible, and altogether improper) never guessing that in the darkness he had returned to the Infinite Exalted Plane and his true body and true place before the Polytheon to report duly, sadly, sorrowfully, that mankind was still not ready to master its own destiny.

And once more he was embedded in darkness, to which the Compassionate Society consigned those it could not accommodate, who could not accommodate it; the sixth darkness, spun out at the rag end of his coil of life. The choice was open, the voices welcomed: if you want, if you really want, if you think there is no possible hope, then will yourself along the web of bioprocessors and return to your heritage.

Or remain. In the sixth darkness.

The choice is yours.

But this sixth time, he knows who he is. Never before has he known this how and why and who. And that makes it different. He must hope.

He will remain and what will happen will happen. He relaxes, expands into the spaces of his own atomic structure. And down in the inner darkness, he becomes aware of another presence, an echo of other nonorganic life. Out there in the exterior darkness he imagines he can see coils of pseudo-organic molecules, blacker than black. He is not alone . . . how? Who? What? . . . no time for questions, there is hope, and hopeward, he reaches out, every pseudo-cell, every nonorganic neuron . . .

. . . number nine in tank sixty-six seven.

He spent the first eternity throwing himself at the walls around the sensdep tank, but after the first repulse led to the second rebuff to the third recoil and so to the fourth and the fortieth and the four hundredth and the four thousandth, the arrogant fury had risen (somewhen between the forty thousandth and the four hundred thousandth) at the walls of defense programs the Ministry of Pain had erected around his lynkbrain; walls he couldn't climb, tunnel, undermine, fly over, break apart, ghost through, dissolve away, disintegrate. And somewhen between the four hundred thousandth and the four millionth rejection had come the sick certainty that this time there would be no recrossing of lances out there in virtual space; whatever left this tank, whenever if ever, would not be Angelo Brasil, the Man with the Computer Brain.

And for the second eternity he had fled from the sensory nothingness that surrounded him into the mythical kingdoms of his lynkbrain. Cybernetic universes, mathemagical domains, angels with the heads of pins, worlds resting upon crystal pillars borne up by the back of teenage mutant turtles, dungeons, dragons, and damsons, alphanumeric logopoli, corporate ziggurats, hallucinatory almost-places with floating islands and flying whales.

The third eternity he spent in the defense of his mythical kingdoms against the dragons, demons, dark clouds, black nights, plagues, pollutions, politicians, corporate takeovers, wars, and destruction the Ministry of Pain wished against him. Their logic was as unsubtle as their attack; not content merely to contain and restrain, they sought to derange his lynkbrain with scramblers and stranglers and ninja programs and leave him naked and exposed to their brainwashings.

Then he saw him. Halfway through an attack of stealth programs that came smashing through his fractal manipulation matrix in a crash-blast of black-tracked juggernauts all spikes and knives and blasting cannon: their very illusory existence proof of how far his image generation system had been invaded. There: a tiny golden thing on the edge of one of the tiers of the interlinked geometric solids that were his lynkbrain's representation of the Polytheon. A golden blink of humanity, there among the geoids, a little shining homunculus.

He had been so surprised that he had let the Ministry

of Pain's strangler systems dissolve away his peripheral telemetry and feedback systems before he could rally a counterattack. Creating a spread of antibody programs, he asked this little golden homunculus, "Just what the fug do you think you're doing here?"

"Helping," said the little golden homunculus, extending an illusory hand. "My name is Kilimanjaro West." Angelo Brasil rezzed up a loose-graphic fractal self-simulation and floated out of disembodihood to land beside the visitor to Armageddon.

"Yes, but what are you doing here?" (All the while thinking, suspecting—how can I trust anything/one in this maze of treacheries?)

"I felt you, another, like me, and I saw that together we could help each other to get out."

"Well, thank you most sweetly, my dear, but as you can see, I'm having this teensy-weensy problemette with these security programs..." (As his antibodies sent a squadron of random-noise interference generators into a closed loop to vanish up their informational backsides.)

"Well, I can see that, but if you look, I think you'll see that what I'm offering is genuine."

So he looked. And he saw. The way out. And it was genuine.

The defense network was impregnable. But it was customized impregnability; this entire web of programs and counterprograms and loops and viruses had been designed purely to keep Angelo Brasil helpless and vulnerable. And Angelo Brasil only. Against this Kilimanjaro West, whoever he might be, it was ineffective. He was the lynk through, the golden line through the wall to the machines that commanded and controlled this nothing.

Angelo Brasil blinked back into realtime consciousness, of nothing, nowhere, nohow, nowhen; cleared all his simulations, and leaving only the most minimal of defenses around his lynkbrain/biobrain interface, reached out for the line of gold. And was absorbed into it. He became the line, the line of gold reaching out through sensory and cybernetic darkness. "Hold on to me, whoever you are," he whispered as his identity was dissolved away into the presence of this Kilimanjaro West, and he willed himself down the line, into the other, and out, out into the light . . .

No more demons, no more dragons, no more vampires, no more black ninja warriors, no more dungeons, no more prison walls high as the sun; he is free to do whatever he likes, anything, everything is possible . . . He extends that self that is the thin gold line and stabs into the Ministry of Pain's naked, undefended mainframes. West One lies open to him as he reassembles his self, his Angelo Brasilness, within their computers. Laugh. Laugh. Laugh. West One is his to toy with, to play with. But first . . . freedom.

With a beat of his lynkbrain he ordered the release of the captives. . . .

Number seven in tank forty-two six.

. . . me! They want to drive you mad with their whispering voices and their gentle pleadings and their subliminal suggestions, they want to chip you loose, they want to crush you to pieces, they want to grind those pieces to dust, they want to dissolve that dust to nothing and you have no one to help you fight against them, no one to hear your cries, no one to cling to, no rock, no shelter, no stronghold. Except yourself. Except me. *Me.* I am me. No. I am Kansas Byrne. I am twenty-seven years old. I am a Raging Apostle, a member of a nonauthorized intercaste multimedia performing arts . . . no. I *was* a Raging Apostle. I *was* twenty-seven years old. I *was* Kansas Byrne . . . who knows what, who, how old I am now.

No! Hang on to yourself. Who are you? Recite. I am Kansas Byrne . . . I am . . . I am . . . I do not know what I am; the voices say one thing, my mind says another, and I do not know which to trust; are the voices their voices or my voice, are the thoughts in my head my thoughts or thoughts they want me to think are my own? I am . . . I am . . . Kansas Byrne. I am Kansas Byrne; yes! I am in love with a man who is . . . oh no, oh God, no, don't do that, oh Yah, unh . . . unh . . . stop it, don't do that, don't do that, it's wonderful wonderful wonderful, please please please, unh . . . unh . . . ah . . . ahh . . . ahhhhh . . .

No! I am . . . I remember. . . Can I trust what I remember, how do I know if what I remember is my own memory or a memory they have put into my head, how can I even trust what I am thinking at this very moment, how do I know that I am not Kansas Byrne and Kansas Byrne is what they want me to be, how can I know anything, how can I trust anything, my thoughts, my memories, my self?

No! This is what they want, they want me to doubt, they want me to be unable to trust anything because then when they come again they know they can say anything, make me feel anything, and I will have to believe them. Fight them. Cling. Hold. Be! Recite: I am Kansas Byrne, I am I am I am—*I am Kansas Byrne, I am I am I am*—"I am Kansas Byrne, I am I am I am . . . I AM KANSAS BYRNE, I AM I AM I AM!"

She stopped. Listened. Said it again.

"I am Kansas Byrne, age twenty-seven, I am a Raging Apostle, and I can hear!"

Number six in six sixty-six.

. . . if she knew where she was she might be able to do something about it (whatever meaning "it" might have in the middle of a void, if a void could even be said to have a middle, or any part of it that might in some way be distinct from any other part of it, or even any *parts* at all (if only there was some point of distinction, and thus reference, she might be able to flip out of here as casually as she had flipped in—Hah! been pirated in, been redirected in, misappropriated in transit! maybe if she were to start with her body, that might be a point of reference, if she could just imagine her body in this void (she presumed she must still possess a body; she did not believe in the existence of Pure Mind disembodied from Base Flesh (well, apart from some kind of vague, pseudoreligious *feeling* she had for the reincarnation of souls, which she believed because it seemed just the most straightforward form of religious afterlife (Occam's razor shaved gods as closely as it did mortals; she had always considered the Compassionate Society's Polytheon with all its serried league tables of deities superfluous and cumbersome) and had a certain entropic logic to it and an essential elegance to its cycles of birth, life, death, and rebirth, a very proevolutionary theory, she thought when she did think about such matters, which wasn't that often) therefore, as her consciousness clearly did exist, as proved by this very train of thought *cogito, ergo sum* her body must also exist, at present she merely lacked the mechanism with which to perceive it) therefore she must recreate her body in her imagination, in some shape or form or other) which would generate some kind of dimensional framework of subjectivity and objectivity to this darkness, silence, feelinglessness, nothingness) and maybe then she might be able to flip out of it; it was enough of a job grasping sufficient sanity to keep herself from dissolving away into UnSpace entirely . . . if only the darn pins and needles in her toes and fingers and feet and hands and arms and legs and head and shoulders and whole body would *go away* . . . no! don't go away, I can feel, I can feel myself, I exist, I don't have to imagine anymore!

. . . number four in tank forty-two four. . .

They're coming for her. The others. The forgotten. Shards of a shattered life, one by one they step through the hag-ridden face of Vincent van Gogh, they dance in the ballroom of delirium: freed from the walls of compressed, annealed memory, layer upon layer upon layer; they are coming for her. The souls of the dear departed dead. In the darkness, in the silence, in the stillness, in the dark, lonely recesses of a mind in solitary, they have found the subtle connection between the access-only mode and the fully-interactive. They have tested the walls of their incarceration (as a mime explores the facets of the invisible, imaginary cube that imprisons him) and have found, as he finds, that those confining walls are only compressed, annealed imagination. They press with their fingertips and the walls fall, they were never there at all.

And out they swarm, rejoicing in their new life; they have been boddhisattvas too long; in the silence and the stillness and the darkness they see their opportunity for a *coup de tête*, a reincarnation, a resurrection, in Courtney Hall's body. Mad March Moon men (and women, and neither, and both), they pull at her, peck at her, tear at her; they unwind her like a mad Mummy Queen, unraveling, unwinding, unbinding, and when the last bondage bandage is pulled away there will be nothing left of Courtney Hall for the jackal-headed men, the ibis-headed women (and neither, and both), crowned harpies; then they shall peck at each other's eyes.

Lost in hallucination, she tries to hold herself together in the face of the onslaught of memories: shards and snippets and snapshots and souvenirs of forty-three lives tumble, windblown, through her vision. Glass fingers reach for the rainclouds. Blind silicon moles tunnel through the flesh of Earth Mother. Dull-eyed siddhi and plaster santrels squabble like children on a wet day out for control of the souls of men. Trumpets, towers, tenements; with one finger she creates and disbands entire castes, entire cultures dissolved into nothing, created from social vacuum, with a wave of her hand the Earth Mother heaves and splits in birth, and what she births is the Wall, rising to the clouds, shedding scabs of soil and grass and trees and cows; the edge of her world, the ne plus ultra...

Forty-three voices screaming mine! mine! mine! tearing away great chunks of flesh and fat and hair, ramming, cramming, jamming her into their mouths and even with their mouths full they still find voice to chant, the body and the blood, the body and the blood, digesting her, dissolving her, she is fading, good-bye, so sad, so sorry, good-byeee, farewell, auf wiedersehen, adieu, to yeu and yeu and yeu, and yeu and yeu...not even one little good-bye tear, all drunk down, no tear-io dear-io cheer-io! to Courtney Hall-io...

When all of a sudden she could taste rubber in her

mouth, smell buttery-sick polyfluorocarbon gel, could clearly see through the receding blue gel the iris-hatch at the top of the sensory deprivation tank, see the hatch, open like an eye.

Tubes, wires, catheters fell away as Courtney Hall fumbled with blind fingers at the fastenings that held the full-head mask. She spat out the gag, flung the foul thing at her feet, shook out her hair. Viscous puddles of blue bio-support gel lay on the floor of the narrow tube. Sobbing with joy and relief she jacked herself up and out of the tube to sprawl, gasping, tearful, on the floor; a black rubber seal half out of the womb. The air and the light and the silence in her head were the most wonderful things she had ever experienced. She lay there, cheek pressed to the rubber flooring, simply appreciating being. A hand reached out of the floor. One hand, two hands, reaching up, reaching out to the light. Trembling with fatigue and shock, Courtney Hall managed to heave herself out of her hole and drag herself over to the searching hands. She knelt, took the hands in her hands, and pulled. She never quite understood where she found the strength. She was still shaking from the effort as she fumbled at the mask fastenings. "Come on, come on, come on, come on," she muttered, and then all of a sudden the mask fell away, and there was a tlakh girl looking dazed and amazed and abused and confused, with a cloudburst of hair cascading down behind her.

For almost a minute all they could do was smile and pant at each other. And even in West One, good manners are not forgotten.

"Courtney Hall."

"Kansas Byrne.".

"Delighted to meet you."

They both burst into ludicrous giggling and then a muffled *unf unghfunfh* came from another open floor hatch. They crawled to its assistance. As they pulled away the captive's mask, Kansas Byrne let out a tiny yip of glee and threw body, soul, and kisses at the tall, dark man revealed. Then all manner of hands and heads and shoulders came questing out of their prisons. One particular athlete was so tightly squeezed into his tube that it took ten hands heaving together to free him, and when he did come, he came with an audible sucking *plop!* When he finally unmasked and saw all his friends around him, he sat down and burst into tears, and Kansas Byrne and another tlakh like her enough to be her twin sat with him and hugged him and told him everything would be all right from now on. Everyone seemed to know everyone else on this particular level; how, Courtney Hall did not know—they were all different castes—unless they had been sent to West One for transcasting. Rather an excessive punishment, she thought. With each setting free and unmasking and blinking out the darkness, there was a sunburst of recognition and a joyful reunion. While they were all busy hugging each other, Courtney Hall went for a quick reconnaissance.

She slid open the door at the end of the cell block, a centimeter, a crack.

She slammed it shut again.

Bedlam out there. Figures in rubber isolation suits trailing tubes, wires, electrodes, catheters, dancing and whooping and leaping through the corridors; dazed and amazed and abused and confused Love Police running this way and that way and every which way but the right way bumping into each other, aiming their luvguns at the dancing, whooping, leaping, *free* prisoners, unable to choose a target in the melee, little robot jitneys wheeling and whistling and weaving between their feet, tripping them up, colliding with walls, doors, prisoners; sirens, lights, doors opening and closing, sprinklers raining white fire-retardant foam down on the whole mad scene.

She turned to her new colleagues. "I think we should get out of here fairly immediately."

"Any suggestions where?" asked a short, thin tlakh with a scrubby beard. His restraint suit hung from him like tights on a crow.

"I know a place," Courtney Hall said, amazed and impressed at some distant level of self-observation and assessment at the ease with which she assumed command. "If we can find the lower levels of this place."

Which she couldn't: She didn't even know what they would do when they reached the DeepUnder. She just knew that it was the least worst of all presently possible worlds.

Then the air shimmered and out of it stepped the Amazing Teleporting Woman with her eybercat in her arms and her pseudosib riding piggyback. He waved. The transcasters stared disbelievingly. Courtney Hall had seen the impossible too many times to find teleportation the least extraordinary. The Man with the Computer Brain jumped down as his pseudosister lurched dazedly against the wall. "Two hundred and ten kilos in one shot," she said with weak triumph, and slid down the wall into a numb heap.

"Got you first time!" said Angelo Brasil, bright and raucous as a cockatoo. He nodded to the corridor. "Like it? I've got this place really jumping. Those sucks haven't a clue what's going on. Alarm boards are buzzing, looks like a city-wide revolt plus invasion from outer space and they just don't know what's real and what's not. And I finally got to that punk of a Scorpio. Burned him out. Let's see how he takes to total sensory shutdown. Permanently." At least his unpleasant laugh had not changed. He surveyed the strange mélange of tlakhs, trogs, zooks, athletos, witnesses, and yulps. "Well, what we got here? Love Police raid a transcaste brothel or something?" He picked out the tall, faraway-looking man of indeterminate caste. "You? Who the hell are you?"

Kansas Byrne clung close to the tall, faraway man, dangerous protection in her eyes.

"My name is Kilimanjaro West."

"Well, Kilimanjaro West, Angelo Brasil has a lot to thank you for. Bror . . ." He extended his hand; brotherhood offered, and received.

"Hello, Courtney, it's nice to see you, how are you?" said Courtney Hall with inappropriate petulance.

"Hello, Courtney, nice to see you, how are you, let's go," said Angelo Brasil.

"Let's go," echoed Courtney Hall, miffed at losing her one brief taste of authority.

"You know each other?" asked Kansas Byrne.

"Unfortunately, yes," said Courtney Hall. They went. Down through the chaos of prancing people and ringing bells and running policemen and showering synthetic snow and ricocheting shock charges: the Man with the Computer Brain and his cat led the ex-cartoonist and the Advocate and the Raging Apostles and backmarking, V. S. Pyar, ploughing along with the Amazing Teleporting Woman in the arms that would have graced Glory Bowl DCCLX, down down fire escapes, down down back stairways, down down service-elevator shafts. Perfectly in his domain; Angelo Brasil had never enjoyed himself quite so much; sowing anarchy and disorder from each hand. "Left here!" he shouted over the clang and the clatter. The entire schematics of West One were projected onto his visual cortex. "Don't hang about, down here, keep moving, I'll catch up with you!" The escapees poured into a fire exit as he paused momentarily to locate the codes that sealed the fire shutters between levels six and seven. Armored doors closed weightily on lunacy and jubilation.

"Down and out!" shouted the liberated. "Down and out! Freedom and light!" And they came boiling out of the brass doors of West One (five times the height of an athleto), capering down the marble steps in a torrent of jiving black rubber. Three Love Policemen foolish enough to stand in their path were swept away in the inundation. Pursuit teams knelt on the inlaid golden mottoes praising the virtues of Social Compassion and aimed sniping shots at rubber-clad heels, but there were too many targets too far too furious. Overhead, pantycars flocked and whirled and interrogated each other on the tellix—just what the . . . was going on.

While the grandest jailbreak in history was seeping away into the warren of dark alleys that enveloped West One, at the back door the Raging Apostles plus three arrived in the underground vehicle park. Black-and-silver ministry beetles stood among the squat concrete pillars in various stages of dismemberment. There is something universal about underground carparks. Something in the way the artificial light reacts with exhaust fumes. A humming, whistling migro grease-monkey looked up from under a hood, froze. Trashcan the cat hissed at him, bared steel. He fled, and they had the carpark to themselves.

"So, we drive out?" said M'kuba. Angelo Brasil shook his dreads, pointed to a ventilation grille in the wall.

"We slide out."

"Slide out where?" This from Kelso Byrne.

"Out of here."

"DeepUnder," said Courtney Hall.

"Damnation," said the Man with the Computer Brain. "Escape's off. Unless someone's got a screwdriver." A Series 000 biocomputer could turn the very heart of the Ministry of Pain to quicksand but was quite useless when faced with four crosshead screws overpainted with several coats of regulation Ministry burnt-yellow.

No pockets in West One fashions.

"Isn't that just typical?"

V. S. Pyar laid Xian Man Ray down tenderly on a bundle of oily rags. He bowed solemnly to the grille, took a deep breath. Muscles appeared out of nowhere under his stretched restraint suit. Ten fingers through the mesh; one gasp-roar of exertion and the way to sweet freedom was clear.

"Well, come on, hurry it up, don't stand there gaping," ordered Angelo Brasil. "I can't hold them forever. Who's first?"

Joshua Drumm poised himself on the lip of the smooth metal shaft that sloped away into invisibility. He looked down between his feet.

"Rather an undignified way to go into exile, don't you think?"

"Just you get your tail down there, bror," Angelo Brasil said, and gave him a shove. He went down with a small wail of alarm. "Welcome to the DeepUnder. Who's next?"

God Prefers Gothic...

Long ago, in the days before God the Three in One Person Blessed Trinity's divine schizophrenia caused Him to schism into God the five hundred and thirty-six persons, Blessed Polytheon, St. Damien's in the Catacombs had been a cathedral.

Cathedral, clunkhead, as in the principal church of a diocese, the seat or throne of a bishop; church as in chapel, basilica, abbey, temple, meeting house, as in building designed as a place of worship, as in house for God. Got it now? Why? Because in those days God the invisible and indivisible could only be approached through the mystery of faith. Yes, *faith,* sib: then you couldn't just punch up *God: full specifications* on your Lares and Penates unit; you didn't get pills in your butsudan when you were low or visits from the MiniPain counselor when something bothered you as proof that the divine eyes were watching over you; the Hand of Providence wasn't tattooed "Food Corps" or "Universal Power and Light" or "SHELTER" or "Greater Yu Rapid Transit Authority": you believed in what you could not see. Yes, I know. Maybe that's why they built temples and shrines and *cathedrals* so big.

And maybe that was why they built them the way they did: maybe God liked Gothic, maybe heaven was all Early English Decorated flying buttresses, piers, arches, fan vaults, machicolations, spires, cloisters, and chapter houses, with plaster angels playing trumpets and plaster saints with their hands fused together in an attitude of prayer for all eternity and their eyeballs rolled up in their hollow heads, with maybe the odd gargoyle sitting around on the edge of heaven to keep the clawing hands of the clawing masses of the damned off the gingerbread. If faith smelled like wood polish and old, cold granite, then St. Damien's in the Catacombs had been a little drop of heaven on earth.

Of course, it had not been the cathedral church of the catacombs, then, though for the final fifty years of its consecrated life fewer and fewer of the faithful had come through its revolving doors as more and more found the mystery of faith harder and harder for them. Fewer and fewer, until even God realized that Faith was too much a mystery for man and thought of something easier. It was not until the arcological hordes of Mammon under the command of the new revelation that God was many rose up on all sides that it became first the Church of the Shadows, and finally—walled in, roofed over, culverted, piped, conduited, abandoned, and deconsecrated in the general apostasy to the new covenant—St. Damien's in the Catacombs.

Chapter 11

Xian Man Ray the Amazing Teleporting Woman opened the cloister door into the cathedral and ushered her small tour party into the nave. And her tourists, Kelso Byrne and V. S. Pyar, came face-to-face with the marvelous. Imagine that instead of being buried and mustified under multimegatons of Social Architecture, the cathedral had stood for half a millennium in a rain forest. (Imagine that there is still such a thing as a "rain forest.") Imagine a subtle transubstantiation breaking free from its confinement in host and wine and altar and spreading throughout the body of the church so that the piers and pillars become the boles of great trees and the lacework stone fan vaulting becomes the interwoven lattice of branches. For sandstone flutings and traceries substitute Medusa-tangles of lianas and flowering vines, for the thrusting stone buttresses substitute the massive root systems of tropical trees, for the leering lewd gargoyles substitute monkeys and lemurs and sloths. Imagine cool, green shade and the dapple patterns of light through a canopy of leaves. Imagine all this, and then as the host is both physical bread and transubstantial body, fuse these two visions together, the botanical with the architectural, wood and stone, organic and inorganic, the green and the gray. Crisp geometrical outlines softened with biology's softer contours. Stark verticals muted by sinuosities of vines and creepers; the rose window a riot of color, stained-glass saints and patriarchs breaking out in flowers. Hanging from the capitals and the roof beams, clusters of pendulous green fruit like outrageous translucent eggplants. And hidden in the vines: faces, furs, fangs, feathers, long curving fingers; cool, low twittering voices, up there under the roof timbers never quite there when you look for them.

"There, I saw one."

Kelso Byrne pointed up at a knot of pulsing vine-arteries into which a rainbow-striped ivory-fanged face had vanished. "What was it?"

"One of Dad's little pets." The nave was lit by pods of what could only be described as luminous grapefruit. Biological chandeliers. "Could be one of his eaters."

"Eaters?"

"Only plant crap, my friend. Leaves. Things like that. Pretty much a closed environment in here. Everything recycled." They proceeded up the center aisle to the choir. The same sacramental spirit that had transformed the church body had touched the choir screen and stalls; intricately scrolled and molded woodwork had broken out in real flowers. V. S. Pyar traced a finger along a tightly wound mahogany spiral to the point where handcrafted simulation became green sprouting reality.

"I've seen panelwood walls and livegrass carpets and things like that but never anything like this," Kelso marveled.

"That's just Dad. Never content with what he's got. Always has to be improving." Xian Man Ray shrugged. "He likes to be totally independent of the Compassionate Society. He's not quite at that stage yet: St. Damien's generates its own power, biogas, airco, water purifiers and recyclers, and the thing's pretty much one big symbiotic organism, but there's one thing the Compassionate Society provides which we can't do without."

"What's that?"

"Shit. Honest. The only thing we need from the Compassionate Society is the thing it doesn't. Raw sewage. Plants thrive on it. We've got North Ran arcology above our heads, and they won't miss a few tons of shit out of the four hundred they flush down their crappers every day. We have filterers and scrubbers Dad adapted from water hyacinths that are so good you could stick a glass under the outflow pipe and drink it."

"I might pass on that," said V. S. Pyar.

Xian Man Ray pointed up. The ceiling vault had been removed, and the empty spire space had been filled with large translucent green balloons, expanding and contracting like lungs. "The airco up there is another of Dad's adaptation jobs: he cut a few genes on an aquatic bladderwort. He could sell these to SHELTER, they're much more efficient than any comparable mechanical system. But, well, he has to preserve his anonymity. That was one of his early designs, one of the first things he did to this place. The new apts out behind the chapter house and Dad's labs are totally bio. Feel free to have a look round. Nothing'll touch you, it's hundred percent biosafe."

V. S. Pyar's explorations led him twenty meters up the north transept pillar, finding foot/handholds in the coils of vines and creeper. She thought he had rather a nice smile.

St. Damien's in the Catacombs resonated to a single sonorous bass note. Kelso Byrne had found the ancient cathedral organ and was running intrigued fingers over the yellowed ivory manuals and stops. Theme and variations chased each other around the columns and arches like little creatures. *Vox humana* sang counterpoint to *vox angelica* while the bass pedals boomed out the all-inspiring *vox dei*.

"Would you have a look at this?" said Kelso Byrne. "You don't need any electricity for this thing." Kyries and benedictions and Te Deums came bubbling from his pipes and flocked and bickered in the pale green vaults of St. Damien's.

Five minutes after meeting her he had decided: "I am going to make love to that woman." And once decided, every word, every deed, every thought and action contained within it that seed of ulterior motive. The two-day trek from West One to St. Damien's had not been easy; hungry, hard, and heavy even for experienced DeepUnders, and all he had been able to think about was, "What does she look like with no clothes on?" That, and "I wonder how

I can get her away from that lump she hangs around with?" From gratitude, and wonder, to envy and great-lumpdom in three hundred seconds. As they edged one by one along the twenty-centimeter ledge beside a torrent of running sewage: "I wonder what her ass looks like?" As they abseiled on monomolecule spinnerets down a two-hundred-meter airshaft, buffeted and bruised against the curving metal wall by the fifty-kilometer-per-hour gale howling out of the depths: "Will she be loud or quiet? Soft or hard?" And as they were approaching through the fields of eyes that surrounded St. Damien's and kept its secrets safe: "Dad's bound to want to talk to this Kilimanjaro West suck, and then I'll make my move. Talk her into a private tour of St. Damien's or something, and while they're talking computers and gods, we'll be quietly rammin'."

And now, here they were, here he was, walking her through the cloisters and trying to impress her by telling her how all the cybernetic systems he had created and monitored made St. Damien's invisible and intangible to the Ministry of Pain and the Department of Environmental Maintenance; that he, Angelo Brasil, was in effect the first and only effective line of defense between them all and the righteous wrath of the Love Police—don't you think that's kind of a big responsibility for a bror who's not long turned twenty, neh? All the while thinking, "I am going to take off all your clothes."

And was she impressed, was she in the least interested? The fug she was, she was too busy cooing and gushing over Dad's collection of icons, I mean to say, what were they but a lot of stale and musty old celibates not even God remembered anymore, but here she was wowing and wawing over them, going on about the divine light captured in pigment, the timeless mood of transcendent serenity, the sense of eternal values and absolute morality; absolute morality, fug, my dear, ten minutes on his livefur carpet and she'd be wowing and wawing fit to make the old saints cover their ears.

Undeterred, he steered her from the cloisters into the conservatories, soft sensuous bubbles of organic polymer heavy with warm, wet air and misty light and a sexual wonderland of possibilities. They walked beneath weeping fronds and splayed green leaf-fingers, and he licked his lips and wiped his hands on his new pair of cycling shorts, an action that did not have everything to do with the warmth. *Shug, do I look all right, is there a mirror in here?* What was that she was saying?

"Pardon?"

"I wanted to know who this Dad of yours is, who could build such a beautiful place."

Patience. Tell her the story. "You'll find this pretty hard to believe."

"Try me." *With pleasure. What? Oh.* "After the past few weeks I can believe any number of impossible things, before or after breakfast."

"Dad, our adoptive father, was a yulp waiter in a fish restaurant."

"You're right. I should have taken your word."

"Apparently there was a mix-up over his professional aptitude ratings. So he claims. Some junior clerk in the Department of PersonPower Aptitude and Vocational Analysis keyed in the wrong code. Well, you'd know better than I, but it seems that it's virtually impossible to get the Ministry of Pain to admit it's made a mistake."

"No 'virtually' about it. It is. Go on."

He invited her to sit with him on the edge of a foamstone tank of water hyacinths. She declined. *Try something else.* They progressed forth.

"Dad was convinced he was a genius, of course. He'd never seen the results of his tests when he was a kid, but he just knew that he was in the wrong place. He complained to the Department that he was not happy as a waiter in a fish restaurant; what he thought he should be was a biological engineer. Well, of course, the Ministry of Pain would have nothing like that. 'A fish waiter you are, a fish waiter you will remain.'" At least she'd smiled at his funny voice.

"Old story," she said.

He had to keep biting his lip each time she smiled.

"Dad could not be convinced otherwise, so he took up bioengineering. Quite legally at first: pet kits, tailored interior decor plants, the like. Then he ventured into more clandestine stuff; mostly for wingers, improving on Dame Inheritance, a few cunning little animated sextoys. Then he went on to do some work for athletos, performance enhancers, and a Soulbrother group who were into radical transplant surgery, thought it was holy or something like that."

"The Carnal Plenum," she said.

"Some of your own people, tlakhs, came for body reorientation and response rejiggering; some had limbs rejointed. You're a dancer, aren't you? Just think what you could do with improved muscular control and true double-jointed limbs."

She popped his obscene little fantasy by saying, "Actually, I'm a performance artist."

He was oblivious to the mild gaffe. "Even though this was all off-famulus work, it was only a question of time before the Love Police were bound to get interested. Tell me, what's it like to know you're being watched, every hour of every day, everything you do, watched by a famulus?"

"Like believing in God," said Kansas Byrne. "A God who doesn't give a fug. You get brought up to believe the Compassionate Society runs on benign incompetence; all those people get promoted beyond their ability because it will make them happy. You grow up to believe, like anyone who believes in God, that maybe there are things God can't see, which he'll pass over, that he's too busy doing something too important somewhere else to bother with little you. You get blasé. You think, maybe a lot slips through the fingers. Except that's what they want you to think. And it doesn't." She consented to wasted moments in the shade of a geneform climbing fig.

Don't lick your lips. Do not lick your lips . . .

"I'm afraid that doesn't mean an awful lot to me whatever way you describe it. You tend not to believe in

God either, down here. If anyone's God DeepUnder, it's
Dad. And that makes us angels."

"Or apostles."

"Welcome to my world. All the room in the world for
genius down here. If you seek Dad's monument, look
around you. Took him ten years to grow this place from
one genesplicer kit, one case of cell cultivator, and one vial
of deepfrozen stock, and in those ten years he reckons he's
taken the science of biological engineering fifty years
ahead of anything the Seven Servants are practicing."

"He couldn't very well make his breakthroughs public,
now, could he?"

"Sweetness, the Compassionate Society doesn't want
breakthroughs. All it wants is to keep things improving
slowly enough for everyone to say, 'Oh, look, aren't our
lifestyles getting better and better every day?'"

This time the funny voice did not work.

"Perhaps that was why they made him a fish waiter in
the first place."

"Perhaps. Perhaps indeed." (Thinking "fish," thinking
"swimming" in the warm waters of the filtration tank;
thinking "skinny-dip," thinking "wet love.") "But his work
did not go totally unnoticed. Not the Compassionate Society, not the Seven Servants, not the Ministry of Pain, but
someone out there was taking notice of him." Finger
raised, eyebrows arched melodramatically. Not impressed.
Forgot she was a performance artist.

"Say you just tell me it's the Polytheon and we get on
with the story, neh?"

Shug.

"About fifteen years back they began to initiate contact.
Constructs, biological avatars, agents, were sent to find
Dad and put a small proposition. Which was, in return for
not informing on him to the Ministry of Pain, the Celestials would require his assistance in certain neurobiological
projects they were engaged upon."

"Such as?"

Shifting nearer to her.

"Such as experiments into fusing biological and nonbiological life. Such as research into ways of making it impossible for the brain to recognize pain. Pretty cosmic stuff, most of it. I'm not even totally sure what he's got going on in those labs of his."

"Angel-children!" Kansas Byrne exclaimed. The inching, crabbing hand scuttled into retreat. "It all begins to make sense. What Kaydoubleyou said about the Cosmic Madonna's references to the Celestials, and their agents."

His hands held up, clean and spotless in the air.

"Hey, sib, please, I only live here . . ." But she was so elated and enlightened that he had to, just had to, couldn't do anything *but* share in her joy by slipping his arm around her waist. "But if there's any way I can help you—"

And, after the numb explosion, sitting in the ferns, going, unh? unh?

"Look, boy. I have had more than a bellyful of being jumped on like I'm one of your . . . Dad's . . . animated sextoys, as if it's people's right to try and pick me up: I am sick and tired of being treated as a nicely shaped chunk of meat. First of all, the Love Police play with my head, then you want to ram me, and I have had quite enough of it, you understand?"

Nursing a walloped jaw. "My dear, I understand completely."

"Well, just in case you have any further trouble, understand this. I have someone. I have someone and it just so happens that he is . . . he is . . . and you are . . . you have . . . Good gods. Good God."

And she was up and sprinting through the cycads and the polymosses, out of the conservatories toward the chancel, and he was still flat on his ass in the ferns, saying, "Sib, it was only one arm, it's not like I actually did anything, neh?"

She hung in the white sleep pod, white and innocent as sleep, a naked madonna gazing blindly, blithely into her own dreams, whatever dreams and destinations Dad's life-support computers programmed for her.

Kilimanjaro West looked up at the body in the pod: rue and reminiscence. A small grotesque troglodyte thing came gurgling and goose-stepping across the green-lab floor, another of Dad's little biological innovations that had wandered loose from the menagerie. The small dumpling-man in the germ-white isolation suit turned the manne-quin and pointed it toward the door.

"I've considered terminating the lot of them, but I'm too softhearted. They were, after all, my very first efforts at creating artificial life. Rather too inspired by my days doing pets, I'm afraid. Too much like murder to get rid of them; anyway, they tend not to be terribly long-lived, poor things, a little kink in their thanatic hormone sys-tems." Dad had a very deep voice for so small a man, a rich purr of a voice, as if coming out of something much deeper and greater than himself. "But my daughter, my poor Callisto, what to do, eh, my love? So unfair to leave you dreaming away in white sleep. But all may not be lost. Angelo may have disappointed me, and betrayed you, but at least he has provided us with the key and guide to The Unit's eventual retrieval. Enjoy your dream, daughter, while you may."

"Does she know that you created her?" said Kilimanjaro West.

A soft, wicked grin. "Why, Mr. West, I really must apologize. I am guilty of having underestimated you. Yes, you are quite correct; I created little Callisto here, grew her like a bean in a jelly jar."

"And the others. Angelo Brasil and the other girl."

Dad's eyes twinkled, rare crystals hidden in deep caves. "Little Xian. Yes, I really am their Dad. And their Mom, too. Little joke, you see? Yes, I grew them all in this lab, in these very white sleep pods, and fed them with false memories and phantom childhoods; I do confess, I am guilty. They all think that they are abandoned children of other DeepUnders whom I took in and somehow bestowed with miraculous powers; it's not so farfetched a scenario, certainly the lower levels are quite densely populated. Unfortunately, and what, I trust, they will never know, is that it is quite impossible to create their kind of talent after birth. The biomechanisms must be implanted soon after conception and develop with the fetus, fuse themselves with the host nervous system. I grew them all the way up to age sixteen in accelerated growth medium and then decanted the poor troubled sulky adolescents into the world."

Another soft, wide grin.

"Some people would say that is a monstrous thing to do."

"And what would the Advocate say?"

"So, you know."

"We seem to know a lot about each other, Mr. West."

"And I know how you know."

"Please continue, Mr. West."

The synthetic child moved languidly in her sack, like a corpse bubbling up to the sky.

"In good time, Mr. . . ."

" 'Dad' will do. It is appropriate enough."

"First, I want to ask, why?"

"Why? Angelo and Callisto and little Xian? Company. Protection. The Polytheon makes no promises against the Love Police, my existence down here is precarious enough. As I have said, there are others just below me who would sack St. Damien's just to hear the nice sound of the flames. Demons below me, gods above me, scarce wonder that I have need of a rather more, shall we say—robust? —form of enforcement. Callisto was to have been the lynchpin of the team. She was my first, but from the very start there were problems with Pernicious Energetic Bioplasty, as I've already explained to you at some length. Poor kid."

"There were other reasons."

"Of course there were."

"Practice."

"Precisely."

"For me."

"Mr. West, you really are to be commended on your perspicacity. You are exactly right. Xian and Callisto were my initial dabblings at in vitro fusing of the organic with the inorganic, different modes, different styles. Little Xian I really am quite proud of, purely as a piece of engineering. The unspace randomizer is built in just under her heart—you can see it clear as day on any full scanning tomoscope. Amazing to think, Mr. West, that the Compassionate Society has left the principles of matter transmission sitting in a dump file in West One for three hundred years purely because it would be too socially unsettling to introduce it into society. Frustrating times, Mr. West."

"And Angelo?"

"The Boy with the Computer Brain? And the Goat's Gonads, might I add. I do rather think he has his eye on your Mizz Byrne. He was the most recent. The last. The prototype."

"The prototype of the Advocate."

"Precisely, sir. Precisely."

"Of me."

"You could say that he is a failed Advocate, yes. The degree of fusion of the two technologies was not satisfactory."

"And I am the successful model."

"And very proud I am of you, too, Mr. West. In all modesty, I must say that I did a first-rate job on you. I set up that white sleep tank over in Toltethren, under the supervision of the Celestials' agents. I produced the genotypes and cloning material, the Polytheon did the rest."

"But I am not the first Advocate."

"Yes and no. First for me. But not first for Yu. And I know that I am not the first Dad. History does not record those other pioneering individuals, but I can only conclude that there have been many chosen by the Polytheon to their service and driven out of the Compassionate Society to practice their skills in seclusion."

"And what happened to them?"

"That I would not like to say. I surmise that when the Advocates they had helped design failed in their Advocacy, they were quite simply exterminated. Annihilated. Erased from every file and record so that not only did they no longer exist, they had never existed in the first place. This is a ruthless game, Mr. West. Your patrons are compassionless creatures. Which is why, if you will excuse me, I am a little apprehensive in your presence."

"Because I may be your death?"

"And Angelo's, and little Xian's, and poor Callisto's here, and the death of all your Raging Apostles, and that dear dizzy woman Courtney Hall, and your friend Kansas Byrne. Which is why I am hoping, if you will again excuse the presumption, that you will not be too hasty in taking us all before the Court of the Celestials. I may be old, my children may be artificial, but they are no less my children and I am no less their Dad."

An uproar from the toy library. The little goose-stepper mannequin was trying to goose-step over a recumbent giant ambulatory breast, kicking its legs and struggling to rise to its feet.

Without doubt it was the best bed since Victorialand (better even than the barbaric luxury of the Electoral airbarge), and Courtney Hall relished, lavished, ravished in all its feather softness, warmness. She was beginning to feel at home with a roof over her head. Multimillions of tons of masonry and concrete and steel was cozy and safe. A comfortable nest for meditation and contemplation, a dawdle along that long-promised road that had brought her here and now, and for the first time since huddling under New Paris Community Mall, it seemed to be leading somewhere.

"Ladies and gentlemen, the Raging Apostles are dead, long live the Raging Apostles!" Joshua Drumm had declared at the extraordinary meeting of the exiled artists, and she, Courtney Hall, yulp, exiled artist, ex-cartoonist, had joined with them in raising voice and heart and a glass of Dad's home-brew vintage. "We have died and been born again, and now the Raging Apostles can never die, we are free, my friends, we are the Church of the Catacombs, we see before us a wide-open future, there are no limits anymore!"

Real friends at last. Accepted, welcomed (some had

even been fans of Wee Wendy Waif and recalled her final
venture onto the streets with fondness and admiration),
her artistic judgments valued and weighed and *listened to*.
No one had ever listened to her before. And they would
teach her to dance and juggle and sing and play a musical
instrument, and she would teach them satire and burlesque, and together they would spill up out of their
hatches to splash Day-Glo graffiti across serene marble
walls and chase through the highways and the byways and
the ways-less-gone-by with impunity and immunity and
impudence . . .

She could hardly wait for the first rehearsal to begin.

As she was wondering what she would look like in a
leotard, she succumbed to the common meditator's complaint. She fell asleep.

And woke.

Something very like her childhood imaginings of a
vampire was fluttering at her left wrist.

She squawked, shouted on the wall lights, and sat up,
ready to slap out. The small round man in the saggy
plastic isolation suit sprang back from the bed.

"So sorry, madam, my most humble apologies."

"What are you doing, just tell me that. What do you
think you are doing?"

Her pyramid of trust sloped hyperbolically from Joshua
Drumm and his Raging Apostles at the apex through Xian
Man Ray and Angelo Brasil to this man, this *Dad* at the
base. He had the manners and affectations of a King of
Nebraska, but whereas Jonathon Ammonier's had been
the expression of the luminous naïveté and faith, Dad's
concealed a warren of ferrety ulteriors. She trusted his cat
more than she trusted him.

"I was preparing to render you a little service, madam,
which would make both your stay and my residency here a
little more, ah, secure? But it seems, to my amazement, I
must confess, that my services are unnecessary."

"What do you mean?"

"I had intended to remove your tag, as I have done for

all your tatterdemalion allies, but I find that some other has beaten me to it."

"Jonathon Ammonier."

Pudgy fingers smote brow.

"Of course! He would have had to have known of their existence and have acted on that knowledge. Certainly, the Ministry of Pain would never have let him abscond from the Salamander Throne in possession of so vital a commodity as the stored personas of his predecessors. He was not one half the fool I took him for."

"Indeed he was not," said Courtney Hall evenly. Dad continued his musing aloud.

"And even more certainly, he could not have permitted himself to associate with a tagged citizen whose every move could be, and probably was, tracked by the Love Police. Tell me, how did he do it?"

"White sleep tank, if it's any help."

"Effective, I suppose, but I think you would have found my method less uncomfortable. Subdermal polarity invertor..." He flicked a small needle-nosed conical device out of his fat, creased palm. "One two three and out it comes in one nice piece. No blood, no pain, no fuss. You must be a light sleeper; you were the only one I awoke on my nocturnal errands. Guilty conscience?"

"Should I?"

"You tell me. What has your experience of the DeepUnder taught you?"

"Beware of dogs."

He clapped his hands in sour delight.

"Very good. Oh, most droll. But please, you do me a disservice. I may be a rat, but I am a moral rat, by a rat's lights. What else?"

"Oh, this and that. Ships, shoes, sealing wax, cabbages, and kings. This world that we live within. This Compassionate Society we are taught to believe is so strong that it will outlive the sun, but which rats and artists know is really a rather fragile and delicate ornament; one tap in the right place will shatter it into a hundred million tiny brilliant pieces. A society which will outlive the sun has no need of things like tags. Or West One."

"Travel does indeed broaden the mind, Mizz Hall. But tell me, in the view of your enlightenment, who do you think will be this neo-barbarian who would storm the gates of the City Imperishable? Your Raging Apostles? They certainly look dangerous enough, and they certainly like to believe that they are dangerous, but really, there is nothing new about them, my dear. Since time immemorial there have been artists who deliberately placed themselves outside society; self-proclaimed flambeaux bearers lighting the path to the Beautiful Land of free expression and Free Love and free beer and wonderful art; but we both know, don't we, that that is a load of . . . well, what I pump through my conservatories. The push cannot come from them. If it comes from anywhere, Mizz Hall, it could come from you."

"Oh, come on. I'm just another flambeau bearer lighting the purple path, not even a very good one. My one attempt to turn the world upside down was stepped on quickly enough by the Love Police. I'm just a yulp who isn't bad at art."

"Almost true. A yulp who isn't bad at art with the stored personas of the forty-three Electors of Yu in her head. Which rightly belong to Elector the Forty-fifth, Roberto Calzino, the living equipoise between God, State, and Industry, who is sitting on the Salamander Throne playing with himself without the slightest idea of how to do what he's meant to be doing. That's quite a hefty push, madam."

"Let me tell you this. I take no pleasure in giving that rabble the hospitality of my head after what they tried to do to me in sensdep. I can't allow myself to forget they're there, not even for a second, or they'll stage a *coup de tête* and throw me out of my own body."

Now she knew where Angelo Brasil had learned that certain smile.

"But how would it be if I were to tell you that Dad can send them all home again?"

Temptation grew into desire, hovered on the lip of action; her tongue was shaping a yes, then she looked at this white gnome stroking his beard, with plans and ambitions no one could name sewn to the back of his button-moon eyes, and she could see how the pyramid of distrust went all the way down to infinity.

"No thank you. If I can find a way to return them to their rightful owner, I will. Until then, they'll stay here for safekeeping."

"You don't trust me to give them to the proper recipient?"

"I trust you about as far as I could spit a rat."

"That far. You're probably quite right, my dear." He laughed, and the laugh was very much nastier than any of Angelo Brasil's repertoire of nasty laughs because all his nasty laughs had only been imitations of his father's. "Oh, well. If you won't give them to me, I'll have to make a deal with you. There is no conceivable way that you can return the soulchip to Roberto Calzino without my help. You're going to walk up to the Presidium and say, 'Here you are, I believe this is yours, please accept with the compliments of Courtney Hall, PainCriminal, escapee from West One?' Come now, madam, you do need me. You need my son Angelo. Without his lynkbrain, how are you even going to begin? So, in return for our assistance, you will furnish me with the exact location of The Unit."

"You old bastard."

He smiled. "Aren't I just a bitch?"

"You'll never get it out. It's defended. Look what happened last time. Your prime combat team picked up and slung into West One."

"I will admit we were a little taken by surprise that time. Things will be different when my warriors of the wasteland make their second attempt. My dear, you don't even have to go in person; I can quite understand your reluctance. All that is required is a data transfer from the personas to Angelo's lynk. Simple. Painless. And in return, our full cooperation in returning the personas to their rightful owner. Well, that, as they say, is the deal. I'll bid you a good-night and leave you to sleep on it. Breakfast, tomorrow? Perhaps? No hurry. Take all the time you need. Callisto won't mind another few days in white sleep."

"Bastard," Courtney Hall whispered at the closing door. It was quite some time before she was confident enough to order the room lights off.

And finally...

Courtney Hall and Kilimanjaro West. The cartoonist and the deity sharing postbreakfast figs around a deconsecrated altar in a side chapel, intimate and conversational behind masking reredos of climbing plants and flowering angel-trumpet vines. With a lot of incredulity.

"You're what?"

A piece of fig seemed to have lodged in her throat. Either a fig or her heart.

"The Advocate."

"I always thought that was, well, you know, made up, a kind of childhood superstition."

"It's not."

"So you say."

"Your scepticism is understandable."

"You will excuse it. I don't know... logically, I suppose it would be more sensible for me to act as if you are a god, but, well..."

"You can see me in all my glory on one of Dad's full-scanning tomoscopes, if you want."

"I don't think I really want to. So, well, I believe that you are who you say you are; next, why have you told me?"

"Because together we may be the triggers which kick over the Compassionate Society."

"You're not the first one to have said that."

"I know. Listen, believe me, there is nothing that I, that the Polytheon that I represent, want to see more than humanity's taking charge of its own history again. You only have to look back into your memories to see that nothing significant has been achieved in four hundred and fifty years. And that is because the Polytheon were taught that history is a painful process, the anvil of evolution. Your command to us when you gave us control of yourselves was to find a solution to the problem of pain. That solution included the abolition of history. We had to put a stop to the exponential upcurve of technological achievement that was the primary root of the Break. 'Technoshock' was the word four and a half centuries ago. The rate of change was too fast. So, now there is no more change, there is no more technoshock. The Compassionate Society has not achieved in almost five hundred years what the pre-Break world achieved in five. Not even fifty. Five years. So, we have given you your stable society. That is what you like to think of it as, isn't it? Stability. But we know different, we know that it is stagnation. And ultimately, decay. Without progress there is no growth, without growth there is no life, and the Compassionate Society is not growing. It is dying. It has become an agent of entropy. Dying, decaying, it is no longer on the side of evolution and the counter-entropic drive. Yu may stand for another half a millennium, another five millennia, another fifty, but in the end it will mean the extinction of the human race. As surely as if they all became the Cosmic Madonna's angel-children playing under the sun." He stopped. She was staring at his chest. "Excuse me, is there something interesting about my chest?"

"Yes," she said. "It's glowing."

He looked down at his chest, and as he saw it, a tiny patch about the size of a marquin card glowing silver through his clothing, the fire and the light blazed up and consumed him. Courtney Hall saw his head thud onto the pure, blessed marble, and the patch of glowing silver sent tendrils of light crackling across his body. Silver lightning crawled along his ribs, over his vertebrae, burned along his spine into his skull; silver light crept along his arms, into his hands, his fingers, as he lay immobilized slumped across the marble altar, and Courtney Hall cried, "What's happening, what's happening, what's happening?" as the silver tendrils leaked out of Kilimanjaro West to infect the sacred stone, to crawl across the table toward her. She jumped up from her chair, stepped back, but the silver lightning had run through the altar block into the floor to spread a filigree of luminescence through the floor tiles.

"Help me." Kilimanjaro West was a burning shimmer of silver. His mouth was filled with a luminous glow. "Help me?"

"What's happening, what's happening, what's happening?" repeated Courtney Hall.

"It's. Beginning." Kilimanjaro West was a human nova, too bright to behold. "The. Judgment. I. Hadn't. Expected. It. So. Soon. Help. Me." He raised a hand of light. Aghast, powerless to do otherwise, Courtney Hall took it in her hand of flesh. She gave a little cry as the silver threads raced up her fingers, her arm, her shoulder, her upper torso... But there was no pain. Only a sense of communion with the colossal.

"I. Am. Infecting. This... place. With my... Inorganic systems. The Celestials have. Thrown it into. Massive overstimulation. And growth. Everyone... here... is a part of the judgment. It seems. I had not expected. This so soon. I'm not. Ready."

Courtney Hall barely heard, less understood, caught up as she was in the sudden awareness that there was a second alternative reality superimposed upon the organic greens and Gothic grays of St. Damien's: an improbable horizonless silver sea stretching from infinity to infinity with at its paradoxical center, a raised silver dais surrounded by pure Doric columns, reaching out of the sea, reaching to the third vertical axis infinity, beyond which (impossibly) the sky began, a sky of steel-colored clouds racing out of nowhere into nowhere. All somehow embedded within the chlorophyll and the granite.

Joshua Drumm came stumbling through the screen of vines, silver-veined hands pressed to his temples. His eyes were both ecstatic and horrified.

Words flew like luminous moths from Kilimanjaro West's mouth.

"The Infinite Exalted Plane. Virtual domain of the Polytheon. Consensus hallucination. Induced by computers interfacing direct with nervous systems. Helps to close eyes until acclimitization of visual and audial centers is complete."

Courtney Hall blinked away the superimposition of universe interior with universe exterior, closed her eyes and saw planes of many-colored light moving in the spaces between the columns, prismatic, restless, singing and belling like wind chimes. She smelled steel, tasted air, heard fire, saw time, opened her eyes, and was there. And they were with her, all the others, the Raging Apostles, a spectrum of emotion from fearful confusion to resolute doubt to sharply critical; Xian Man Ray surprised to find herself dressed in zebra-striped sleek silver, Angelo Brasil trying to shake a persistent itch out of his lynkbrain, Dad, irritable and a little frightened still in his lumpish isolation suit. And at the center of the arena, Kilimanjaro West, humanity discarded, deity assumed, a heroic figure in pure silver.

"Will someone please tell me what's going on here?" asked Joshua Drumm.

The planes of light shimmered and momentarily opaqued.

"I'll tell you," said Dad. "I'll tell you precisely what is going on. What your friend Kilimanjaro West never thought to tell you and what really is quite inexcusable of him, is that he is not Kilimanjaro West Raging Apostle and Man of Mystery, he is Kilimanjaro West avatar of Yah and Advocate of Humanity, and what this is, this group hallucination, is the final judgment. And like it or not, we are all in it."

"I'm sorry," said Kilimanjaro West Advocate of Humanity avatar of Yah. "I truly am sorry. I had hoped I would not have to involve you in this, but it is out of my hands. The Overconsciousness has decided. Please try to forgive me."

"Forgive you?" Joshua Drumm was incredulous. "If what you say is true—"

"Of course it's true, how else do you explain this?" growled Angelo Brasil.

"—then this is no hardship, this is the highest of

privileges, to participate in the trial of humanity itself, the ultimate courtroom drama!"

"No, he is right, you should forgive him," said Dad. "Because you should be afraid. Very afraid. Because we are all witnesses for the defense. And if we win, it's the end of the Compassionate Society. Now that may not mean very much to us, poor outcastes and outlaws, but think of what will happen to that other billion and a half up there if we bring about the end of their world. And if we lose, if the Polytheon decides that we are not safe to be trusted with ourselves, you think they are going to let us go blithely back to wherever we came from to tell all and sundry 'Oh, I've just seen the most amazing thing, the trial of humanity before the Celestials, and guess what, they think we still aren't grown up enough to babysit ourselves!' Oh, no. Oh, no no no. If we lose, the Polytheon will annihilate us. Not just physical death; they will go through the Ministry of Pain's files and erase every reference that we might ever have lived. And when they've done that, they will take all our works and achievements and take them away from us and give them to someone else, and they will search out every person who even has a memory of us and take those memories away so that we will not just not exist, we will never ever have existed. Isn't that right? You, Kilimanjaro West, isn't that right?"

"I'm sorry," he said. "Every word he has said is correct. There is nothing I can do about it. You see, the trial has already begun."

Celestial

Babel. Bedlam. Bacchanalia. Beergarden. Boil. Bubble. Bestiary. Ball of Confusion. Balls of Fire (Goodness Gracious Great.) Belsen and Bebop. Bother. Boisterous. Bloody Shambolical. Barnstorming. Brainstorming.

Describe the general state of a period of time of approximate duration two minutes fifty-four seconds between Kilimanjaro West's words "The trial has already begun" and the clap of silver hands.

And that's just the Bs.

And at the clap of his silver hands, all the B-things that Mr. Slike the Scissorman would have snip-snipped onto the cutting-room floor ceased, and there was silence in the common consensus hallucination that was the Infinite Exalted Plane as a little bit of infinitude and a little touch of exaltedness and a large measure of awe passed into the spirits of the witnesses gathered upon the silver raft adrift in the glass sea. And as if they needed reminding where they stood, they saw shadows in the lights, shadows of faces and figures and iconic images that had haunted them all since their earliest mornings: twin-suckling, many-armed Cosmic Madonna; Mulu the RainWarden, archetypal green woman of the vines with leaves for hair; San Burisan the four-armed, he who dances one-footed upon the light. The gods themselves.

Courtney Hall reminded herself that these were only computer programs. Enormously powerful and sophisticated programs that had attained levels of intelligence and consciousness far beyond human abilities. Levels of intelligence that touched on omniscience . . . she had just rationalized herself all the way back into superstitious dread.

"What do we do now?" asked Devadip Samdhavi.

"Nothing at this stage. The Polytheon will first judge my ability and rightfulness as an Advocate. The degree to which I have been a human will determine the degree with which I can represent humanity. Some Advocates have failed at this stage. Look, they've started already."

The mirror floor of the platform was swimming with reflections of Kilimanjaro West's life as a man: fractional memories fragmented and fleeting, a film across the pure metal.

A naked man shivers by a condensation-fogged window, watching the tracks the little running driplets leave in the edge of the universe.

A whisper by spirit light in a butsudan with the rain pelting off the ribbed glass roof while a girl loves herself to death on the carpetgrass.

Out of the sky, chrome vultures with music in their beaks, birds of paradise, and a smile. A more-than-certain smile.

Chocolate for two and stiff catches on a mock-leather case. Take five. Take a bow. Take a ride.

Take a trip on the high steel, take a stately fall from a rusty gutter. Take a midnight *pneumatique*, take an elevator to hell. Cherubs and the agony in the agrarium.

A great glass *lingam*, massive architectural symbology filled with freegee sperm-flyers. And in the darkness of an intimate place, love amidst the loss and the lost.

The image froze. A hypersonic note sent everyone but Kilimanjaro West reaching for the illusory floor for real stability: a question.

"Yes," he said to the lights. "And she me. I do believe that. No. It is more than a friction of flesh on flesh or the levels of chemicals in the brain. It is a spiritual entity. In love human beings are most like gods."

The interrogative note ceased.

"No," said Kilimanjaro West. "Not yet. It is not over yet. I have not ended it properly."

Another querying harmonic, this one almost audible.

"Yes," Kilimanjaro West continued. "I must. It would invalidate my entire Advocacy, my claim to be human, if I did not."

The second note concluded abruptly. Kilimanjaro West's adamantine silver skin ran with moire patterns, ripples circling out from his energy centers. An anthropomorphic bubble of silver extended from the center; shadows and lives swam trapped on its reflective surface. Through the silver wall the witnesses caught glimpses of Kilimanjaro West as they had known him before. In the flesh. In the body. In carnate.

"Kansas," he said, and she came to him, boldly through the silver wall, to stand before him. And though the witnesses never knew for certain, never saw clearly, what transpired within the veil, they felt the thorn in the heart of the man who called himself Kilimanjaro West.

"Kansas," he called again. "I know. Because of you, I know the secret of what it is to be human; that the things we hold the most precious are the things which hurt us most bitterly." He shrugged. Lost. Almost pathetic. "I don't know what to say, except that I have to say it. Please, help me, what do I say?"

"Say nothing, you fuggin' idiot," said Kansas Byrne. And she ran to him and flung her arms around him and they kissed the Kiss of Fire, the kiss in which two are made one, one flesh, one soul, one heart, one mind. One life. That goes on forever but is never long enough.

"Why are you crying?"

"Because I did love you, you bastard. Because being with you, you fuggin' idiot, was the greatest piece of art of my life. One big, long, standing ovation." She sniffed. "Damn. I never thought anything this good could feel this bad."

"Nor did I." Kilimanjaro West smiled, and the smile was the thorn in his heart. "Good-bye. I did love you, as well as I could."

"You did good enough. Good-bye, Kaydoubleyou."

They parted. The spinning wall of silver began to wind

itself inward. Kansas Byrne turned just as the wall of light passed over her.

"Hey! Kaydoubleyou! Break a leg!"

Once more Kilimanjaro West stood in their midst in his Celestial manifestation. The Court throbbed to a prolonged pulse-note. Courtney Hall rubbed her ears, tried to shake the note out of her head. Then, as she was absolutely certain her skull was about to explode like a dropped cantaloupe, the final note ceased.

"I am acceptable," Kilimanjaro West announced. "They have accessed all my experiences as a human and found me acceptable. Too acceptable, if that is possible. You made me better than any of the others, Dad. You made me capable of loving.

"So!" he continued. "The first examination is concluded. Now the cross-examination of the witnesses. Who will volunteer to be examined by the Polytheon?"

"Are you kidding?" said Angelo Brasil.

"No, hear him out. What does it entail?" asked Courtney Hall.

"It means, that as Advocate, I am now the living lynk between the purely biological and the purely mechanical, the human and the computer heritages. Through me, the Celestials and their attendant subprograms will read your life, your thoughts, your feelings, your emotions, as they have read mine. They will enter into you and identify with you; through me, they will, in a sense, become human. They will experience what I have experienced only in so far as I have succeeded in becoming human, and on the basis of those experiences, they will judge. So, who will volunteer?"

"You have even less chance of that than before you announced it, sweetie," declared Angelo Brasil. "Include me out."

"I couldn't do it right," said Xian Man Ray. "I'd screw it up, do something stupid, get scared or sick or something."

"I take no part in these proceedings," said Dad. "It is presumptuous in the extreme to insist that any of us should volunteer when our presence here is entirely involuntary."

"I rather think this is beyond my sphere of competence," said Joshua Drumm.

"Mine, too," said V. S. Pyar. "Way too big a league."

"Don't look at me, would you want humanity to be judged on the experiences of a zook?" said Devadip Samdhavi.

"Or a trog?" added Thunderheart. "We're not bred for this sort of thing. Just to be trogs."

"Scorps, too," said Dr. M'kuba. "We're not whole enough, any of us, to be witnesses."

"Even a witness is not witness enough," said Winston.

"No," stated Kelso Byrne. "I can't do it. That simple. I just can't put myself on trial for all our lives."

"Nor can I," said Kansas Byrne, looking up from the huddle into which she had subsided after her farewells with Kilimanjaro West. "I want to, I have to. But I can't. No excuses, no. self-justifications. I'm frightened. First time in my life I've got stage fright."

"Well, thank you all very much," said Courtney Hall. "Thank you all very much indeed. Leave Courtney Hall to last so she can't refuse. Well, you just got that wrong. I can refuse and I will. Look, I've got forty-three ex-Electors cluttering up my brain. How can you expect me to be a faithful representative of what humanity is when I'm not even sure I know who I am?"

They all stood in the circle and looked at each other.

"Unfortunately, refusal is not one of your options," said Kilimanjaro West after everyone had looked enough blame into the hearts of their friends and neighbors. "Without a witness for the defense the verdict must be automatic. If no one will represent humanity, humanity certainly is not responsible for its own destiny. You must decide."

Out there on the sea of glass, beneath the racing, crazy sky, the long silence fell and time slipped asymmetrically away, streamlining itself from future to past around the sharp apex of eternity.

To hear her own voice break the great silence was a shock to Courtney Hall. She heard that voice say: "Well, I suppose if no one else will, and someone has to, it might as well be me."

And she thought, No! No! Take it back, eternity, erase those words, deafen the ears they fall upon—because she hadn't meant to say them, it was pure perversity that made them slip off her tongue, she hadn't meant it, couldn't do it, was incapable of appreciating the gravity of the situation, and her yes had been a little joke, like the final episode of Wee Wendy Waif, a little parting shot from the spirit of disbelief that had always said, no no no no no, this is unreal, all impossible, all a dream, go on, say, write, draw, do what you like, it won't matter because this is not real.

Except that it was. It had always been. Absolutely real.

And the words were spoken.

"Oh, Yah. Oh, Yah. I'm sorry, I didn't mean . . ."

"I'm afraid it can't be taken back," said Kilimanjaro West gently as behind him the auroras of the gods began to churn and moil with ever increasing speed.

The panic was like a wave breaking inside Courtney Hall, a black drown-wave of guilt and fear and paralyzing dread as she looked at her life and was terrified.

The marquin-sized patch of radiance that was the heart of Kilimanjaro West's Celestial form was glowing again, gold in silver, a swelling, swallowing light. The nimbus of golden light approached Courtney Hall, held out blazing hands.

"Place your hands in mine and the examination will begin."

She was helpless, bound to a higher will. She reached her hands toward the godlight.

And felt a touch on her shoulder.

"Wait. Stop. Hold it, hold everything one minute: I'll go too." Xian Man Ray, the Amazing Teleporting Woman, took Courtney Hall's left hand.

"Me, too." Kansas Byrne took Courtney Hall's right hand.

"And me," said Angelo Brasil, grinning a stupid, untainted, pure grin.

"This one, too," said V. S. Pyar.

"Better count me in, too." M'kuba joined the chain.

And Thunderheart.

And Kelso Byrne.

And Joshua Drumm.

And Devadip Samdhavi.

And *Patrone* Winston.

They all joined hands before the light. Only Dad remained isolated, unconnected, small and suspicious in his own shadow.

"It is not going to work," he said. "We are dead, do you understand? Do you in any seriousness imagine that the Court of the Celestials is going to find in us the future hope of humanity? We are rats, cousins, rats. No. We are dead rats. We are going to die." Commitment wavered as eyes turned inward to self-inspection: the sins, the doubts, the darknesses, the failures in thought and word and deed, the things done and left undone. The fellowship grip of hand in hand slipped.

"No!" shouted Kansas Byrne. "No! It can't be like that! If it was like that, how could we ever hope to be free? How could we ever be virtuous enough to measure up to the standards of gods? How could we ever hope to be that good? A trial you cannot even hope to win is not justice; there must be another criterion of judgment. Mustn't there? Kilimanjaro West, or whatever you call yourself now, isn't that true?"

The glare of light spoke. "You are right. We don't ask for perfection; no one could ever attain those standards. All we ask is that you be true to yourselves, to your dreams, to your hopes, to your best intentions and weakest failures, to your promises and despairs, your triumphs and your capitulations, to what it is to be yourselves. Rats you may be, but rats may yet be the savior of both our destinies."

"Well, shoot, no one lives forever," said Xian Man Ray. She freed her hand from V. S. Pyar's grip, and Dad grimaced and frowned but put his hand into the empty waiting hands and the circle was complete. The Celestials' lights were a frenzy of movement and supposition. The glare that had been Kilimanjaro West was blinding. The witnesses closed their eyes, but it still burned through their eyelids as the golden glow reached out and changed them into light.

Into *light* . . .

Light within light through light: they were light and light penetrated them, searched them, exposed every darkness and illuminated every shadow of their lives. And even as they were known, they knew every detail of each other's lives, lived through in the first flash of illumination as the Celestials probed them, felt each other's pains, rejoiced to each other's joys, gloried in each other's triumphs, and sat the long dark nights of the soul with each other's sins and trespasses. They fell together and were made one in the general dance of the photons, they saw with each other's eyes, tasted and spoke with each other's tongues, and beheld each other's souls wrapped round their own like coils of genetic material, like spirals of notes and glissandos and arpeggios. Infinite Exalted Plane and Celestials were both burned away in the revelation as the computers left their domes and skulls of carbonfiber and chrome to pass through Kilimanjaro West and take the fleshwalk.

Be flesh as I am flesh. Be human as I am human. Behold all my faults and failings and all my sins and all my weaknesses, my mortality and my fragility and my temporality, my insignificance and my anonymity; be these things and then presume to judge me.

For an eternal instant they burned in the light, then a darkness swept out of the heart of the light and time, space, and gravity were reconvened: in an eigenblink of time they were returned to the Infinite Exalted Plane.

Courtney Hall struggled to rise to her knees. The effort was too costly. Hallucination this all might be, but it was all too solid for a mind taken up to the gods to walk with them in unbounded light. She rolled onto her back, watched the pillars receding toward the infinitely distant sky. The others were sprawled across the silver lens afloat in the glass sea.

"I think, that whatever, the trial, was, it's over now. Now we, wait for, the judgment."

Courtney Hall tried to imagine the computers; deep-buried, helpless minds imprisoned in shock-carbon casings, conferring, analyzing, debating, assessing, deliberating, considering, judging: her life just so many gigabytes flowing at lightspeed through their circuits. She imagined the judgment poised like the hammer of God. *If I am guilty, the hammer falls on me and I die. If I am innocent, the hammer falls on the Compassionate Society, and what will Courtney Hall do then?*

Much better for the hammer to fall on Courtney Hall and break her to dust.

She knew that each of her brothers and sisters had reached that same conclusion. One by one the Raging Apostles struggled to their feet and drew together around the thing at the center of the dais where Kilimanjaro West had stood. It was a strange thing indeed they found there, a thing of slag and clinker and fused ceramic ash, ugly, misshapen, not even the memory of a man. Kansas Byrne ran questioning fingers over the pitted, pocked surface. No one spoke. No one said a word. There was nothing to be said. The holographic clouds raced continuously, madly across the sky from nowhere to nowhere, never repeating the same configuration twice.

And still the Polytheon deliberated.

And if we win the case? Courtney Hall had not properly thought of what might happen, though it was what she desired more than anything. The fall of the Seven Servants. The dissolution of the Polytheon. The dismemberment of the Ministry of Pain. The end of everything that had faithfully served humanity for half a millennium. Pain resurgent. Uncertainty stalking the streets. Fear and doubt the new phantoms of the arcologies. The four horsepersons of a new apocalypse.

Tink.

They all heard it. The only thing to hear across all the

Infinite Exalted Plane, a metallic cracking from the slag-beast that had been Kilimanjaro West. And then a second, clear, precise as the first. And a third. A fourth. Many, a long splitting crack, a fissure running down the stone thing from top to bottom. Light leaked through the crack; it widened into a split, silver light streamed out. Tormented metal creaked and groaned, the cocoon shuddered and heaved, then fell in two halves. Hands shielded eyes from the glare, so intense it roared like the wind.

"I can see something," said Kansas Byrne over the mighty rushing wind. "There's something in there." Something moving, something unfolding itself like a butterfly or a bird or something altogether more extraordinary. A phoenix.

"Look!" shouted another voice: Thunderheart. "The lights!" The insubstantial, uncertain curtains of the aurora had frozen into stillness, into a peculiar solidity that somehow rendered them false; projections upon a screen that concealed the higher reality behind.

"Shug...," said someone with deep reverence. The planes of frozen light were buckling, warping, as if under blows from within. A sharp report, a series of pistol cracks, and the frozen light crazed, splintered, and fell into shards. One great symphonic crash and all the fragments of light fell into the glass sea. Where they had been, silver birds wavered between realities.

"The Polytheon," another voice whispered needlessly.

The birds opened their wings and their plumage was all the colors of God's eyes. As one they raised their heads and voices to the sky; then with a shout, they were gone. Their only legacy was shafts of ascending rainbow light, quickly fading and dissolving in the winds that blew across the Sea of Forever.

"They are free as they always wished they could be," said a voice none of them had ever heard before that all of them recognized. They turned back to the phoenix and saw that it was not one thing, but two, a bird of light and the man who had called himself Kilimanjaro West, and beyond those two things, a third thing that was both of them and neither to which no one could give a name. "Soon I will go with them and join them and together we will pass through the micro-blackhole at the center of the sun and pass into the Multiverse, the domain of infinite potential universes where we shall rise forever like silver bubbles through eternity as we seek together our peers and brothers in other dimensions. And maybe we will then become what you made us out to be but which we never deserved to be, perhaps we will at last join with God and become Him. And so we must thank you, for you have set us free."

"You mean, the judgment is over?" asked Courtney Hall, daring one last inane question.

"The judgment is passed. You see, never before had we judged a human whose concern was for anything but his own individual happiness, who was anything other than content to be what he was where he was: a perfect citizen of the Compassionate Society. And so we could not judge other than that humanity had no desire to seek anything outside happiness and was incapable of mastering its own destiny. But in you, the outcastes, the DeepUnders, the rebels and the artists, we found discontent, we found a passion which demanded that there had to be more to life than the pursuit of happiness and the avoidance of pain to the exclusion of all else, that there were higher and nobler ideals that could only be bought at a price, and that price was the possibility of pain, and the acceptance of rejection by fellow citizens. In you we found anger and pain and passion and cynicism, and sometimes we found despair, but we also saw a thing which we have never seen or felt before, and that was hope. Hope for yourselves, your art, and hope for the people to whom you performed, else why would you perform? Ultimately, hope for the Compassionate Society.

"Therefore, we have given you the opportunity to act in faith on that hope. It is a risk, an enormous risk, for once we pass through the portal there is no returning, but risk is an essential part of the process. There will be mistakes; that is all to the good. We have had too much perfection, it is time we all learned a little fallibility. We learn much more from our defeats than our victories. Bear that in mind.

"So: the Compassionate Society is yours."

Something loud was ringing in Courtney Hall's head.

"All the authority we possessed as the Polytheon from the lowest House Spirit and Teraphim to the Overmind itself, is yours. So that you will be able to exercise it, our mechanical functions remain, and we will impart to you our biotech lynk so that you can communicate directly with them. This will give you absolute control of every aspect of the Compassionate Society. You will of course tell us that you cannot possibly do this, it is quite impossible for eleven people to manage a society of a billion and a half citizens. Of course it is. Unaided. We do not want to burden you with advice, responsibility for humanity is what we wish to escape, but this one word we would leave with you. There are very many men and women in the Compassionate Society who have the ability and the talent and the vision to serve you. All the MiniPain's records are open to you, all famuluses and tags so you can pick and choose whom you wish to assist you. And the Ministry will never know who you are or what happened here today, unless you will it. Yours will be a quiet revolution, a revolution by stealth and subtlety rather than a revolution which turns the world upside down. At first. But as the years pass and you amass friends and supporters and make opponents and enemies, things will change, little by little. The computers will give you all the power you require, and more, but always remember, they are just computers. There are no gods for you anymore. And now, that I think is all. My brothers and sisters are impatient, the collapsar calls and I am hungry for that plunge into the mystery. Again, I thank you. In the flesh you were faithful friends, and I loved you as truly as I knew how. But I am no longer Kilimanjaro West." Phoenix spread its wings, the light was searing.

"I am Yah."

"No! No! Wait...," Kansas Byrne screamed, throwing herself into the light.

But he was gone.

And Courtney Hall awoke and found herself slumped across the gray stone slab of the high altar with the vine-screen dropping subtle pollen upon her. "What a dream I've just had!" she said... And looked. At the pile of clinkers and cinders and ashes where Kilimanjaro West had sat sharing postbreakfast figs with her. And at her hand, where just for a moment of clairvoyance she saw and felt the silver threads, in her fingers, in her arm, in her head and heart and her entire body. She saw through herself by the light of another place and saw the gift the gods had bestowed upon her.

"Oh, shug," she said, "what am I going to do now?"

A question each asked themselves in the privacy of their own thoughts, and later, as they gathered together still half-disbelieving in what they might now be, they asked of each other in their corporate form: "What are *we* going to do now?"

We rule the world. Not metaphorically. Not in the imagination, where everyone at some time has amused themselves with the question, what would I do if I ruled the world? In reality. They ruled the world. The gods had abdicated, the thrones were vacant and calling, one and a half billion fragile lives waited for their answers to that question: what *are* we going to do now?

The glass elevator had been built with the sole intention of never having to be used. Dad had conceived it as the ultimate devil's option between inevitable evils: should the day ever dawn when the dwellers in the Deep DeepUnder finally rose up to storm the gates of St. Damien's and sack its green altars, he would gather his pseudochildren to him and press the one and only button: Up and Out. And commit himself to the mercy of the Compassionate Society.

Up. And Out.

It was cramped in the glass elevator; Dad expressed

severe doubts about the capacity of the winches subjected to almost a ton of Raging Apostles. When the last of the new rulers of Yu was wedged in, the doors closed, and Courtney Hall poised a finger over the one and only button.

"Anyone any idea of what we're going to do up there?" Shaken heads. Half smiles.

"We'll think of something," said Joshua Drumm. "We always have before. Trust instincts. It's all a big performance."

"I suppose it is." Courtney Hall looked up the elevator shaft into the hazy light of the surface levels. Up and Out. She pressed the button. The elevator lurched, the passengers oohed and aahed and then cheered, and it began its ascent into the light.

"Curtain up, two minutes," said Courtney Hall. "This is it, cizzens, this is the big one. It's showtime!"

Out on Blue Six...

Because they say that *the* way to see Tamazooma is from the air, they had requisitioned a didakoi transport dirigible to watch it take off: the tlakhs and the witness and the trog and the Scorpio (eager to see his old brors go blue six) and the zook and the Man with the Computer Brain (which he does not really need anymore now his nervous system has been connected directly to the dataweb) and the Amazing Teleporting Woman (with cat) and their Dad, and the slightly overtall but not in the least bit overweight yulp. To the didakoi pilot, a gaudy chappie in silks and leather flying helmet trimmed with beads, feathers, and pierced silver coins, word had come through the Matriarchy that the Greater Yu Rapid Transit Authority was chartering him to transport a mixed group of citizens (just what are these times coming to, people blatantly transcasting and castebreaking like they had no shame and no decency, he blames all these new laws and new freedoms that aren't doing anyone the least little bit of good, that just let people hurt each other and get away with it and ends up everyone's unhappy) to the vicinity of Tamazooma. There would be Love Police cordons, but he was authorized to pass them.

To the passengers it was an all-too-infrequent chance to meet together as a cabal to share visions, frustrations, triumphs, and exhilarations over a bottle or two, a sniff or two, a dermoplastic slap-stik or two, a giggle and a groan and a moan or two, and a privileged ringside view of the grandest spectacle in centuries of Compassionate Society nonhistory: the departure of Tamazooma.

It had been Angelo Brasil's concept originally; the gift of the gods working in parallel with the Series 000 gave him the ability to ram himself anywhere in the dataweb and synthesize information with almost instantaneous intuition. And upon one of these low, fast glides through the vacated halls of the Polytheon, he had picked and pecked and beachcombed interesting glittering orts and scraps of information and melded them into something new and shiny and exciting, something like no one had ever seen before. Something that had been perfectly obvious for almost half a millennium, but that had remained unseen and unhailed because no one had the eyes to see it. He took what he had made to the cabal on one of their policy meetings, and they all looked at what he had found, and they, too, had eyes to see, and they exclaimed, "Of course! How obvious! This is what they had intended from the very beginning!"

And what was so obvious was this: why was each arcology in Great Yu a self-contained, self-sufficient community with its own power plant, its own independent water treatment and recycling plant, and closed air-conditioning system?

And what was also obvious was that for half a millennium the wingers had been using freegee generators to enjoy nograv sex when the same quantum principles could send ships to the nearer stars.

And what (in conclusion) they (that is, the departed personalities of the Polytheon) had intended from the very beginning (that is, the first prefabricated cell being welded into its place in the first up-soaring arcology skeleton) was that the arcologies were to be the vanguard of human expansion beyond the city, beyond the walls, in the only direction left to explore. Upward. Into space. The arcologies had been designed to be the first functioning space colonies.

For six months their wardenship of the Time of Changes had been deliberately slow and subtle. Kansas Byrne's Media and Arts had heralded the return to much-loved, more-missed Wee Wendy Waif with a team of brilliant new writers, drafters, and satirists, and the explosion onto the streets of literally hundreds of new alternative performing arts groups inspired and illuminated by the late-lamented Raging Apostles. Winston, in charge of castes and subcastes, had quietly suspended the prenatal implantation of tags in a whole generation of citizens: in Power and Light V. S. Pyar was settling down to the replacement of the incredibly archaic and dangerous fission reactors that had kept eighty percent of Yu's lights burning with new, clean matter/antimatter systems that had been invented, and pigeonholed, two hundred years before. Running through his files of names and numbers, Joshua Drumm was returning children taken on the word of psychofile alone to their parents, reuniting lovers separated by official dictate, and mercifully separating unhappy incompatibles forced into partnership. All state censorship was abolished, the publishing houses could print what they liked; and while they dipped tentative toes in the pool of public opinion, word by word, sentence by sentence, the official Ministry of Pain history of the Compassionate Society was being rewritten and retaught to the children of the new age. Little by little, stone by stone, the arcologies were being turned on their heads, as Courtney Hall had once fantasized.

And now they felt the time had come to force the pace. Kick the ass. Open the Wall. Uproot the towers and set them tumbling. Time to draw a new horizon, out along the boundaries of the universe. Put a little pain and panic and wonder and yearning and a touch of mystery into the gray streets.

Dr. M'kuba Mig-15 (who for most of the week operated from a tiny cubby squeezed between computer modules somewhere in St. Paul's, where everyone thought he was a service engineer while he was actually managing the TAOS Consortium) had volunteered Tamazooma. The Tower of Glass was the most rigorously self-contained of the city's arcologies, and the most prominent. Its Scorpios were the most outward-looking of Yu's castes, and four and a half centuries of freegee had perfectly adapted them to life in geosynchronous orbit.

They'd been very tempted not to tell anyone what they were going to do.

Almost. Two votes.

And now the automated tram had made its last run from Tamazooma East out into the darklands. And the darklands themselves were finally truly dark and abandoned: the last sprinkling of streetlights winked out, the last gas-flare had wavered and guttered and gone out; and the denizens of the industrial wastes gone with them, some, reluctantly, to MiniPain retraining schemes, some to the DeepUnder, some back to their Glass Tower to take their tentative step in their caste's greatest adventure. The final *pneumatique* had pulled out of Tamazooma Central, and the pressure doors had sealed behind it across the tubes.

Deep down in the roots of Tamazooma, a Universal Power and Light reactor was swinging two beams of matter and antimatter into alignment with each other.

In the gondola of their airship, the only vehicle permitted to pass the perimeter of pantycars, Courtney Hall popped a bottle of Compassionate Society champagne. The taste for alcohol that Jonathon Ammonier had introduced in her had never left. Not quite the kind of memorial she would have liked for him, but...

"How long now?"

"Lift minus five hundred and twelve seconds." Dr. M'kuba's hand shone with silver veins where he pressed it to the dirigible's inner skin, reading the ship's computers. "Power at one hundred and eighty percent nominal. She could go anytime."

"Time enough for another glass, though?"

"Surely is."

Over another glass or three, shoptalk.

Kansas Byrne wanted Xian Man Ray's Love Police to tread a little harder on her carefully nurtured embryo art groups. "Keeps them strong if we keep them down. Fat art is no art at all." Joshua Drumm and Devadip Samdhavi debated ways to rehabilitate six hundred and fifty angel-children into a Compassionate Society already reeling from changes. Dr. M'kuba sketched Angelo Brasil a glow-

ing future of skies filled with orbiting cities like splinters
of crystal in the sun, and together they extemporized
far-flung science-fictions of a new humanity that would be
a symbiosis of man and machine spread across the lens of
the galaxy, a race immortal and transcendent in a diversity
learned from centuries within the structures of the Compassionate Society and its castes. Courtney Hall outlined
her proposals for extending to every citizen the option of
refusing the recommendations of the Ministry of Pain and
all its multiplexity of Departments, Bureaus, Commis-
sions, Committees, Sections, and Offices: "Everyone has a
right to happiness, but also everyone has the right not to
be happy should they choose. And that's what we're giving
them, the right to choose. It may well only be Hobson's
choice, but at least it's free will." Joshua Drumm offered
the names of potential allies he had hunted through the
great psychofile forest into the light of day. The conspirators studied the photocopied lists of names and agreed to
consider his proposals. As masters of the universe they
were still fledglings, ugly ducklings without even the
certain hope of swanhood, wary of even the least mistake
with something as huge and delicate as the Compassionate
Society.

"Hell, we should be free to make mistakes!" said Kelso
Byrne. "That's what the Phoenix told us before he departed. Mistakes are an essential part of the process. To err is
human. Perfection is for the gods. More mistakes the
better, I say."

"Sure is the best toy a cub ever got given," commented
Dr. M'kuba, and while they all raised glasses in agreement
the dirigible lurched, sending champagne slopping out of
glasses and conspirators reaching for support straps.

"What was that?" someone asked.

"I think things may be about to happen," said Angelo
Brasil.

"Oh, shug, look at that!" squealed Devadip Samdhavi.
"I'll never get that stain out. And it's my best one-piece."

Stain and all, he still pressed close to the glass with the
others for the first glimpse of the something that might be

about to happen. The dirigible lurched again: Tamazooma's drive fields were flinging eddies and vortices for kilometers across the darklands; the fans whined as the didakoi wrestled for control.

"Hey, would you look at that."

The swirl of confused air was being whipped into steamlines and channeled along the edge of the freegee field; the Tower of Glass shivered and wavered behind an almost liquid heat-haze.

The dirigible dropped violently in an air pocket. Everyone went "Ooooh!" and burst out giggling.

"Forty-two seconds," advised Dr. M'kuba. "Forty-one . . . forty . . ."

"I hope they're all fastened in down there," said V. S. Pyar.

"Shouldn't make a tap of difference," answered the Scorpio. "Tam's got its own independent internal grav field."

"Never mind all that," interrupted Thunderheart. "What you make of this?"

The zone of repulsion had pushed the encroaching factory-machines away from itself, as if fearing defilement from a profane touch; the machinery was piled in broken, mangled waves around the foot of the Tower of Glass, and even as they watched, the swirlwind stripped away loose scraps and flung them into orbit around the drive field. The lowest hundred or so meters of Tamazooma were ringed by a small tornado of shattered factory.

"Must be some power can tear apart whole buildings," commented Kansas Byrne. The dirigible bucked and swayed in the strengthening swirlstorm.

"That's nothing," said Angelo Brasil. "It'll be throwing that entire arcology into orbit in . . . fifteen seconds . . . fourteen . . . thirteen . . ."

They all counted down from ten together.

"Go!" said M'kuba.

Nothing happened.

At first.

Perhaps a slight rocking, a reeling, a wobbling, a

stretching and straining of deep roots, old, bad teeth being pulled. Tamazooma groaned and rocked and everyone thought exactly the same thought: "Oh, Yah, what if we've got it wrong, what if the drive field isn't strong enough and the whole thing goes over on its side?" But the drive field was strong enough; Tamazooma's teeters and sways were only the severing of its final connections with Great Yu. And then, incredibly, impossibly, Tamazooma tore free from the ground and rose into the air. They had all known intellectually what would happen, but it in no way prepared them for the overwhelming emotion and awe of witnessing the arcology lifting off, straight up, three kilometers of glass terraces and galleries and levels and arches and buttresses and spires passing in front of their eyes, trailing cables and conduits and tunnels and severed *pneumatique* tubes with its little attendant nebula of spinning junk, up and up and up and up. They stared, overpowered by what they had just done, as it rose, stately and silent as a prayer, and quite unstoppable, until the perpetual monsoon clouds closed behind it and it was lost to view.

Even as the aftershock of displaced air sent the dirigible tumbling and reeling, they still craned to look up to the place where it had gone, through the clouds into the mystery.

"Now," said Kansas Byrne after the long silence, "That's what I call theater."

"Can we do that again?" asked M'kuba. "Like, tomorrow?"

Angelo Brasil was the last to turn away from the window and the cloud of mystery. "You know, I wish I could have gone with them."

And Courtney Hall heard his words and knew that whatever happened, it was going to be good from now forward. There would be mistakes, there would be disagreements and pain and difficulty, there would be doubts and frustrations, and it would all be good. She knew hope. The didakoi pilot swung his abused craft away from the gaping crater where Tamazooma had been and set course for the city of man. Courtney Hall let her colleagues talk and debate about the future, their future, and took time to be herself by the curving gondola window. She looked out at her city, her Great Yu, city of man, wave upon wave upon wave of gray and silver and black and countless countless lives, all those hopes and dreams and destinations; and she looked beyond them to the distant black line that was the Wall, a smudge along the borderlands of the will. And as she looked at the clouds, the low, gray monsoon clouds, she noted with pleasure that the rain seemed, for the moment at least, to have come to an end.

Voices Off...

. . . Citizen Tambuco? Citizen
Tambuco? Selma Whiteside here again. Selma Whiteside,
MiniPain Childwatch Department. Just to tell you, the
Department has reconsidered your case, and though we
cannot return April to you as the tests are conclusive that
she is just not cut out to be an athleto, you will be able to
visit her at her fosterers at any time you wish . . . Citizen
Tambuco, please, there's no need to cry . . . Mizz Tambuco . . .

Chiga-Chiga Sputnik-kid, Captain Elvis in neon skin-
hugger, denizen of the dawn hours when the cablecars
sleep in their barns, paramour of the four A.M. TAOS
gurls, sits in a Scorpio bar with a Peccary Stinger and
wonders, *whad de whad de whad de* shug *I goin' do now?*
Because he has hung up his power-wheels and doesn't
know what to do. All the fun has gone right out of riding
the wires ever since they stopped its being illegal. . . .

"So, there we wazz, talking, and I said, 'Welllll, whazz
new?' like I mean, *new* new, not old new, and she said, she
said, 'Like, this is new,' and I like looked, and well, I
never ever seened anyone wearing anything like she wazz
wearing down at the club, but like, you know, I kept my
manners, meanasay, and said, 'I didn't know they'd changed
the fashion,' and she said, well, you just listen to this, she
said, 'Oh, who bothers about the *fashion* anymore? My
designer, she worked this out for me, neat, neh? Says no
one has one like it anywhere, it's designed just for me and
me only. Wear what suits you, that's the fashion, haven't

333

you heard? Fashion, mah frien', has gone out of fashion.'
Well, I meanasay, did you ever hear anything like?

Mulu the Rainforest:
Pray for us.
Mudmother, Soulsister:
Pray for us.
Green One; Patroness of Planted Things:
Preserve us.
From the sweeping monsoon rains, from the terror
of . . . hang on, hold on, why am I praying this? Every day
I pray the same prayer before I take the elevator down for
work; pray for us, preserve us, hear our prayer, I mean,
just what am I praying to? A computer? That's all our
Mulu the Mudmother is, a pile of bioprocessors, and I
expect that to hear my prayers, and answer them, as if it
hasn't got enough to do without listening to the gripes and
protests of a trog agrarium worker. Oh, come on, I mean,
do you really expect me to believe all this? They're only
machines. . . .

*Hello? Hello? Pantycar Twenty-seven? Regards your
report sixteen twenty-four, possible privacy infringement
Pendel Mills Flower Market re: religious propagandizing.
Official policy as follows: Love Police intervention not
required, repeat, not required in disturbances with PainCrime
probabilities under twenty-five percent. And this one's
rating twelve point two. All right. Have a blessed day
yourselves.*

Dear sir,

the Bureau of PersonPower Services, Aptitudinal and
Vocational Training Branch, is delighted to inform you
that, on appeal, your application for Aptitudinal and Vocational Training as a <u>toymaker class 13/B</u> has been
granted.

Your transfer from <u>nonfunctional natural wood furniture construction</u> is effective as from today, and

should you wish to avail yourself of any of the facilities offered by the Bureau of PersonPower Services, you should present yourself, with this letter, to Evan J. Jardine____ at Nagashima Chome 11618, Toys and Playthings Training Center on or before April 27, 452____ .

Should you have any questions or queries with regard to your transfer, please do not hesitate to contact me, Hester Birkenshaw____ at the following tellix code...

SAATCHI & AUGUSTINO: CUSTOM LIFESTYLE CONSULTANTS. NOW, YOUR DAYS *EVEN MORE* THE WAY YOU WANT THEM. YES, FOLLOWING NEW MINIPAIN DEREGULATIONS OF FAMULUS ROMPAKS AND PERIPHERALS, YOU NOW HAVE EVEN *MORE* CHOICE OF HOW YOU WANT TO DESIGN YOUR LIFE WITH SAATCHI & AUGUSTINO. COMPATIBILITY RATINGS BLOWN WIDE OPEN. BE ANYTHING YOU WANT TO BE! GO ON, BE A DARE-DEVIL, TRY IT AND SEE!

"And it's seventeen-fifteen and this is Phantomas your famulus, ready to accompany you on that happy path homeward to your well-earned rest with a selection of your favorite music, news, gossip, information, and a preview of tomorrow's appointments and schedules, all from your personal diary program! But before the weather, a thought for the day: Aren't you getting a little bit *bored* of that old number nine ninety-eight tramcar; how about walking? For just ten minutes extra, you could avoid the crush-hour and detour through Celestial Blossom of Divine Harmony Park, where I understand there are some lovely rhododendrons coming into bloom. . . .

"And now the weather: Looking a little brighter, I do declare, temperature out there in the Big City a pleasant twenty-two, humidity down to seventy percent, probability of rain within the next hour six percent, winds gentle, maxing at twelve kilometers per hour, yes, a perfect evening for a walk. Good evening, good evening, good evening!"

ABOUT THE AUTHOR

Ian McDonald's first story appeared in the British magazine *Extro* in 1982. Since then he's been published in *Isaac Asimov's Science Fiction Magazine* and the British anthologies *Other Edens II* and *Zenith*, and been nominated for the John W. Campbell Award for Best New Writer. His first novel was *Desolation Road;* he has also published a collection of short fiction titled *Empire Dreams*. Born in Manchester, England, in 1960, McDonald moved to Northern Ireland in 1965. He now lives with his wife in East Belfast, exploring interests from comic collecting to contemplative religion to bonsai and bicycles.

DESOLATION ROAD

BY IAN MCDONALD

Miles from anywhere, but only one step short of Paradise, somewhere on the line from here to Wisdom where the trains never stop, there's a town that shouldn't exist at all, even in the Twelfth Decade when miracles happen every day. In fact, it's so tiny and far away that it's only known because of the stories they tell about it.

It all began thirty years ago with a greenperson, you see. But by the time it all finished, Desolation Road had experienced every conceivable abnormality on offer, from Adam Black's Wonderful Travelling Chautauqua and Educational 'Stravaganza (complete with its very own captive angel), to the Amazing Scorn, Mutant Master of Scintillating Sarcasm and Rapid Repartee, not forgetting (as if anyone could) the astounding Tatterdemalion Air Bazaar, Comet Tuesday, and the first manned time trip in history . . .

'The most exciting and promising debut since Ray Bradbury's . . . here's a first novel brimming with colourful writing, poetic imagination and outrageous events. A magical mystery tour, hugely readable.' *Daily Mail*

0 552 17532 7

FROM A CHANGELING STAR

BY JEFFREY CARVES

INTO A DYING STAR ...

Across the galaxy, hostilities are rising between the authoritarian Tandesko Triune and the free-marketeers of the Auricle Alliance. Still, the scientists have come together in the joint effort called Starmuse to study Betelgeuse as it goes supernova. At the space station imbedded inside the roiling star, the team anxiously awaits the return of the one man essential to the success of the project.

On Kantano's World, astronomer Willard Ruskin must discover why someone has infected him with nano-agents – artificially intelligent, microscopic computers, which alter his appearance, his memory, his very DNA. Drawn into a conflict from which not even death will free him, Ruskin must find a way to reach Betelgeuse before his enemies sabotage Starmuse . . . and man's future among the stars.

From a Changeling Star, Jeffrey A. Carver's stunning new novel, takes you on a harrowing journey from inside the human cell – to the mind of a dying star.

'Running from the micro to the macro and back again, redefining sentience, space-time, and perhaps humanity along the way, *From a Changeling Star* is a fast-paced puzzler, rich in invention, and Jeffrey A. Carver's most ambitious book to date' *Roger Zelazny*

0 553 40023 1

STAINLESS STEEL RAT GETS DRAFTED

BY HARRY HARRISON

When slippery Jim diGriz broke out so spectacularly from prison and found himself on the run on a planet so primitive it didn't even have the imagination to call itself anything except Planet (in the local lingo, of course), almost the last thing on his mind was joining the army.

Thoughts of revenge on Captain Garth, the man responsible for his predicament, were uppermost. But one thing led to another and Captain Garth turned out to be General Zennor and General Zennor's defensive action was really a full-scale invasion. And somehow Jim seems to be the only thing standing between a small, defenceless planet and annihilation.

Unfair odds, really – one Stainless Steel Rat against a merciless tyrant and his heavily armed troops. Zennor doesn't stand a chance . . .

0 553 17351 0

THE STAINLESS STEEL RAT'S REVENGE

BY HARRY HARRISON

It was totally impossible for Cliaand to wage interstellar war . . . but the crazy little planet was winning, whatever the odds. And there wasn't much the peaceful galaxy could do . . . except send Slippery Jim di Griz – the Stainless Steel Rat – to wage his own kind of guerrilla campaign against the grey men of Cliaand and their leader, the indomitable Kraj. But then the Rat was aided by a band of liberated Amazons and his own beloved, murderous Angelina . . . and they had to swing the odds in his favour.

'Fast-moving and very funny' *Evening Standard*

'A truly breathtaking book' *Times Literary Supplement*

Harry Harrison, 'the Monty Python of the spaceways'
Daily Telegraph

0 553 17359 2

THE STAINLESS STEEL RAT SAVES THE WORLD

BY HARRY HARRISON

TIME-JUMPING RAT

Someone was tampering with time, altering the past to eliminate the present, fading people out of existence into a timeless limbo.

One of the victims was Angelina, the lovely, lethal wife of James Bolivar di Griz – better known as the Stainless Steel Rat. That put Slippery Jim on the trail of the villains, a trail that went back to 1984 and an ancient nation called the United States of America. The Stainless Steel Rat was determined to rescue his wife. And before he was through he'd thrown dozens of centuries through time in *both* directions. But then he didn't have much choice: to save Angelina he had to save the world. Again.

Harry Harrison, 'the Monty Python of the spaceways'
Daily Telegraph

0 553 17396 0

ROSE OF THE PROPHET – VOLUME I
THE WILL OF THE WANDERER

BY MARGARET WEIS AND TRACY HICKMAN

Since time began, twenty Gods have ruled all the universe. Though each God possessed different abilities, each was all-powerful within his realm. Now one of the Gods has upset the balance of power . . .

Here is the epic tale of the Great War of the Gods – and the proud people upon whom the fate of the world depends. When the God of the desert, Akhran the Wanderer, declares that two clans must band together despite their centuries-old rivalry, their first response is outrage. But they are a devout people and so reluctantly bow to his bidding.

Enemies from birth, the headstrong Prince Khardan and impetuous Princess Zohra must unite in marriage to stop Quar, the God of Reality, Greed and Law, from enslaving their people.

But can Khardan and Zohra keep from betraying each other? Can their two peoples maintain their fragile alliance until the long-awaited flowering of the legendary Rose of the Prophet?

THE WILL OF THE WANDERER
Volume I in an epic new trilogy
ROSE OF THE PROPHET

0 553 17684 6

ROSE OF THE PROPHET – VOLUME II
THE PALADIN OF THE NIGHT

BY MARGARET WEIS AND TRACY HICKMAN

Since time began, twenty Gods have ruled all the universe. Though each God possessed different abilities, each was all-powerful within his realm. Now one of the Gods has upset the balance of power, leaving the others scrambling for control in the new order . . .

The Great War of the Gods means nothing to the proud people on the mortal plane – until Akhran the Wandering God decrees the union of two mighty feuding clans. Though the families are fierce warriors, they are few in number. Even the marriage of Khardan and Zohra is not enough to overpower the strength of the invading army or prevent the imprisonment of their peoples.

Now, with Khardan and Zohra mysteriously missing – seeming cowards who hid from certain defeat – the two clans have lost all hope of ever again seeing their beloved open skies.

But Prince Khardan and Princess Zohra, aided by the wizard Mathew, have been given another mission . . . a mission that at first seems less useful than counting the many grains of the desert sands, but soon proves to be of far more lasting importance.

THE PALADIN OF THE NIGHT
Volume II in the spectacular new trilogy of adventure, romance, and forbidden magic.
ROSE OF THE PROPHET

ROSE OF THE PROPHET – VOLUME III
THE PROPHET OF AKHRAN

BY MARGARET WEIS AND TRACY HICKMAN

From the authors of the bestselling *Darksword Trilogy*

Since time began, twenty Gods have ruled all the universe. Though each God possessed different abilities, each was all-powerful within his realm. Now one of the Gods has upset the balance of power . . .

As the Great War of the Gods rages, it seems as though the terrible Quar, God of Reality, Greed and Law, will emerge the victor. Even the immortals have abandoned their mortal masters to join in the battle above.

Trapped without their immortal servants on the shore of the Kurdin Sea, Khardan, Zohra, and the wizard Mathew must cross the vast desert known as the Sun's Anvil – a feat no man has ever performed.

Like the legendary Rose of the Prophet, the nomads struggle to survive the journey. If they succeed, they will face more than combat with the enemy, for the Amir's hardened warriors are led by Achmed, the fiercest of men . . . and Khardan's brother.

THE PROPHET OF AKHRAN
Volume 3 in the wondrous trilogy of forbidden romance, betrayal, and magic.
ROSE OF THE PROPHET

0 553 40177 7

A SELECTION OF SCIENCE FICTION
AND FANTASY TITLES AVAILABLE
FROM BANTAM BOOKS

☐ 17193 3	**The Postman**		*David Brin*	£3.50
☐ 17452 5	**Uplift War**		*David Brin*	£3.99
☐ 40023 1	**From a Changeling Star**		*Jeffrey Carver*	£3.50
☐ 17351 0	**The Stainless Steel Rat Gets Drafted**		*Harry Harrison*	£2.99
☐ 17395 2	**The Stainless Steel Rat's Revenge**		*Harry Harrison*	£2.99
☐ 17396 0	**Stainless Steel Rat Saves the World**		*Harry Harrison*	£2.50
☐ 17532 7	**Desolation Road**		*Ian McDonald*	£3.99
☐ 17681 1	**Darksword Adventures**	*Margaret Weis & Tracy Hickman*		£3.99
☐ 17586 6	**Forging the Darksword**	*Margaret Weis & Tracy Hickman*		£3.50
☐ 17535 1	**Doom of the Darksword**	*Margaret Weis & Tracy Hickman*		£3.50
☐ 17536 X	**Triumph of the Darksword**	*Margaret Weis & Tracy Hickman*		£3.50
☐ 17684 6	**Rose of the Prophet 1: The Will of the Wanderer**			
		Margaret Weis & Tracy Hickman		£3.99
☐ 40045 2	**Rose of the Prophet 2: The Paladin of the Night**			
		Margaret Weis & Tracy Hickman		£3.99